# THE SHAPE OF

# DARKNESS

HEAVY LIES THE CROWN one

BY D. FISCHER

ISBN: 978-1-952112-45-4

*I dedicate this book to Amanda M.*

*You are the very definition of a best friend.*
*I do not deserve you, but you know too much and now you're*
*stuck with me.*

*Everything in this book is fictional. It is not based on true events, persons, or creatures that go bump in the night, no matter how much we wish it were...*

# Contents

# CHAPTER ONE

At the base of the Northern Kadoka Mountains lies Chickasaw, a quiet ice-mining village situated in the fork of the frozen Kadoka River. Snow swirls in every direction, great gusts that squeeze between houses and thick, towering tree trunks.

The frigid temperature bites at any exposed flesh and makes Nefari Ashcroft's fingers stiffen and painfully numb. She wiggles them to generate warmth while she glares at the situation stretched out before them.

Together with all the other Chickasaw villagers lined up along the river's edge, everyone's wrists, including hers, are bound tightly with rope. Together, they wait, seated in the packed snow for further demands of the small Salix army unit.

The army had invaded at first light. Their lion sigil is not a symbol Nefari would soon forget. But still, and as predicted, they took the village swiftly just as Nefari had hoped they would.

Smoke from the hovels' chimneys are carried away, and the mountains tower over Chickasaw like a god seated on his throne. The breeze carries the scent of the surrounding pine trees, and behind them, the ice speaks, creaking as the gentle current underneath pushes against the thick, frozen sheet.

The prisoners shiver as an oncoming storm is crawling along the sky. Most of the snowstorms do not come from the mountains. No. They build and travel from the Frozen Fades, a place even the brave do not go.

This particular storm, with dark gray and puffy clouds, stretches on the horizon like a large wraith's outstretched hand.

Some are superstitious enough to believe the crones who live in the Frozen Fades taint the Divine Realm's atmosphere with their wicked ways. As if nature itself sucks up all crones' evil, churns it in the clouds, and releases it across the land as punishment for buried and exposed sins.

Nefari knows better. She knows the evil isn't rooted in the Fades but eyes the storm with distaste just the same. Unlike her companions in the Kadoka Mountains, she's seen more evil – more devastation – than most would in an ordinary lifetime. Probably more than these soldiers hovering over the abused and beaten villagers while the others finish raiding their homes.

The soldiers guarding the villagers stand too close, bodies tense. And with good reason, she supposes.

Before Nefari had been bound, she had put up a good fight. And though she was meant to get caught, she hadn't been able to resist getting in a good punch or two. It was with pleasure that she had taken down three of theirs. The dead bodies still lay bleeding in the shadow of a hovel, and their blood creates rivers in the sloped snowy paths. The bodies had been dragged there, dropped, and left entirely forgotten.

When they finally managed to obtain her, her many weapons had been taken along with her beloved sword. The weapons carried by the other villagers were also pilfered and stored inside the hovel near the line of captives.

A terrible choice, in Nefari's opinion. Weapons shouldn't be placed so close to them, but Nefari is well aware that those of

9

the Salix's army who travel this far west are usually the least skilled.

One crooked-nosed soldier stands out to her, though. Unlike the others, his posture is wide and confident – authoritative, one might surmise. He glares at her now, and Nefari glares right back.

Patrix Eiling, a satyr and the only person she knows within the sobbing and frightened group, leans to discreetly whisper in her ear. "We better pray to the Divine that they come for us before we're marched off to Caw's Cove by these fools." He juts his chin toward the mountains in emphasis.

Caw's Cove, the largest slave trade on the Divine Realm, is feared by anyone who has enough breath in their lungs to scream. Nefari fears many things – though she pretends otherwise. Caw's Cove isn't one of them.

She looks to the mountains with him and nibbles on the inside of her cheek, knowing he's right. She and Patrix could easily get out of captivity, but the other villagers . . .

"Haven't you heard? There's no Divine left to pray to," she mutters back, mindful of her expression. One wrong move – one misplaced twitch – and the soldier eye-balling her will draw his sword and relieve her of her head. He's twitchy enough as it is because it wouldn't be the first time an entire village tried to take on the army, but this soldier needn't worry. Not one of those villages had been successful. They hadn't stood a chance.

Recently, it's been noted that half of Salix's armies are possessed with darkness. It angers Nefari that those who are possessed are often her own kind: Shadow People. It's an entirely different form of slavery, forcing those possessed to do things they wouldn't normally do. The realm calls these people – be it Shadow Person or human – harvestmen.

Harvestmen, or harvestwomen, are people whose minds are controlled by dark divine magic. A single wraith carries this magic, and a single touch from them makes the individual a puppet for eternity.

Patrix chuckles darkly. The sound is raspy from years of sucking on his pipe. Nefari switches her attention to him and visually traces his goat-like features. His ears are large and pointed, but their tips stretch far past the top of his head. His nose is nearly flat against his face, a long bridge and slits for nostrils. Black paint circles his slitted eyes, and his scruffy beard is rugged and lengthier than the last time she'd seen him.

The satyr's calloused fingers grip his ropes while his hooved feet sprawl out before them.

Out of all of his features, Patrix's hooves are her favorite. They're delicate compared to his muscular frame and scruffy and furred legs.

She and Patrix often find themselves in enemy arms. On purpose, of course. They're usually sent out together because they work well as a pair – one trained to protect and the other skilled in strategy.

Satyrs, by nature, are supposed to be neutral beings. Serene, even. Anyone born and raised in Loess is immediately trusted, for the country itself has refused to pick sides in the battlefield that has become the Divine Realm.

Patrix is so trusted that he can waltz into any kingdom without being questioned. He's a confidant to kings and queens if it suits him and often returns to the mountains carrying the secrets they share with him. If it wasn't for him and a few other spies peppered across the countries, the Kadoka centaurs wouldn't know about Salix's attempts to stretch its influence this far west. If it wasn't for him – if he hadn't received word from a friend in Urbana – this entire village would be marching to Caw's Cove,

11

sailed across Widow's Bay, and given an ax to work in one of Salix's gold mines or a pitchfork to harvest their fields.

Nefari is determined to not see that happen even if they do get paid for protecting the villages around Kadoka Mountain's – the Rebel Legion's – territory.

"I suppose one could say we could pray to you, then," Patrix teases.

"Don't you dare." Nefari lifts her bound hands and uses the rough ropes to scratch an itch on the tip of her nose. The soldier jolts at the movement and grips the pommel of his sword, shrewd lips sneering. The human woman next to her flinches at the soldier's wordless threat, but Nefari pays him no mind.

Nefari hushes her voice until it sounds more like a threat. "I am the last person you – or anyone – should pray to."

His burly shoulder bumps into hers, and the leather of his meager armor pokes at her skin through her black cloak. Without the usual clank of their weapons being jostled, the gesture feels empty. "You're the closest thing we've got, little shadow, whether you own that you're Fate-blessed or not."

"That would be a 'not'." Nefari's nose wrinkles, and this time, she narrows her eyes at Patrix. She hates it when he calls her 'little shadow.' She much prefers the other nickname he had dubbed her when they met ten years ago at the entrance of Kadoka City. Fari is what he had nicknamed her, and it's what nearly everyone else in the mountains has adapted since then. She likes it much better, for she sounds more fearsome than she feels on the inside.

Indeed, Nefari is Fate-blessed, a fact she promptly ignores and a fact others have begun to push on her. Fate was a fool for giving his magic to her and destroying himself in the process. She is only one girl – one woman, barely eighteen. Nothing is going to save this realm, especially not her. That sort of thinking is what got her parents killed and their kingdom destroyed.

His hooves click together. "Ah. There's a bit of that temper I remember. For a moment, I feared you had turned into a stiff like the rest of the Kadoka centaurs."

"I'll show you temper," Nefari growls.

A villager behind them makes a shushing sound. "Are you trying to get us killed?" the man asks.

They ignore him.

Patrix dips his head, and the tip of his messy beard touches his exposed and hairy collarbone. His lips barely move as he sternly says, "No magic. Remember what Bastian said."

A small, sly grin spreads across Nefari's lips. Bastian had warned against it, but defying the centaur leader – the Rebel Legion's leader – is her favorite pastime.

"Fate is inside you, Nefari," Bastian had said when they left Kadoka City yesterday. "Your magic is the only thing that can kill a wraith. As you are our most valuable weapon, you are also our most dangerous. If she were to find you . . ."

Nefari shakes Bastian's warning from her mind. "Bastian says a lot of things these days. That doesn't mean I have to listen to them. I'm an adult and, therefore, no longer someone he needs to hover over and protect. Besides, I'm already using magic to hide my features. What's a little more?"

And Nefari is glad for it. If these men were to realize who and what she is . . .

Nefari's magic is a gift from the stars – a sort of magic that hasn't been seen for centuries, according to Swen Copsteel, the old and wise records keeper of Kadoka City. It's bright and hot, and if she wields it correctly, she can cast shadows and shape them to her will, including across her own features. It isn't enough to make her look entirely like a new person, but it's enough to shade her tell-tale shadow people features – white hair and ice-blue eyes – until she appears like any other ordinary human.

If she were to someday forget she had this magic shrouding her face, her enemies would know more than her race. They'd know the secret she keeps, for she is the Shadow Princess long thought dead. The very Shadow Princess the Queen of Salix sought to destroy the day she invaded her people's kingdom.

"Fari," Patrix chastises. "Cut your nonsense. If I so much as see light dancing at your fingertips, I will dump you in the river, soldiers with pointy sticks be damned." He glances at the oncoming storm. "That much magic will bring the wraiths. It is what Bastian warned you of, and you know it."

Grumbling under her breath, Nefari straightens her spine and sags her shoulders. "Fine," she relents. She searches the surrounding trees and then studies each soldier dragging more and more villagers to the collective captives. At least, the villagers have kept quiet about who and why she and Patrix were there.

One woman, in particular, holds Nefari's attention. She grinds her teeth as she watches this woman being dragged along the path by her brown hair. The person dragging her is one of Nefari's own kind – a shadow person turned harvestman. And in this shadow person's eyes is the vacant look Nefari always sees in all who were unfortunate enough to be touched by a wraith. They see nothing. They're playthings to a greater mastermind, to the Queen of Salix and her continued push to rule the entire realm.

All shadow people have two forms. One is humanoid, and the other is shadow form. For a decade, she hasn't seen a single shadow person shift to their shadow form. Not since the Shadow Kingdom fell. No one dares because it's magic, and magic is

14

detected by the wraiths. These wraiths prowl the skies until they feel the magic pulse in the atmosphere, and then they're drawn to it. It takes seconds for them to harvest the magic wielder and anyone unfortunate enough to stand beside them. It is their sole purpose to ensure all the power is sitting on Salix's throne and nowhere else. Magic is Salix's bane, and any shadow person left unharvested is a threat.

The shadow form is a beautiful form, though. Nefari misses the black skin that sparkles like a galaxy. She still sees it in her dreams, but those harvested never wear it, for reason's Nefari isn't privy to. She remembers it all though; the shadow jumping, the great tales of shadow royal magic, and the messages she would sometimes get from her parents, sent through the shadows. She tries to not think about it.

The woman being dragged along screams and kicks. She's making such a ruckus that every soldier turns or glances briefly to watch the scene unfold. The soldier who had been glaring at Nefari chuffs and marches over to her and the harvestman. He raises his hand and strikes the woman across the face. The force of the hit causes the harvestman to release his burden, and the woman drops to the ground, clutching her face.

The harvestman doesn't flinch. His expressionless eyes look down on the woman, and his long white hair sways in the snowy gale.

Nefari's blood boils, and she feels her magic rising to the surface.

"Fari," Patrix warns as Nefari's fingers clench into fists in her lap. "Wait for the others to arrive. Do nothing. Sit still and –"

The crooked-nosed soldier strikes the woman again. His face is twisted in amusement, and a blaze of white-hot anger travels through Nefari's bones. "I can't," she growls.

15

A sliver of her starlight magic seeps out of the skin of her hands. The falling snow obscures its brightness, but it's only enough to burn away the rope binding her wrists. The rope disintegrates to ash, and Nefari leaps from her seat on the ground. She dashes to the soldier and tackles him in the midst of kicking the woman's ribs.

With a thud, Nefari lands on top of the man and quickly scrambles to straddle him. His sword's pommel digs painfully into her inner thigh, but she squeezes her legs as tight as she can to keep him still.

"Run!" she tells the woman still lying, gaping, on the snow. Then, she draws the short knife from the soldier's hip and presses it to his throat. Nefari leans close to the man's face and snarls, "Move, and this blade will touch your spine."

The woman struggles to stand, and in those precious seconds, the harvestman recaptures her.

Still with the captives on the sidelines, Patrix Eiling battles his binds as he watches Nefari threaten the soldier. By the Divine, this woman is going to get him and everyone else killed! The older she gets, the more unpredictable she becomes. He should have known better than to request her for this mission. The last time they were involved with liberating a village of invading soldiers, she had been reckless, too. At the time, he had thought it was a youthful outburst, but now he knows that isn't true.

She's near incapable of following orders, and that in itself could be as deadly as a sword in the heart.

The rest of the soldiers draw their blades, but they hesitate to approach. Patrix blinks as his mind works for a solution. He hadn't planned on Nefari's rogue actions.

But the soldiers aren't attacking, and when Patrix studies for the reasoning, he realizes the only reason they haven't is because that man – the man under the Princess of the Shadow People –

16

is important to them. They need him alive. They've been ordered to *keep* him alive. Why?

It dawns on Patrix, and he bites back a curse. *Of course! Of course, Fari would attack the lieutenant of this small raiding unit. A lieutenant! Foolish, foolish woman!*

Knife still tight against his throat, Nefari Ashcroft feels her heart skip a beat at the Lieutenant's order. "Kill her!" the lieutenant orders the others. His face is a shade of pure white, but his cheeks are bright with anger. "Kill her now!"

A bowstring snaps, and an arrow whizzes through the air. Nefari's sharp senses pick up the sound a fraction of a second before the arrow can find its mark. She tilts her body an inch and catches Patrix's wince when it knicks her shoulder. The arrow embeds in the frozen dirt ten feet past the lieutenant's head.

Nefari hisses at the pain, and blood seeps into the sleeve of her cloak. She doesn't release her hold on the blade as most would, though. Instead, she presses the blade farther into the man's neck. Beads of red slope down his filthy skin.

"Fari," Patrix barks. He gathers himself to his knees.

That one word is enough to break Nefari's concentration. The lieutenant frees one arm and elbows Nefari in the jaw. They tumble through the snow, both grappling for the upper hand. The lieutenant dwarfs her, and if it wasn't for Nefari's quickness, it wouldn't be an even match.

But then, she gets stuck underneath him.

Shouts rise from the crowd, and the soldiers turn toward them, readying to strike down the next person who dares make a stand.

Patrix struggles against his ropes again, cursing under his breath about hot-headed young females. The tip of a sword is pointed at

17

his neck, and he stops moving. The soldier wielding the sword snarls at him, a clear threat.

"Don't," the soldier warns him. Patrix swallows thickly, his Adam's apple brushing against the blade.

A horn is blown in the distance, and the village's writhing panic seizes. The sound came from the other side where the trees hold their ground against the North's frigid bite.

All falls quiet except for a child's tiny cry.

Nefari and the lieutenant look to the woods at the same moment, and then Nefari's face, bruised and cut, spreads into a feral grin. She peers up at the lieutenant whose fist is raised.

"What is this?" the lieutenant demands. True fear finally settles in his expression. "Who are you?"

Nefari plunges her borrowed blade into the man's chest. The warmth of his blood gushes across her palm. She whispers quietly enough so only he can hear, "I am nobody. To the realm, Nefari Astra Galazee Ashcroft was never here. She is dead." It takes a moment for the man to recognize the name. It takes even less time to recognize her face – the face of her mother – when she drops the shadows shrouding her features. He's old enough to remember who her mother was and what she had looked like, Nefari is sure. And when he does, his eyes widen while he gurgles on his own blood.

She grins wickedly and answers his other question louder, "And that, in the woods, is the Rebel Legion." She plunges the knife in deeper, twists it.

When he grunts his last breath, the shadow princess pulls out the knife and pushes the lieutenant's body to the side. He drops, limp and motionless beside her. She glances once at Patrix and notes his displeasure. Satyrs have excellent hearing, Patrix's greatest asset in his line of work. By his expression and the tick of his jaw, he had heard what she said.

"Prepare yourselves!" the foot-soldier holding his sword to Patrix's throat shouts to the unit. The thunder of many hooves quakes the ground, and the soldier leaves Patrix's side to join the others.

With the soldiers distracted, Nefari liberates the lieutenant's sword from its sheath and dashes back to Patrix. He says nothing about her disobedience. Instead, he snorts at her.

"Don't get all goat-ish on me," she chastises with great humor. She cuts the rope around his wrists first and then hands him the sword while she dashes with the blade to the beaten woman and uses it to free her. A bruise is spreading rapidly across her cheek, and Nefari touches it lightly when the woman is free of her ropes.

"Take this," Nefari says quickly to her. "Free the others, and then hide in those trees. Do not stay here." She points over the woman's shoulder to the forest across the ice where all is as quiet as the grave.

The woman shakily takes the blade with one hand, gripping Nefari's wrist with the other. "Thank you."

A smile tugs at the edge of Nefari's lips. "No one deserves the fate of Caw's Cove, nor what comes after."

Nodding, the woman turns to the villagers and begins the process of freeing them.

Satisfied, Nefari whips around.

At the edge of the forest, the first centaur emerges. Then another and another, each carrying weapons and shields double the size of a human soldier's. Their circular shields are dented from past battles, but their plain swords are as sharp as the day they were forged.

The centaurs have been trained for battle since they were young boys and girls, vowing to protect the innocent once they officially joined the Rebel Legion. Nefari is fortunate to have learned from them – lucky to be counted among their numbers.

Each roars with war cries as they gallop toward the soldiers. The soldiers shout back, and as one – both possessed and unpossessed – they dash to meet the centaurs halfway, weapons raised.

Metal clashes against metal as the two sides meet. Swords reflect the trees while breath mists into thick clouds, and blood peppers the snow in a spray of fat, red blobs.

The princess watches the battle for a second, and then she dips inside the nearby hovel where the weapons were hidden. She presses against the wound on her shoulder. It throbs, and the tumble across the snow with the lieutenant hadn't done it any favors.

The orange flames still roar in the hovel's fireplace, and the heat inside licks at Nefari's cold cheeks.

There, on the crooked wooden table, are the weapons stolen from the villagers. Seated next to the table is a soldier. At her sudden intrusion, the gangly youth nearly drops the sword he's holding – Nefari's sword. He trembles as she approaches, her eyes narrowed with unspoken accusations.

"I believe you have something of mine," she snarls.

"I – I –" The soldier regards Nefari's sword, blinking rapidly as if he isn't sure how it had gotten into his grubby hands in the first place. She had bought it from the black market at the edge of Caw's Cove the last time she and Patrix had traveled through there. The odd man who sold it to her assured her it was one of a kind, and Nefari hadn't questioned him. Sellers in the black market don't lie, for if they do, it ensures their death.

20

The black pommel is unique but simple; the cross-guard is black strips of twisted metal that swirl and twine together like vines. The blade itself is made of the finest steel, but when the light hits it just right, there's a substance mixed in with the metal itself that sparkles blue and purple. It had reminded her of the Shadow Kingdom, and she had to have it right then and there.

"I – I –" Nefari mimics. She strides to the man and punches him in the nose. The man falls off the chair and thumps to the floor, and as he does so, his hand releases the pommel. Nefari catches the sword before it has the chance to clatter to the floor, and then she swirls it once in the air just to hear the whoosh.

She stares down at the man whose hand hovers over his nose. His eyes are wide, and he frantically scoots away from her until his back hits the cupboards.

"You shouldn't take what's not yours."

"They told me to!" the soldier pleads. Finding some semblance of bravery, he squares his narrow jaw and clambers to his feet. "They told me to protect the weapons. I won't let you take them."

Nefari cocks a hip and tips her head to the side. "You won't?"

"No. The Queen of Salix had sworn me –" A blade flips through the air and sinks into the soldier's open mouth, cutting off whatever he was going to say next.

Huffing, Nefari's lips thin when the man's body falls in a heap to the floor he just crawled off of. "He was just getting to the good part," Nefari says as Patrix steps up beside her. She leans to study the blade's hilt. "Is that the blade I handed the woman? The fool. She should have kept it."

Patrix grunts as he sifts through the weapons scattered across the table and finds his own blade. As he frees it from the tangle of weapons, half the pile teeters and falls to the floor. Patrix sighs, steps over an ax and three swords, and says, "The villagers are all in the forest now, in case you're wondering."

The battle has reached further into the village, and the shouts grow louder, but Patrix pays it as much attention as he does to the mess he made. Instead, he toes the young soldier's leg upon passing. "You're like a cat. You toy with your food before you eat it."

"Life's too short to be as efficient as you are." Nefari bats her lashes.

"Mmhmm." Patrix strides to the door and whirls her to face the battle raging outside. "I don't know what is going on with you, but this – all of this – could have been less messy if you had just gone with the plan, little shadow."

"I like you, Patrix, I really do, but if you call me little shadow one more time, I'll –"

He sighs and pats the top of her head. She bats away his hand and smooths her shadow-shaded hair. "Come on. Let's help them finish this and get the hell out of here."

Nefari exits the hovel and stops abruptly. There, just off the path, is a shadow person. His body lay twisted in the snow, and his unseeing eyes stare back at her. The world falls quiet as it always does when she's reminded of all the death in her past, present, and certainly her future. Memories bombard her, sharper than any blade. Nefari swallows thickly to the sounds of her dying people rising in her head and the way it had echoed down the halls of the shadow castle.

"Fari?" Patrix calls. He hadn't noticed her stop and spins to face her. He follows her line of sight, sighs, and returns to her side to grip her shoulder. "He was harvested just like the others, Fari. We both know death is far easier than a life harvested. Push it from your mind like Sibyl taught you."

Saliva pools in Nefari's mouth like it always does when she feels guilt. Nodding, Nefari blinks away the memories, freeing the breath she'd been unknowingly holding. It fogs around her face as soon as it meets the winter air.

She lifts her sword, and together, they dive into the dwindling battle for this village's freedom.

# CHAPTER TWO

Nefari stares at the fire while she leans against a hovel's outside wall. She barely hears Fawn Whispersong when she asks, "Is that the last of the harvestmen?"

Fawn, the centaur who cares for the Rebel Legion's armory, has been Nefari's reluctant companion since the moment she arrived in Kadoka City with a handful of other mentally scarred shadow children. As far as Nefari knows, she and those children are the only remaining shadow people without shackles permanently around their wrists. Fawn wasn't one of those who had rescued them, but Nefari knows underneath all the snark is a woman who doesn't know how to show she cares. She struggles to build relationships beyond one-night-stands in another warrior's bed, be it man or unwed woman. Perhaps she's a woman who thinks she has something to prove. Perhaps she's a woman who fears connection. Most likely, it has everything to do with her past.

Rubbing her eyebrow, Nefari turns to the centaur. Fawn's braided red hair whips in the wind, and the fire raging behind her makes her rust-colored fur appear orange. The storm is getting closer now, and the closer it gets, the darker this part of the realm becomes. They'll have to leave for the mountains soon if they plan to reach Kadoka City before the heart of the storm prevents them.

"Yes," Nefari answers tiredly. Her shoulder's throbbing is far less than before. A healer had already tended to it. The cut hadn't been deep, but she was still rewarded with a needle and thread.

Fawn throws the last of the logs onto the already flaming fire that's burning the bodies of the harvestmen. If they don't burn, they will rise again. That's the last thing Nefari wants. She can't fathom what kind of dark magic it takes to accomplish such a feat.

"And the other soldiers?"

Sighing, Nefari points behind her to the other side of the village where the corpses of the unpossessed are enduring their own flames. There were too many bodies to burn in just one fire, and since Nefari knows Fawn is obsessed with order, she had asked the other centaurs to separate harvestmen from regular men. Thankfully, they agreed without question. Everyone avoids Fawn's shrewd gaze when they can.

Truth be told, they're lucky there's a storm. The wind is carrying away the smoke as quickly as it rises. No one will know for days what has happened here though Nefari has no doubt the gossip will spread quickly. The pungent scent of burning flesh, however . . . Well, there's nothing to be done about that.

Patrix approaches with a half-eaten loaf of bread in his hand and a wad of food bulging from the inside of his cheek. "Where did you get that?" Nefari breathes excitedly. Her stomach rumbles and gurgles at the sight of food.

He tosses her a purse of coins – her share in the village's agreement for protection.

All the villages in the Kadoka's territory pay a fee once they're saved. At first, it had made Nefari sick to her stomach, knowing she'd be compensated for saving someone's life, but as she grew wiser, she understood. The people of the Kadoka Mountains cannot survive on their trade of ale and sheep. They need coins to survive. It's a disgusting trade but a trade nonetheless.

Nefari tucks the purse into the inner pocket of her cloak.

"There was a lady I rescued so valiantly," he claims, wiggling his eyebrows. "This is my reward, among other things." His grin spreads wide, cheeky and full of chewed food.

"My Divine, Patrix," she mumbles under her breath, grimacing with disgust. She shouldn't be surprised. Patrix can pretend to be anyone he wants, and even though he has large pointed ears, it doesn't stop him from charming his way into anyone's bed. But here? Now?

A shiver runs down Nefari's spine. He used to hide this side of himself from her. She supposes there are many sides of herself she's previously hidden from him, too.

Fawn chuckles and snatches the loaf from his hairy grip while leaving them to themselves. She murmurs her greeting to Bastian Pike as she passes him. Nefari knew Bastian was close by – knew he'd been watching her, waiting for the right moment to chastise her behavior today. She could feel it, and so far, she's been successful in avoiding him. She's had enough of Bastian's lectures to know when another is coming. She isn't ready to endure one more.

"Rude," Patrix grumbles while he watches the female centaur stride away. He rubs his hands to free them of crumbs, and Nefari notes the fresh rope burns on his wrists. How hard had he fought against his binds?

A little guilt slivers its way into Nefari's chest, but she raises her eyebrows instead of thanking him for having been concerned for her safety. "Are we ready to leave? The wind may be carrying away the evidence of the day's events, but if the bone criers show up . . ."

She lets her sentence trail off there. She doesn't need to say more. The large black birds give everyone the chills and not just because they eat rotting flesh. Their caws sound like a woman's scream, and they can scent death from miles away.

Once they're done feasting, there's nothing left but a garden of bones. Nefari has seen this for herself. Of course, that particular village wouldn't have been wiped out if the raid had gone according to Salix's plan. They didn't have to die, but the villagers were outnumbered. It was either death or slavery. Nefari often wonders which she would choose if the situation was ever taken from her hands.

At the thought of the possibility, she runs her thumb over the black diamond ring resting on her middle finger. A ring her mother had gifted her.

"Almost, but they may not show up at all if there's nothing left to eat." The satyr turns to her and considers her expression with a thoughtful one of his own. He asks softly, "Why did you freeze back there? The dead harvestman. Why does seeing one still affect you so?"

Shrugging, Nefari endures the swirl of bad energy gripping her stomach. Though he was dead, she was sure his unseeing eyes had peered into her soul – into her past. It had felt that way to her. "It was nothing," she says aloud.

"Nothing?" Patrix leans in. "The Fari I know wasn't here tonight. You were reckless, and when it was time to execute the only part of the plan you followed, you hesitated at the very sight of the men you were meant to kill. Why?"

"I've changed," she grumbles. It's all she'll admit.

"I see that. Why?" Patrix narrows his slotted brown eyes to study her under great scrutiny, and then realization dawns across his goat-ish features. "You're eighteen. The birthright?"

Nefari glances away. "It's nothing."

Patrix pokes the tip of her nose. "It's not nothing. You're of age to truly be the Queen of your people, but instead, you're killing them." She pushes his hand away. "Look, I get it. It's nothing to be embarrassed about. You're a princess who consistently has to murder the very people you were born to protect."

They both examine the blaze, and the princess closes her eyes to the flames burning holes in her heart. It was only part of the truth, but Nefari says, "It doesn't matter now, does it."

"I told you. Whether you claim your fate or not is up to you. They may all be pressuring you into it, but ultimately, the choice is yours."

"Her fate is many things," Bastian's deep voice grumbles behind them. His long and dark red hair is tied to the nape of his neck with a leather strap, and the muscles under his leathery brown skin ripple with each shift of weight. The dark slits of his green equestrian eyes narrow as he glares down at her. "But her birthright is only one of them. And one she thinks she can outrun."

Patrix rises on the tips of his hooves. "The Fate-blessed princess of rage and wrath and all that nonsense," he says, reciting part of Nefari's prophecy. The prophecy had been told to Nefari's mother ages ago, declared by a crone who had first reported it to the Queen of Salix. "But is your prophecy truly the reason you don't want your crown?"

She knows he means the shadow crown, for the other physical crown is presumed to be destroyed.

Shadow queens and kings had two crowns. One was a physical crown, steel twisted like vines with black diamonds embedded in them, and the other was the shadow kingdom's crown. The shadow crown is conjured by royal magic and appears like black smoke atop their heads. Nefari hates wearing that particular crown, but thankfully, only Sibyl makes her.

Before Nefari can defend herself, Bastian says, "She doesn't want her fate – both to her throne and to the realm – because she's frightened of it."

"Of course, she is." Patrix looks taken-aback. "Only an insane person wouldn't be frightened of those kinds of expectations." He leans closer to Nefari and whispers not so quietly, "This is why I don't stay in one place for too long, ya know. People start expecting things out of me."

Nefari's fingers ball into fists. "I am not scared of my birthright."

"Sure, you are," Patrix counters. He points his thumb over his shoulder, indicating the fire engulfing dead harvestmen. "Everyone's scared of something. What is it, Fari? If it's not your prophecy, what frightens the fearless?"

Nefari snorts as the echo of her prophecy rises in her thoughts. She hadn't learned of her prophecy until sometime after living with the centaurs. The centaurs had tried to hide it from her – Bastian in particular, but Sibyl had refused to harbor the truth from her for long. Sibyl may keep most of the truth from Nefari, but she's never been one to refuse such life-altering information.

*Fate-blessed,* Nefari nearly snarks aloud. *As if that means anything to anybody now.* She keeps those thoughts to herself, however, because villagers are nearby, and she doesn't want them to fear that the Divine they pray to – Fate, Choice, Hope, and Despair – are no longer around. Except for Despair, of course, and the only ones who pray to him are the crones. Everyone knows the Queen of Salix herself is harvested by

Despair. But not many believe they live in a realm where their prayers go unanswered.

With fear comes wild hope. Nefari avoids both for reasons she refuses to say.

Ten years ago, the other gods learned of Despair's malevolent plans. He had tried to take over the other realms. It had sparked a war, and those realms had risen in the challenge to rid their land of the evil that was trying to rot it. When he lost, he came back here and possessed the Queen of Salix in his last attempt at ruling his realm.

During the Realms War, Fate had discretely guided the leaders of the battles who had destroyed the corrupt fee who ruled the realms. Those Fee once lived here, children of the four gods, or so the story goes. Her mother used to tell her about it as a gruesome bedtime story, and even after ten years, Nefari has never forgotten them.

Despair had learned of Fate's interference in the Realms War, and instead of waiting for his death, Fate had blessed the unborn child of a Shadow Queen with all his significant gifts. It is a fate Nefari never asked for. It is a prophecy Nefari ignores. And the shadow crown is a weight she will never be able to balance on her head. She's not fit to be a queen. She's done too many dark and unforgivable things just to survive, including killing her own people for the sake and safety of others. Some may call that heroic. Nefari knows it's damning, but this realm is no place for the weak and fragile.

Only death is a reliable sanctuary.

That is why she froze, for in those dead eyes of the shadow man, she was reminded of all of this. Reminded of what she's become. Reminded of how the true Shadow Kingdom crown is gone, assumed to be dust on an abandoned castle's cobbled floors. Reminded how unworthy of that crown she would be if it still existed. But she'll never tell Patrix this. It is her burden to bear, and Bastian's attempts to convince her otherwise will be just that: Attempts.

"Rage and wrath are appropriate," Bastian grumbles.

"Indeed." Patrix squints at her. "She's turning a precarious shade of red."

Nefari rolls her neck and toys with the ring her mother gave her. It's what she always does when she's afraid, a fact both Bastian and Patrix are privy to.

"Perhaps the prophecy will come true then," Patrix chimes, slapping Bastian on the shoulder. "If that temper continues to go unchecked, you may have what you desire at last! A Fate-blessed princess risen indeed."

Bastian curls his lip at Patrix's hand, and Patrix slowly drops it back to his side, cringing.

"You'll see to it, won't you," she says angrily to Bastian. "But not all of us like to give hope to others only to later break those promises made." Nefari looks at Bastian's palm in emphasis. "Some of us have more pride than that."

Patrix's grin fades, and he, too, peers at Bastian's hand. Bastian curls his fingers into it, obscuring the evidence there.

Across his palm is a scar as black as night. The scar would have faded to pale pink had he not broken the blood vow to her mother. Nefari remembers that day just as well as all the other horrific events on her eighth birthday.

Bastian's jaw flexes as he peers down at Nefari. She's never let him forget about his broken blood vow, and he's never been able to make her see that his choices were to ensure the survival of her people so someday, "she can be the sword who cleaves the darkness."

That'll be difficult to do if she continues to refuse her birthright. She has every intention of continuing to do just that.

"I'm told you had used magic to break your binds," Bastian murmurs, mindful of the villagers watching them. "You disobeyed me."

"And I'd do it again," Nefari spits. "He would have killed that woman for no other reason than her display of terror to keep the others in line. I wasn't going to let that happen. Tell me, Patrix, how many villagers died today?"

"None," he says sheepishly.

"Exactly. I took my chances, and look," Nefari points to the sky, "No wraiths. We're fine."

"No, we're lucky," Bastian growls. He places his hand on the pommel of his sheathed sword and grips it with significant strength. The large sword is as insignificantly detailed as all the other centaurs' weapons, but there is one detail that is different. Etched into the metal before the sword meets the pommel is the crown of the centaur's leaders, a crown Bastian never wears.

Bastian likes to touch his sword when he wants his word taken as law. Nefari braces herself for his decree. "You should not use magic except in the safety of Sibyl's home, Nefari. And since you keep disobeying my order, I will be confining you within the mountains until I can trust you to follow the rules laid out for your own safety."

Nefari glares, and Patrix whistles uncomfortably. She stares long enough for Bastian to leave, and once he does, she turns back to Patrix. "Did our horses run off?"

He shakes his head, his long and stiff brown hair shifting to frame his face. "They're still in the village stables."

"Good." She begins to stride in the horses' direction and Patrix follows. "Tell me you have another assignment. I'm not ready to go home and endure more of Bastian's lectures or lessons."

Patrix rubs the back of his neck while jumping out of the way of an unruly toddler dashing from his mother. "I do, but it's one I'm taking myself."

"Oh, come on," Nefari whines. Her shoulders slump, and she slows her pace.

He sighs and pinches his lips to the side as he considers his friend. "He has a point, Fari. You've been fortunate so far, but that will end. Many could have died today. Was the one woman's life worth everyone else's?"

"Yes," Nefari growls without pause. She feels her answer down deep in her soul because Amoon would have been worth it. Vale would have been worth it. She'd be damned if she repeated Bastian's mistakes. "Who are we to decide the worth of a single life?"

Sighing, Patrix looks skyward. "All right."

Assured, Nefari diverts the subject while ducking into the path between the bakery and the butcher shops. "Where's your assignment?"

He pockets his hairy hands. "Vivian."

"The city of wealth and slave trade," Nefari says with distaste. "Whatever will you be doing there?" It's said sarcastically because everyone knows Patrix likes the taste of a higher life from time to time.

Vivian is the capital of Urbana, and its higher-ranking people are responsible for the slave trade of Caw's Cove. Nefari has never been able to stomach their lifestyle. They throw endless parties, indulge in narcotics, and toss their coin at frivolous things, all for the sake of status. That wealth could go somewhere else like

33

improving the slums of their poorest neighborhoods. But they won't. If the wealthy are short on slaves, they snatch the poorest people from their homes, and the slums are the first place they go.

When Nefari was a child and her kingdom still prospered, they had prided themselves on trading the most luxurious wool and jewels. In her teens, Nefari had learned her father was also trading in Diabolus Beetles, glowing bugs that had replaced fire in the Shadow Kingdom's lanterns. The bugs are poisonous but, if diluted enough, a strong narcotic.

Nefari had heard the beetles became overpopulated in the Shadled Forest – a dry forest within Urbana's borders that was once her playground, full of deep shadows and plump purple leaves. She shouldn't be surprised that the royals of Urbana took over the trade. Before, Urbanians had left the Shadled alone for fear of the Shadow Queen's – her mother's - magic. Now that there's no one to protect it, they had greedily taken over the trade.

Patrix grins as they reach the paddock next to the village stables. "I'm not allowed to discuss it."

The paddock is a ramshackle square with rotted logs keeping the horses within. Packed snow is peppered with horse feces, the horses crowded at the far end to generate warmth against the chill.

"Will you at least be home for Shadow Mourn Eve?" Shadow Mourn Eve is the event the centaurs had thrown a few days after the Shadow Kingdom fell to honor their friends who had fallen. The centaurs of the mountains and the shadow people of the Shadled had been friends for eons. It wasn't just Nefari and the other shadow children who had lost people that day.

His grin turns sad and sympathetic. "I will try, but I make no promises."

34

Pausing with her hand on the paddock gate latch, she squints sidelong at him. "Secrets never stay secrets for long. I'll find out where you're going and why, eventually."

"As you always do. But I'll be back before you know it." Nefari lifts the latch to open the gate, but Patrix places his hand overtop hers. "Listen, I told Bastian about this, but I doubt he'll tell you. The villagers told me Grundy was raided a day before we arrived here."

Her horse, a sturdy cremello mare, whinnies inside the small square paddock, a greeting which goes unanswered with the new tidbit of information. Grundy is a smaller village than Chickasaw and about ten miles north of here. Nefari's heart sinks with grief. "Were there any survivors?"

"No." Patrix shakes his head and rubs the mare's muzzle. "Those who weren't taken were left for the Bone Criers."

Nefari surveys the direction of Grundy. The snow has begun, and it's too thick to see down the road leading to it. "Why is Salix traveling so far north? I mean, we all knew they'd eventually try the west, but why north?"

"I have a theory, but you're not going to like it."

"Oh?" Nefari asks. She gives in to her mare's demands and produces a sugar cube from her pocket. She passes it to the horse.

Patrix puckers his lips. "I received word that someone from Salix's court might be traveling to the Fades."

Nefari blinks dumbfoundedly. Of course! If someone important from Salix had indeed crossed Widow's Bay to travel to the Fades, they would have brought armed escorts of mass proportions. No one from Salix would risk passing so close to the centaur's mountains without heavy protection, let alone endure the Fades where the crones make their home. It stands to reason they'd raid the villages for supplies and for slaves to profit from.

"Do you know who?"

"Rumor has it it's the princess."

# CHAPTER THREE

*Nefari dreams.*

*Within the Shadow Castle, her mother brushes Nefari's hair in the princess's chambers. Like it always is in their kingdom, it's twilight outside her windows, but the lanterns full of the glowing Diabolus Beetles brighten the large space as well as the flames roaring in the fireplace.*

*The large canopy bed is dwarfed by the chamber's size, but everything in Nefari's room is soft, white, and clean, all gifts from the people when she was born.*

*While playing with her dolls in her lap, she peeks at her mother's face in the mirror of her vanity. Her mother's eyes sparkle like a million stars, filled with a love even a child can comprehend.*

*"Do I have to go to bed, Momma?" Nefari whines again. Nefari knows something isn't right with her mother. Usually, Amala's lady, Beau Timida, brushes her hair before Amala tucks her in for the evening. Tonight is different.*

*"Nefari . . ." Amala scolds. Nefari bristles at it. She doesn't like to be scolded. "I already gave you my answer. Do not ask me again."*

*Nefari tugs gently on the doll's yarn hair. Gen Riversdale had sewn and gifted them to her for her last birthday. Her son, Vale had teased her about them, and she teased him back when he insisted on playing with them, too. She especially loved when they snuck into the hidden tunnels of the castle and played dolls in the room of treasures and old dusty books. The treasure would wink at her, a reflection of the lanterns they took with them.*

*The last time they were down there, Vale's father had caught them. Both were put on stable mucking duties for a week, for both knew it was forbidden to travel down there without the King or Queen. He filled them with stories of monsters who roamed in dark places, and ever since then, Nefari couldn't stand the darkness of her own room at night.*

*"Why can't I stay up a little later? Tomorrow's my birthday. I think I deserve it."*

*Through the reflection in Nefari's mirror, she spies her mother's grin. "You deserve it?" her mother repeats. There's a teasing tone to it, and Nefari perks up hopefully.*

*"Yes."*

*Amala playfully pinches Nefari's nose. "In this realm, no one deserves anything. Nothing is fair. Nothing is just. It is never wise to fancy yourself deserving."*

*"Why?" Nefari asks, but she already knows the answer.*

*Her mother bends and moves a stray lock of hair out of Nefari's vision. She whispers, "Because, silly girl. All the good we receive in this life is a blessing, and all the bad is a lesson. But no one – you, me, not even your father – deserves what we have, for that is presuming we are better than others."*

*The words touch something deep inside Nefari, and even at seven years old, she understands the weight on her mother's* shoulders. She knows that someday, the weight will be hers to bear. Her's and Vale's.

Beau shifts her stance in the corner of Nefari's room. The princess glances at her and returns the grin Beau wears.

The smile fades from Nefari's lips as her young mind peeks at the shadows moving inside her room. She's never once told her mother, but the shadows . . . they call to her, bend toward her, wait for her. What they wait for, she doesn't know. Her mother never seems to notice them. "And what about when we are afraid?"

"Are you afraid?" Nefari nods. "What are you scared of?"'

Everything, Nefari wants to say. But chiefly, the things her mother won't discuss in front of her. Nefari hears what she says anyway. She always listens closely, even if she pretends otherwise. "That the scary monster will come and get me, and I'll never get to see you again."

The brush in Amala's hand clinks against the vanity surface as she sets it down. Concern is etched in her eyes, but she cups both hands to Nefari's cheeks. Her mother's frame is blurry with the oncoming tears, and she wonders briefly if her mother thinks she was talking about the wraith that had made it into their kingdom. "Do you know what I want you to do when you feel alone and afraid, Nefari?"

She shakes her head.

Amala kisses her forehead. Her lips are warm against Nefari's skin. "I want you to be brave."

Brave? How can Nefari be brave? "I'm not brave. I'm not like you or daddy, momma. I'm not brave."

The queen clucks her tongue. "I have something for you then." She stands from her crouch and strides to Beau. Something is passed between them, but Nefari can't see from *this angle. Amala turns back to her daughter, hiding whatever is in her hand behind her back.*

*Nefari sits up straighter, and the fear that had threatened to cripple her banishes like fog in the morning sun. The dolls drop to the floor with this new position, and Nefari barely notices her toy left forgotten. "What is it, Momma?"*

*"An early birthday present." Amala kneels in front of Nefari's knobby knees and she shows her the gift. It's a small square box. Nefari has seen boxes like these carried by shadow women who leave the kingdom's jeweler.*

*Her heart leaps with joy. She plucks it gingerly from her mother's hand and removes the lid. Inside is a black diamond. It winks at her when it reflects the fire's light. "It's beautiful!" Nefari gasps.*

*"Just like you," her mother says while touching the diamond. "It was mine, my mother's, and her mother's before that."*

*Nefari picks up the diamond. She hadn't realized it was a ring, for the band had been buried in the box's cushions.*

*As she continues to lift it from the box, a chain comes with it, looped through the finger's hole. She moves slowly as she removes it completely from the box. Her mother grasps the chain, and Nefari releases the ring. Glee dances in her chest when Amala slips the necklace over her head.*

*"When you're afraid, I want you to press your lips to this ring and remember that you are as sturdy as the silver, as sharp as the stone, and as wise as all those who have worn it before you." Nefari says nothing, too transfixed with the ring resting against her chest. "Nefari? You need to promise me."*

*"I will, Momma. I'll remember."*

The springs of her mattress wobble precariously when Nefari jolts up in her bed. In the darkness of her room, her hand covers her heart, and heavy beads of sweat cling to her back. She can feel her heart's rapid beat pushing against her ribs, but somehow, feeling the life beneath her palm calms her – forces her to remember where she is.

The dream was a memory, one she had once cherished the days after her mother's death. Now, it's one that torments her, especially on the days following the events of freeing villages.

Her mother wanted her to be brave always, but Bastian asked her to be nobody.

The princess pushes her hand through her damp hair. She had told the lieutenant she was nobody, too, right before she revealed her true identity upon his death. After her kingdom was destroyed, and she and the remaining shadow children were walking through the hidden tunnel to the Kadoka City, Bastian had said, "You are nobody, Nefari Ashcroft."

She remembers it like it was yesterday. She knows it wasn't said without love. It wasn't meant to hurt her. In fact, there had been tears in Bastian's eyes. In these tears, she could see her shadow skin reflect back to her. But it did. It did hurt her. That is until she found the freedom of being just like everyone else.

Still, her youthful self had scoffed at his words while she absorbed the cave's darkness and the shadows jumping out at her. Nefari didn't know until years later that she had been the one who made those shadows move, but Bastian knew. Even if her mother didn't, he knew. Her power had awoken at the base of their mountain, erupted in a blast of light that trembled the snow around them. He had been watching for more magic, more instances that she might lose control.

And though the magic always awakes in a shadow royal child on their eighth birthday, Nefari had never told him the shadows had bent toward her for as long as she could remember. It wasn't part of this awakening. Somehow, she knew this wasn't normal.

But Sibyl knows the full truth. She had seen it in her cave atop the mountain the very first day she was sent there for lessons on controlling her own magic-made shadows and the light that casts them. She had been delighted about it, to say the least.

Her thoughts drift back to the memory while her eyes stray to the embers breathing in her bedroom's fireplace.

"You must be nobody," Bastian had continued. "Do not let my words scare you, Nefari. Everyone will know you're their princess – their rightful queen – but there's a reason why you must be nobody. The realm believes you dead, and with your death, no one will come searching for you. Do you understand?"

Nefari's nose had wrinkled, but her anger had banked. "Fine. I don't want to be a princess, anyway," she sniffled.

"But you are and so much more." Bastian had glanced down at her. "It is too much to ask for a child to bear the weight of an entire kingdom's death, but someday when you've grown, you will understand, and you will be able to pick up the pieces. That day is not today. Nor is it tomorrow." He held out a hand. "Come. I have a room for you in my hut. It isn't as fine as your room had been in the Shadow Castle, but it will do."

Nefari blinks away the memory as she glances about the room Bastian had given her ten years ago. It looks exactly the same except her dirty tunics are draped over the broken rocking chair shoved in the far corner. She's often considered moving into her own hut within the city, but truth be told, she only comes home to sleep. There would be no point. She supposes now she has the time since Bastian has grounded her until further notice.

She wrinkles her nose at the idea.

Maybe tomorrow.

The small fireplace barely heats her room or reaches her tiny bed. The room is tall and wide, and sometimes Nefari feels like it's swallowing her. The wooden planks that make up the floor are dry and drafty, and during the day, meager light filters in through the window to smear across them.

Across from the bed and against the far wall, there's a trunk full of the belongings she's accumulated since she first arrived – leathers, coins, old swords, and sharp knives.

Sighing, she climbs from her bed and walks to the filthy window that overlooks the city.

Off in the distance, the secret tunnel is tucked within the city's forest though she can't see the trees at all through the storm. On foot, the city is only accessible through the secret tunnel. A path winds from it that leads through the main parts of the city erected in a valley between the peaks of the Kadoka Mountains. The city isn't large, but the huts themselves are.

Through the spiraling snowflakes, she can make out the sharply pointed roofs of many huts. The roofs' angle helps keep the snow from gathering too heavily, and each hut is sandwiched between beaten and snowy paths and large, sharp boulders. But this early in the morning, before the sun has even risen, the city appears grey with the storm still raging. When it's a clear day, everything glistens brightly in all its fine glory. The air is always crisp and clean, however, and the tall trees throughout the city block the majority of the victorious gales that happen to make it over the mountain.

Nefari touches the window and traces the nearest hut's roof. Her finger moves from the window and runs along the rough wood of the hut's structure; tree trunks stacked on tree trunks like the cabins Nefari often finds abandoned while on journeys for the Rebel Legion.

When she first saw them, she had wondered how these huts had managed to stay upright, but as she grew older, she realized the trunks fit together like a puzzle piece. When she had brought it up to Sibyl, Sibyl had said in her crackling childlike voice, "Everything in life is a puzzle, Nefari. It is our job to proceed with caution and assemble it properly."

She looks back out the window again.

Centaurs are already milling about. There are duties to be done, and a little snow and wind won't stop the massive creatures built to live in such environments. If Nefari doesn't leave this hut soon, she'll never hear the end of it.

They had made it back just in time yesterday. Though, visibility of the storm had started to become a problem on the narrow paths up the side of the mountain. At one point, she had to hop off her mare and guide the animal the rest of the way by the reins. They're lucky no one fell to their death, and if it hadn't been for Nefari's meager height compared to the others, they surely would have plummeted to the villages below. Being so low to the ground had made it easier to see, and they had used the mare's tail to form a chain.

In the pane, she can see her reflection. She never wears shadows on her face when she's in the city. Here, it's safe to be who she is – to be no different than the rest of the few shadow people. Her white hair is back to its normal shade, and her ice-blue eyes sparkle as vibrant as a clear sky. The triangle markings still etched, albeit smeared, around her eyes make them appear more-so.

She looks exactly like her mother. Her mother always appeared regal and cat-like with a normal-sized nose that was flat atop the bridge and reached up to curve delicately into her smooth eyebrows. Nefari's mother's lips were always bunched when her mother concentrated on a task, but they would thin into a flat pressed line when she thought about something harrowing.

44

Nefari's favorite part of her human form is her ears, though. She likes the way their points stick out from her tangled, long, and rebellious hair.

The bedroom door bursts open, and before she can think, she grabs a small knife from her hip and flings it at the door. It embeds into the wood inches from the familiar face staring at her in shock.

"Divines, Fari," Dao breathes. "You could have killed me."

Dao Pyreswift is one of the shadow children the centaurs had saved. Her friend's short hair is cut so each lock is uneven. It's longer in the back than the front and frames his face the way delicately plucked feathers curl. His pointed ears poke through his white hair the way Nefari's does, but his are twitching with agitation.

Some might think he's attractive with his pronounced jaw. It angles toward a sturdy chin and seemingly props up high cheekbones. His full lips are like half-opened rosebuds, but the other shadow people in the city who find themselves lusting after him will be disappointed when they finally understand that Dao doesn't return their feelings. One shadow woman, in particular, comes to mind.

Nefari grimaces, strides to her knife, and yanks it roughly from the wood. The wood is already marred from impromptu target practices on past days such as this when restless urges grip her. "Try knocking next time?"

Shrewdly, Dao peers down his nose at Nefari. He's only a foot taller than her, but somehow, he manages to appear so much bigger when he looks at her that way.

She tosses her knife onto the bed. Immediately, it's lost in the fur blankets heaped and tangled at the edge. "Next time, I won't miss on purpose."

She knows her words won't hurt Dao. He's the only friend of Nefari's that she trusts, which is something that doesn't come easy for Nefari. The last time her mother had trusted someone, she died. The traitor, a longtime family friend and confidant, was Vale Riversdale's mother, Gen.

It had only proven to Nefari that anyone can be bought to do the most despicable deeds, but she's never seen Dao fold to such pressure. Not even when pushed to do so. He's always remained on Nefari's side.

Though Dao has admirers, by the near-constant intensity of his eyes, Nefari knows he only has feelings for her. Feelings she cannot return. Her 'feelings' were meant to belong to the man she was intended to marry this year. A man dead.

Vale's features pop into her mind's eye. Although his intense eyes, sharp nose, and thick lips are distorted by time, she can still fill in the blanks. Every year that passes brings another thing she forgets about him, but she refuses to forget his face.

She shies away from Dao's gaze. "What are you doing here? Did Bastian ask you to talk some sense into me?"

Dao crosses his arms and leans against the door frame. "He mentioned something. The whole city is talking about it, and not necessarily in a good way."

She has never understood why they call it a city. Salix's capital is far more populated and, from what she's heard, more extravagant and civilized. Truly, the centaurs aren't a prospering species, and they're certainly heathens. As warriors, there are some years when more die than are given life. Besides, the valley within the mountains isn't large enough to host more than a hundred more than it already has. Not unless they sacrifice the trees that keep a majority of the city hidden.

Amused with his response, Nefari snorts. She strides to her trunk for a change of clothes. "I'm assuming you're talking about the

46

magic. I don't know why he cares so much. It was only a little bit, and as I told him, the wraiths never came."

"The magic, the arguing with Bastian, the fact that you didn't wait for the others . . ." Dao trails off. "You shouldn't undermine Bastian's authority, Fari. The others don't like it, and eventually, they will see him unfit to lead because of his soft spot for you. The Rebel Legion doesn't need a war between its own people."

Digging around a bit in the cluttered trunk, Nefari pulls out a tunic and a pair of leather pants. She tries hard not to let his word sink in, wishing he would give her some slack instead of trying to shape her into someone she doesn't want to be.

Patrix is right on that score.

Without being asked, Dao turns his back to her, and Nefari strips from yesterday's grimy clothes. She hadn't bothered to change when they returned home. After she stabled her mare, she had flopped in her bed and immediately fell asleep.

Nefari dips her hand into the water bucket Bastian had gotten for her last night and rings out the cloth. The frigid water loudly plops back inside.

None of the huts have bathing chambers – the one thing she misses most about the Shadow Castle – so unless she wants to make the trek to the communal hot springs . . .

She quickly wipes herself down with the cloth, careful to avoid the stitches, and scrubs at her raw face. Her cheeks are still wind burnt and chapped from the blustering wind.

Water splashes out of the bucket when she drops the cloth back inside. Nefari rises to his disapproving mood, which seeps into the room like a rotting stench while he waits for her to finish. "Everything worked out the way it was supposed to. No one died, Dao."

"Only because you were lucky," he grunts. His words echo down the wide and tall hall which stretches to the rest of Bastian's hut.

"Would you have done anything differently?" The words are muffled by her tunic as she shoves her head through the hole.

"Yes. It isn't my job to question those wiser than I."

She huffs. It's the main reason she's not attracted to him. He's too comfortable with authority that he doesn't question it when it collides with morals and common sense.

"You weren't there. No one in their right mind – Look, you didn't see –"

"Were you, Fari?" His voice is soft but petulant. "You were there, yes. But were you in your right mind?"

Fully dressed, she grinds her teeth while shutting the lid of her trunk. Dao turns around and leans against the doorframe. He continues, "Can you blame him for trying to keep you safe? Besides, if he did treat you like everyone else, he would have dragged you before the council as soon as you returned. You would have been destined for the shame post."

Nefari bristles, knowing he's right. The wooden pole outside of the Council Hut is where those who've broken meager laws get tethered for everyone to witness their crimes. Nefari has never been subjected to the shame of it, and she never wants to. There are some things she proudly avoids.

She ignores his mights and maybes and answers his question. "He doesn't need to try. I don't know how much clearer I can make it. I don't need his guidance. I never asked for it, and frankly, I don't want it." Nefari puts her hands on her hips and breathes deeply. She can feel her magic stirring as her agitation grows.

"You need to find a way to get over the blood vow."

Get over it? Nefari gapes at him. "He could have saved both, Dao. We've all heard the legends. We've all seen him fight. He could have killed those crones and saved all three of us. He chose not to. He chose to break his blood vow and let them die."

Her mother, Amala Ashcroft, had asked one thing of him: to save the shadow children should the kingdom fall. And when that time came, he left Amoon, Nefari's cousin and best friend, to die. She was eaten by the crones who were sent to kill Nefari on the Queen of Salix's orders, all because Bastian used her and Amoon's similar appearance to make a quick and unnoticed escape. Bastian tossed Amoon to the crone's feet, and they had pounced like starving dogs to a bone.

Nefari's cousin wasn't the only one he left behind, either. No. When the screams from the throne room traveled down the hall and spilled into Nefari's chambers, Nefari had hidden inside her closet with Vale Riversdale. Vale was her age, and they were promised to be wed once they both turned eighteen. Even at such a young age, she knew she loved him, but as Bastian leapt from the castle window with both Vale and Nefari on his back, Vale had fallen off and tumbled right back into her chambers.

Vale never made it out of the castle that day. He wasn't among the children who were fortunate enough to be saved by the centaurs. Nefari was the last person to see him. The last person to touch him. He was the last person who wiped away her tears.

She's probably the only person left who remembers him – who still loves him even though he's dead.

These actions had made Bastian break his vow, and he'll wear the black scar until the day he dies as a reminder to all around him of what he'd done. But instead of being punished by his people – or seen as untrustworthy – the Rebel Legion dismissed it, claiming he could have done no differently in order to save Nefari. No one batted an eye. She had even heard some whisper, "Sometimes, promises cannot be kept," as if it were a righteous explanation for two dead children.

But Nefari will. She's been delivering his punishment ever since. She'll never trust Bastian, care about what he wants, and will always take pleasure in disobeying nearly every command. He didn't give her mother that luxury of trust, and she won't give it to him, either.

"It wasn't as simple as that, and you know it." Dao shakes his head disapprovingly.

"Because I'm the Fate-blessed princess," Nefari mocks, complete with hand gestures. It's the same old conversation they always have when Bastian asks Dao to talk some sense into her. "I'm so sick of hearing that. The only gift Fate gave me upon his demise was power. Power that, so far, only makes the shadows attracted to me. Power that, even if I did know what it could do, I can't use because –" She holds out her arms and emphasizes the world.

"The shadows are attracted to you?" Dao cocks his head to the side. His question goes unanswered.

The fight leaves Nefari in a huff, and she glances away and softens her voice. "What did Fate expect me to do? Take his power to Salix and destroy Despair? If it were easy, he could have done it himself."

"You and I both know Fate had his reasons. Just because we don't know what they are now doesn't mean –"

Tiredly, Nefari swipes a hand through the air. "Enough. Okay? Enough. Your point – Look – I don't want to be queen of anything. I'm doing what I can to help keep others out of slavery, but that's as far as I go. I'm only one person."

Dao steps into the room and drops his arms to his sides. "You don't want to save our people?" Just like her slip about the shadows, she's never said that to him out loud. Until now, she's let him assume that someday she'd save their people from slavery and harvest. "I knew you had no desire to be queen, but I didn't think . . ."

Her gaze turns hard at his wordless accusation. "Like I said, it's not something I could do alone, and you know it."

He chuffs, and red splotches blossom over his cheeks. "Your choice to be alone is also self-inflicted."

She laughs and pushes past him to retrieve her sword resting by the fireplace. "I would never ask the Shadow People here to help me. The chances of you guys getting caught and enslaved are too high." She straps her sword to her hip. "It's not like I can hunt down Choice and Hope and demand their help. Sibyl was very clear. The Queen Sieba Arsonian – Despair, to be more accurate – has Hope. A smart person would devise that Choice is dead. Or fled entirely. Finding Choice isn't in the cards, unfortunately." Quite literally, actually.

"You put too much trust in Sibyl."

Nefari shakes her head and briefly closes her eyes. "She's been nothing but good to me."

Everything Sibyl does is to help Nefari move on from her past and embrace what's left of her future, and though she's set on Nefari picking up her crown like the others, her urging feels entirely different.

Sibyl had used her fate card to see if she could discover Choice's whereabouts, but all the card showed was an organ – a beautiful gold heart.

The fate card is an interesting piece of magic. It's a blank rectangle that shows a symbol of the fate one wishes to see. In a swirl of fog inside the card itself, an object will appear. Most often than not, Nefari can never decipher what the object means, but this is why Sibyl is the seer and not Nefari.

Dao rubs at his jaw but drops the topic of Sibyl entirely. "How do you know Choice isn't simply hiding? How do you know Choice didn't do what Fate did and bestow their power onto another?"

Sword fully fastened to her side, she then tugs her hair up and ties it with a leather strap. "Don't you think we would have known by now?"

"No." He shrugs. "No one knows you're still alive."

She casts her attention to the ceiling, exasperated. Dao unhooks her black fur cloak from beside her bedroom door and hands it to her as she says, "The realm is large and plentiful, Dao. If Choice had chosen someone, a wise person should still consider it impossible to find him. But still, Hope, captive as she is, is untouchable." She sweeps her arm out. "So here we are. My decision is still final. I will remain in the Rebel Legion as nothing but a warrior because there is nothing I can do." She said the last few words between her clenched teeth. She may be close to Dao, but he doesn't need to be burdened with the other reasons for why she wants nothing to do with sitting on a throne and freeing people on a fool's errand to save this unsavable realm. "Now, can we go?"

Without another word, Dao turns, leading them from her room and through the rest of Bastian's hut.

The hut is larger than the others in the village, telling of Bastian's higher position. However, in a resemblance to Nefari's bedroom, there is little in the way of belongings and cherished possessions. Dao's hut is vastly different.

Like Nefari, all the other shadow children were taken in by other centaurs who reared them until they grew. She and Dao are the only two who still live in the same huts they first arrived in.

Old and wise Swen Copsteel, the city's record keeper, had taken in Dao. Swen knows all the history that stretches from one end of the realm to the other. Over the past ten years, he's taken the time to pass the information and engrain the knowledge onto his young charge, who continues to show a great interest in the subject. Perhaps the record keeper's wisdom of the past is why Dao is so cautious to break the rules given in the present.

They pass the many bland and large cushions in the main section of the hut. The cushions rest against the floorboards and are larger than she is.

To their right, in the kitchen, is an extremely high slab of wood that makes the dining table. It's where Bastian has his morning tea, and empty mugs are religiously left there. From years of exhaustive carelessness, the wood is marred with the dark herbal stains. Nefari often thinks this is the sole reason Bastian doesn't have a wife. Being a slob is repellent to most women. Perhaps, none will have him.

The centaur in question is nowhere to be found, and Nefari wonders how early he had woken or if he had even gone to bed in the first place. As leader of the centaurs, she's aware of how little sleep he gets.

Nefari huffs as they reach the massive door. There's a hole in the bottom where the planks of wood don't quite form together, and a small pile of fresh snow rests in their path. Dao's boot squashes it.

"Any word on the Salix's court? The one who was riding through the area?" Nefari asks.

Over his shoulder, Dao quirks a brow. "You mean the princess of Salix?"

"So Patrix says. It could be a rumor, Dao," she quips. She and Fawn had discussed it as soon as Patrix took off on his horse in Chickasaw. Both had drawn the conclusion that Patrix may not

53

know everything, no matter what the spy claims. "We don't know if it was the princess. No one knows what she looks like. No one has seen her face. No one even knows her name. We shouldn't believe it to be the princess because it would be foolish to think Queen Sieba had let her leave. Besides, what would the princess of Salix be doing this far west, headed toward the Fades?"

He holds the door open for her, and gusts of wind blow more snow inside. "You think she was headed toward the Fades?"

"That's what Patrix deduced." Nefari pulls her cloak's hood over her head, steps out into the storm, and shouts into the wind. "But like I said, logic would reason that it isn't the princess. What business would the princess have with the crones?"

"But still, the court was headed toward the Fades."

"Rumors, Dao. Rumors."

They lean into the push of the storm as they head down the wide path, weaving between jutting boulders and toward the morning meal in the great mess hall a few huts down.

"The crones are allies with Salix. Maybe the princess is negotiating with the crones on Queen Sieba Arsonian's behalf."

"It's not the princess!" Nefari growls. "If there were negotiations to be had, she would have sent her son, who is set to rule if the crown-wearing hag ever dies. *If* negotiations needed to be had, it would be Prince Philip Arsonian in the lion-crested carriage."

He peeks at her from inside his hood. "Don't you trust anyone?"

She grits her teeth and squints down the path. "Yes, Dao. Yes. I trust death."

Dao chuckles without humor and shakes his head.

# CHAPTER FOUR

Patrix Eiling saddles his horse. Here, where the Kadoka Mountains meet the Shadled Forest, the close-sewn trees block the storm entirely. They also block the day's light, and the only reason he knows it's morning is due to his internal clock.

The pleasant aroma of the trees tickles his sensitive nose, an alluring scent that tricks passersby into believing the forest is harmless. He hadn't had a choice but to take shelter inside the forest. This is the last place he wanted to be, and he barely slept because of it.

Paranoid, he peers at the trees over his shoulder before turning his gaze in the direction of the Sea of Gold he and his horse will cross this day. The sharp blades of grass are harmless to hooved creatures, but they still make the spy nervous. One fall from the horse and he'll have hundreds of bleeding cuts. The Sea of Gold isn't forgiving, and it's never his favorite part of his journeys. This evening, he'll be thankful to see the glistening green water of Caw's Cove.

While he repeats the demands of Bastian to himself, he pats his sleepy horse's neck and dips underneath it. "Soon, brother," he murmurs to the horse. "Soon, we'll be in the heart of Urbana, and you'll be stabled in Vivian's castle. You'll have your belly full of oats soon enough." He straightens the twisted stirrup and then startles when a twig snaps.

Both he and the horse look in the direction of the noise. The Shadled trees create near eternal darkness despite the tendrils of flames that still eat at the burnt logs in the meager fire he had built and slept beside.

The two stare for a long while, frozen. Patrix strokes his horse's shoulder with his knuckle and murmurs to soothe them both, "Probably just an unfortunate animal." After all, he can't be the only one who sought the trees' shelter.

Turning back to the task at hand, Patrix readjusts his reins when a soft cackling laugh crawls up his spine.

Eyes prick the back of his neck.

He whips around. His horse knickers and dances as the sense of danger reaches them both. "Who – Who's there?" If it's a Salix soldier, he'll kill him just for making his heart march out of his chest.

Sliding his hand under his cloak, he grips the pommel of his sword. The horse rears, and soon, Patrix is scrambling out of the way from the beast's flailing legs.

"Whoa, whoa!"

The horse doesn't listen to his pleas or the hand gestures accompanying them. Mid-rear, the horse turns and gallops down the path they were to travel on today.

Cursing under his breath, Patrix flares his nostrils as he whirls back to the dark forest. He pulls the sword from its sheath. The off-feeling continues to curl around his gut.

"Hello?" Patrix calls again. "What do you want?" With any luck, the cackle will have come from some maiden who lost her way and found his fuzzy ears funny.

56

His breath fogs the space around him, the atmosphere as chilly in these parts as Kadoka Mountain itself.

Seconds tick by, and not a peep reaches his ears. Not a sound. As Patrix starts to chuckle at his own fear and re-sheath his sword, a rough but feminine voice says over his shoulder, "Satyr."

Patrix stumbles over a protruding root. His sword flies from his hand, and his rump hits the ground. He scrambles back, eyes wildly searching for the voice that now cackles inhumanly from every direction, and then . . .

The telling stench reaches his nose.

"Crone," Patrix growls into the forest, gripping the parched dirt of the Shadled Forest floor. They patrol these woods now that Nefari's people are gone, but he's never seen one this close to its edge.

He scrambles the short distance to his sword, grips the pommel, and quickly rises. "Come out and face me!" He angles his sword this way and that, readying himself for the great chance that this may very well be his last breath.

The crone's laughter increases in volume.

"What do you want?" he demands. "Where are you?"

Heartbeats tick by. Frantic heartbeats that roar in his ears.

"Here," the crone barks, and strong but withered hands shove him into a tree's trunk. The movement was too fast, the forest too dark for him to see her coming. The crone holds him there, the stench stronger, and soon, he can make out her features when her nose runs up his neck. "You smell of sweet, sweet stars, Satyr. There is only one individual I know of who would smell so sweet."

The crone's hair is wild, but part of her head is bald as if she snagged it on something and ripped it out without a second thought. Her skin is aged and deep grooved, a resemblance to tree bark, and her teeth. . . *My Divine, her teeth.* They're jagged nubs like the shards of broken glass.

Patrix lifts the pommel of his sword and rams it into the crone's ribs. The crone hisses and stumbles backward. He whirls and slashes his blade into the darkness that enfolded her, but all it meets is air.

The crone is gone.

He growls while turning in a crouched circle. "End the games, hag!" The pop of his dwindling fire follows his voice, but he knows she's still there, watching him, waiting in the shadows too dark to see through. "End them now, and I'll let you live!"

"Let me live?" Her laughter booms once more, but Patrix can't tell where it comes from. "Do you truly think you can kill me?"

Turning in a slow circle, Patrix grins wickedly. "I do not know, but I assure you, if you are the only one to walk away, it won't be whole." He wordlessly prays to any Divine who might still be alive.

*You smell of sweet, sweet stars, she had said.* It was enough to make Patrix's blood run cold because that one sentence means she knows more than she should. She can't be allowed to live. Even if Patrix dies, she must be wounded enough that she, too, won't make it out of this forest.

"I don't much like to eat satyrs. Too boney, you see. But it's been a while, and my stomach assures me you'll make a delicious meal." It's too late for Patrix to move out of the way. Too late to sidestep or swing his blade. The crone drops from the tree branches and lands on top of him.

In a messy and tangled heap, they hit the hard and frozen forest floor peppered with snow. She straddles him immediately, her rags slipping off her thin frame. Her fingers dig into his shoulders as he wiggles and tries to dislodge the crone. Blood wells where her nails puncture his skin, and she bends lower to laugh gleefully in his face.

Grunting, Patrix cranes his neck to get away from her stench and the spittle that splats against his temple.

"You indeed smell of sweet, sweet stars. Do you know what this means, Patrix Eiling, spy to all kingdoms?" Patrix stiffens at her words. "Yes, yes, I know who you are. *I can smell it*."

"Get off me!"

She laughs once more. "Try as you might, but the spider has caught its fly. Still your movements, and maybe I'll let you live."

Patrix's nostrils flare, and he whips his gaze back to hers. "Why?"

"Because a spy is always useful, you foolish, foolish man."

He considers her expression, a mix of wickedness and innocence on a face so wrinkled with age.

From his position, and her closeness to his face, he can't make anything out past her head. There could be more of them, more crones who will pick apart his flesh like the bone criers scenting impending death from hundreds of miles away. He needs to get this over with. If the bone criers do come, the wraiths and the Salix soldiers will follow.

"What do you want? Who are you?"

"Raygelle is my name."

Patrix's face pales. He knows who she is.

She eases her sharp nails out of his shoulders. "You know that I know, don't you. You've touched her. Loved the child of stars like a little, itty-bitty, helpless sister." She cocks her head to the side, a strangely animalistic gesture.

"No," he says firmly through his teeth.

"You stink of lies. So many lies; I cannot weed through them all. Tell me, satyr, does she still live?"

"I already told you. I don't know who you are talking about."

Raygelle glares. "Do remember that your life is in my hands. And if your life isn't enough incentive, I will feast on those who are. Those you care for. I can scent lineage, Satyr. Not just those you've come into contact with." She runs a nail down the vital vein in his neck. "I know whose blood runs through your veins. And I will not stop until I have my answers now that I smell her scent – her mother's unforgettable scent – on you."

Patrix flexes his jaw. If he lies, she'll know it, and he'll die. If he dies, this mission will never be completed, and the Rebel Legion will never get their answer. "Yes," he hisses. Guilt curls in his stomach like sour milk. "Yes. Okay? Yes, I know who you speak of."

"We thought as much. *I* thought as much. The girl's flesh I tasted ten years ago didn't taste nearly as lovely as it should have. Not for royal blood." She wistfully studies the very shadows the Shadow People used to jump through. "We still dream of her, you know. We still know she breathes."

When he struggles underneath her once more, she inserts her nails back into the wounds. Patrix hollers. "If you had known for sure, your sister would have shared it with Queen Sieba." Wrenchel Withervein, the crone who governs over all three crone factions is her sister. The very crone who first uttered Nefari's prophecy right here in these very trees. He raises his head until his nose nearly touches hers. "If you had known for sure, you

60

wouldn't have needed my assurance. Or maybe you've kept your mouth shut because you ate the wrong girl."

"Little hooved man." She licks the skin beside his nose. "You are too arrogant for your own good."

"Despite what you think, I am no fool. Your sister is the reason there is nothing left of the Shadow Kingdom. Your sister is the reason Despair's darkness was able to reach every nook and crevice of this realm. The only reason I assured you was because I know you have no idea where she's hidden."

"The Shadow Kingdom may be riddled with the ash of her dead, but it still stands in the pocket of Shadled Forest shadows. She will come for it eventually. She will desire to know what became of it and, perhaps, what . . . *trinkets* were left behind."

Patrix exhales through his nostrils. "You truly haven't told Queen Sieba you think she's still alive, have you." The crone's silence is answer enough. "Why?"

"Oh, Satyr. For a spy, I am terribly disappointed in you." The crone's tone takes on an offended quality, which morphs to rage in the flip of a hat. "Why would we tell the Queen of Salix – Despair – that the Fate-blessed Shadow Princess still lives? Do you think we'd blindly follow a God who needs us? We – the three factions – need nobody."

"I assumed so you can end the prophecy the Queen had once feared." Patrix blinks as a thought hits him. "No. No, you wouldn't because you need the princess for something, don't you?"

The wicked grin returns, and the crone eases her fingers out of the punctures they created. "There are many who need her, Satyr, each for different reasons. But we will get her first, and when we're finished with her, she will die the death she was always meant to. The queen will be none-the-wiser, and the darkness will continue to spread. No one will be safe. Not even your beloved centaurs."

Patrix blinks, and in that sliver of a second, the weight of the crone leaves his chest. He sits up abruptly and searches the dark for Raygelle's retreating back.

"You won't get your hands on her!" he shouts to the dark and then whispers to himself, "I won't let you."

# Chapter Five

The great mess hall smells like tea and smoked meats, and the atmosphere is jovial despite Nefari's sour mood. Coins rattle in purses. Weapons strapped to hips clank against each other. Laughter booms, and conversation flows.

Shoveling the last of her eggs into her mouth, Nefari watches everyone around her. Dao hasn't said a word since they sat at their table, and the two have been content to remain silent.

At a table by the kitchen, Fawn stands, gambling with three other centaurs. Dice are rolled between them, and at Fawn's next turn, she angrily slams her fist on the table. The coins stacked off to the side fall over.

More of the Rebel Legion's centaurs move through the line of splayed food across a large table, passing over good coin for their meals into the palm of the butcher named Nio when they reach the end of the line. The dry cracks along Nio's hands are always stained red from animal blood. Nefari can see them from where she sits and knows it's a hazard of his job.

Numerous scars are slashed across Nio's face. When Nefari was younger, she had once asked him about the scars. He had told her he squabbled with a crone in his youth. A cluster of crones had wandered too close to Kadoka City. That particular crone hadn't walked away, and by the time his alarming story was over, she promised herself to never test the patience of the butcher.

Standing and alone at another table, gray, aged, and bent Swen Copsteel eats while pouring over an ancient book laid open in front of him. He shakily lifts a spoon of eggs and shoves it into his beard-clad mouth. Nefari often wonders if the man, his mind as sharp as any blade, will outlive them all.

She moves her focus away from Swen. There are only a few tables meant to accommodate those with only two legs. They're hip height and, thankfully, have chairs. The other tables reach Nefari's shoulders, and since the centaurs cannot sit, they stand while they joke, gossip, and shove each other around like wild heathens. Nefari often grins at it, but not today. The memory of her dream constantly invades her thoughts, teamed with the argument she and Dao had.

When Dao finally speaks, it startles her. He shoves away his empty tray. "Are you meeting with Bastian this morning?"

She twirls her spoon between her fingers and leans back in her chair. "I've been ordered to."

He peers at her sidelong. "Are you going to listen to this order?"

Smugly, she mutters, "If I ever want to leave the city, I'll have to."

"What's he teaching you today?"

She glances briefly at him, stands from her chair mid-stretch, and hands him her spoon. She's already late, which means she'll have to feed Astra, her mare, after her lesson. If it hadn't been for her and Dao's argument earlier, she would have been on time. She just hopes the horse will forgive her delayed appearance. "He's never divulged the details of our lessons before. Why would he now?"

Dao grins up at her and then stacks her tray on top of his. "That's because he doesn't want you to prep for it. Surely you've noted that already."

Chuckling, she turns from him and strides out of the mess hall. "Of course, I know," she says to the wind as she pushes the door open. "Bastian loves the element of surprise."

Bastian has been training Nefari since her mother died. Her mother had told her stories when she was still alive – stories of The Great Bastian Pike, Leader of the Centaurs. He had trained her, too, and Nefari's grandparents.

When she first arrived, he and the other centaurs allowed the children a few weeks to grieve, but after that, they trained right alongside the centaur children. Nefari was often paired with Fawn because of their similar determination and broken spirits. Fawn's own parents had died in the same crone battle Nio received his scars from, and it had made her personality as hard as a rock.

Their similar pasts and shared personalities have never made them as close as sisters, but it did teach them how to respect and listen to one another. Nefari supposes Fawn's the only female friend she has here, but Bastian's urging to bud a close relationship between them was fruitless.

There are many legends surrounding Bastian. No one knows how old he truly is, for the centaurs have a longer than average lifespan. He's certainly not as old as Swen. His fight has always been about the betterment of the realm. Some believe Choice – the Divine who created the hooved creatures – had bestowed Bastian with superior abilities to fight and lead, but Nefari won't go as far as that superstition.

Hard work and diligence had made Bastian the warrior he is and nothing more. It is the only thing she respects about him.

From an early age, Nefari has learned to be a warrior – a killer when she must, a savior when she could – by Bastian's pushing. Each lesson varied from the others. Some were hand-to-hand combat. Sometimes, she trained with a bow. And sometimes, she wielded a sword. The sword lessons had always been a favorite of hers despite enduring her teacher. Wielding a blade reminded her of the shadow dances performed in the Shadow Kingdom – like the sword itself was an extension to the dance.

The teachings she isn't particularly fond of are the lessons of the mind and spirit. Each of those lessons makes her feel graceless. In her opinion, her personal depth doesn't go far beyond self-preservation.

During the time she was in the mess hall, the storm had begun to pass. The wind doesn't howl, and the snow doesn't sting her skin. She weaves through the huts, avoiding the city's main path that will be teaming with centaurs.

At this hour, gatherers will be rushing to the mess hall, carrying baskets full of traded crops slung over their backs, and elsewhere, merchants will be calling out their handmade goods to all who jingle with coin. Nefari's patience is thin enough already. It's best she avoids situations where she might snap on unsuspecting and innocent sellers.

Once outside the heart of the city, she follows the path to where Bastian had said he would meet her when he dropped off the bucket of water in her room. The path leads up a sharp hill that the jagged white mountains tower over. Great pine trees are speckled throughout, and because of them, the snowdrifts hadn't buried the path.

There are many paths outside of the main parts of Kadoka City. Some lead to nowhere; others lead to somewhere, and some wind and curl until the treader finds themselves back to where they started. Getting lost in these woods would be cumbersome. Once, when she herself had taken the wrong path, she was forced to follow a bleating herd of sheep trotting back to the stables for their daily feed.

The trek is blissfully quiet. She leisurely walks while trailing her hands along the lower branches' piney needles. When the weather is favorable, she likes to gather the needles, stray sticks, and stones and make crowns similar to the Shadow Kingdom's crown – the one destroyed in her mother's blast of magic.

Her mother never wore the physical crown, though. It was more of a relic than anything else, and Nefari had often wondered why but dared not ask. Her father didn't like it when she asked too many questions.

Nefari doesn't know why she's fascinated with recreating the true Shadow Kingdom crown. Perhaps it's so she never forgets what it had looked like though she could just ask Swen. He'd have a picture somewhere in his many books. Perhaps she makes them to honor her fallen mother since there isn't a grave or place to visit. Perhaps Nefari just likes to punish herself with the reminder of what she fails to become: Worthy.

The path eventually spills out on a small cliff that overlooks a large flock of fluffy black and white sheep. Bastian waits there, his hand on a tall, protruding boulder jutting at an angle. He watches them nose through the fresh snow for scraps of food.

The livestock wander aimlessly here, free to roam. There's no point in keeping them in pens when the only way out of the city is through the tunnel. The only animals stabled are the horses because they can be a pain to hunt down, especially when there's no warning for when the Rebel Legion must depart on rescues.

"You're late," Bastian grumbles quietly. The soft wind ruffles his hair tied neatly at the nape of his neck with the usual leather strip. The sheep pop their heads up to blink at the sound of his voice but then return to their meager breakfast when they're sure he doesn't carry a bucket of grain.

Nefari says nothing as she strides to his side. He doesn't have any of his usual weapons with him. Normally, he carries a bow over his shoulder, a quiver full of arrows over the other, and a sword as tall as Nefari at his front hip. Today, his free hand grips a normal-sized practice bow and only one arrow.

He passes them to her, and she takes them questioningly. "Are we hunting today?" *And with just one arrow?* Nefari doesn't add; she's already in enough trouble.

Lifting the arrow, she wrinkles her nose at it. Sure, Nefari is good enough to take down an animal in the first shot, but when she goes hunting with the others, they carry numerous arrows and bring back many animals. It takes much to feed this city and many skins to trade for the goods they cannot grow themselves.

Bastian peers down at her, and she studies him in return. Centaurs have the most marvelous skin. What appears to be tattoos across their torso and upper arms are actually an ingenious camouflage thought up by Choice when he had created them. The markings change shades and patterns to blend with their surroundings. Right now, Bastian's markings resemble the thin needles of the trees embracing them. They shift and wave as if the gale itself is stirring them underneath his skin.

"Yes and no," Bastian answers. He kneels near the edge of the cliff and then lowers his other half until his belly is resting on the rocks and snow and his hooves are folded underneath him. He pats the space next to him. "Come."

Curiosity outweighing her distaste for him, Nefari obeys and adjusts her cloak to cover her legs. The ground is frigid against her leather pants, but she's thankful she's not some primping girl who wears only fine dresses. She's met a few of them in Caw's

Cove's Black Market. To say she wasn't impressed is an understatement.

"Take aim," Bastian orders.

"We're hunting sheep?" She's never hunted the village's livestock. They're normally killed in a more traditional fashion and only if the wild beasts beyond the mountain are scarce. The livestock are never butchered for such frivolous things like her lessons with Bastian. Skewering them with this dull practice arrow would be a prolonged and painful death – something no creature deserves.

Surely, he means something else. She squints past the sheep, searching for another animal who may have strayed into the city's perimeter. A large bird, perhaps.

Bastian crosses his arms, and each word that follows is clipped. "Shoot a sheep."

Anger bubbles in her chest. "Why?"

The heat of his breath fogs the air when he sighs. "You know how to take a life to preserve your own, Fari. I've taught you to take care of yourself. What I haven't taught you is how to take the life of someone who doesn't necessarily deserve death." Bastian peers down at her again. His eyes trace the arrow clenched in her grip. The arrow's dull metal tip glints back at him.

With a hairy finger, he points to one particular sheep. "Shoot that one."

Nefari follows his line of sight. This sheep is plump. Its kid leans into her hip, and it's too large eyes blink up at them. The kid, not more than a few weeks old, is unaware of what might happen next. Unaware of how its life will change in a split second, should Nefari obey.

Her grip on the arrow slackens as her decision is immediately made. "No." She doesn't want anything to do with a lesson like this. "I'm not a monster. If I kill the mother, the kid will die."

He purses his lips. "What if I told you she's sick and she'll infect the rest of the flock."

"Is she?" He only shrugs. "What is this, Bastian?"

"Fari –" She watches his fingers curl into his palm and brush the scar.

"I have morals," she chuffs. "I won't kill a mother because of those morals."

"But you'll risk the longevity of the flock for one mother and her child? You'll risk the life of a village for one woman?"

She blinks and then snarls at him.

He holds up a hand. "The choice you made to save that woman was the noble one, but there are choices that won't always be so simple. And, there are some circumstances that won't come with choices – like your mother's."

Nefari looks away and grinds her teeth. "Don't you think I know that?"

"Sometimes, I think you forget," he says gently. "Sometimes, I think you resent your mother for it. Now, will you kill the sheep's mother? Or will she live? Do you save the flock to feed your people? Or do we go hungry so the child may live to nibble on his first piece of grass before he, too, dies?"

Her grip on the arrow tightens dangerously. The slender wood groans. She says, "Move the sheep and her child to isolation if you're worried about illness. See what becomes of it because there are other ways to save the flock. Dooming the young sheep isn't one of them. They're both as worthy of living, of taking breath as the rest of them."

70

"You're missing the point."

"I'm not. You're telling me that dooming that kid is better for every other animal in the herd. And I'm telling you that other precautions can be taken. This isn't one of those impossible circumstances, Bastian. This is simple." Quickly, Nefari stands and moves to stride down the path. She won't do it.

"Nefari?" Bastian calls. His tone is unusually even, calm, and Nefari glances over her shoulder for this very reason. She had expected him to order her return. Expected punishment for her disobedience. Instead, a small prideful smile gleams across his face.

She turns back to him.

Muscles shifting and swaying, he gathers his legs underneath him and crosses the distance between them. He clasps his hand on her shoulder. "Perhaps someday, you will heed your own advice and see your own worth. Your mother did."

Insulted, Nefari blinks, and the bow nearly falls from her hand. "That's it? This was the test?"

Bastian tries to hide his smile. "You've been reckless lately. Patrix had concerns . . . I wanted to make sure I could still trust you. I wanted to be sure –"

She narrows her eyes. "I assure you that you can still trust me despite what the gossiping satyr says." Nefari has half a mind to send him a raven just for talking behind her back.

"And now I know for certain. You're eighteen, Nefari. You're of age to claim your throne, and because you are, you're reliving your past and allowing it to influence your actions. Don't, because, despite your similar appearances and your strong, stubborn heart, you are not your mother. She didn't have choices. You do. If you continue to hold yourself to impossible standards or, more accurately, continue to blame her for something she couldn't control, it'll turn you into someone you hate. Don't let your mother's sacrifice cripple you. You are worthy of your title, Nefari Astra Galazee Ashcroft, and she knew that. You are capable of being more than she ever could. She would be proud to see the decision you made today."

*Be brave*, her mother's words echo. It is all she had ever asked of Nefari.

Shouldering her bow, she says, "I'm not ready ..."

He drops his hand back to his side. "I'm not asking you to be queen today. I'm asking you to be queen, *someday*. If she were here right now, she would have said the same thing."

Nefari's eye twitches as she peers at the nearest tree. "What do you think she would say if I told her I just wanted freedom?"

"She would say you are as free as they come. It is everyone else who is not."

"I won't be if I wear a crown."

"Ah," he says softly, and it's enough for Nefari to return her attention to him. Then, he throws her words back at her. "There are other ways to save a flock, and unlike your mother's situation, you have the freedom to save your people in more ways than one. There are many paths. You just have to choose one because being a warrior in the Rebel Legion will only get you so far."

There's a pause between them as Nefari toes the snow. Her voice comes out small when she says, "I miss her."

He gently taps her chin. "We all do."

Nefari watches him walk away, his hooves softly clicking on the path. She grinds her jaw while his words replay over and over in her head. "Is the sheep truly troublesome?"

He grins over his shoulder. "Only if the sheep continues to believe it's only a sheep."

She chuffs. *You are nobody,* he had told her so long ago. And now . . . now he wants her to be somebody.

"Does this mean I'm no longer bound to the city?" she hollers down the path.

"No," he shouts back. She curses under her breath and kicks at a pocket of snow. His laughter booms among the trees.

# CHAPTER SIX

Ducking into the armory, Nefari sighs contentedly at the warmth of the forging fires within. Her frozen nose burns with this new change in temperature, and she wets her chapped lips as she glances around.

Fawn Whispersong has the fires at full blaze, and the sound of her hammer striking metal rings in Nefari's ears.

On the wall to Nefari's left are rows and rows of weapons: bows and arrows, swords, axes, and glinting throwing knives. They're all perfectly aligned, and all of the metal pieces reflect the flames.

There's a centaur-sized table a few paces from the door where patrons stand to make deals with Fawn. She doesn't like it when others invade her space and had erected this table to halt any unwanted advances into her forgery. Its wood surface is nicked and scarred from several years' worth of swords and arrows tossed onto it, and the floor itself is half ash and half dirt.

The armory hut smells of burning wood, metal, and sweat, and Nefari often wonders if the heat and the smells seep into the small attached room in the back where Fawn sleeps; when she sleeps here at all.

The door shuts behind Nefari, announcing her arrival, and Fawn looks up, hammer half raised. Her expression of concentration deepens into a frown, scrunching her lovely features slick with perspiration and smeared with ash.

From a young age, all the centaurs are trained well in combat, but there are still some females who prefer cosmetics and perfumes once they reach adulthood and begin dreaming of a family. Those females giggle in the presence of an attractive male, but Fawn has proudly distanced herself from being included in those numbers.

*She could be*, Nefari thinks to herself. Fawn has the beauty to be part of the simpering herd who prowl the taverns at night, but the ever-present ash smudges across her cheek and the scars along her arms have branded her as someone else. Someone who isn't interested in something so frivolous as true love. Someone who would rather have glory than a promised future with just one man.

And still, despite it all, Fawn has never had trouble finding someone to warm her bed. Who was it last night? The baker's unwed son? One of the warriors who had gone with them to Chickasaw?

Though . . . Nefari can't deny Fawn has some interest in a relationship. Everyone knows why she sneaks glances at Bastian with a certain longing in her eye, but she's never once made a move. She respects her teacher too much to do so, and for that, Nefari respects her. Innocent itches scratched is one thing, but understanding Bastian's disinterest is another. Bastian is married to his leadership and nothing more.

Fawn sets her hammer aside and wipes the sweat from her brow. Her red hair is a tangled, sticky mess around her face, and her naturally green lips are streaked with clumpy soot. Nefari sets the bow and arrow on the table. The table comes up to her shoulders, and the snarky welcome she had readied upon entry evaporates with the feeling of being so small and insignificant in front of it.

The centaur strides over. The clomping of her hooves sounds as loud as the hammer was. "Back so soon from your lesson?" she asks, peering at the practice bow and arrow. "And with no sheep, too?"

"Oh, there's a sheep," Nefari grumbles. "The sheep is with Nio, being skinned as we speak, but I didn't butcher the one Bastian asked me to, nor did I use this." She nods toward the dull arrow. A simple snap of her chosen sheep's spine had sufficed. It was a clean death, but she will never admit to the thanks she mumbled to the sheep and the long regard she and the little sheep shared afterward. The little sheep hadn't blinked an eye as if, at such an early age, he had been accustomed to death. Nefari envied it – had thought about that shared look the whole way back to the city with the dead sheep slung over her shoulder.

Fawn touches the tip of the dull arrow. "I'm going to assume Nio didn't thank you."

Nefari chuckles. "I don't think our butcher has ever thanked anyone. Not even the Divine." Nio would have known Bastian took her hunting. He and Bastian are good friends, and if she hadn't brought back something for him, she'd be getting eggshells in her breakfast every morning for a week.

A spark twinkles in Fawn's eyes, and she smirks.

Nefari traces a deep nick in the table's wood. "I saw you at breakfast this morning," she proceeds cautiously. "You should have warned me about the crap Bastian was going to pull today." She knows he would have told her, too, because he came to Fawn for the practice weapons.

The centaur slides her hands into her apron's pockets, and the mischief vanishes from her face.

Outside, drums begin to beat as another Rebel Legion party returns home. Nefari ignores them because returning warriors are a daily occurrence. Instead, she holds the gaze of the centaur until she finally speaks. "He's just trying to help, Fari. That's all he's ever done." Nefari flexes her jaw, and her earlier anger returns. "Everything he does and everything he teaches you is for a reason. Bastian doesn't waste his time for anyone. Aside from Sibyl, you're the only one he's ever taught for this long." Fawn glances at the window as the returning group passes by it. "He's trying to prepare you."

Nefari's irritation heightens to profound resentment. She grips the edge of the table tightly. No matter where she turns, someone is always pushing her toward a destination different from her own desires.

Magic snakes under her skin. The shadows dance in the corners as if a giant had come along and blown into the room. A weak light pulses once from her skin, and the weapons along the wall rattle as it washes over them.

Fawn staggers a foot to the side and blinks in surprise at her. When she regains her composure, she slaps her palm on the table. The arrow quivers from the force. "Fari! What the hell are you doing?"

"I – I –" She frowns at the walls of the hut, at the shadows that move and dance until they finally settle once more. "I didn't mean to."

Curling her top lip, Fawn pins her with a deep glare. "Do you want to alert the wraiths? My Divines," she spits. "Your recklessness will get everyone killed!"

"I said I didn't mean to," Nefari growls. The fading drums pound to the same rhythm as her heart. "Drop it."

Hissing with outrage, Fawn snatches the bow and arrow from the table. In her hands, both seem miniature and delicate. Her posture holds her rage as she marches to the wall and hangs the bow in its proper place and drops the arrow in the bucket with the other practice arrows.

The hut is quiet, aside from the sound of the crackling flames, and the two women use the reprieve to gather their wits about them. Fawn adjusts the bow's dangle with the tip of her finger, aligning perfectly with the others. When she turns her head, her gaze flits to the hand Nefari rests on the hilt of her sword.

Nefari follows her line of sight and grips it tighter.

"Is that the Black Market blade you bought?"

"Perhaps." She juts her chin. Fawn has never asked about it before. "Why?"

Swinging her rump around to fully face Nefari, Fawn swishes her braided red tail. The strands of it shimmer. "I've heard about it. Some of the others claim it sparkles when the light hits it just right. I haven't had a chance to see it for myself." A grin spreads across Fawn's face, one that tells Nefari she's about to be teased endlessly for adoring a sparkling blade.

"It doesn't sparkle," Nefari huffs. "There's something embedded within the metal itself. Some sort of substance."

Ash and dusty dirt rise as Fawn slowly returns to her spot on the other side of the table. She peers down her long nose at Nefari. "Can I see it?"

Raising her eyebrows, Nefari considers her request. She doesn't use it aside from Rebel Legion rescues, but it's always strapped to her hip, even when she's practicing with a training sword with the other warriors in the open space that sprawls beside the Council Hut. Fawn avoids anything remotely close to idle conversation, and now they're tapping dangerously close to one. But, Nefari supposes the conversation is about weapons, and weapons are where Fawn's fascination lies.

Choice made, Nefari shrugs and pulls the blade from its sheath. The metal rings until she sets it on the table.

Together, they study it. The sword does sparkle, Nefari will admit, but in the oddest way. Like it's living – throbbing – shimmering blue and purple within the silver in a way that resembles thick frost gleaming along the pane of cold windows.

Soundlessly, Fawn bends over the sword. She runs a finger over the smooth metal, and the odd substance inside it almost appears to . . . flare. "This is not normal steel, Fari."

"Have you ever seen anything like it?"

Shaking her head, braids fall into her face, and she tucks them behind her ears. "Did the merchant say what was forged with the steel?"

"No, and I didn't ask. The Black Market isn't a place to linger."

"The criminal life isn't for you?"

Nefari chuckles. "Contrary to popular belief, no."

Indeed, the Black Market at Caw's Cove's edge is infested with criminals from across the realm. Mostly pirates, but what's most scary is that Nefari can never pick out the assassins from the normal folk. The best killers often blend in with their surroundings. At least, some of the pirates make it easy to pick them out among a crowd.

The thought redirects Nefari's attention. "Did you hear about the pirates, too?" She isn't sure if the rumor had spread throughout the city yet. Before they had left for Chickasaw, she had heard about it in the morning's market.

"I did," Fawn answers while she traces the black strips of metal swirling above the pommel. "They say they're shipping slaves to Salix now."

Nefari rubs at her face to keep the color in her cheeks. "As if plundering villages for long lost treasures wasn't enough." She looks out the window and studies the way the clouds move across the sky.

The Rebel Legion hasn't encountered any pirates before. Not directly. If they someday do, Nefari isn't entirely sure who would walk away. The pirates live and breathe for gold and rare trinkets, and like the centaurs, they're capable of handling themselves.

She returns her attention to her sword. "Look, I'm late to see Sibyl, and I still have to stop by the stables. Do you want to –"

Fawn nods without Nefari having to finish her sentence. "I'll clean it but only after I look into this substance."

"Okay. Um – thank you," she responds as she backs away from the table. Nefari doesn't trust everyone, but she does trust Fawn when it comes to her belongings – mysterious sword or not. Besides, she hadn't cleaned the sword after their return from Chickasaw. Bastian would be outraged if he knew her sword hadn't been cared for before she plopped onto her bed.

Inside the stables, it isn't as chilly as the mountain's atmosphere. Its short ceiling and tight spaces help keep the warmth of the animals within its four walls made of both stone and wood.

The stable's far wall is the base of a gagged cliff, and the remaining three are logs stacked on top of one another. A tree juts up in the middle of the open space between stalls, its branches used as support beams for the roof itself.

Nefari rubs Astra's muzzle with the back of her knuckles, opens her stall gate, and throws a rope over the mare's neck. The horse lazily follows her lead without a fuss and stands untied outside of the stall. Nefari hums a tune – one her mother used to sing to her – and snatches a rag from a nearby tree stump the shadow children used to use were they too young to hop on their horses' backs from the ground.

She brings the cloth to Astra's flank and begins wiping away the barn's dust and the dried sweat from the saddle of yesterday's trek.

The mare's coat is thick but shines like it's laden with gold. She's a prized possession of Nefari, and many would have paid several purses brimming with coin for her. Nefari would have too if she had boughten her in the traditional fashion.

The Black Market isn't just for selling illegal things. Often, there are gambling tents where wine and ale distributors pass around their goods for extra sale. Some of alcohol is illegal and some can be found in any court or village. Either way, the patrons from all over the realm flock to the tents like the bone criers to the dead.

The day she bought her sword, she and Patrix snuck into the gambling tents. It had been Patrix's idea originally, seeming just as drawn to them as all the others, but Nefari hadn't disagreed. The games had looked fun – mischievous and rebellious, both things Nefari is attracted to.

Once they had snuck past the tent's burly guards, they had gotten particularly inebriated while they played cards against a woman with an interestingly feathered hat and a wicked gleam in her eye. She had been young, like Nefari, but a life at sea had aged her darker skin with too much exposure to the sun. She was a pirate and a young one at that.

It was a night Nefari will never forget, especially the brawl that had broken out toward the end of the game. She had long suspected Patrix began the fight, but she hadn't been paying attention to anything but the cards in her hands. The feathered-hat woman had engaged in the brawl, and when Patrix peeked at the woman's cards left sprawled across the table in her haste to defend herself, they had gleaned her losing hand. The game could have easily tipped back into the woman's favor with a few lucky draws from the stack, but . . .

Nefari still remembers the grin Patrix shot her way. She knows that grin. Whenever he grins like that, trouble follows. They had shrugged at one another, and Patrix had eagerly collected their prize without speaking another word to the woman. The prize was Astra, a beautiful mare born in the breeding guilds in the heart of Sutherland. Nefari hadn't been positive the feathered-hat woman had boughten the mare in the first place because she didn't appear particularly wealthy. Besides, what would a pirate need with a horse?

By that point, both were staggeringly drunk. The pair had hopped on the horse, plump saddlebags strapped to the saddle, and rode into the night. It hadn't taken long for Patrix to name her. Astra is part of Nefari's name: Nefari Astra Galazee Ashcroft. Nefari hadn't disagreed because it meant he was giving her the horse to claim as her own. "An early birthday present," he had told her.

She never learned what was in those bags. Coins and gold, probably. She had never asked Patrix when he took them for himself, making excuses about how he could use the coin while on his many travels.

Nefari's fortunate she won. The only thing she had left to gamble was her life… or her new sword. At that point in her life – a particularly low point – she's not sure which one she would have chosen. Her dreams and memories had been worse then, especially since her seventeenth birthday was only a few days away. She remembers thinking she had one more year until . . .

Nothing had felt lonelier than her seventeenth year.

The mare nudges her side, and Nefari clucks at her in response. "Stay here," Nefari says in a soft and loving voice while she begins the task of mucking her stall. Astra shakes her head, and her long mane shifts like ribbons of silver and gold, an impatient gesture for the hay and oats she knows will come once Nefari is finished with her stall.

Out of everything in Nefari's seventeenth year, Astra is the only thing that had never changed. She was her constant, a predictable beast who never minded Nefari's company. Sure, she had Dao to lean on, but over the years, Dao had changed and continues to change as he matures into the man he's being morphed to be. She doesn't fit so well by his side like she used to. And Sibyl . . . well, Sibyl is Sibyl. She knows everything, especially the things left unsaid. It's not always pleasant to be around her.

So, in the absence of a devoted friendly companionship, Nefari has always turned to the mare to share her weaknesses. She speaks to Astra about her dreams, about the ring slipping around on her finger and where it had come from. She murmurs her fears to the horse and the details of faces belonging to those she's killed. The mare listens without judgment, and best of all, she can't respond.

Nefari often has dreams about her past, snippets of memory that haunt her, as if it's a grave she constantly visits just to punish herself. Now, with each toss of her shovel, they flip through her mind.

After a while, Nefari sighs and asks the half-asleep horse, "Do you think I'm damaged?" Astra doesn't twitch an ear. Her bottom lip droops, and her eyes are hooded. She leans further into her shovel's handle. "What kind of person can't let go of the past?" she whispers. "Who refuses to become the person they're meant to be if it means they can save their own people?"

Falling silent, she rubs warmth into her nose with the back of her hand. Then, she peers at the black diamond ring and shifts it around on her finger. Her mother had told her to kiss it every time she was afraid. "Be brave," her mother had asked of her. With her uttered questions still hanging in the air, her mother's request feels like her answer.

Nefari brings the ring up to her face and presses her lips gently to the cold diamond. She is afraid. If she were honest with anyone who asks, she'd tell them she's afraid, and not just of one thing but everything. It's not just feeling unworthy as Bastian had so painstakingly pointed out. She's scared of the dark. She's scared of her memories. And . . . she's scared of the fate everyone wants her to grasp.

The world is a place her mother had shielded her from. When her parents died and she came here, the world's problems had plopped into her lap as a future task left only for her. The Rebel Legion helps where they can, but they can't free those already enslaved. Nefari knows this. Nefari knows Bastian spoke truth; if she wanted to free her people, she couldn't do it here. The centaurs don't have the magic to rise against the darkest evil any realm has ever seen. And for some odd reason, Fate believed she could, and would. But Fate hadn't accounted for the fact that she may not want to, she may be too frightened to.

Here, in the Rebel Legion, nobody bows to her as a royal of the Shadow Kingdom. To most of them, she's a simple warrior. Those individuals don't expect anything from her besides completing her duties on rescues and guarding their backs while doing it.

To be more would be admitting she's alive. She'd be admitting she's somebody instead of nobody. Hope would blossom across every kingdom when she picked up the task her mother had left for her. And when that happens – when hope is shone through the enslaved's eyes, she'd have no choice but to find a way to destroy the darkness she so fears. There would be no turning back. There would be no returning to this life she lives.

Would her people forgive her? She's remained free for ten years while they've endured the worst. How worthy would they see her once their shackles are removed and they realize she'd let them rot while she so selfishly hid among the centaurs?

Blowing out a breath, Nefari continues her task more roughly than she had previously shoveled the mare's scat. Soon, the door opens, and a fierce gale slips inside and licks at the sweat beading Nefari's temples.

Astra's snaps awake and peers at the stable doors. Footsteps swish against the straw scattered across the stable floors. Astra knickers warmly, and a hand comes into view to pat her muscular shoulder.

Dao peeks his head inside the stall. "Hey," he murmurs. His voice is warm and soothing. "How'd the lesson go?"

Nefari huffs and rubs the back of her neck. "Well, I passed." She wipes her sweaty fingertips on her leather pants.

He attempts a grin, but it doesn't reach his eyes. He steps closer and rubs Astra's neck. She hooks her head over his shoulder. "Look, about earlier – our argument –"

She waves him off and props her shovel against the wood of the stall. "Already forgotten." A lie, but Nefari isn't interested in talking about it.

Nodding, he surveys the clean stall, holds up a finger, and disappears for a moment. Nefari nibbles the inside of her lip and frowns at the mare. Then, she peeks over the stall boards and watches Dao gather an arm full of straw to replace the soiled bedding Nefari had removed. Dust rises in the air with his misty breath.

When he returns, he enters the stall and pauses beside her with his burden. Words hesitate on the press of his lips, and his brows pull together as he sorts through whatever he wants to say. He eventually turns his head and peers into her eyes.

Their bright blue depths have speckles of brown, and she fidgets under the heat of his study. She swears the stall warms a degree.

"I'm glad you're not angry." He's close enough that his breath fans her face. Nefari glances away. It's not that he's repulsive, but his subtle hints of desiring more from her . . . Nefari doesn't know how to turn him down without losing her friend.

The stable doors burst open again, and it snaps Dao's attention away from her. He steps away and layers the stall with the straw bedding in his arms. A laugh filters in – a deep laugh Nefari recognizes.

In the shadows of the stall, Nefari and Dao glance exhaustedly at each other, but they slip out of the stall anyway. There are chores to be finished if she wants to get to Sibyl before Sibyl's patience wears thin and she marches down the mountain in search of her. Sibyl detests leaving her cave, and the last thing Nefari wants is to endure her wrath.

Though she wants to, Nefari refuses to hide from the owner of the laughter. She heads to retrieve an armful of hay mounded in the middle of the aisle between stalls while Dao strides to the barrels of oats.

Over the mound of hay, Nefari can just make out the top of Kaymen Liptonstone's head. Three of his usual friends, shadow people, stroll to their horses' stalls. A chorus of low and rumbling whinnies sounds in the barn, and thankfully, none of them notice Nefari or Dao.

She dreads it when Kaymen and his devoted posse are around. It's not that she can't handle her own when it comes to Kaymen's taunts and his friends' sneers. She's the best of her age with her sword and her fists. But it's exhausting to suffer through his very presence, and more so, grueling to not punch the smirk from his face when he thinks he's won whatever point he tries to make.

Begrudgingly, Nefari will admit Kaymen is not a notorious bully. He's quite the opposite. Over the years, especially in his teens, he may have had a few choice words to sling at Nefari, but his frustration over her refusal to guide her people – to give them hope – infuriates him.

He's always had a quick tongue, though. His opinions are loud, and the other shadow people in the city … well, they have to follow someone who is stubborn enough to take charge. Nefari isn't that person – has never tried to be.

Their continued laughter is jarring in the quiet stables, and a draft slithers in from the door they left wide open. With a quiet snort, Nefari is about to go close it when Cyllian Timida sneaks inside, leaving the door ajar.

Cyllian's heart-shaped and lovely face lifts when she flashes a timid smile at the Shadow Princess. In return, Nefari nods her greeting to the petite shadow woman, still stunned every time she sees her. She looks exactly like her older sister, a living reminder of Nefari's childhood. Her sister was Beau Timida, Nefari's mother's lady, a devoted servant and most trusted friend. But Beau died with everyone else.

A year younger than Nefari, Cyllian was too young to work in the castle, but Nefari remembers how she would visit often. The cooks would sneak the girl freshly baked rolls, but the adults didn't know Cyllian was only there to listen to courtly gossip. She was small for her age and often went unnoticed. Nefari had envied her invisibility and lack of supervision and obligations.

Once, when Nefari, Amoon, and Vale had asked if she wanted to play with them, Cyllian had turned them down. At the time, Nefari couldn't understand why, but now, as an adult, Nefari realizes the girl was simply too shy to play with the princess. It had taken her nearly all ten years in Kadoka City to work up the nerve to look Nefari in the eye.

Moving away from her memories, Nefari blinks and grabs an armful of hay.

Kaymen stops as soon as he sees Nefari, and the laughter dies from his shrewd lips. His three friends stop with him.

Lace Liptonstone, Kaymen's grandmother, had served on the Shadow Council. The council had guided her parents on making wise decisions. Unlike Kaymen, she had always been kind to Nefari, but like the rest of the shadow children who survived the destruction, Kaymen lost everyone that day, including Lace. Nefari is sure he blames her for it.

A gust shoves through the ajar door and ruffles his short hair. White tattoos stretch across his throat in the sketching of a spine, and two additional white tattoos slash across his chin. His features are rugged and square, which match the set of his hard, blue eyes.

"Fari," he sneers. He takes one step in her direction, and she's just about to do the same when Dao's hand grasps her shoulder.

"Don't," Dao warns quietly enough so only she can hear. He squeezes once, a reminder to keep her wits about her and to not engage no matter how he taunts. She's already in enough trouble with Bastian. Any more, and he won't be so kind in her punishments.

"I hear you think you're untouchable now," Kaymen grumbles distastefully, arms loose at his sides. "From what I remember, your father thought the same." Nefari flexes her jaw and flares her nostrils. She's heard this taunt throughout the years – had even heard the centaurs whisper about it when she was younger.

Her mother had spent years warning her father about the dangers that lay ahead – about the trouble Fate had promised before he blessed Nefari inside her womb. Her father had ignored her warnings until it was too late to correct his mistake.

"Not all of us enjoy following orders," she says too sweetly. The atmosphere of the barn sours. Out of the corner of her eye, she sees Cyllian stiffen by the door. She pinches her fingernails while jerking nervous glances between her princess and Kaymen.

Kaymen narrows his eyes. "You aren't untouchable, Nefari. If you keep disobeying Bastian, others will begin to, too. I care enough about our people to listen to orders. I'm playing my part. What is it that you're doing? How do you compare, Princess?"

"Shut your mouth!" Dao barks. His hand clenches Nefari's shoulder tightly.

"I never said I was untouchable. As you so pointed out, it's in my blood to disobey."

"And the 'boyfriend' weighs in," Kaymen says to Dao, ignoring Nefari's words completely as he takes another step closer. "Tell me, Dao Pyreswift, have you confessed your love yet? Or are you still waiting for it to unfold naturally?"

Nefari blinks, and in that second, Cyllian blushes. Nefari knows she's one of the shadow people who fancy Dao but has made no move to confess her own adoration. Instead, she stares at him from afar every chance she gets, and Dao goes completely unaware of the feelings stirring from the quiet girl.

Kaymen continues, "Or perhaps you have not yet learned that Nefari doesn't care for anyone else but herself."

"A lot of talk for someone who doesn't have a pot to piss in," Dao grumbles angrily. "Are you still crying in your sleep for your grandmother, Kaymen? Or have you finally grown out of it?"

Kaymen's face hardens, and his fists ball at his sides. "Talk about my grandmother again and I'll —" he gathers himself and takes a deep breath. "You won't stand for anyone but yourself, Nefari. Dao will eventually see that." His voice lowers into a growl. "The only reason he still stands next to you is because he hopes someday you'll wake up from this self-absorbed behavior and listen to reason. Tell me, Nefari, what are you going to do? What's your plan to survive all this darkness and evil across the realm? If you don't embrace your fate, what do you think will happen? An army will rise in your place? Because I have news for you. Queen Sieba owns the realm. Despair owns the realm. And your fate - your prophecy - is the only sliver of faith those of us fortunate enough to live here have left."

Rage quakes Nefari's bones. "Have you forgotten the ending of my prophecy? "Death will yawn across the realm?" Does that sound like something you should have faith in?"

Kaymen steps closer and scrutinizes her from head to toe. "Who ever said it was to be *our* deaths?"

A throat clears and snaps the tension. Bastian stands in the stable doorway, his posture straight and his eyes narrowed. His shadow spills across the straw scattered under their feet, and the tattoos across his abdomen dance until they settle into something that resembles strips of hay.

Without further order from Bastian, Kaymen backs away. The beseeching edge to his gaze wordlessly advises her to consider the option that perhaps the death isn't to be theirs.

Exhaling the tension pent up inside her, Nefari peeks at Bastian. They say nothing to each other. There is no need. Bastian knows how the other shadow people challenge her, but he also knows she must stand on her own two feet if she wants to continue to defend her choices.

Nodding once to her, Bastian leaves.

"Don't let him bother you like that, Fari," Cyllian mumbles. She stoops and gathers hay in her arms for her black steed. Nefari and Dao look at her, and when she rises, Cyllian shrugs under their attention. "He's a scarred child like the rest of us. He'll say what he must to make himself feel like things are changing for the better."

They watch her walk away. "She's right," Dao murmurs and then sighs. "Go see Sibyl. I'll finish Astra's stall."

# CHAPTER SEVEN

With his hood firmly shadowing his face, Patrix Eiling enters the tavern known as Deeds. The air of the tavern is stale, but at least it's warm. Fires are lit in every hearth, and laughter rises to the beams, both things he's missed on his short but disturbing journey here.

Deeds is named after the owner, and not necessarily after the happenings within. As the Black Market's least popular watering hole, many disturbing things occur here. Prostitution, drugs, and things of a similar nature to name a few.

Whispered conversations dissolve and glances are thrown Patrix's way as he weaves between the many seated patrons. Patrix couldn't care less what they're saying about him – the new-comer who hides his face. All they know is that he is a satyr, and satyrs are not often seen this far North.

It is wise to hide his identity here. With all the many faces he wears, he will surely be recognized by someone, even in places like this.

On the other side of the bar, Savage Deeds nods to him as he fills another patron's mug. Patrix sits several seats down at the bar, and as he does, the bitter scent of the ale stuffs its way up his nose.

From under his hood, he studies the old dark-skinned man who used to be a pirate. Patrix knows Savage isn't his birth name, and Deeds isn't his surname. There are rumors about the man and who he used to be, and Patrix knows most of them to be true.

Savage Deeds was captain of the Wench, the main and most wicked ship in the entire pirate fleet. There are also rumors that he faced the Widow Maker, the dark and mysterious creature swimming in the foggy regions of Widow's Bay. More legends surround the old and aged scars slashed across his face. Savage definitely had survived at least some of the rumored fights with infamous warriors during his reign as Pirate King.

One of those rumored fights include the Red Reaper of Salix, but Patrix isn't sure that particular story is true. The Red Reaper never loses and never leaves anyone alive.

But as rumors and legends go, they all have an end, for Savage's title as Pirate King was stolen and given to another. There was a mutiny among his ship. His daughter, Luxlynn Billihook, had begun it, her surname one she had given herself.

Luxlynn had convinced those on the ship to overthrow her father and place her as captain and honor her as Pirate Queen. She promised them great gold and exceptional treasures. She promised them an enchanting life of thieves and adventures to places unexplored. Savage had gone soft, the story goes. He grew morals. He was tired of stealing and sick of the blood dripping from his blade.

Once successful in uprooting her father's position, Luxlynn and her new crew cut off his legs and dumped him in Widow's Bay. His story had been interrupted before the teller had gotten to the part about how he managed to survive in the deep waters without any legs.

Patrix studies Savage's face. Luxlynn was blessed with her mother's facial features and figure, and a mix of both her mother and father's shade of skin.

Female pirates are not unheard of, nor is it seen as unlucky to have them on board. In fact, Luxlynn is one of the craziest pirates he's ever met, and he has met her although he wishes he hadn't. The last time he and Luxlynn were in the same room, Patrix and Nefari stole a horse from her. He's had finer moments, but that lie to Nefari had scarred him more than the truth would scar her.

Savage's wooden legs clomp against the tavern's floor as he approaches Patrix from behind the bar. "Hadn't expected you for days," he says, his voice as gruff and gravelly as his aging features. "You passing through or are you going to stay for a while?"

"Passing, my friend. Just passing." Patrix takes the mug of ale from Savage's offered hand and brings it to his lips.

Nodding, Savage strokes his grey beard. "Unusual."

Indeed, it is unusual. Patrix always stays and buys one of Savage's women for the night with a bag of the retired pirate's best narcotics. "I was called to Urbana," Patrix lies. "Vivian, to be more specific. I have business with the General."

Savage raises his eyebrows and looks at Patrix meaningfully. He leans in and mumbles, "Just the drugs, then?" His eyes flick to the door before returning to Patrix. "What kind?"

"Whatever you have." He doesn't have the time to waste on anything but what's already been prepared for the day.

Drugs have always been a nasty habit of his, one that he can't break and one that no one knows he struggles with. Well, except

94

for his father, who had disowned him as a teen. It's the true reason he left Loess. It is also how he had fallen into the business of being a spy. One drug led to another, and the next thing he knew, he had more 'friends' than he could manage and more names than he could remember.

"Coming up." Savage hobbles away, his wooden legs clanking to the beat of a common heart.

Out of the corner of his hood, Patrix watches him approach a young boy leaning against the wall. He bends to whisper briefly in his ear before hobbling to the kitchens to grab Patrix's purchase.

The young boy pushes off the wall and dashes from the tavern.

Patrix grins at the bar's surface when the tavern's door opens and closes. Grins, because all of his instincts tell him something is off and that his plan is working out far more easily than he had hoped.

The twinkle in the young boy's eyes as he was whispered to had been hopeful. The boy had looked hungry and haggard. No doubt, he's being paid to run messages for Savage to feed his family in the slums of Vivian, and each errand would gain him a coin.

For as long as Patrix has known Savage, he'd never gone into business with anyone. Savage Deeds doesn't split his profits. Not even with the panhandlers on the streets. It begs to question why the sudden change, but it matters not; Patrix's objective is still the same, and the information he had received about Savage's new ways ended up being fruitful.

Savage Deeds no longer answers only to himself.

Standing from his stool, Patrix slowly takes a step toward the door. Then another. Then another. He can feel the patrons curiously watch his odd behavior, but he pays them no mind. He wants to be in a position where he's ready to endure what comes next.

The door bashes open, and a salty breeze flows in. There, with the sun glaring in the background, is a pirate. A hoop is pierced in the man's nose, and behind him, two more men wait in the street.

"Wick," Patrix greets. His voice is unsteady, just as he had practiced. The man's face is twisted in a cruel half-toothless smile, and the tattoos extending across the pirate's face stretch further.

Wick earned his name for obvious reasons. He likes to make things explode, particularly innocent fishing boats who happen across the fleet's path.

Patrix backs up a step, more acting for the pirate to eat up.

Hands outstretched to grab him, Wick lashes forward. Patrix swings, and his knuckles scream as they slam into Wick's jaw. The pirates rush forward, and it's everything Patrix can do to dodge their punches. Lanterns crash, glass breaks, and chairs crumble into splinters. It doesn't take long before their rhythm is no longer synched and Patrix is forced to endure blow after blow to his ribs while being pinned to a wall.

Wheezing from the last punch, Patrix is forced upright. His face is slammed against a support post, and his arms are pulled roughly behind his back.

"Did ye think we'd forget?" Wick asks in his ear. The stench of rotting teeth and stale alcohol reaches Patrix's sensitive nose.

"A man can always dream," he answers while still trying to catch his breath. He tastes blood against his tongue.

Savage comes into view, his arms crossed over his broad chest. "Sorry, Pat," he grunts.

"Truly?" Patrix growls.

A purse is tossed at Savage, and he catches it with ease. The coins clank inside the bag. Savage peers inside and then glances at Patrix from under his scarred eyebrows. He shrugs. "Business has been slow with the Salix court this side of the Bay. No one wants to get caught with things they shouldn't."

"We square?" Wick asks. At Savage's nod, Patrix is yanked away from the wall and pulled from the bar.

As the glare of the sun burns his eyes, Patrix hopes that the person he planned to get him out of this mess doesn't come too soon. Or too late.

# CHAPTER EIGHT

Having finished Nefari's morning chores, Dao leads Astra back into her stall and locks the stall door. The mare knickers to him, but soon her head dips down to the hay waiting by her bucket of oats.

He then puts the supplies away and starts to stride from the stables. He's already missed tea with Swen, but if he rushes, he can make it before the rush of everyone heading to the temple for today's sacrifice. Everyone, that is, except for Nefari. Nefari doesn't pray to the Divine, and frankly, Dao isn't sure why he does either. They don't answer his prayers, and how could they?

"Dao!" a soft voice calls from within. He turns while walking backward out of the stable's door and shields his eyes from the sun poking through the clouds. Cyllian jogs up to meet him, stride for stride. "Can I talk to you?"

Frowning, Dao stops. She nearly bumps into him. He spies a piece of hay stuck inside a few tangled white locks, and he has the urge to pluck it away. He crosses his arms instead. "What about?"

She pulls on her fingers. "I'm worried about Fari."

"Oh?"

Interrupting their conversation, the beat of drums begins to pound, announcing this morning's sacrifice at the temple. It's a steady rhythm, and even from this distance, Dao can feel it rock against the beat of his heart. They both briefly look.

"We all heard about what happened in Chickasaw." She glances at Kaymen, who is leading his horse back to the stables. He and the others are returning from checking on the roaming livestock. "I don't want to admit that Kaymen is right, but he does have a point. If she keeps going the way she's going to . . ." She lets her voice trail off, and shame colors her cheeks.

Though slight-figured and fragile-looking, Cyllian has seen her fair share of dead bodies. That is what she fears here – that Nefari will be the next body she prepares to burn in front of the city's Temple. As the only two-legged healer in the village, the duty would fall on her.

Like all the Shadow Children, she was taken under the wing of another. Cyllian was brought up by the women in the healer's hut and trained to work right alongside them. Because of her small size, she's useful – able to dig into wounds otherwise too little for a centaur's big hands. And she's canny with eyes that miss absolutely nothing.

Dao runs a hand through his hair and sighs. "I'll talk with her. Come on, we should get to the temple before we're late."

"Wouldn't want that, would we?" Kaymen says beside them. He passes his horse off to the others, and they dip inside to put the animals away.

Nearly groaning, Dao clenches his jaw. "What do you want?"

"Is our highness going to attend?" He nods to the crowd starting to head down the main path. "Or should we expect the same disregard toward the Divine as she's always displayed?"

Dao grabs Kaymen by his cloak and slams him into the outer wall of the stables. "She is one of the Divine, Kaymen. Or have you forgotten?"

"I haven't forgotten anything," he sneers. "It's difficult to ignore, in fact. The realm is in destruction, and the only person who can do something about it chooses to ignore it."

"You have no idea what she went through – what she saw and witnessed ten years ago." Dao releases him roughly.

Kaymen chuckles. "Of course, I do. We all went through it. We all saw the people we love die."

"You still don't get it," he shakes his head. "She witnessed the people she loved being eaten. She was forced to choose her life over all of theirs – forced to leave them behind against her will. And what does she have to show for it?" Dao holds out his arms. "A kingdom of ruins, a fate meant to shape the darkness, and a heavy crown – a birthright – bleeding with the blood, sweat, and tears of our people. Tell me, Kaymen. Which pieces would you pick up first?"

"Her heart is shattered," Cyllian adds. "It's been this way for a long time, but only now is she beginning to pick up the pieces and examine them. Allow her the time to mend and accept that if she wants the realm to be right again, she's going to have to build it anew."

Kaymen exhales slowly as he studies her. He straightens his cloak. "Regardless, time is not a luxury we have. I like you, Dao. Our parents got along well. But our people are out there – shackled, harvested, being put to death. I won't stand for it much longer." Kaymen steps closer to Dao. "Fix her – do something about it – or I will be forced to stand in her place." Snow crunches underfoot as he storms off toward the temple.

"I want her to be our queen too, but not until she's ready," Cyllian admits while they watch him disappear into the crowd. "It could do more harm than good to force such a role onto someone who doesn't want it."

"Yeah," Dao murmurs. He loops his arm through hers, and it isn't long before they find themselves skirting around the others within the temple. Dao squeezes himself next to Swen while Cyllian remains at his side. Nio is to Swen's left with Bastian and Fawn. Out of them all, Fawn is the only one to raise an eyebrow.

"Where have you been?" Swen asks softly. He thinks better of his question and waves his hand in the air. "Don't answer. I already know what you will say." He's aware of Dao's love interest, for Nefari is often the reason he's late to anything. Dao suppresses a grimace and settles in for today's sacrifice.

Arms raised, the priestess clad in wine-colored robes speaks in a tongue long since dead. Her voice caries to the high ceiling like a god's. There's a baying sheep tied to the podium behind her. It paces and tests the strength of its rope with huge, frightened eyes.

Dao doesn't pay attention to any of these things. His attention discreetly swivels to his right. Cyllian is standing where Nefari used to. Her stressed features soften in the priestess's words, and she doesn't seem to mind that his arm is still linked with hers.

He misses the days when their lives were simpler in Kadoka City. Perhaps, if he had been braver in his youth, he could have confessed his feelings to Nefari before her life was riddled with choices and paths that don't line up with his own. Everything would be different if he had. She would be the one linked arm in arm with him, even if she doesn't believe in the ceremonies.

The priestess pulls a long-curved knife from deep within her robs. It glints in the light seeping through the many tall and wide windows. The sheep beseeches her, aware that his end is near.

101

When she brings the knife to the sheep's throat, Dao closes his eyes. The baying is cut off, and heavy liquid splatters the stone around the podium. The hair on his arms rises. If the sacrifice unnerves Dao – reminds him of his past – he can't imagine what it would do to Nefari.

The sacrifice used to be performed to appease Despair's appetite and keep the people who participated protected from his wrath, but obviously, those days are over. Still, the tradition lives on.

The coppery aroma of the sheep's blood stirs memories behind Dao's eyelids.

He wasn't in the shadow castle when the bloodshed began. He had been celebrating in the purple, green, and blue cobbled streets with the rest of the villagers while everyone waited for the famed shadow dance that would have taken place at the end of the castle's festivities. He had been excited to watch because his mother told him that when the shadow dance came to a close, Princess Nefari would be officially eight years old, and her magic would emerge.

While they waited, ale and wine had been passed around between their people. Music had been strung from loots, and great songs had risen from the voices of his elders. People danced, celebrated, and laughed. "The princess will burn brighter than all the stars combined," he had heard his mother exclaim quietly to Kaymen's parents.

The darkness had worried everybody. The rumors had spread that the Queen of Salix had managed to reach their hidden kingdom because a wraith had found its way inside days before.

Even then, at the young age of ten, he knew why they were so excited – why they danced with such joy despite this news. The Fate-blessed princess was their hope, for who better to cleave the darkness than a princess with magic predicted to outmatch all of her ancestors?

Their joy quickly faded however when the cloaked darkness had settled over the ever-present twilight sky of the Shadow Kingdom.

*Wraiths.* He still remembers their stench, their wrongness, and he squeezes his eyes a little tighter against the memory.

Screams had erupted and people began to flee. But they had run right into a line of crones who had blocked them from their homes.

The rest of the memory is hazy. His mother had shouted at him to run and hide, and then she was attacked from behind. A crone had jumped on her back and sunk her teeth into her neck. He remembers his hot tears and his own screams, pleading for his mother's life. And then a centaur came from nowhere, his sword raised.

In a blink, the crone's head had rolled to Dao's bare feet and left a trail of blood splatters in its wake. He was plucked from the street and set on the back of the centaur. As they rode away, Dao had locked eyes with his dying mother until the creep – the black swirling shadows that transports them into and out of the kingdom – had swallowed them whole.

"Dao, are you all right?" Cyllian whispers.

Her voice startles him. His eyes fly open, and when they meet hers, he nods curtly. Sweat coats his neck, and she examines it.

"Are you sure?" Her grip on his hand tightens. When had he grabbed her hand? He glances at their intertwined fingers. "You're pale. And you're sweating."

"I'm fine." He removes his hand from hers and tucks it into the sleeve of his cloak.

The temple service is over, and the sacrificed sheep is gently carried away. The priestess takes the bowl filled with the sheep's blood and steps down from her platform. The crowd parts, and she strides gracefully to the door where she will stay until everyone exits. Upon their exit, she'll dip her fingers in the blood and mark everyone's forehead, a four-pointed star, which represents all four Divine Gods.

"May the Divine bless you," she will whisper to each.

She and Dao move into the line to be blessed with the sheep's blood, but his feet feel numb with every step.

*She will burn brighter than all the stars combined*, his mother's voice echoes in his head. If only she had known she wouldn't be around to see it. If only she knew . . . everything.

# CHAPTER NINE

The bag that was placed over Patrix's head is ripped off. He squints as his eyes adjust to the sun's bright rays. Though it's warmer in Urbana than it is near the Kadoka Mountains, it still endures seasons. It's currently encroaching upon spring though winter's snow still occasionally threatens the area.

Emerald green water splashes against the dock he was forced to kneel on moments before, and there, in front of him, is Luxlynn Billihook herself.

She's as beautiful as he remembers. Her long, flowing brown hair is as rich as chocolate with eyes to match. She's slight and slender, almond-colored skin, and if she were a lady of any court, she'd have men with great riches begging for her hand in marriage.

Patrix gazes beyond her at the ships tied at every dock cleat. The salty sea breeze whips the flags of the few pirate ships counted among their numbers. These flags are black, proudly displaying the white femur that's forged into a sword and the ribcage shield behind it; the pirate fleet's sigil.

The largest among them is the Wench. Water bobs against the ship, splashing onto the dock. Slaves are marching up the

105

gangplank, filed like cattle into a slaughter pen. All of them are human, Patrix notes. Dirty, beaten, and bruised humans.

In the other direction, on the land the Black Market stretches across, the crowd moves from carriage to tent to table without pause. They know not to get involved with pirate affairs, but one particular merchant snags Patrix's attention.

By height and broad shoulders, he can tell this person is a man. He's hooded in a thick cloak, features tucked so deep within that Patrix can't see the shape of his eyes. This man watches them, and Patrix swears he gleams the ends of long white hair poking from the hood. White hair which belongs to only one race . . .

For a better second glance, Patrix blinks to readjust his vision, but when he opens his eyes, the man is gone, disappeared back into the masses.

"I would have thought you'd never show your face here again, Mr. Eiling," Luxlynn coos. Her voice is as sweet as any seductress, dripping honey. He can see why the men on her ship follow her every command.

"I'm not surprised you remember me. Everyone remembers this handsome face. But . . ." He cocks his head to the side. "How do you know who I am?"

She laughs. "Of course, I know who you are. I know the names of all those who cheat and steal from me."

"Just as I know all about you, Ms. Billihook. I know some of your deepest secrets. Tell me, because I've always been curious. Do you know who your mother is?" She stiffens but says nothing. He smirks. "I certainly do. Shall we share the happy news with your crew?"

"What's he mean?" Wick asks the others. Patrix's grin broadens.

She bends and snarls close to his face, "Games may be your favorite pastime, but they're not mine. Where is my horse? Where are the drugs that were on the horse?"

The adrenaline surging inside Patrix banks. He was hoping she'd be wise enough to realize both were long gone.

Last year, while browsing in the Black Market with Nefari, Patrix had overheard two gossiping merchants. They had gotten word the Pirate Queen was traveling with a saddlebag full of narcotics straight from Urbana's castle. He couldn't pass the opportunity up, not when he was desperate for a fix.

Nefari had no idea the true reason Patrix wanted to go inside the gambling tents. It was too easy to convince her to sneak inside with him. All he wanted to do was discover which horse was Luxlynn's and then steal a few bags of narcotics for himself. But then, Nefari sat at one of the tables and played against the woman with the feathered hat. The woman was Luxlynn Billihook.

'Til this day, Nefari still has no idea she was gambling the Pirate Queen. And with Nefari as inebriated as she was, the princess had never suspected, nor questioned him when he took the entire saddlebag for himself. She even bought the lie about needing the coin she thought was in there.

It wasn't until later that day he realized how wrong everything could have gone. It wasn't until later, when he was stoned and staring at the stars, had he realized what a target he had painted on Nefari's back by starting the brawl and by stealing the horse.

So far, he's been lucky she hasn't returned to Urbana. *No.* No, he's lucky Nefari kept her wits about her during that game, despite how much wine she drank. The shadow magic shrouding her shadow born features could have easily been forgotten about – could have easily disintegrated and slipped entirely off her face for how drunk she was. Then, they both would have been dead.

Patrix shrugs, and before he can finish the gesture, Luxlynn backhands him across the cheek. His head whips to the side, and he spits blood from the reopened gash inside his mouth. With this new angle of his face, he spies a slave stumbling along the gangplank of the Wench. The slave nearly falls to his knees.

"Slave trade, huh? I would have thought slaves weren't the right kind of treasure for a pirate with a reputation like yours."

"Slaves are a big business, Patrix," she says. Her chest puffs with pride.

The feather on her hat flaps, and he watches it for a moment. "So I've heard. Still, it's a bit beneath you."

"It feeds my men and women. Do you wish to join the slaves?" She points to the ship with a jeweled finger. "We sail for Salix come dawn. I'm sure they'll have a need for a horny, thieving satyr such as yourself."

Patrix laughs, but the sound comes out weak from sore ribs. "Is that all you got, Luxy? My, my, you're becoming as weak as your father."

Her pupils flare. "Perhaps we will find the Widow Maker along the way and feed you to her to sustain her appetite. Or maybe I'll let the pyrens have their way with you." She runs her tongue along the edges of her top teeth. "I hear the finned women are still after handsome young men such as yourself."

He shrugs again to suppress a shiver. Both deaths would be horrifying. "A fine death, either way, I'd think," he lies. "One worthy of being sung around fires."

She chuffs. "I already know where the drugs went, but tell me . . . where is my horse, Patrix?"

Without thinking, Patrix tries to gather his hooves underneath him. Wick's hand clamps down on his shoulders, and he forces him back onto his knees. Patrix bites the air where Wick's hand had just been and then answers, "Somewhere you'll never find her."

"She's still with your friend, isn't she? What is the girl's name? She was a pretty thing. Your lover, perhaps?"

He mocks a gag. "Despite what you say, you cannot discover everyone who has stolen from you. If you could, you'd know she's no lover of mine." Another backhand to Patrix's face, and this time, he laughs through it. "You'll never know, Captain – Queen – whatever you go by these days. I'll never tell you."

Squatting, Luxlynn grabs Patrix's beard and roughly yanks his face back to hers. She plants a kiss on his lips, a rough and painful one. The blood from the corner of his mouth transfers to hers and dribbles down her chin as she says, "Then, the bubbles of your last breath shall sing the truth in the cold waters of Widow's Bay."

"Oy!" a voice shouts in the distance. Patrix fixes his eyes on her even when she reluctantly looks to the man who calls. Patrix recognizes the voice. He has no need to glance, but hiding his glee is a struggle. For once, the boy is on time.

Standing, Luxlynn shields her eyes from the bright sun and purrs, "Emory Vinborne, what a pleasant surprise."

Emory Vinborne is Urbana's General's son. A weakling, scrawny and gangly, he's nothing like his father, who's a brutish and loud man. The young man comes to stand beside Patrix, his headdress tightly wrapped around his head. His cloak smacks Patrix's side when he whips it authoritatively. Patrix fights the urge to roll his eyes.

"Are you trying to steal the very man I requested an audience with?"

"An audience," Luxlynn says humorously. "With this thief?"

Emory crosses his arms over his thin chest. "Why, you shouldn't talk about your own kind like that, Luxlynn. Thieves should stick together. The only reason you're free to roam is because my father says so. Shouldn't this man be afforded the same luxuries by my own word? Or are you here to challenge that, too?"

"Your father and I have a deal," Luxlynn growls between her clenched, perfect teeth. "Along with payment, I help him move the slaves, and any past, present, and future crimes committed by my crew are waved."

"Then perhaps, if you wish the deal to remain, you'll give me the satyr." Patrix mentally applauds the boy. In the short time it's been since he last saw Emory, he seems to have grown a spine.

Luxlynn narrows her eyes and grinds her jaw while Patrix looks back and forth between the two. To Emory's credit, the boy stands his ground. Seconds tick by until finally, Luxlynn nods curtly. She sizes up Patrix. "You and I aren't finished."

Turning on the toe of her boot, she waves for her men to follow her, and as they head to the Wench, Patrix hollers, "Maybe next time you can put your lips somewhere a little lower!"

Whirling, Luxlynn walks backward while giving Patrix a particularly rude hand gesture and then continues on with her men back to her ship. The dock weaves and bobs with the waves, and Patrix sags slightly with relief.

"You have my undying gratitude," he says to Emory.

"She would have murdered you."

"I know as much." Patrix holds out a hairy hand, and Emory grips it, yanking the satyr from the dock planks. Patrix dusts his tunic off and then points inches from Emory's nose. "You will speak of this to no one unless it has a happy ending." Patrix wiggles his eyebrows in emphasis.

Emory suppresses his beam, but his expression quickly sobers. "You're lucky I came when I did. I waited for you at Deeds. When you didn't show up, I was worried." Unlike Emory, Patrix is always on time.

"That's because Savage gave me over," he says too chipperly.

Emory gapes. "He gave you over to his daughter?"

"I know. That was also stroke of luck." They begin walking off the dock and back to the land teeming with merchants bellowing their illegal goods.

Emory's face falls into a frown. "Wait. You did this on purpose, didn't you?" His only answer is a slap on the boy's shoulder. "My Divine, Patrix. You have a death wish!"

"What was so pressing that you wanted to see me before I arrived at the castle, anyway?" Patrix asks, changing the subject. When Patrix left Chickasaw, he hadn't planned on roping anyone else into his scheme. However, when Emory's raven came carrying news he wished to share in person, he couldn't pass up the opportunity to use the boy's presence, and title, to his advantage. "How did you manage to sneak away, anyway?"

Emory's father is always on him about taking on more duties. It's rare when he doesn't have an eye on him.

"My father thinks I'm interested in the Princess of Loess. He thinks I'm traveling to see her." He scrubs at the spotty stubble along his jaw.

Patrix chortles. "Your father still believes it's women you're after?" All Emory has ever voiced to Patrix is that he wants a better world, and he'll dedicate his life to it. The slave trade disgusts him. The Black Market disgusts him. Urbana siding with the Queen of Salix disgusts him. The boy was Nefari's age when the Queen of Salix destroyed his kingdom by murdering the royals at Nefari's birthday ball. All the kings and queens of the realm were murdered so Queen Sieba Arsonian could wrap her dark grip around each kingdom's seat of power. Urbana is the only country that bows willingly.

Emory chuffs. "I could get a woman if I wanted."

"Sure, kid, sure," he answers distractedly, because he swears, just for a moment, the mysterious hooded white-haired man's head poked above a crowd down the way. But just like before, in the space of a blink, he's gone.

Annoyed at the tricks his mind is playing on him, he returns his attention to Emory. He grabs his arm and stops him. "Look, I'm not ungrateful, but . . . You told your father you were traveling to Loess. That's several days' ride, boy. Why? Why are you disappearing for such a long period of time?"

Emory leans in. "Because the information I have needs to be told to the Rebel Legion, Patrix, and you're going to take me there to tell it. Do you have a horse?"

"I do." Patrix wiggles his eyebrows. "It's a delightful story full of more rare luck. Come, I'll tell you along the way while you spill your guts on what you've heard."

"Tell me you didn't steal another horse." Emory stumbles and nearly falls in his haste to keep up with Patrix.

"I did not!" Patrix turns on the path to Deeds where the horse he found is still tethered. "I do believe I somehow managed to borrow this one, however."

With the horse in view, Emory squints at the saddle. A lion is branded on the leather. "Let me guess. It belongs to Salix filth."

Patrix grins wide, blood caked between his teeth. When he veers to head inside instead of to the horse, Emory tugs on his cloak. "What are you doing?"

Glaring at the boy's grip, he says, "I'm getting what I came here for."

Emory matches his expression and then steps in closer so the patron exiting the tavern doesn't overhear. "Drugs? You're here for drugs? Are you a fool?

"There are many titles I bear, but fool isn't one of them."

"Do your friends in the mountain know about this habit of yours?"

"There's nothing to know." He rips his cloak from Emory's grip. "I like a good time."

"You're going to get yourself killed one of these days." Emory shakes his head woefully. "Straddling this line you so bravely and regularly cross . . . It may not be your addiction that ends you, but it'll be a deal you cannot unmake or a lie you cannot hide from."

Patrix slaps him on the shoulder. "We can't live forever, Emory."

# CHAPTER TEN

The wind is brasher this high up the mountain, and Nefari curses as her hair whips against her face. Her feet shuffle and grind against the mountain's rocky path, and she grasps at the skinny trees to ensure she doesn't fall.

To catch her breath, she leans against the last tree near the entrance of Sibyl's cave mere feet away. She turns and squints through bleary eyes at the city below.

The gale rushes up the side of the mountain and pushes her cloak from her head, stealing her breath away.

"Why must Sibyl live so high up?" she hisses.

The large huts are tiny dots along the white valley, red roofs gleaming. Her world tilts. She's used to heights – Bastian had trained her to not be fearful of them, but no one, not even the centaurs who have lived in the mountains for years and years, could ever get used to this degree of cold nor the near thin-to-unbreathable air. Flesh, lungs, and beating hearts aren't meant to endure it, Nefari is sure.

She lifts her gaze. She can see over the mountains and to the land beyond, too. The purple treetops of the thick Shadled Forest fleck the right, and if it wasn't snowing, she'd be able to see the glare of the Sea of Gold beyond it. Its border reaches the flatlands of Urbana.

Nefari remembers the Sea of Gold in vivid detail, mostly from her youth. The grass is indeed gold, but it is not typical grass, nor is it typical gold. Each blade is as intense as the sharpest knives in Fawn's armory, and like most things in this realm, nothing is free. The blades of grass drink the blood of those who try to cross, and in turn, the crosser endures the wounds for days to come, unless they have an excellent healer, which is rare for the realm. Crossing that field is deadly on foot, except for those who were born blessed with hooves.

Gritting her teeth, she turns back to the dark cave entrance. The basket she hauled up here drops from her shoulder and into her hand, swaying and bumping against her thigh.

This cave is guarded to hide Sibyl's magic and warded to keep out unwanted magic. Aside from having this luxury, Sibyl Withervein and her species and ancestry should frighten Nefari, but Sibyl has been nothing but helpful, especially for a crone. She is nothing like her grandmother, Wrenchel Withervein, the crone faction leader. She asks for little and gives much back.

Two centaur skeletons loom over Nefari as guards of the entrance. It is told these two centaurs had died when the citizens of Kadoka City formed the Rebel Legion and fought the crones who tried to invade – the same battle in which Fawn lost her parents and where Nio earned his scars.

The skeletons make the Kadokians nervous, however. Those who want nothing to do with Sibyl and her ways have spread rumors that she makes them come alive with her dark magic. These very people swear they've looked up to the cave's entrance and seen the centaur's striding across the platform before the cave.

115

Both have swords made of bone in their hands, the tips nearly embedded in the rocky platform. She's never seen the skeletons move as the others have claimed, but she's always felt like they've watched her. Judged her. Perhaps they do if they truly do guard the crone within.

Sibyl Withervein is the only crone in the realm who isn't governed by the three crone factions. As far as Nefari knows, she's the only crone who doesn't live in the Fades, and the crones themselves don't know she's alive.

In all the time Nefari has met with Sibyl, her appearance hasn't changed. Sibyl is a child and always has been. Dao had read up on it. He claims crones live longer than most and mature into their adult bodies at a much later age. Nefari hadn't believed him at first, but as the years went by . . .

Aside from Sibyl, who has distanced herself from the reputation of her own people, crones are a plague to this realm. Ripe with dark magic, they often feast on their victims just like they did with Amoon and Vale. Some say the flesh gives the crone's strength. Others say it gives them immortality. Bastian believes neither. He believes, as Despair-born creatures, their darkness is rooted to their core. The more dark deeds they do, the more haggish they become. Because of his beliefs, Nefari has often wondered why he allows Sibyl to live among them, for fear that someday, she may turn into the very being she was meant to become: a true monster.

Nefari nibbles on her bottom lip. Contrary to Bastian's theory, Sibyl assured her crones are born with black hearts, but sometimes, there are a few who aren't. She didn't have to mention she believes herself as one of the exceptions.

Visually tracing the cave's entrance, Nefari wonders how long Sibyl plans to stay with the centaurs. In his research, Dao had told her Sibyl had been brought back as an infant from the Divine Islands two decades ago. The Divine Islands are four volcanos that float in the bay between the Shadled Forest and Sutherland's edge. Every child-bearing crone travel's to Despair's island to give birth, and then they leave their child there for three moons. If the child survives, he or she is worthy of the factions. If he or she dies . . . well . . .

Swen had weighed in on the story from his position on the cushions of his hut. The ancient centaur had said Bastian was visiting Fate's island when his boat sailed by Despair's island. He had felt drawn to it, and once ashore, he found the child abandoned and alone. He took her without a second's hesitation and brought her home to the city swaddled in his cloak. He then raised her for ten years and allowed her to stay when her power became ripe. The situation reminds Nefari of her own.

She was moved to the caves when the wraiths started hunting the few magic wielders who roam the realm.

Crones are always born with some kind of magic. How much magic the crones have, in addition to how black their hearts are to be believed, are what tells which faction they will belong to. Patrix swears even the lesser faction is dangerous.

Nefari lets go of the tree and shuffles onto the mountain cliff's platform. The cave is dark like a damp hole in the realm that promises to swallow the person who enters. It brushes up against Nefari's fear. It makes her hesitate. It makes her remember too many things all at once.

The shadow princess grits her teeth once more. "Grow a spine," she grumbles to herself. She steps past the guards and into the cave's entrance, clutching the basket tightly in front of her. The smell of the food within rises to her nose, along with the damp moldy scent of the cave itself when its darkness folds around her.

The torches along the cave's wall immediately flash to life, and the fear threatening to pull Nefari under eases just a bit.

She begins walking.

From cave floor to hip height, skull after skull lines the walls. Each is in various states of expression and apparent agony. Finger painted drawings are scribbled above them in faded red, yellow, and blue dye. The dye is made from flower petals of a nearby village, and the poorly drawn, simple sketches are made by Sibyl herself.

The illustrations are of battles - past or present, Nefari isn't sure, but one particular drawing has always given Nefari a shiver. It's of a woman painted in red with apparent tendrils of wispiness curling from her body. At least, Nefari thinks it's a woman. Her head is that of a lion's.

This woman hovers over splashes of red, and in the center of the red is another person, the color blue. This finger-painted person is bowing, arms cover their head as if they're in pain.

Nefari strides past the scene without glancing in its direction again. Femurs of various sizes and creatures dangle from the tunnel's ceiling, and they clink together as she passes underneath them.

The cave's tunnel winds and twists, and the further she goes in, the narrower the tunnel becomes.

Whispers swirl through the space, too. They creep up Nefari's spine and tickle against her ear.

Quickening her pace, she eyes the skulls suspiciously and then breathes a sigh of relief as Sibyl's dome-like room comes into view at the end of the cave's tunnel.

Here, the air is more damp. Frost clings to every surface, making the remaining path slick and forcing her to tread carefully.

"Sibyl?" she calls when she enters the dome-shaped space. She sets down the basket of food and straightens, tugging her cloak tighter around her. "Nio sent smoked boar today."

118

A small bed, dresser, and circular cracked mirror sits on her left. The bed is already made, but there's a dip in the blanket where someone had been lying.

Nefari turns to the right and frowns. The divinity table is empty though the fate card and the skull of omens casts deep shadows across its surface, flickering with the single torchlight that had lit up upon her entry.

It's quiet. Too quiet, except for the water dripping from somewhere. She exhales shakily, her breath fanning out around her. "Sibyl?" Is she too late to see the crone? It's not often Sibyl goes to the city but maybe –

"Right here," a raspy child's voice crackles from everywhere and nowhere all at once.

Nefari's heart slams into her ribs. She whips around, and her hand flies to where her sword usually rests against her hip. When she grasps air, her other hand wraps around the neck of the shorter person in front of her.

The person, shrouded by the cave's darkness, chuckles. The sound is delicate and girlish, vibrating against the cold jewelry biting at the crook of her palm.

*The jewelry . . .*

Shock crosses the princess's features. "Oh, Sibyl!" She uncurls her fingers from around the girl's throat. "I'm so sorry. You caught me off guard." She places her hand over her heart to calm the rapid beat within.

Sibyl adjusts her jewelry, grinning. "I caught you crippled by fear, not off guard. You are always frightened when you're surrounded by things you cannot see and events you cannot anticipate. Complete darkness is only one of them. It is becoming boring. *You* are becoming boring."

Nefari backs up a step, offended. "I am *not* boring!"

119

"Fine. Predictable, then." Sibyl steps into the light. Her hair is as black as night and reaches her hips in a tangled mess. A few tangles fall around her face, nearly obscuring her eyes and the words scribbled across her forehead. There are always words scribbled there – pieces of a prophecy currently on the girl's mind. Sometimes, the letters are backward, and sometimes the words shift and rearrange themselves.

Nefari can read the first line, however, and she visibly cringes at the sight of them. It's her prophecy – Nefari's fate. And the bane of her very existence.

The crone sniffs in the direction of the basket resting at their feet while Nefari continues to study the child. Her small nose is short and button-ish, and her pale skin is nearly translucent enough to see her veins. How long has it been since the sun last touched her skin?

A gold necklace wraps around her neck so many times that it reaches from the top of her jaw, and dangling from it is a chipped piece of the skull of omens.

Nefari once asked her about the chipped bone. "It channels my foresight," she had spat as if the answer should be obvious. But crone magic isn't obvious to anyone. It must be taught. Sibyl had to teach herself by ancient books Patrix had stolen for her.

The crone licks her chapped lips at the smell of the smoked meat, wraps her boney fingers around the handle, and carries it to her bed while murmuring about a grown woman fearing the dark.

The way she walks has never settled well with Nefari. She scuttles like a spider as most crones do.

"So, I don't like the dark. What of it?"

"That's only because the darkness reminds you of the wraiths. It reminds you of a pitch-black closet. It reminds you of the things you've seen which creep into your nightmares." The crone turns back to her and grins as the memories of people screaming echo in Nefari's head. "We all have nightmares. Be glad yours still interest me."

"Truly?" Nefari glares. "Are your nightmares of memories?"

"We all have memories we don't like." The torches inside the dome flare fractionally brighter, and with her decree, the blurred edges of the shadows sharpen into crisp lines. Nefari glances around and feasts her eyes on all of the gruesome and gothic drawings sprawling across every surface.

She looks back to the crone and raises her eyebrows. "You've been busy."

Sibyl grins wider, teeth still white. When she was a child, Nefari had met other crones. Their teeth had been jagged and broken, presumably from gnawing on the bones of their victims.

She tips her head toward the basket. "Will this be enough until our next visit, or shall I send someone tomorrow with more food?"

"This will do," she says. She narrows her eyes at the top of Nefari's head. "But your appearance will not. We do not hide who we are in my home. Change or leave. Oh, wipe the sneer off your face. You know my rules."

"What sneer?" she grumbles.

"The pinched and snarky one. The one that tells me you're keeping spiteful words in your head instead of sharing them aloud."

Pressing her tongue to the roof of her mouth, Nefari rolls her shoulders. Her joints crackle and pop, and her true nature comes forward. Pale white skin darkens to pure night black, and stars speckle every inch of it.

In her shadow form, the shadows of the cave lurch toward her like blown flames before they settle once more. The real flames of the torches, however, remain untouched – unaware of the magic that called their own shadows to bend toward the will of another.

Sibyl squints at the top of Nefari's head. "Fari . . ."

Making a disgusted sound, she retorts, "Do I have to? It's not important."

"In my home, you will not hide who you are. You will not pretend to be something you're not. You will not be half of someone you are. You will wear your shadow crown, or you will get out." The last two words were said slowly, the harsher letters clipped but heavily annunciated.

Nefari growls as she wills the shadow crown to flare atop of her head. The vivid memory of her parents' shadow crowns press against her thoughts, and she fights the tears that usually come with them.

In the mirror of the crone's room, she briefly watches the tips of the crown wave like black flames. She can almost see the Shadow Kingdom – tucked in the pockets of the Shadled Forest's shadows – surround her. Just for a moment, the cave becomes twilight, and the Diabolus Beetles glitter like a thousand stars.

The image is gone as quickly as it came. A lump forms in her throat.

"Good," Sibyl hums. "Come. Let us begin."

Nefari follows her scuttle to the divinity table and takes a seat across from the chair Sibyl crawls onto. The chair rocks unevenly underneath her, but she's used to it. The cave's floor is uneven, and tiny pebbles often get caught under the chair's legs.

Sibyl rests her elbows on the edge of the wooden slab and squints across the table at her. The table is just a sheet of rotting wood balanced on a protruding, narrow boulder. Nefari has never figured out how it remains balanced, but it doesn't matter. Whenever Sibyl is around, odd things occur.

She traces Nefari's features with her uncanny eyes. "You are tired."

"Is it obvious?"

Sibyl smirks. "Maybe not to most, but to me . . ." Nefari glances down at the table to avoid the truth in Sibyl's eyes. Because of her self-induced seclusion, she sees more than others. "You're having the dreams again. The dreams of your past."

She nods and rotates the black diamond ring on her finger. "The last one was about the ring."

"Bah. The ring that's diamond was forged by rock not made of rock?"

A long time ago, Sibyl had asked to hold the ring. At the time, it was still on the chain it had been hanging on when her mother had gifted it to her. Nefari will never forget the look on Sibyl's face when she licked, sniffed, and studied the diamond. She's been reminding Nefari of its value ever since, insistent that the diamond is unusual. How unusual? She's never said.

Nefari regards her skeptically, and Sibyl continues, "Your dreams are never about an object, Fari. Have you learned nothing in the past ten years?"

"Then what?" She peeks at the crone from under her white lashes. "What's it about?"

Sibyl leans her stomach against the edge of the table. The table doesn't rock. "What did your mother say to you in the dream, little one?"

123

Bristling at being called 'little one' by someone who looks vastly younger than her, she squashes the urge to lash out. "To be brave, but that's nothing new. She told me that throughout my childhood."

"And have you been? Brave, that is? The truth only, please."

"Sometimes," she admits. "I cannot banish what cripples me, Sibyl. There is much I fear, and I swear to you this realm knows it." If the girl caught Nefari lying to her, their sessions would end. Even though every time Nefari leaves this cave, she's more exhausted than when she entered, she doesn't want that. She doesn't know why, but she needs Sibyl, clutches to her wisdom like it's the only thing that keeps her sane.

Sibyl holds up a finger. The pad of her index finger is smudged with red ink. "How many times do I have to tell you; fear is not a bad thing, Nefari Astra Galazee Ashcroft? Fear is what makes us move forward. It is what drives our actions. The fact that you're fearful means you're not as much of a monster as you think you are. Those without it succumb to greed. Succumb to dark desires. Those without it see nothing wrong with their selfish ways. You, however, feel guilty for your continued selfishness, and this guilt is driven by how little you think of yourself." She settles in her chair, satisfied.

"I do not –"

"Lies!"

Nefari considers her from the corner of her eye. "But what if what I fear most is the darkness that created the wraiths? The wrath of the Queen once she discovers I'm alive. That kind of magic . . . How do I fix this fear?"

"Why do you want to fix it?" the girl challenges. A gleam flashes in her eyes.

Thumping her fist against the table, Nefari growls, "So I don't hesitate when I'm surrounded by it, and nothing more. Stop implying –"

Sibyl flicks a hand, and pain blooms in Nefari's temples. She grips her head and grunts her pain.

Lowering her hand, Sibyl grumbles, "Do not bring your tantrums into my home." She straightens herself and plucks up the fate card as if nothing had transpired between the two. "That is why you're here, is it not? I promised to help you through what ails you, to work through your past so you may someday embrace that particular fear. I did not ask for anything in return, and therefore, I deserve your respect."

"You're right," Nefari agrees begrudgingly. "But you cannot deny you want what the others want. Do you? Do you deny it? Do you desire for me to be queen – to revolt against the very thing that makes me tremble?"

The crone watches as Nefari's jaw ticks, but she doesn't answer her. Nefari supposes her silence is answer enough.

"Touch the skull."

"No." She shakes her head and leans away from the table. "No."

"Touch it. Be reminded of who you are. Embrace your fear, for if you do not fear, you have nothing left to lose and no one left to love."

Nefari closes her eyes, not wanting to hear the words the skull of omens has to say. It says the same thing every time she touches it. And every time it says those words, her heart chips away a little more.

"Touch the skull," Sibyl demands in the voice of her mother.

Relenting, the princess reaches and rests her middle finger against the skull's forehead. The skull opens its wide mouth and

125

gasps a breath. In the voice of someone Nefari will never forget, the skull imitates Sibyl's grandmother, Wrenchel Withervein's hissing tone. "She will shape the darkness – this Fate-blessed princess of rage and wrath – for she is the crown of endless night and the memory of woeful shadows. Echoes of clinking chain and metal. The sharp sting of leather. The bitter taste of tears will feed despair, but the hopeful shards of a broken kingdom will find the fated queen, and then death will yawn and swallow the realm."

Nefari draws back her finger and vigorously shakes her hand. The skull emanates an electrical current, like lightning itself, whenever a person seeks its guidance for their own prophecy. The feeling is unsettling, no matter how many times she touches it.

"Death will yawn and swallow the realm," she mimics while clutching her hand.

Not everyone has a prophecy. A fate, yes, but some people are just players in a game far greater than themselves – pawns for those who have larger destinies. These people don't warrant the need for prophecy, and they should thank their blessed stars for it.

Dao had touched the skull once and was disappointed at its silence, and Bastian . . . well, Bastian refuses to see if he has one of his own. If Nefari had been given the choice, she wouldn't have wanted to know her harrowing future either.

"You mock it, but it is the part of the prophecy that has never settled well with you. Don't you think maybe it's the reason you fear the dark the most?"

"Of course, it is! My entire kingdom is gone because of that fate. Because of Despair's darkness and their desire to see me and my prophecy dead! At least the Queen of Salix believes she was successful. If I do nothing, if I don't allow the prophecy to unfold, I'll live!"

"Do you think you can avoid it? Do you think you can outrun the darkness?" Sibyl considers her with narrowed eyes. "You are not to blame, Fari. Your prophecy – your fate – isn't the reason your kingdom fell."

"No?" She holds her arms wide, embracing the realm. "Then whose is it?"

"The crones'. Despair's. Queen Sieba Arsonian's," the girl ticks them off with her fingers. "The queen was already corrupt before Despair came along. He had been planning it for quite some time. It would have fallen with or without your birth.

"My prophecy is what urged Despair to move faster."

Sibyl curls her fingers into fists and rests them against the tabletop. "All is not lost. Not yet. If you do nothing, if you do not embrace your fate and learn to cope with the darkness, the realm will indeed fall and you with it. Then, you truly will be to blame."

"And how do you know?" she growls.

"Because –"

"- Because you know things." Nefari mocks, having heard the child say it more than once whenever Nefari questions her foresight.

She glances at the shadows, and the voices of her past whisper within them; Vale speaking her name, Amoon's conspirative giggle, and lastly, the screams of her people being slaughtered in the throne room and halls of her castle.

The fight leaves her, and Nefari shakes her head and mumbles, "It doesn't matter."

"Is that what you think? You don't matter?"

127

She slides her gaze back to the child. "It's what I know. Hope is captured, and Choice is . . . well, we don't know where Choice is. Dead, probably. I am only one person, Sibyl! Embracing my fate is a death's errand. I cannot do it on my own, and there is no one left powerful enough to help."

"If Choice were dead, I'd know about it." She nods curtly. "You are more than just a warrior, Nefari, and you constantly overlook this fact. You are cunning. Able. You are Fate-blessed and, if you so wish it, the Queen of the Shadow People. There is nothing more powerful, and if you accept these sides of yourself, you might be able to cleave the darkness."

Licking her lips, Nefari softly says, "Kaymen thinks the darkness part of the prophecy might not mean – He thinks the death foretold to yawn across the realm might not be *our* death."

"And? You're only making my point, Fari."

"And!" Nefari huffs. "Do you have any other opinion on this? Or are you going to continue to imply that I am a fool?"

"Kaymen is smarter than you give him credit for. The fact that you brought it up makes me believe you think his opinion should be considered."

Silence stretches between them. Indeed, she had considered it the whole way up here.

Scanning the fate card near Sibyl's hand, she tips her head to it. "You've seen Choice?"

"You know the fate cards don't work that way. They show objects meant to be deciphered, just like dreams. But, to answer your question, yes, I have seen something."

Nefari pitches forward. "Can you show me?"

128

"Are you sure?" At Nefari's glare, Sibyl shrugs. She brings the card up to her mouth and blows across the flat surface. As Sibyl lays the card flat on the table, Nefari shimmies closer.

The card is the size of Nefari's hand, and stars dance around the inside of it. At the command of Sibyl's breath, gold swirls and shimmers around the edges. Fog creeps forward within the card's stars like clouds over an evening sky.

There is only one fate card in the realm. In the hands of a powerful seer such as Sibyl, the card materializes an object to be divined by the seer herself. The magic has always fascinated Nefari, but it must be a great burden for Sibyl to try and piece together whatever the card shows.

Now, as the fog churns and churns, an object creeps forward. "A gold heart?" The heart isn't a shape. It's an organ, and underneath it, the words "the heart" is scrawled.

She reaches to touch the card's surface, but her hand is slapped away.

"Indeed, it is a heart," the girl spits. She doesn't like it when others touch her things. "The card sought my intentions through my breath. Time and time again, I've wished to seek information on Choice, and no matter which way I've tried to angle my thoughts in hopes of being shown something clearer, the heart is all it ever divulges."

"And what does it mean?"

Lovingly, Sibyl traces a finger over the heart. "How badly do you want to know?" she asks too sweetly.

"Tell me," Nefari growls.

"Very well," Sibyl chuckles. "If I had to guess, I would say Choice is no longer a spirit roaming this realm."

Blood whooshes in time with her heartbeat and floods Nefari's ears. "You think – You think Choice took the same measures Fate had?"

"I do."

The shadows bank and bend toward Nefari when a jolt of adrenaline rattles her nerves. "How do you know for certain? And what does this have to do with a gold heart?"

She holds up a finger and quirks a brow and then leans to touch the skull. The skull gasps again and says in Sibyl's voice, "Born to have a heart as black as coal, the Choice-chosen's purity will have unending pull. A heart so gold is foretold, hidden in places where there's nothing but cold. She will be the sympathizer of both the enemy and kin, a shield for those shackled and sold. And with the wolf as a guide, she will choose to stand by those who wish they had died."

Breathing heavy, Nefari asks, "Is it you?" Sibyl shakes her head, and Nefari slumps in her seat. She snaps her glower to the crone. "How long? How long have you known Choice had chosen a crone?"

"I admit that you figured it out more quickly than I had guessed."

"The black heart and the mention of cold gave it away," Nefari grumbles. "You didn't answer my question."

Sibyl shifts her weight in her seat, but her posture remains confident. "I've known for a while. Prophecies are not something everyone should be aware of. Knowledge of them comes at great cost as you know. I didn't think it necessary until now when you practically melted into a puddle of tantrums. With Salix's push toward the mountains, and the Fades, and your insistence that you cannot possibly rise against the darkness, my hand was forced."

"I had the right to know when you first discovered this!"

"Why?" she whispers angrily. "You don't accept your role in this, so why would I believe you had the right to know? The only reason I told you now is because your self-pity is annoying. But it would seem divulging that information did me no good. You're still annoying."

Nefari chuffs and snarls at the shadows lurching toward her. "And Hope? Do you know Hope's prophecy?"

"Of course, I do." Sibyl touches the skull once more. Again, in the girl's voice, the skull says, "In years of pain, the Hope-favored has been a silent witness to the darkness's violent reign. Both powerless and powerful, she will be the hope to the captives who cower. On her eighteenth birthday, she will rise with the very shadows she befriends and become the enemy of her own kin."

"Well, that's immensely not helpful," Nefari mutters as goosebumps rise across her starry skin. "We know where Hope is, and the prophecy just confirmed it."

Sibyl shrugs. "Indeed, it does sound like the Queen of Salix has her as a pet, but, if you had listened carefully, you would have noticed that Hope has also given herself to this person."

"Oh." Nefari's lips pinch together. "Still, we cannot do a thing about whoever this Hope-blessed person is."

"Indeed, we should direct our attention to the Choice-chosen"

"If Choice-chosen is with the crones, wouldn't that mean she's under the Queen's thumb, too? The crones are loyal to Despair after all."

Sibyl shrugs again. "I do not know everything, Nefari, but I doubt it. Whoever is Choice-chosen would keep the information to themselves. The crones only bow to Despair. Divulging that information would result in their own death."

She's right. If the crones were to discover someone among their midst as Choice-chosen, they'd be dead within seconds for fear

131

of weakness and Despair's inevitable wrath. "What does the fate card show for Hope?"

"A gold sword."

"I see. Well, that's immensely not helpful, either."

Gripping the edges of her table, Sibyl mutters hopefully, "These prophecies change everything, don't they."

"Perhaps." More than perhaps. It changes Nefari's outlook on her entire future.

"Imagine what the coming days would look like if the three of you combined –"

Nefari rises from her seat. "Thank you for your wisdom." She turns on her heel and begins to march off, clenching her fists underneath her cloak. She doesn't want to hear this. Not from Sibyl. Not when she hasn't had time to process this information herself.

Sibyl thumps her small fist on the table. The fate card and skull rattle. "Check your fate, Shadow Princess, for if you don't embrace your fate, it will embrace you, and not in a way you'll like."

Her steps slow until she stops before the tunnel. She looks over her shoulder to the crone whose hair has returned to covering most of her face. Her tiny shoulders rise and fall with the anger of being abandoned so soon.

Tentatively, Nefari asks, "Do you think the court traveling to the Fades is the Princess of Salix?"

"Does it matter?"

Nefari chews on the inside of her lip. "Do you think -" she angles her body just a bit so her words can carry further over her shoulder. "Do you think the dark magic used to harvest my people can be undone?" All it takes is a single touch from a

132

wraith, and a person is harvested. But, Nefari has always wondered if there was anything left of the person – some part of their brain that tucked away the person they used to be – or if the person is just . . . gone.

Sibyl moves away from the divine table and crosses her arms, a very adult-like posture for someone so small. "I do not know, but it is not just your people who are enslaved, harvested, and forced to endure all this." She hesitates and then asks, "I am curious. . . If you could, would you free them all?"

Nefari doesn't say a word as she turns and leaves. She doesn't see the skulls or the dancing shadows of the torchlights squirming from the gale pushing into the tunnel. She doesn't see the drawings scrawled above them, either.

*If you could, would you free them all?* Nefari doesn't know, and it makes her feel terribly guilty.

# CHAPTER ELEVEN

Swen Copsteel's hut is attached to the Temple and far more elaborate inside than Bastian Pike's has ever been. Dao Pyreswift knows he's had years to acquire all the baubles, pictures, maps, and books from across the realm before it had been conquered by Salix.

When Fari visits them, she loses herself in examining the decorations, cultures, stacks and stacks of books, and historical objects that rest on the many shelves collecting dust. Dao likes watching her interests expand.

It makes sense, he supposes, that someone with Swen's occupation would hoard such trinkets. Every time Patrix returns, he gifts the old man with more trifles from his travels. Dao has never asked how the satyr acquires them because it goes without implying it wasn't legally.

Sometimes, he wonders if Fari envies Patrix and his ability to be whomever he wishes, but Dao holds no such desires. He likes his life here, likes to read about the history of their realm and hold pieces crafted at the beginning of time.

By Swen's large hearth, Dao watches Fari as he lifts the ladle from the boiling pot over the fire and fills a mug of tea herbs with hot water. Despite having traveled up and down the mountain, her white hair flows like water down to her hips. Her leather pants cling to her thighs just visible by the angle of her cloak slightly off-centered, and her high cheekbones are chapped and dusted pink from windburns.

A drop of hot water splashes onto his hand. He bites back his shout of pain and shakes it off. To his relief, Fari hadn't noticed, too lost in the objects he's seen since he was a child. He often ponders if she's searching for relics from their home, but he's never been brash enough to ask. If he asks, then she'll inquire if there are any. He doesn't want to see the disappointment on her face when he tells her there isn't. No one has been back there in ten years, and even if they had, he imagines all they'd find is dust and ruins.

Sighing, he hands Nefari the mug and helps her remove her black cloak. She smiles shakily at him when he drapes the cloak over a hook.

Something is wrong.

She had burst into the hut thirty minutes ago. Her skin had been whiter than snow, and a haunted look had settled in her eyes. But to Dao, the biggest sign that all was not well was the way she gnawed on her bottom lip. Having studied her for years, he's aware of her nervous ticks as well as if they're his own.

"Are you sure you're okay?" he murmurs. "Talk to me, Fari."

She lifts the mug to her nose and breathes in the soft aroma of herbs. "I'm fine," she whispers into it.

He leans his shoulder against the bookshelf she had been examining and crosses his arms over his wide chest. "You didn't seem fine. You still don't. What happened?"

Turning back to the shelf, she traces the crack on a book's dry leather spine. Then, she moves her hand to the crown of twisted pine needles she had made and given him last year. She has a fondness for making them, will sit for hours in the middle of the city's patchy woods while she weaves and twines to her heart's content. Dao hasn't had the courage to toss it yet even though the needles are brittle and flaking away. If making those crowns is a way of weaving meaning into her past, then he won't be the one to take that away from her.

"Sibyl's usual doom and gloom but with an extra twist," she finally says.

"Fari . . ." He touches her shoulder and steers her to face him. She's reluctant to peer into his eyes. Why won't she just talk to him? Why is it so hard for her to open up? "What happened?"

As she sighs, the loose, brittle pine needles fly off the shelf and float to the wood floor. "She's been lying to me."

He frowns down at the pine needles. "Sibyl?" He rubs the edge of his jaw uncertainly. "She never lies. She might dance around the truth and keep secrets, but she never outright lies."

"Secrets, lies. Does it matter? They're the same thing. She had information I needed to know, and she didn't tell me until just now."

"I see," he says, dropping his hand. "Is that why you're here?"

She sniffs her tea's steam, exhales, and returns to viewing the books. "I'm here because after what she said, I have questions."

"Why didn't you ask her your questions?"

"I did." She twists her lips to the side. "She didn't have the answers."

Understanding crosses Dao's face. "You think the answers pre-date her?" Nefari nods, and he rolls his neck as stress settles at the base of his skull.

Sibyl knows everything – he's never asked her a question she didn't have the answer to. Not that he asks the child crone many questions. He makes it a point not to be around Sibyl and her unsettling ways as much as possible.

The firewood pops, and he asks, "What's your question? Maybe I can help."

The two glance at the hallway as shuffling hooves along the floorboards head their way.

Emerging with a wicker basket full of aged scrolls in his arms, Swen Copsteel blinks in surprise at Nefari's presence. "Ms. Ashcroft," he murmurs, his bushy white eyebrows drawing together. "What an unsurprising pleasure."

Nefari grins weakly at him and watches as he continues carrying his basket to a desk in the far corner. He lights one of the candles squatting on its surface, and she turns back to the conversation with Dao. "I want to know if the harvestmen – if their possession – can be reversed or if their minds are truly gone forever."

Dao blows out a breath and blinks hard, but it's Swen who answers. "Are you planning to be queen, Fari?" To busy himself from such a loaded question, Dao heads to the hearth to fill a cup of tea while the old centaur pinches out the match he used to light the candle.

"No," she says firmly. "It's just a question I can't put out of my mind."

"Oh, but don't you think it's time?" He picks up a scroll and sniffs it. He always sniffs them, but Dao has never had the desire to be *that* close to history. Perhaps the vellum holds the scent of the past and stirs the senses that dull with age.

The record keeper turns and takes the offered teacup from Dao and then allows the aid of his young charge to guide him to the many cushions along the wall. As he sits, he sighs in contentment. "Why else would you have these questions?"

"Because I'm not a monster. I don't want to kill if there are other ways. If I choose to help them, I want to know if it can be reversed. That doesn't mean I want to be queen."

Grimacing at his scalding sip of tea, Swen peers at her from under white lashes. "There is never a choice with fate, child. You are Fate, the very essence of him. Your choices are limited, and this particular one is set in stone whether you want it or not." He sets his mug down on the nearby wooden stand and folds his hands contentedly across his slender belly. He then twirls his thumbs around one another. "If you do not bear your shadow crown, if you continue to resist your fate, everyone and everything around you will die. The harvested people will no longer be the only regret you have."

"Swen," Dao cautions.

The centaur holds up a hand. "It is time she accepts it, young Dao. Inaction can have more consequences than action. We have seen the evidence that the darkness is stretching its fingers to the Kadoka Mountains. The group who returned this morning was not able to save everyone in Polk. The pirates–"

Nefari starts and then breathes out the question, "There were pirates? In Polk?" Her eyes move to the floor, searching the worn and aged wood planks.

"Were there any deaths?" Dao asks.

Returning his hand to his stomach, Swen raises one eyebrow, causing wrinkles upon wrinkles to stretch and fold along his forehead. "Does there need to be death for action to be taken? How long do you think it'll be before we're next on Queen Sieba's conquering agenda? Those of us who have seen much in our long lifespans are surprised she hasn't tried already."

138

"Yeah, well . . ." Nefari huffs with her hands on her hips. "I thought you two might know something more, though. A way to reverse dark magic. Some sort of spell. Some kind of amulet. Nothing? You have nothing?"

"You've been listening to too many of the city's wild tales, child. If we did, don't you think we'd have used it by now?" Swen challenges.

"She's right, though." Dao thins his lips in consideration. "There has to be a way. Fate wouldn't have blessed her if he didn't think she couldn't find a way."

"So, why not give my mother all the answers then?" she barks as she returns to treading across the living space. "If he had them, he would have said something to her."

"Perhaps it wasn't safe to do so," Swen answers into his mug. "Perhaps there was no time."

Abruptly, Nefari stops and peers at the wall adjacent to her, a look of wonder on her face. "The court traveling to the crones." She whirls to face them. "Despair – the Queen of Salix – already believes me dead. What are the chances Despair is searching for more things that could destroy him? I mean, look at us; we're all but talking about it. If we – mere tiny pawns of the realm – are tapping dangerously close to the topic of Despair's destruction, it has to be Despair's main concern, too. He already has Hope. Choice is in the Fades."

"That's disheartening," Dao mumbles. "But how would Despair know of the same prophecy the skull of omens whispered?"

"He wouldn't." Swen squints at Nefari's expression. "But, I do not think Ms. Ashcroft believes Despair is going after Choice, young Dao. Not directly."

Nefari ignores them. "Are there objects that can find the Divine? Some sort of compass?"

141

Dao's heart skips a beat, but Swen's eyes brighten. He's always been charmed by Nefari's quick wits. "There's rumors of Divine objects all over the realm. Who knows what these objects can do? But searching for them is pointless. If there are such things, the Divine wouldn't leave their possessions where anyone could stumble across them."

Nefari nods and nibbles her lips. "The court headed to the fades, the pirates allying with Salix . . . It isn't all a coincidence, is it? This is Despair's doing. He's looking for an object that'll help him find the other Divine to ensure his survival, and both the crones and the pirates are aiding him."

"If he did find such an object . . ." Dao's voice trails off because they all know what that would mean. Nefari's life would be in danger. Her secret would be out. Despair would know she's alive. "Why do you think Choice chose a crone and not a hooved creature?"

Sighing, Swen adjusts his cushion. "I imagine he had his reasons just like Fate had his."

"Who do you think Hope is?" she murmurs.

His mind whirling and his gut in knots, Dao heads to the hearth and stares into the flames. Swen says nothing because, truth be told, whoever the Hope-favored woman is, well, she could be anyone.

"What if we get to whatever this object is first?" she asks, disheartened.

"We don't know what it is, Fari," Dao says softly. He rests his arm on the mantle. "There's no point. Whatever they're searching for, we have no way of knowing."

The conversation dwindles as all three lose themselves in thought. The fire crackles, and the smell of their tea permeates the air, and soon, the sky darkens outside the window.

Eventually, Swen unfurls himself from the cushions and heads to bed. Nefari moves to his space, snuggling into the warmth as she stares at the ceiling, sifting through everything she's learned today.

Dao watches from a chair by the fire as her eyes drift closed, and once the soft breaths of sleep slither through her nostrils, he throws a few more logs onto the fire, grabs a wool blanket, and drapes it over Nefari. It's not the first time she's spent the night here, and sometimes, he wonders if she prefers to sleep in the company of others. Perhaps she likes being close to Dao. He can only hope that's the case. After all, he is the only shadow person she enjoys being around. He knows more about her than all the others do, and that cannot be without reason.

He watches her sleep for a moment longer, brushes the hair from her forehead, and then extinguishes all the candles in the room before he heads to his own bed down the hall.

Under the warmth of his fur blankets, it doesn't take long for sleep to claim him, too.


Nefari dreams in the darkness of the hut. The part of her mind where the only purpose is to torment her picks up the pieces of her shattered past and forces her to examine them.

The piece it chooses this time is no different than the others. It's a memory of her time as a child in the Shadow Castle. She's in the hallway outside of her mother and father's chambers, the stone cold on her small, child's feet. Amoon and Vale are bickering quietly behind her, but she ignores them.

Through the crack of their bedroom door, Nefari can just make out her parents. Both emerge from the secret tunnel within their chambers, clad in the shadow form which blends with the room's dimness.

143

Tears stream down her mother's face, and her father's is red with anger. "I just want her to be safe, Davan."

At her mother's words, the dream morphs and twists. Wraith cloaks, ancient whispers, and purple Shadled trees wisp about until the dream settles on another memory.

It's her birthday ball. She's plucking at the many entrees spread out before her, all brought from across the realm. Nervous butterflies flutter in her stomach, making a slight bout of nausea swell up her throat. She scans the dining crowd, and there, watching her from a mere foot away from Bastian, is Wrenchel Withervein.

Her mother had told her about the crone when she had been giving the crazy woman a tour of the castle. At eight years old, she couldn't figure out why there was a crone there in the first place, but her mother had assured her that all the guests were invited, so she hadn't voiced her concerns aloud.

There, in near shadows, Wrenchel grins wickedly at her, but the dream shakes and wiggles back to darkness once more.

The darkness doesn't change. Nefari's subconscious waits for the next memory, but it never comes. The darkness swirls like the ripped and holey cloaks of the wraiths, and in this darkness, she can hear them breathing, smell their stench.

Nefari's child voice screams in her dream.


Waking abruptly to the sound of screaming, Dao tumbles out of his bed, dashes through the hall, and skids to a halt in the living space.

On the large cushions where he had left Fari, she writhes in her sleep, her mouth open in terror as the sound of great fear erupts from a deep place within her.

Dao's heart thuds fast, and his eyes bulge. He knows she has terrible dreams, but never has he seen her like this . . .

He dashes to her side and shakes her shoulders. "Fari! Fari, wake up!" She clutches the cushion, and sweat beads across her neck. He shakes her again, and finally, her eyes open, wildly searching her surroundings.

The look of terror on her face would have brought him to his knees if he wasn't already on them. He gathers her up and presses her cheek to his bare chest. "It was just a dream," he reassures hurriedly. "Just a dream."

# CHAPTER TWELVE

The next morning, Nefari wakes before the sun. She's surrounded by the many candles Dao had lit after he calmed her from her nightmare. The fire had dimmed to glowing embers, and the candle's wax is nearly gone.

Tucked underneath many furs, she finds herself feeling a little uneasy. She wets her lips, sits up, and pushes her hair from her face.

She blinks at her surroundings, remembering her nightmare.

*The nightmare* . . . It's as though broken shards of herself had been scattered in her mind, and at some point in the dream, perhaps from the moment she fell asleep, she began assembling them back together. It was painful. *So painful.*

After Dao had lit the candles, he had asked if she wanted him to stay with her for the rest of the night. She had told him she'd be fine – a lie, of course – and he hesitantly returned to his room. She had drifted off into a dreamless sleep shortly after. The dreamlessness was what had woken her so early. It was unusual for Nefari to dream of nothing, and it left her feeling empty and wary.

146

The hut is silent. Dao and Swen aren't awake yet, so as quietly as Nefari can, she eases herself from the cushions, slips on her cloak, and slides out into the dark city. She needs to get out of here. She needs to get away from the false comfort of Swen's home. This isn't her home. This isn't where she belongs. She isn't sure where that is anymore.

The cold immediately bites at her cheeks and fingers, but she quickly rushes to the stables, feeds Astra with the promise of a clean stall later in the morning, and then climbs the nearest steep path.

The path isn't as long as the one to Sibyl's cave, and soon, she finds herself watching the sun rise over the foggy Frozen Fades. She moves away from the tree trunk she briefly rests against and pushes snow aside with her boot before sitting down on the cold rocks.

She soaks in the sight before her, enjoying the peace of the land while everyone still slumbers. Fading bright blue auroras shift and sway in the sky. It won't last, she's sure of it. Soon they'll disappear. Animals will rise. The Kadokians will bustle, and the day's responsibilities will truly begin. But as the fog churns and swirls like the land is breathing and puffing its haze toward the auroras, Nefari basks in what it offers her in this moment: Quietness to think.

The Frozen Fades are always like this on snowless mornings, serene enough to ease the most hardened hearts. As far as the eye can see, the Fade's tall trees are specks that blanket what the fog does not. Jagged ice rocks jut through every now and then, random and menacing as they thrust toward the vanishing stars.

At the edge of the horizon, just a sliver of the sun shows itself. The sliver looks large, touchable even as if she could just reach forward and snatch it for her own. If only her life were that

147

simple. Perhaps to others, it appears so, and that is why they push her. But it's not.

Beautiful as it is, she has no interest in traveling to the Fades, and she can't imagine why anyone from Salix would either, despite their queen's demands. The centaurs certainly avoid it. Anyone foolish enough to wander into its depths deserves the fate within, a bloody and vicious death.

Nefari blows out a breath – as if it could reach the fog, whisk it away, and betray the hidden crone factions within. She often wonders what would happen if she ever ran into another crone. Would she avenge her family's death? Would she spill their blood across the land in payment for what they've done? Avenge her kingdom to the fullest extent?

The crones had betrayed her kingdom by starting the massacre, which inevitably began the harvest of her people. That can't easily be forgotten. Every time she thinks about it, her blood simmers with rage. Indeed, if she were to ever meet another, it wouldn't be a pleasant experience.

Nefari picks up a chunk of snow and squeezes it in her fingers. If their theory is true and the Salix Court is traveling there, most of its soldiers will never return. It is probably why they took so many soldiers – to feed the hags and appease their needs. But if the crones know of something that could find the other Divine . . .

A shiver creeps over her, and dread fills the pockets of wariness in her gut. She chucks the ball of snow and thumps her fist against her thigh. She's angry. Angry about everything. Angry that fate is finding her just as Sibyl said it would, and choices are being taken from her just as Bastian predicted.

Perhaps she chose the wrong view for her morning. The dawn's rays hitting the purple trees of the Shadled Forest would have been a better alternative, but the mere thought of glimpsing the forest that once belonged to her people might heighten her internal turmoil.

The Shadled is no more dangerous than the Fades.

Though the Shadled was her playground as a child, the forest could easily turn on any shadow person. Her mother had tried to hide the deadly creatures who could survive in a forest where there is no water for miles, but she couldn't, however, hide the bodies that would sometimes be carried back by hunting parties.

Occasionally, the hunters became the hunted as with all things in life. Nefari had seen too many bodies return home mangled or husked, both as a child and as an adult here in the city. It just depends on which beast catches their scents while they are tracking another, and there's always something or someone watching.

It was just like her mother to try to hide all the scary parts of the realm. 'Be brave,' she soundlessly mocks. She had never given Nefari the chance to exercise it. Not until she died. She's not entirely sure what her mother meant by it.

Without thinking, Nefari raises the ring to her lips and kisses the black diamond. The familiar gesture eases the tightness in her chest. "I'm trying," she whispers over the mountain because maybe, just maybe, her mother might hear it on the Death Realm.

"What a nasty view," Dao says as he approaches behind her. She startles. She hadn't heard him sneak up the path on the mountain, but then again, she's the one who trained him to be as silent as her.

Clad in his cloak and thick fur boots, he takes a seat next to her, groaning when he's forced to sit on rough mountain rock. "I thought I'd find you in the stables. Instead, I only found Astra with a mouthful of hay. It's a rare day when you've done chores on time."

149

"I woke up and couldn't get back to sleep," she lies. In truth, she didn't want the questions about what, exactly, she dreamt. Fleeing was easier. Thinking them through herself was easier because, past the anger, in some deep part of herself, she wonders if this assembly of memories is her own way of working through her own forgiveness. She's worried that, when it is fully assembled, her time as nobody will come to an abrupt end.

Nefari puckers her lips. Bastian, Dao, Swen, Sibyl, and Kaymen were all getting to her. But maybe they're not wrong. Maybe she is.

Dao's words are as crisp as the air. "It was the Shadow Kingdom, wasn't it? Your dream, I mean." Nefari says nothing, and his posture slumps. "I see it in my dreams, too, you know. It's nothing to be ashamed of. Do you," he swallows, "Do you think we'll ever get over it?"

"Get over not going home?" She peeks at him from the corner of her eye. "Or get over the fact that there's nothing to go home to?"

Eyebrows pulled together, he says, "The Shadow Kingdom was never a shadow person's home, Fari. The royals were. The people were."

Dumbfounded by his wise words, Nefari blinks.

Knowing his advice reached some deep place within her, he bumps his shoulder against hers. "You are our kingdom, Fari. You are our fate. It is the only reason each of us fights for you when you refuse to fight for yourself and what you deserve – what we all deserve."

"I know." Her voice is so small that she barely recognizes it. She picks up a rock and chucks it over the mountain's ledge. "Do you ever miss them? Your parents?"

Shocked, he gapes at her. "Of course, I do. I'm not heartless."

Shortly after they had come to live here, Dao had told her the story of how his mother died. It was the first secret he had ever shared with her, and as a child, he had sobbed through his entire story. Nefari had been too broken herself to comfort him.

She peers at her hands nearly numb with cold. If she willed it, warm light would dance between her fingertips, magic quite similar to her mother's.

A shadow royal does not have unlimited magic. There is a limit, and if the magic wielder tries to push beyond it, they die. That is what her mother did. Her mother's magic was blinding and hot – the light of the stars just like Nefari's. But Nefari has never tested its full limits, has never found the bottom of it, nor had the opportunity to see if there was one.

She remembers the bone criers swooping over the Shadled for days afterward when her mother's magic reached its end, exploding like all-stars do when they burn too hot. The bone criers couldn't enter the kingdom, however, but the stench of death still seeped through the shadows of the Shadled.

Sibyl assures Nefari that her magic is far greater than all of her ancestors combined. Because Sibyl's cave is protected, she had been able to practice there a few times when she was younger but hadn't done anything significant. "Fate's magic mixed with your own," Sibyl had divulged when she saw how Nefari's starlight could dance across her skin. The shadows had bent toward her, waited like living servants, and Sibyl's marvel increased. The crone's deep interest had unnerved Nefari, made her feel naked.

The exploring of her magic had come to an end, however, once Sibyl became aware the magic was too great for her cave to contain. Those lessons had ended, and diving into the destruction of her past had begun.

"I didn't mean to offend you by inquiring about your feelings, but sometimes," she scratches her chin and then turns to meet his gaze, "sometimes I feel like I'm the only one who does miss my parents. I feel like the only person who can't let go of the past long enough to plan for the future. Do you ever have that, Dao? My parents loved me. They truly loved me, and they're gone, and my mind just can't wrap around that fact. Ten years, and I still feel like the same little angry child who . . ."

He leans closer, and Nefari can feel his breath on the bridge of her nose. "You're not, Fari. You're not the same child. Angry, yes. But you're not helpless, and there are people here who love you. I just don't think you're allowing space for anyone else to fill the void your parents once had. In your eyes, compassion is weakness. Displaying love, no matter the form, is weakness because inevitably, all good things come to an end."

She licks her chapped bottom lip and murmurs, "Because everyone I had chosen to love died. How can I endure that possibility again?"

More light extends from the horizon and makes the whiteness of his hair shimmer like the snow around them. She's aware of how close he is. His ice-blue eyes spark with a certain sort of interest that thickens the air between them. Nefari parts her lips. Goosebumps rise along her skin, but not for the same reason as his might.

Dao closes the distance, and panic fills her thoughts. Just as his lips almost touch hers, she turns her head away. His kiss presses against her cheek, and a blush rises to her face.

She feels his chest, pressed against her shoulder, stiffen. "Dao," she whispers, her voice cracking.

He veers away. "I – Fari – I -"

Nefari had never been kissed. As a child, she had hoped it would be with …

*No.* No, she won't think about Vale Riversdale. Not here. Not while Dao's embarrassment colors his skin a pale red.

Grinding her teeth together, she looks him square in the eye, furious she has to explain this. "I do not feel the same way about you as you do for me. I care for you deeply but as a friend – a brother, perhaps – but nothing more." She watches as his throat bobs and adds more softly, "I am sorry if I led you to believe otherwise."

He opens his mouth to say something, but a horn is blown above the city. The sound is coming from the mountain tops on the other side where a few centaurs keep watch over the tunnel entrance. From this high up, it echoes loudly, vibrating everything around them.

Nefari and Dao turn to peer down at the huts.

"A returning Legion group?" she asks.

Dao frowns, "They're not set to return until high sun."

She stands at the same time he does. She brushes off the snow from the backside of her cloak. "An attack?" she guesses again. Her heart pounds in her ears at this irregular warning.

He shakes his head, and they begin to take off down the mountain trail. Nefari's pace is far quicker than Dao's, and he jogs to keep up with her. She weaves between the dark trees and hops over the drifts of snow. Sheep bleat their outcry when she races through a flock crossing the path.

"Fari, I didn't mean to overstep," Dao shouts from behind her. Is that why he thinks she's running? Isn't he worried about the warning horns as much as she is?

She peeks at him from over her shoulder and huffs, "I know."

At the base of the trail, before it spills out into the city, Dao grabs her shoulder and turns her to face him. "Fari, talk to me."

"What's there to say, Dao!" she barks at him. Frustration curls around her every nerve. "It was a miscommunication. What's done is done. I've already forgotten about it." As the last sentence leaves her lips, she regrets it. It wasn't a lie, but his expression . . .

He drops his hand from her shoulder and ticks his jaw. "What is so wrong with being with me?"

"It's not you, Dao." She shies away. "You were right. I have no interest in love."

Stuffing his hands in his cloak pockets, he pauses. "Then, what do you have interest in?"

She doesn't answer, because the person she was meant to love for the rest of her life is dead, and her future with him evaporated ten years ago. Love isn't an option for her. It was taken away, and Nefari has no interest in replacing what was lost.

Instead, she closes her eyes to the question, and when she opens then, her attention catches on something in the distance. Something odd in the village.

The Rebel Legion group has returned, but they're not alone. There's a woman on the back of one of the centaurs. Her hands are bound and a cloth is tied around her face. Dao looks with her, and their labored breathing falls into the rhythm of the drums being pounded by the centaurs in the back of the group.

*A prisoner?* The centaurs take no prisoners. *What makes this one different?*

Nefari tips her head to the side as she senses the wrongness.

Paling, Dao whispers, "Tug the shadows back across your face, Fari."

He doesn't have to tell her twice.

# CHAPTER THIRTEEN

In the Council Hut, the gathered centaurs part for her and Dao as they stride to the front, passing Nio and Fawn in the crowd.

"What is going on?" Nefari demands.

The Council Hut is large, possibly the largest community building in the village aside from the Temple. An open fire burns in the middle, and the smoke rises to an opening in the high roof. Sheep, wolf, and bear pelts drape from beams and the pillars stretching to meet them.

In the front, there is a platform, and on this platform, judgment is often dealt. Nefari has seen it happen before – has watched Bastian sentence his own people to death for thievery or more heinous crimes.

This is where Bastian stands now, tall with a set of shrewd and judgmental eyes. The girl she had seen tied to the back of a centaur is on her knees before him. *Not a girl. A woman.*

Centaurs seem to inch closer, still dressed in their leather armor with their weapons strapped to their backs. Cyllian stands to the right of the prisoner with a tote full of healer's supplies. Her hands tremble nervously, and when she meets Nefari's glower, they tremble further.

155

"Bastian?" Nefari asks as she moves her gaze from Cyllian to the woman on the floor. "Who is this?"

"See for yourself," Nio grumbles from behind the prisoner. By the looks of it, he had taken it upon himself to govern over the prisoner's captivity. Nefari isn't surprised. Nio despises intruders. He rips the cloth from her face, and slowly, the woman raises her eyes to Nefari's.

Nefari steps back, unnerved at the sight before her. Her brown eyes are round and lined with tears, and underneath them, purple bruises proclaim her sleepless nights. Her long, dark hair spills down her dirty cloak and dress. Filth smudges her small chin and her high cheekbones. How long has this woman spent in the wilderness and the unfavorable climates of the North?

She studies the brown and yellow bruises splotching her face, and breath seizes in her lungs. Nefari recognizes her. She's the woman Nefari defended in Chickasaw – the one who was dragged by her hair and beaten in the snow.

Why is this woman here? Why was her head covered? Why –

Her gaze drifts lower, to her wrists bound by rope. The skin is red and raw, and for a split second, Nefari looks back to Cyllian. The healer is here to tend to the woman's wounds, but it begs the question: what exactly happened when they left Chickasaw?

Wordlessly demanding an explanation, Nefari curves her eyebrow at Bastian.

Bastian murmurs, "We found her."

"Found her where?" She places her hands on her hips while Dao slides, unnoticed by the others, up to Cyllian's side. "She looks like she's been to the Death Realm and back. Why is she bound? Why is she a prisoner?"

Sighing, Bastian crosses his arms. "We found her outside a nearby village. She then lied, trying to pass as one of them."

156

"I don't understand." Nefari frowns down at the woman. Her study travels lower to the soiled dress, which was once trimmed with bright colors. By her clothes, she is not someone of importance, but the rich dye of the cloth is not found around here. In fact, Nefari would have to travel to the Black Market to buy such finely colored fabric. She hadn't noticed any of these things back in the village, but it had been chaotic, and . . .

The woman moves her head to peer up at Bastian, and that's when Nefari sees it. She nearly gasps. The Salix's lion sigil is stitched over the woman's heart.

"Salix?" Nefari asks Bastian. He inclines his head, content on letting her guide this sentencing to discover for herself what he already knows.

*Foolish*. Nefari was foolish for defending this woman! She doesn't care there might be more to this captive's story. She doesn't care why the Salix Army hadn't recognized her as one of their own.

Regaining her composure, Nefari bends to be eye-level with the woman. She places her hands on her knees and doesn't bother to wipe the sneer from her face. Anyone from Salix does not have her sympathy, no matter how frightened they seem. She should be frightened. Frightened of Nefari. Frightened of the mountains. Frightened no one from Salix will hear her scream when she's put to death.

She demands from the woman, "Who are you?"

The woman peers nervously around, and Nefari would wager she's the first person with only two legs the woman has seen since captured. Nefari will make sure she isn't comforted by that. "My name is Kristal Timpleton." Her voice is soft, and her words flow flawlessly from one to the next with an accent from the people of the East.

"And?" Bastian barks.

157

At Kristal's confusion, Nefari asks on Bastian's behalf, "Are you a spy, Kristal?"

Fear crosses the woman's face. She can't be much older than Nefari, but her age does not sway Nefari's hatred. She supposes she has the answer to her earlier question about what would happen if she were confronted by those who have done her wrong. Kristal Timpleton may not be a crone, but Salix blood will do.

"No! No, I'm not a spy, I promise."

"Do you know what we do to liars?" she asks.

Kristal's lips firm to the question as she narrows her eyes. "I imagine it's the same that happens to traitors where I come from."

Nefari grins. "First and foremost, we dig out the truth. Our butcher, Nio, is most adept at such things." She points to Nio, and Kristal swivels to peer at the man in question, an intimidating sight, she is sure. He towers over them, ready, waiting for Kristal to make the slightest move.

The fear returns to Kristal's eyes.

"He takes one of his best knives and carves into the flesh of the liar," Nefari continues, "hoping the truth eventually spills out." Nefari leans closer. "And it always does. Always. So, I will ask you again, Kristal Timpleton of Salix. Are you a spy?"

Kristal speaks through clenched teeth. "I am not a spy. I sought refuge in Chickasaw. They – they didn't know who I was or where I came from. Thought I was some poor maiden passing through. I didn't want any trouble, and when they started to discover who I was . . . I didn't want to endanger them."

Nefari cocks her head to the side and touches the tip of her tongue to the edge of her teeth. Her white hair spills off her shoulder and tangles in the button of her cloak. "Then who are you?"

"I'm just a handmaiden."

"To who?"

"To the princess of Salix." Kristal quips and then focuses on Bastian. "What I told you is true. I ran – escaped from the traveling court – because I couldn't take it anymore – the darkness, the slavery. All I desire is refuge."

Murmurs spread across the Council Hut, but Nefari doesn't hear it. Her vision swims for a moment, and as she slowly stands, her body goes numb with shock. Patrix was right. Dao was right. Sibyl was right.

*The princess of Salix is indeed traveling to the Fades.* Nefari's fingers curl into fists. Who better to send to retrieve a Divine object than the daughter of darkness?

A hand settles on the curve of Nefari's shoulder, snapping her from her thoughts. She glances up to see Fawn's grave expression, but her grip firms, a steady support for Nefari's wobbling knees. "Are you all right?"

"Quiet!" Bastian yells to the room.

Nefari doesn't answer Fawn. Instead, she invades Kristal's space. "You're lying." She grabs the woman by her cloak's collar and tugs her upright. "Tell me the truth!"

"I'm not," Kristal vows angrily. "I've been with the court for as long as I can remember."

"Nobody knows who the princess is," Nefari hisses.

"If this girl ran, they probably invaded Chickasaw to find her and claim their fugitive," someone says in the crowd.

"No!" Kristal says, eyes pleading. "I was very careful!"

"Not careful enough," someone else growls.

"You –" Kristal says, after a moment of studying Nefari. "You're the one who saved me! Tell them – tell them I'm not a spy."

Silence stretches inside the Council Hut, and Nefari's heart thuds in her chest.

"What is she talking about?" Bastian demands.

"I had no idea who you were," Nefari growls to Kristal. Over her shoulder, she says to Bastian, "She was the woman I saved in Chickasaw."

She ignores the comments fluttering through the crowd. She wouldn't have saved her if she knew she was a Salix woman. Everyone in this room knows that despite their grumbling.

She returns her attention to Kristal. "Nobody knows the princess's name or what she looks like. And you want me to believe we somehow caught the handmaiden to the princess?"

"I am telling you the truth." Kristal's brown eyes shift back and forth between Nefari's.

"And I'm telling you I don't believe it." Nefari studies the girl's expression, her small nose, her heart-shaped face, but what catches Nefari's attention the most is the too pale color of her skin. Nefari slowly releases her. "Are you sick or something?"

Kristal blinks as she readjusts her bound hands. "I have been for as long as I can remember."

Nefari whips around to Bastian. "You brought in a woman who is ill! To the city? A Salix woman! Are you mad?"

As if called, Cyllian steps forward with her supplies. Dao acts like her shadow and moves with her.

"No, no!" the woman quickly says. "It's not like that. I – just – my body cannot endure exertion for as long as yours can. I tire easily, and I must rest a lot. It has been a long few days on my own, and . . ."

Nefari snarls, cutting the woman off before squinting at Cyllian for confirmation. The healer shyly shrugs. "What do you want to do, Bastian?"

"We can't let her wander around," Fawn cautions. "It would be unwise."

"I am not evil! I am not like them. All I want is refuge. A place to sleep, food. I won't bother anyone!"

"You can get that out there," Nefari nods her head, gesturing to the land extending out from the mountain and the villages that dot it.

"If she was a slave," Cyllian whispers, "then, they'll still be looking for her. She cannot stay in the villages or we will have more repeats of Chickasaw. It would put them in more danger than they already are." Her steps are tentative as she approaches the woman. She circles her, studying the condition of her dress and cloak. "When was the last time you've eaten?"

Nefari doesn't allow her to answer. "This is a mistake," she growls, and the words seem more feral with a crowd who holds their breath.

The clomp of Bastian's hooves is loud when he steps forward. "I must agree. We cannot let you roam around, but we do provide sanctuary here. The council will convene and decide your fate."

Glee tingles in Nefari's wiggling fingertips.

"My fate?" Kristal asks nervously, a fly caught in the web of a spider.

Nefari grins wickedly as Bastian asks someone to fetch Swen. "If you'll stay. If you'll be tossed out. If they want to dig the truth out of you or squish you under the weight of boulders. Either way,

161

settle in, Salix, because those ropes are staying around your wrists."

The leather of Fawn's armor groans when she bends to Nefari's ear. "We need to talk."

She peers over her shoulder, nearly nose to nose with the female centaur. She hisses, "About what? I'm not leaving here until this is dealt with."

"I'm not asking you to leave right this minute, but we need to talk about your sword." Fawn watches the centaurs of the council as they detach themselves from the crowd and disappear into the dark hallway leading to a private meeting chamber. Nefari has never been in there, has never wanted to be.

"My sword?" She had nearly forgotten about it.

The rest of the attending Legion disburses once the council has left the room, all filing out of the large main entrance door with their heads bent close together. Their gossip sounds like the rustling wind traveling over the Sea of Gold. With the door open, cold whisks inside, causing the fire to flare. When the Council Hut is near empty and the doors close, Nefari squints at who remains. Kaymen and his three friends prop themselves against the far wall, and Kaymen and Nefari's gaze meet.

"This is a terrible idea," he growls across the fire. The orange reflections of the flames hover across his face.

"For once, we agree," she spits. "But it's not your decision to make." She'd love nothing more than to see this woman die, but defying Bastian is one thing. Defying the entire council is another. Kaymen is aware of this even if his entire being – his posture, the curled lips, the crossed arms – radiates distasteful rage. The fact that he held back his opinion until now is impressive.

Kristal's wild eyes pass back and forth between the two, and Nefari wonders what she sees there.

There's a taut pause, and Fawn is the one to break it. "Go find something else to do, Kaymen."

His tongue runs over his teeth, and he considers his next words carefully. Just like everyone else, Fawn's wrath isn't something he wants to have directed at himself. "Nobody from Salix should be allowed inside the city."

"Again, we agree." Nefari crosses her arms and cocks a foot. "But it is not up to you or me or Fawn who is allowed refuge."

Snarling, he steps closer to the fire's light. His friends stay tucked in the shadows, watching the scene unfold without a peep. "Letting traitors inside is what got our people killed in the first place. Or have you forgotten?"

Nefari's fingers curl into fists underneath her arms. She wants to wipe the arrogance off his face, but she says nothing – refuses to take his bait – and when she doesn't answer, he chuckles and shakes his head. "I shouldn't expect more from you, should I?"

She visibly bristles.

"Don't," Fawn advises, her voice so quiet, only Nefari can hear her warning.

Surely, Kaymen wouldn't reveal who she really is to someone from Salix? Doing so would be foolish. Doing so might very well damn himself in turn. But he doesn't. Instead, he chuffs, waves to the others, and together, the four of them leave the hut.

Once they're gone, Fawn sighs through her nose. "He's always trying to get a rise out of you, isn't he? Don't listen to him. He's colored by hatred."

So is Nefari, but she doesn't say that out loud. "I know. But he's right. We shouldn't trust her, and if we can't trust her, then she shouldn't be allowed to remain."

"You lot are Shadow People, aren't you?" Kristal whispers. Dao, Cyllian, Fawn, and Nefari all glance at her. To her credit, the woman doesn't flinch or shy away from their scrutiny. "The white hair, the bright blue eyes, the pale skin . . . I thought your kind was all . . ."

"Dead? Harvested? Enslaved?" Nefari finishes for her.

Kristal blinks and rubs at her nose with the sleeve of her cloak. "Well, yes." It's said so simply, it's almost offensive.

"Surprise," Nefari says flatly. Sighing, she turns back to Fawn. Her stomach growls loud enough for everyone to hear. She had missed breakfast, but it doesn't matter now. Her appetite evaporated the moment she saw the lion sigil. "What about my sword? Have you finished cleaning it?" Nefari nods toward the woman's front hip. There, sheathed and strapped to her hip, is the sword in question. Nefari would recognize the pommel anywhere.

Pulling it from the sheath, Fawn holds it in the light shining through the window behind her. "I have, and I looked into the mysterious material, too." She holds it out for Nefari to take, and Nefari senses Kristal leaning to peer at it with them.

"And? What did you discover?" Nefari takes it and immediately feels her anxiety drain from her body. She hadn't realized how much she missed her sword at her side, and she's almost ashamed to admit she had forgotten about it over the last few hours. The sparkles within the metal shine brightly in the dim room, and Dao moves to their side to examine it, too.

Deeming it safe to do her duties, Cyllian tends to Kristal's raw wrists. Kristal doesn't complain about the pain as she's poked and prodded by Cyllian's insistent fingers.

"I consulted with Swen before I heard the drums," Fawn begins. "The substance mixed with it does not solely belong to only this realm."

Nefari's hair falls around her face. She blinks at the sword. "What other realm is it also from, then?"

Fawn lowers her voice, but in such a spacious room, it carries anyway. "Swen had translated the book we found. It was written in the language the fee used to use, but from what he could gather, the substance is also made in a land of dreams – a realm of dreams, to be exact."

"The Dream Realm," corrects Kristal. Everyone turns to look at her. Nefari almost snaps at her, but the woman's eyes are wide – more fearful than when she faced the Legion crowd. Before their very eyes, her face pales considerably.

"What?" Nefari asks defensively. "What do you know?"

"That substance," she tips her forehead to the sword, "is made of inferaze."

"By the Divine," Dao curses. "What is inferaze?"

Kristal presses her lips together and eyes the sword like it might reach out and bite her. Annoyed, Nefari steps in her direction and points the sword at Kristal's throat. "Tell me what it is."

"Fari-," Cyllian starts to warn softly.

"She will tell me, or she'll see just how sharp it is."

Kristal wets her lips. "Inferaze is a magical rock. You cannot find it everywhere, but . . ."

When she pauses, the anger rises in Nefari, and the shadows in the room flare. "What part of my threat did you not understand?"

"In every realm, the inferaze does something different," she whispers. "Sometimes miraculous . . . Sometimes terrible."

Nefari edges the blade closer and bites out, "Like?"

"For the Divine's sake," Kristal curses, hissing the words. Her throat bobs. "It's only rumors. All I've heard are rumors."

"Like?"

"My father had told me st-st-stories as a child. On the Dream Realm, it is used to create dream dust."

"The healers taught me about dream dust," Cyllian says. "It was in one of our lessons."

The news of Kristal's truth affirmed by Cyllian is enough for Nefari to ease the blade back a fraction. She asks them, "How do you know they're not just stories? Legends? Folklore? This realm is full of them. That doesn't mean they're all true."

Straightening her spine, Kristal says, "Because it's been found to be sold in the Black Market. My – the Queen of Salix has been trying to banish it since she first became aware of it, but she hasn't been able to locate the seller."

*Interesting*, Nefari thinks to herself. The blade lowers more as the information continues to flow freely.

When Nefari was in the Black Market last year, she hadn't seen anything else like her sword, but then again, there was indeed just one man who was selling it. This man with eyes like clouds had only shown her the sword and no one else. He had appeared blind but seemed to sense Nefari's approach to his carriage, which was separate from everyone else's. Hardly any patrons were striking deals with him for his meager selection of ware.

While Nefari talked with him, she could have sworn the man's cloudy eyes sparkled. There had been something different about him. Something primal deep within, and the wolf he had at his side . . . it was large and unusual and had the same set of cloudy eyes as his owner.

Patrix had been nervous around the beast, had nearly danced during the entire negotiation.

When they had left on Astra, the wolf, the man, and his carriage had been gone. It was as if he was never there. Nefari hasn't thought about that man since then, but he's not one easily forgotten. Who was he? And how did he get his hands on a substance such as this?

Fawn steps closer, her tall shadow looming over the rest of them. "If it's found in the Dream Realm, why is it also here?"

Kristal shrugs, and the way she does it makes Nefari think she's keeping something to herself. "I imagine it's been here since the beginning of time. I've heard whisperings at the docks of Salix's Capital City. A few merchants had found some on Hope's island but left it there for fear of the Divine's wrath." She squints at Nefari's sword. "I suppose not all were worried about that."

"If this inferaze has magic capabilities on each realm, what sort of magic does it have on this realm?" Nefari wonders aloud. She hadn't expected an answer.

"I do not know," Kristal admits softly. "No one does."

Nefari snorts loudly. "Then, how do you know it's magical?"

The Salix woman growls, and Nefari nearly bursts with laughter for such annoyance coming from Salix blood whose life could literally end before sundown. "Because my father told me. My father is many things, but he is not a liar."

"I see." Nefari's grin is as sly as a cat prowling toward a trapped mouse. "And what does your father know of it if he is so wise?"

She sniffs, and her gaze shies away. "He didn't say, only that it sparkles like many stars."

Fawn chuckles, and Nefari elbows the centaur's side. "My sword does not sparkle," she murmurs to the group defensively.

# CHAPTER FOURTEEN

Glaring at the sun, Sibyl Withervein scuttles her way past the group of sparring centaurs who practice their skills yards away from the Council Hut. Their swords clash, and the stench of their sweat and leather reach her sharp senses.

Sibyl had felt the new arrival before the beat of the blare of the warning horns had reached her. From her cave, and gripping the thigh bone of the skeletal centaur, she had watched as the prisoner was marched through the city. The woman who was brought in is certainly tainted by darkness – so thick that Sibyl could taste it from on high where her tangled hair whipped in the freezing gale.

This particular darkness had drawn her from the safety of her cave. Any crone would be drawn to it. Leaving her cave wasn't a choice but a necessity. Something wicked is here. And though she can't perform any magic in the open without drawing the wraiths from wherever they're currently harvesting, she can still taste the tainted trail the girl left behind just the same.

Once more, Sibyl sniffs the air. It's not another crone. No, Sibyl would know it – sense their shared blood before she'd smell them. There is something else that clings to the newcomer like a second skin. A sweet taste of sorrow and desperation that can only be the result of living a life of despair.

Sibyl inches closer to the Council Hut, and her spindly fingers clutch at its log siding. The breeze switches direction, and from here, she can hear bits and pieces of the conversations of those waiting outside the hut's main entrance.

"Bone Criers, they are," Sibyl hisses. "Anxiously waiting for death." Small mercies that no centaur children are running around. The drum's steady beat is a warning to their mothers to keep them indoors. Sibyl thanks her blessed stars for that.

The centaur children are pests – loud urchins who find the ever-moving words on her forehead, her jewelry, and her deformed shape fascinating. They poke and prod to their content when their judgmental guardians aren't watching.

Huffing her annoyance, she sneaks around the curved wall of the hut's exterior. Smoke billows from its chimney. Sibyl slides her way to the large back door of the council hut, opens it enough to slip inside, and shuts the door softly behind her. The voices of the convening council greet her in the wide, pitch-black hallway. The torches along the wall are unlit, and the cold is left to slither along the floor to its own leisure.

She shuffles in the direction of the voices, and soon, the hallway bends, and torchlight from the private chamber spills out into the corridor.

The darkness guides her, beckons her forward. Sibyl continues on as she listens to the convening council's conversation, determined to reach the main area and see this prisoner up close. If she is the stuff of darkness – if she threatens the lives of this city – Sibyl will destroy the woman. Darkness cannot hide from those who are born with it in their blood. She may not want to live among the Kadokians and their busy streets and silly squabbles, but there are people here she cares deeply for.

If someone's presence is threatening them . . .

"Are they traveling so close because of the Shadow Princess?" someone asks, and by the tone, Sibyl isn't sure if it's male or female. She doesn't know everyone in the city, for some completely avoid her.

"Of course, not. We've heard no whisperings from our spies that anyone believes Nefari is still alive," a woman barks. "It has been too long for anyone to have suspected such things." By her emotions, she's clearly upset. *Good*. Despite Nefari's brash actions, the stiff, ham-fisted, old coots are still on her side. Sibyl had worried the council would eventually feel otherwise since the princess consistently disobeys.

"Why else would the court be traveling to the Fades?" another woman asks. This one's raspy voice makes it sound like she'd been smoking from her pipe before she came here. Sibyl can recall her battle-scarred face, but not her name.

Bastian interrupts. His tenor is one Sibyl could pick from any crowd. "We all knew the day would come when Salix would consider traveling this far North. As Swen said, he believes them to be after something – something Despair believes the crones to know about. The fact that we have one of their own might be useful." Sibyl nearly stumbles as this information unfolds. Last night, Swen had sent a raven about what was discussed in his hut. Nefari believes Despair is after an object that could find the other Divine, and Sibyl agrees. But that's not the part of the conversation that halted Sibyl from her advance down the hall.

The prisoner is an enemy – a Salix woman. Only a true Salix fool would be caught in the centaur's territory and the villages they actively guard. Sibyl flares her nostrils as she wonders who this woman could be and why she's still alive. She doesn't have to wait long for the answer.

Bastian's deep voice rumbles, "The girl claimed they're headed there for that very reason, but she refuses to say what the object is that could possibly find the other Divine. We must prepare. We must intervene for whatever they are after. Otherwise, Nefari's life will be in danger."

"She can't stay hidden forever, Bastian," Swen's soft voice rattles.

"She's not ready," Bastian answers. Sibyl can hear dread in his tone. "Not yet."

"Are we sending Patrix to spy on the traveling court?" the woman who smokes asks.

"No," Bastian rumbles. "No. He's already been fruitful by sending the raven about the pirates who are working for the Queen, and he is returning home with news that can only be delivered in person. Perhaps he discovered what they're after in Urbana. The Black Market can be most enlightening. We must be patient and see what unfolds with our new guest and with what news Patrix carries."

Their voices fade as Sibyl nears the main area of the Council Hut. When she approaches, Dao, Nefari, Cyllian, Fawn, and the woman in question turn. Sibyl only has eyes for the woman, though. After what she had heard from the council, she must know more.

From the entrance of the hallway, Sibyl inhales a sharp breath, grasping the corner of the wall with a fierce grip. She had been right. This woman – this prisoner from Salix – is tainted, but . . .

Sibyl blinks.

There's a brightness about her that mingles with the dark. This brightness co-exists with the dark like it's something untouchable. Something hopeful that lives and moves despite the dark trying to smother it.

Sibyl moves, unable to keep her distance. The way Sibyl walks unnerves the woman, but she doesn't care. The child crone scuttles her way across the room, and as soon as she's in front of her, Sibyl stands to full height. The top of her head comes to the woman's slender chin, and she tilts her head back to take in all her features.

She's dirty. And smelly. And sickly.

Quickly, Sibyl snatches the woman's soiled chin and pinches it between her fingers. She twists her head this way and that while she studies the pale-sickness of the woman. Why does the brightness and darkness linger together so willingly? Is it what makes her so ill?

To the prisoner's credit, she says nothing to Sibyl's poor-mannered examination.

"What are you doing here?" Nefari finally asks.

Sibyl ignores her. "Who are you?" she whispers to the woman like the hiss of a snake.

Dao looks to Fawn and then answers, "Her name is Kristal —"

"I did not ask you, boy!" She snaps her eyes to Dao and watches as he blinks dumbfoundedly at her outburst. The fools have no idea — they cannot see what Sibyl sees, and nothing infuriates her more.

"Timpleton," Kristal finishes warily. "Kristal Timpleton."

Sibyl cocks her head in an eerie, overly exaggerated sort of way. Her long brown hair tumbles to the side and falls past her slender, deformed shoulder. "And who are you to Salix, *Kristal*?"

Kristal wets her chapped lips. "Handmaiden to the Princess of Salix."

As if burned, Sibyl snatches back her hand. It explains the darkness surrounding the girl. If she's close to the princess, then

172

she's been around the Queen. "And I suppose you're here for refuge."

"Y-y-yes." Kristal glances nervously at Nefari. Nefari only raises an eyebrow. She swallows and says, "You're a crone, aren't you?"

"Indeed." Sibyl slowly waddles around the woman. "I see much, filthy Salix girl. Tell me, did you grow up next to the Queen of Salix?"

Kristal tenses, and Sibyl halts to observe the girl gripping the rope wound around her wrists. "I already told you. I was the princess's handmaiden. So, yes, I suppose you could say so."

"Why do you ask?" Nefari asks suspiciously.

"It's not unusual, crone." Fawn hooks her thumbs in the shoulder holes of her leather armor. "She couldn't have avoided the Queen the entire time."

Raising her scrawny hands, Sibyl brushes her palms down the back of her arms. "I can feel it. Taste it. She has been witness to such darkness. So much so it clings to her like a foul odor." Sibyl's eyelids flutter closed, and she inhales the girl's distinct scent. She can hear her heartbeat outmatch the beat of the drums still sounding throughout the city.

"Shouldn't that be reason enough to allow her refuge?" Cyllian tentatively asks. "We can give her the safety she's never had."

Sibyl glares at the young healer. She's never had much conversation with her, but surely she can't be so ignorant. There is not good in everyone, no matter how innocent-looking the package or their story. After all, a weak and an ill little handmaiden would make the best spy for any royal. Patrix would agree with her.

*The safety she's never had*? Nefari Ashcroft cannot believe her ears! She doesn't have to reprimand Cyllian, however, because Sibyl's expression is enough.

Cyllian says to Sibyl, "I understand why you're upset, but we cannot toss her over the mountain."

"If you are wise, you would!" Sibyl barks. In such a young body, her outbursts appear unthreatening – laughable even; if the situation weren't so unusual. But Nefari knows better than to point that out. She's never seen Sibyl scared. She's never seen any crone scared.

"It's not up to us," Nefari reminds, her words low and telling to her irritation. It feels different stating the same thing to Sibyl than it had to Kaymen. "It's up to the council."

"Bah!" the crone growls. She turns on her dusty boot heel and scurries from the Council Hut's main room. They watch her disappear back the way she came.

*How odd.* Yesterday, it was Nefari who walked out on her. Today, it's Sibyl who has had enough.

"She's finally cracked," Dao murmurs under his breath. But Nefari doesn't think so. Sibyl has always approached things with grace and perspective.

Chewing on the inside of her lip, Nefari glances at the sword still in her hand.

Fawn nudges her forward. "Go," Fawn mumbles. "Now's the time to ask her about it."

Without hesitation, Nefari takes off after Sibyl and heads into the dark hall. The child is fast for someone so short, bent, and misshapen.

Nefari ignores the conversation happening among the convening council as she passes and jogs faster when the crone slips outside the back door. She follows, and as soon as the wind kisses the tip of her nose, she hollers Sibyl's name.

Wincing, Sibyl halts, and Nefari wordlessly thanks the stars she won't have to chase the child up the mountain. Nefari strides to her. Her boots crunch in the snow as she says, "What is going on? What is this?"

Sibyl whirls around, and the jewelry around her neck sways. "I do not trust her."

"I certainly don't, and no one is asking you to, either."

Pointing to the hut behind Nefari, she whispers in rage, "She is tainted by your enemy, Fari. You cannot allow her to stay. You have no idea how contagious darkness can be – how it can taint a bright star such as yourself."

"I'm not a council member." She steps closer, refusing to acknowledge the bright star comment and the notation that her opinion and decree matters in these mountains. "I'm not saying you're wrong. Just tell me what you see so I can understand."

"It is not my information to tell."

Nefari quirks a brow. "Not yours to tell? Or you're not sure what you stumbled across?"

Sibyl nervously glances around, but passersby pay no attention to their secluded conversation. "If you want those answers, you'll have to seek them yourself. But mark my words, Fari. You will not like what you find about this girl. This I know."

Exhaling softly, Nefari adjusts her grip on the pommel of her sword. "Noted, but I – Look, I came out here to ask you about my sword."

The crone peers down at it with a shrewd, wild eye. "What about it?"

"The prisoner said it's made of inferaze. Have you heard of it?"

Sibyl's nostrils twitch. "Indeed."

"So, it's true? It is magic?"

"It is, but not the sort of magic wraiths can detect."

Frowning, Nefari lifts her sword and twists it this way and that in the sun's light. "What do you mean?"

"Divine magic, Fari. Despite my self-induced seclusion, I have read books upon books. I know where it can be mined on this realm just like the black diamond in your ring. As you see, it's a rock that can be melted and molded."

*My ring?* Nefari's heart beats faster. She lifts her hand, still grasping her sword, and twists her wrists to study the ring. She had said it was made by rock that isn't rock. Is that what it is? Inferaze? Why hadn't she just told her from the beginning? "I thought Fate had gifted the ring to my ancestors. It's been with my people since the beginning of our time."

"Gifted or left in the possession of?" The child crone rolls her unnerving yellow eyes when Nefari responds with nothing more than a bewildered expression. She adds, "It doesn't mean it was Fate's to give."

Nefari flicks her gaze back to the diamond, remembering the day her mother had given it to her. Did Fate truly leave it with her ancestors? Why? What did Fate know, even then, that would have caused him to take inferaze from Hope's island and give it to her people? What was the purpose?

She has so many questions with no ancestors to ask.

"So," Nefari swallows nervously. She doesn't know if she wants the answer to her next question because having answers is stepping closer to the very title she's been resisting. If this object – this rock – is truly Divine magic, well . . . Kristal hadn't known what inferaze can do, but maybe Sibyl does. She asks her.

176

"I do not know," Sibyl answers.

"Then, what do you know?"

"Anything Divine is never ordinary." She sucks on a tooth. "The inferaze hasn't shown its true power on this realm, none that's been recorded, but I foresee implications that it'll soon reveal its nature to you."

"You speak as if Divine magic is a living, breathing thing, Sibyl."

She shrugs. "As I said. Anything Divine is never ordinary."

Searching the crone's face for any hidden truths within, Nefari's stare eventually drifts back to the godly object now weighted on her finger. All this time, she's been carrying around something magical – something undetectable to the wraiths – something Divine. She flexes her fingers tighter around the pommel of her sword so both the sword and the ring glitter together. Did her mother know the ring was Divine when she gave it to her? Or, was she as innocent in the knowledge of this 'gift' as Nefari had been?

She loses herself in studying her possessions, traveling through her memories to find any hints that her mother might have discretely told her.

Eventually, Sibyl scuttles away, murmuring curses under her breath about ignorant fools and their trinkets as she snaps her cloak tighter around her bent form. She pauses after a few feet, however, and Nefari looks up at her.

Where she stands at the edge of the hut, the wind whistles past her, whipping her tangled black hair in every direction. Nefari waits, frowning.

"I may not have all the answers, but I have never steered you wrong." Sibyl peers over her shoulder. "This is your journey now. Keep your shadow tucked tight, Fari. Hide your face. These are dangerous times, and I do not like what little I can foresee.

Pieces of the past, the present, and the future are starting to collide, and I believe your prisoner is one of those pieces. I do not trust her, and I beg you to heed my warning." She hesitates, her tongue darting out to lick the corners of her lips. "Remember, a shadow cannot survive in pure darkness. Remember, for the days to come and in all aspects of life, that darkness cannot dwell where there is light."

*Darkness cannot dwell where there is light.* She's heard the phrase from her mother before, whispered in hope for Nefari's future as she kissed her temple every evening. The words were also scrawled across the Shadow Kingdom's castle's secret chambers, carved into the wall above glittering treasures. Even when Vale and Nefari played together, pretending to be great warriors with exceptional magic, they had spoken those words. It had always been spoken with great valor – with hope and goodness. Now, hearing Sibyl say them, it sounds like an omen – a prophecy – and not one that brings any comfort.

"Okay," Nefari answers simply because what else is there to say?

She watches Sibyl continue back to her cave until the path disappears into the plump pine trees, her gait solemn and utterly exhausted.

Sighing, Nefari turns back to the hut, checks to make sure the shadows are still obscuring her features, and then trudges back inside where meager warmth might chase away the chill in her bones.

# Chapter Fifteen

Since she came back inside, Nefari has been leaning against a wall by one of the few small windows. The stacked logs snag on the shoulder of her cloak, but she hardly notices. It takes all her effort not to glance at the pommel of her sheathed sword or the cold ring on her finger. Instead, she remains quiet, watching Cyllian ask Kristal question after question about her health and the conditions of her lifestyle. Everyone knows servants are slaves, but they don't have it as bad as Nefari's people. Nefari doubts the girl was ever whipped for moving too slow or backhanded for exhaustion. She's heard the stories just like everyone else in the city.

No one here has ever been to Salix except Kristal. No one in the city has crossed the southern forest of the Frozen Fades, nor sailed against the high waves of Widow's Bay. Not even Patrix. Salix is one kingdom he's avoided in its entirety.

Nefari has half a mind to question Kristal about her homelands just to get answers to things unaccounted for in the way Nefari had imagined the place. She likes to know her enemies, likes to know what they do and how they act and what she should expect, should it ever come to it.

Outside the window, centaurs have emerged from their homes and are traveling along the path. The drums had stopped minutes ago, deeming it safe to emerge from the pockets of their homes. They carry armfuls or baskets of goods as they head to their day's tasks of selling or shepherding or any other duties appointed or earned. And as they pass the hut's window, Nefari counts their curious glances.

Kaymen is in view, leaning into the window. He strokes his chin while he watches them.

She glances at the big front door once more, listening to the unintelligible conversations of centaurs gather outside to gossip about Kristal's verdict.

Fawn had left while she was talking to Sibyl. It doesn't bother her that she had not said goodbye. She probably had a hard time being so close to the enemy without being able to cut her down.

She peeks at Dao through the hair half-fallen over her face. As close as he is, his scent is clouding her space, and the familiarity of it banks her uneasiness. It makes her feel guilty because the dying spark in his eyes when she turned him away is something she'll never forget. How long will he stand by her now that she's made it clear she isn't interested? How long will he be around as someone she can lean on? She couldn't blame him if he were to ever walk away from her.

He's remained just as quiet as herself, leaning on the same wall with his arms crossed and staring aimlessly at the scuffed floor. His choppy white hair is in disarray, and each time he mindlessly tugs on the roots near his forehead, it gets worse. He's stressed and with good reason.

When Nefari had returned, she told him everything Sibyl had said. She'd whispered, of course, but the impact was still the same. He's been silent ever since she ordered him not to tell Bastian anything about it. This is her news to share, and if she decides she wants to tell the blood-vow-breaking leader, she'll do it in her own time. Dao didn't like it but agreed.

Still, he makes no pains about hiding his distrust concerning the sword either, occasionally tipping frowns at her hip where the sword is strapped.

She knows what he wants. He wants her to get rid of it. When he finally voices it aloud, she'll refuse. And though she feels guilty about their fractured relationship, he is not her keeper. This is her sword, and if Divine magic is embedded inside, well, all the more reason to keep it.

From where she stands, Nefari can feel his mind working, making checklists to research in Swen's library later. She doesn't have the heart to tell him that even Sibyl doesn't know anything about inferaze. No one truly does except for maybe Kristal, who had clearly been withholding information on the matter. The prisoner won't say a word, not unless she's given something in return, and Nefari doubts it's of much use anyway.

Everyone glances to the hallway when hooves clomp through it. Bastian emerges, and Cyllian and Kristal, both seated on the platform, stand abruptly. Cyllian dusts off the rump portion of her healer's plain dress, and Kristal's balance is awkward as she tries to find her center with her wrists still bound. Nefari doubts those ropes will ever come off, be it a verdict of death or life. She better get used to them.

Nefari nods to Dao, and together they stride across the room to meet Bastian halfway.

"Where are the other council members?" she asks, peering around his torso and into the dark hallway.

"They've remained in the private chambers," Bastian's deep voice rumbles. "There is more we must discuss today than a Salix woman's fate."

Nefari squares her jaw. She could pry as to what else must be discussed, but she knows there'd be no point. Bastian is tight-lipped about matters of importance. Only if it involves her will he divulge anything. "And what was decided, then?"

He challenges her rigid posture with a raised eyebrow. She swears his eyelid twitches. He looks past her and says to Kristal, "You will be allowed refuge."

"Oh?" Nefari breathes. She chomps down on the inside of her cheek and tastes the copper tang of blood. Sibyl isn't going to like this. No one is.

Sagging with relief, Kristal opens her mouth to verbalize her gratitude, but Bastian holds up a palm. "There are conditions to your new safe haven."

"Conditions?" Dao squints suspiciously. It's not normal for the council to allow refuge on conditions, but these certainly aren't normal times. Never has Nefari heard of Salix citizens being provided anything but a swift death before they even make it inside the city's mountainous walls.

"I will meet your expectations." Confident, Kristal squares her shoulders and nods for the centaur to continue. Nefari has the urge to roll her eyes. This is preposterous. Absolutely ludicrous.

"Your wrists will remain bound until we can decide if you're trustworthy," he murmurs. There's a glint in his eye, a brief narrowing, which suggests this will likely never be. Nefari will make sure of it. No one with Salix blood is trustworthy. She'll see this girl thrown out by week's end.

Kristal raises her wrists and frowns at the ropes. The fresh bandages Cyllian had wrapped gleam stark white underneath the twined threads. "I understand."

"I am not finished." Bastian's tail flicks, a snap in the air. "You will shadow another of ours so we may keep an eye on you. One misstep, Ms. Timpleton, one reason to suspect you of bringing harm to Kadoka, and we will put you to death without question."

Her gaze swivels around the room, and a huff escapes her lips. "A bit harsh, don't you think?"

"No." His tone is firm and grave. Goosebumps rise across Nefari's skin. She hasn't heard that tone since she was a child and was caught stealing chicken eggs from Nio's coop. At least Bastian never learned of how many times she'd done so. He only ever caught her that once, but thankfully, her punishment wasn't as severe as it would have been for any citizen. Everyone else would have been subjected to days shackled to the shame post. But not Nefari. Instead, she was unallowed to attend blade practice for a week. That had hurt Nefari's pride more than the shame podium would have.

The eggs she stole were never consumed. Bastian had made sure she was never hungry, but that's not why she stole them. No. She stole them so she could hatch them herself.

As an adult, she understands why she was compelled to raise little chickens – she was trying to be the mother her mother never got the chance to be. She wanted to be someone who would keep the chickens safe and warm and comforted in climates so harsh and impossible.

The eggs never hatched. Not a single one. With the grief and after her punishment . . . she never tried to steal them again.

But Kristal Timpleton is no egg to hatch and bring up as her own. She will find no love from Nefari, nor will Nefari grieve when she's gone.

"You're lucky to be here at all," Nefari barks. "In fact, you're lucky to still be breathing." She has seen Bastian cut someone down for less. "Can I talk to you alone, Bastian?"

Bastian nods. "Dao, Cyllian, please take our guest outside with the others and wait for further instruction."

"Outside?" Cyllian asks, shocked.

Dao scowls. "Shouldn't we take her out back? Where no one –"

"Out front!" Bastian decrees just as the beating drums come to a stop. His voice booms throughout the space.

They give no further argument. Dao gestures for the two women to follow, and as they near the Council Hut's main door, Kristal asks over her shoulder, "Who will I be shadowing?"

Without taking his eyes off the shadow princess, Bastian answers, "You will be shadowing Fari."

A shiver runs up Nefari's spine. It's the first time he's ever called her by the nickname, and Nefari can't help but wonder if he did so to keep her true name a secret or for some other reason that will leave Nefari awake at night trying to figure it out. She hopes it's the former. If the girl stays, it's imperative she doesn't learn who Nefari truly is.

Oh, this is such a terrible idea!

The door shuts behind them, and rage builds inside Nefari. "Me? You want her to shadow me? Have you lost your mind?"

He crosses his arms. "The council decided because they believe it'll benefit the Legion. It was voted, and you will do what you're told. I do not ask for much from you, Nefari Ashcroft, but I do expect your cooperation in this. You must set our differences aside. This is in yours and our best interest."

"She's a threat to all of us even if she's not here for devious plans!" He says nothing, and she snarls like a feral, leashed beast. Her attention moves to the fire still roaring in the middle of the empty room.

184

Terrible idea indeed! Have he and the entire council lost their minds? Do they want the girl dead? Surely, they know Kristal won't last long in Nefari's presence!

Wind pushes against the hut, and the tendrils of it seep through the cracks of the nearby window. The tendrils reach and touch her cheek, a sweet caress that calms her fraying nerves and rising magic.

If the council decided, she truly has no choice. She won't be able to run away from this. "Why? Why me?"

"Who better to keep an eye on someone from Salix than someone who despises Salix with her whole heart?"

Nefari matches his stubborn posture. "And if I kill her instead?"

"You won't."

"Oh?"

"No. Because if you do, you'll be no better than the Queen of Salix. You will be shamed. You will be punished. And best of all, you will never be able to live with yourself."

*I doubt that.* One less Salix citizen is better for the entire realm.

She scoffs weakly, but even to her own ears, it comes out unconvincingly. "I don't want this, Bastian. Please don't make me."

"The duty is yours. You must take responsibility for something, Nefari. Let it start here. Perhaps you will sort yourself out along the way." She says nothing, and the silence pulls their tension taut. Bastian presses, "Sibyl was here, wasn't she?"

"Yes." Nefari runs a finger over the pommel of her sword at the reminder of the crone child. Now, more than ever, she doesn't want to tell Bastian about the sword's oddness. She doesn't want to give him any reason to feel she needs to be watched. Instead, she says, "Sibyl doesn't trust the Salix girl."

He makes a humming sound and sighs through his nose. "Unsurprising."

Nefari spares him a peek. "What is the real reason as to why you want her to shadow me?"

Considering her carefully, he wets his lips as he sorts out what he can and shouldn't tell her. "The council believes you to be right about their hunt for a Divine object that could project the whereabouts of the other Divine. We believe Ms. Timpleton has more information about it than what she's letting on. We want to know what it is."

"So why not just ask her?" she asks tentatively.

"Do you think we haven't?" Bastian eyes her shrewdly. The muscles where his neck meets his shoulders flex once with irritation. "It's the only bargaining chip she has left. If she spills that secret . . ."

"She won't have anything to bargain with for her life later if it comes to that."

"Exactly."

Nefari tries to hide her smirk. She'll just have to make it her mission to find out what, exactly, this newcomer is hiding. "If we find out what it is," she begins, watching the door through which Kristal was led, "I want to be the one to retrieve it."

"I was going to send Kaymen."

"Sibyl said fate is unfolding, Bastian," she beseeches. "If it truly is, I'm not going to leave it in the hands of Kaymen. If you want me to find the truth, you'll allow me to follow it through."

"You think this has something to do with your fate?" he grumbles.

"I do."

He rakes a hand over his face. "Swen believes as much, too."

Outside of the Council Hut, Dao Pyreswift lingers close to Cyllian and Kristal. He doesn't trust these centaurs who are eyeing them with distaste, and though he isn't fond of Kristal being here, he's going to make sure nothing happens to her until Bastian announces Kristal's terms to everyone else. After that, Bastian and the council can deal with any fallout, and then he can head to his scrolls and books and see what he can discover about inferaze.

Kaymen is not far off, leaning against the outer wall by a window while he studies the three of them. His gaze is like little pinpricks on Dao's cheek. He's about to whirl and confront him, but angry voices start to rise in the crowd. Cursing under his breath, he shuffles closer to the women, looming over them.

So far, they've refrained from rushing Kristal. Dao has no doubt she'd be dead in a second if the centaurs didn't respect their betters. Dao also has no doubt Kaymen had told them the verdict before Dao, Cyllian, and Kristal had come outside. He's leaning so close to the window that there's no way he didn't hear. The bastard can rot in the Death Realm for all Dao cares.

"I'm sorry," Cyllian murmurs to Kristal.

"For what?" Kristal whispers back.

"That you're still bound." She points with a tilt of her head to the closest centaurs. "For being the object of attention. This can't be what you wanted."

Kaymen snorts at her apology, but she ignores him.

"It's nothing new." Kristal sniffs nonchalantly. Her accent is foreign and strange to Dao's ears, and it takes him longer than it should to understand her. "I was raised in similar conditions. It's grim, but I survived that, and I will survive this."

He considers the girl carefully. She seems normal, but Dao has seen Patrix change personalities whenever it suits him. He's good at acting the part. A girl who was in servitude her whole life had to pick up a few tricks of that trade.

"Is –" Kristal hesitates before looking Dao square in the eyes. "Is Fari nice? What should I expect?"

He shifts his weight. He doesn't want to respond because, in doing so, he feels like he'd betray Nefari. He's already rattled her this morning with his attempt at a kiss. She feels betrayed, he could see it in her eyes no matter how she said otherwise. He refuses to make her feel like that again even if his heart aches for something that will never be between them.

*Loyalty.* Without it, he's nothing. And he will be *loyal* to her, his princess and friend.

It's Cyllian who answers. "She's cold, but she has to be. She's had a rough past, shaped by . . . well, the darkness as you can imagine. It's difficult for her to be normal." She peeks at Dao. "She hides herself to conceal what's truly broken inside her."

"Cyllian," he warns.

She shrugs. "She's going to be here for a while, Dao. She should know Fari is the way she is to protect herself." She angles her body to face him more fully and crosses her arms. He blinks at her. This sort of boldness was unusual for Cyllian. And her eyes, they spark like the sun shining across ice chips. "Do you not believe she deserves the benefit of being warned?"

"As if that justifies your reasoning to divulge information that isn't yours to give," Kaymen grumbles. He pushes off the wall and adjusts his cloak. "You will tell her nothing more. Nefari's story is her own to tell."

Dao frowns. Since when does Kaymen care?

"Nefari?" Kristal interrupts, and the three shadow people collectively stiffen to Fari's true first name. But then, after a moment's thought, she adds, "That's a beautiful name."

"This is a terrible, terrible idea," Kaymen mutters. Dao is beginning to agree.

# CHAPTER SIXTEEN

The climate embraces Nefari when she steps outside. She hunkers into her cloak and searches for Dao and her burden. He's off to the far side of the path with the others, their faces grim.

She shouldn't be surprised that Cyllian remains, nor should she be surprised Kaymen has added himself to their numbers. Of course, he would. He's probably waiting for Nefari so he can shove this in her face.

She passes by the shame post. Its thin shadow squats while the world underneath it is ever-moving, ever-changing. As she stomps toward her friends, she vaguely notices that Kristal looks like she'd rather be anywhere else than in Nefari's direct path. Her expression most likely isn't a pleasant one.

Beyond them, shortly up the path, there are sparring centaurs. They pay the world no mind, their concentration directly on their teacher or their dueling partner. The clank of metal against metal calls to Nefari, begs her to take her aggression out there and not on suspecting friends.

At her back, the murmurs rise in volume. She doubts the centaurs grouped before the Council Hut know anything about the council's secret agenda, but in her opinion, they should find themselves fortunate to not be stuck with the Salix filth. Their angry mutterings only make Nefari's feelings more aggressive on the matter.

Kaymen's face pinches when she reaches them. He crosses his arms, and she sneers at him. "What the hell do you want?"

"I have a right to know what was decided just like everyone else," he hisses.

"As if you don't already know?" She raises an eyebrow and gestures to the window.

"Look," Cyllian murmurs and then points. "Bastian's coming." They all glance over Nefari's shoulder, and she turns to watch with them.

He emerges from the Council Hut, and Nefari blinks at the crown atop his head, the very one etched into his sword's steel. The crown has been passed down from generation to generation, to each leader chosen, who then swears to protect those who cannot protect themselves.

Metal ribbed horns spike out around the band with a few horns that jut down and press into the cheekbone of the wearer. She imagines it's quite painful if jostled too much. Perhaps that's why he chooses to only wear it when he has news to share others may not like – an intimidating reminder of who is in charge.

Though he never wears it, and though Nefari has only seen it a few times, she's always loved how it looked. Crowns are beautiful to her. Majestic and a generational relic that stands for more than just beauty. A duty unlike any other – an obligation far greater than a single person.

Bastian surveys the crowd before he speaks, retelling the verdict in a tone that begs no question. Instead of listening to what she

191

already knows, she grabs Kristal's elbow and starts to lead her away.

Dao jogs up to her other side and matches her stride for stride. "Did he say anything else?"

"No," she lies crisply. Bastian didn't verbalize it, but she knows what he told her is to be kept a secret. "She's to be at my side until Bastian says otherwise." And though she wordlessly vowed to keep this secret, she gives Dao a look. He blinks at it. Then, his face settles with the understanding that Nefari's only duty isn't to tote the girl around.

"So, there's a chance that –" Kristal begins.

"No," Nefari cuts her off. "The chances of you surviving in a city that hates everything to do with Salix is very slim. I wouldn't get your hopes up."

"And you –" Kristal wets her lips and briefly glimpses behind them. Cyllian and Kaymen are following, listening to every word while she nearly drags the girl along. "You're to watch me the entire time?"

"What? Were you expecting to be under Nio's care?" she asks with a smirk. Five minutes with the butcher, and she'd be spilling all of her guts, quite literally.

To Nefari's annoyance, Kristal says nothing. If she's to find out what Kristal knows, then she'd rather not waste her time, nor have an audience while she does it. Nefari whirls to face Dao, Kaymen, and Cyllian. Kristal stumbles before she rights herself, grumbling her annoyance about the abrupt yank, and Kaymen nearly slams into her. "Aren't you late for practice, Kaymen? You're supposed to spar with Fawn today."

"Fawn can wait a little longer. Why does Bastian want you to keep watch over her? There's better suited, more responsible people who should be her warden."

Nefari barks a chuckle. "Like you, you mean? Does the shepherd boy want to herd around something other than sheep for a change?"

"She's not a prisoner, Kaymen," Cyllian says, her voice small. She huddles inside her cloak and shivers from the gale whistling down the path.

"She kind of is," Dao mutters, mindful of the dispersing centaurs approaching.

"So, which is it, Kaymen?" Nefari challenges. "Are you angry that she stays, or are you jealous you didn't get the job?"

Between his clenched teeth, he grinds out, "I am merely questioning everything I don't agree with. Dao is right." He turns to Cyllian, and his expression softens despite her scowl. "She is a prisoner. Be careful not to forget that."

The group observes Kristal's ropes and then the bandages. Briefly, fleetingly, Nefari wonders if her own people are bound in such ways in Salix. Is it with rope? Chains? Or simply harvesting? Nefari can't imagine they're all harvested.

She brushes the thought aside and says, "Noted."

Kaymen's nostrils flare.

"Give it up." Dao rubs at his jaw in an exhausted sort of way. "Fari isn't going to tell you anything else because she knows as much as you do." It's difficult for Nefari not to grin at Dao's lie, and she bites her tongue to keep from doing so. Despite his earlier attempt at romance, her faith in him to always stick by her side is rejuvenated, and for that, she is grateful. Undeserving but grateful.

When tension pulling between the group becomes too much, Cyllian excuses herself, murmuring her goodbyes and incoherent explanations for returning to the healer's hut. Confrontation has always been something Cyllian avoids. Though lately, she seems to have found a voice.

She strides away, her cloak and white hair billowing in a gusty breeze. As soon as she leaves, Kaymen invades Nefari's space and mutters into her ear, "I don't like to be kept out of the loop. You and I may not get along, but we are of the same people, and we are not enemies on this front. You will not hide things from me. Not when our goals are to be the same."

"This is going to be a real struggle for you, isn't it?" she says, rising on her toes. "Go find Fawn before you hurt yourself trying to think too hard."

Snarling into her ear, he bumps his shoulder into hers as he stomps off toward the sparring centaurs. She watches him go, noting Fawn at the end of the path with her hands on her hips, glaring at Kaymen for being late. Nefari and Dao are supposed to spar together today, but with her new charge, she doubts that'll happen.

She turns back to Dao. He studies the pommel of her sword, a thoughtful shimmer in his eyes. "Are you going to research it?" she asks. She's known him long enough to know exactly what he's thinking.

"I have to. Are they . . ." he lets his voice trail off, but Nefari understands his inquiry.

She nods. "They believe me. They want me to investigate it."

"Investigate what?" Kristal asks.

"Nothing," they both answer.

Loose snow drifts around their calves, and a shiver runs up Nefari's spine. Dao grips both of them by the shoulder before he passes them to leave. "Be careful," he murmurs, and for some reason, Nefari feels like he isn't talking to her at all but warning Kristal.

She frowns at his retreating back. His hair wildly whips about when he passes the Council Hut, and then he jogs.

Kristal clears her throat. "So, now what?"

Fog spirals when Nefari exhales. "Now, we –" she stops when her attention is caught on something else, or rather, someone else. "What?" she breathes, squinting. Someone she recognizes rides down the path and toward them. Through the hood of his cloak, she can make out his telltale facial features.

*Patrix.* But why? Why has he arrived so soon?

And he isn't alone. He's accompanied by one other whose face is wrapped so many times in a scarf that only his eyes and frosty lashes are visible. The horses underneath them leisurely stride along, exhausted and heads drooped low. Clumps of snow cling to both horse and man, and as they pass the merchants, the men exchange half-hearted greetings with them.

"What is Patrix doing here?" she asks herself.

"Who's Patrix?" Kristal turns to investigate what caught Nefari's avid attention.

Sparing the woman a glance, Nefari doesn't answer her. It's none of the girl's business, and she'll be damned if she gives away their best spy's identity. Or his many identities . . .

By the way, Kristal watches Patrix and the man who trails behind him, she's absorbing every detail. They veer onto a path that isn't Nefari's, and when they reach the Council Hut, the two men dismount from their rides. A young centaur boy approaches them at his mother's urging, and Patrix and his companion pass the reins to the boy's waiting hand.

A certain nervousness settles over Nefari, and she presses her tongue against the wound inside her cheek.

With his companion close behind, Patrix strides to Bastian, who hadn't left his position by the Council Hut's main door. Neither glance her way.

The stranger begins to unwrap his face and then pushes back his cloak's hood. Nefari studies him closely.

The layers of animal skin he wears would be laughable on any normal occasion. He must not be used to such harsh elements. The man is obviously from nowhere near here and human at that – slightly younger than Nefari, and as gangly as a newborn tree, but still human. He wears the headdress common to those who live in Urbana, a thick, cream-colored cloth wrapped many times around his head. The color stands out against his darker skin.

"I know who that is," Kristal whispers. Nefari notes the fear in the woman's eyes. Notes how, in the seconds it took Patrix and the young man to dip inside the Council Hut with Bastian, she had taken several small steps away.

"The Urbanian?" she asks, and Kristal nods. If this woman knows who he is, then he must be someone important. Nefari juts her chin and peers down her nose. "Well, tell me, then. I demand to know."

"He's the son of Urbana's General." Kristal swallows. "Emory Vinborne. I've never met him in person, but . . . He's been groomed to take over his father's position someday; although even the court of Salix knows he'd rather do anything but." Nefari quirks a brow and Kristal quickly adds, "Servants gossip."

*Of course, they do.* Nefari remembers courtly gossip well.

She turns her attention back to the Council Hut. Through the window and past the snow piled on the window's ledge, Patrix, Bastian, and Emory hold an animated, albeit private, conversation inside. From where she and Kristal stand, they're not difficult to make out. Bastian must have said something Patrix didn't want to hear because he turns his head toward the

196

window. In doing so, he spots Nefari. Patrix raises his hand in greeting, but she doesn't return the gesture. Instead, she studies this General's son.

In the warmth of the hut, Emory stands fully erect while rubbing warmth into his hands. Patrix's attention elsewhere catches Emory's interest, and he, too, looks at Nefari. His jovial chocolate eyes peer into hers, but his expression remains neutral. His posture is straight and proper, like someone who was indeed raised by all the maidens his parent's wealth could afford.

"Are you sure he's a General's son?" Nefari asks when the men return to their conversation. The boy looks the opposite of someone who would someday oversee Urbana's soldiers.

"Yes," Her voice is weak and small. It's enough to tug on Nefari's curiosity.

"Secrets will do you no good with me," Nefari warns.

"Secrets will keep me alive," Kristal challenges and then waves at Nefari's body. "As I'm sure you well know."

Nefari stiffens. "What's that supposed to mean?"

"How is it that Shadow People have gone unnoticed in these mountains?"

"Because your people have yet to invade it," she snarls. "And they'd be foolish if they tried."

A blush rises to the woman's cheeks, and she shifts her eyes to the left of Nefari's head. "I am not my people. You have no idea who I am. It is bollocks you pretend otherwise."

Nefari's snarling features turn into a feral grin. "Oh, but I have every intention of finding out just exactly who you are."

Kristal rolls her eyes and starts to walk in the direction they had been. "Lay off."

"Not going to happen."

Over the course of the day, Nefari begrudgingly led the girl around. Her company was mixed with a stubbornness that matches Nefari's own, and Nefari rose to the occasion with nasty responses of her own.

In the armory, Fawn had made no pains about showing her complete disinterest. She painstakingly ignored their presence while she carved the tips of large spears. The only time she made a noise was when Kristal had tried to touch one of the centaur's huge bows that line the wall. Fawn had growled and Nefari had chuckled when Kristal looked slightly frightened of the woman's scorn.

They were escorted out shortly after Kristal knocked over the matching arrows and they rolled across the floor.

When they had made their way to the butcher's hut, Nio had grinned wickedly through the smoke curling around slabs of meat dangling from the ceiling. To Nefari's delight, Kristal had turned a light shade of green, surrounded by all the flesh and a centaur twirling a bloody knife.

In Nio's space, Kristal was but a mere mouse, and a certain sort of satisfaction filled Nefari.

The mess hall hadn't been much interesting, but the cooks who adore Nefari had let them taste the evening's meal. Kristal had devoured her sample of battered poultry fried in the fat of yesterday's meat. When she had finally realized they all stared at her, she claimed, "It's bloody lush," around a mouthful of food. Rightfully disgusted, Nefari had still tucked away that information. All day, she had been quietly planning an intervention with the Salix woman. Originally, she envisioned knives playing a vital role, but perhaps Kristal could bribe with food instead.

198

Now, as the sun dips past the mountains, they pass the sparring warriors of all ages and both species. Everyone in Kadoka has a job to maintain. Nefari's had been to teach the young children the art of the Rebellion Legion ways, but with the enemy in their midst, lessons had been canceled for the foreseeable future. Nefari isn't sure how she feels about that. If the Rebel Legion is to carry on, the young will need the knowledge of how to raise a sword and how to draw a bow. It's as important as their history. Perhaps the children's fathers or mothers or brothers and sisters will pick up the task in her absence.

Nefari nearly misses it when Kristal stops to watch them instead of listening to her prattle on about the dangers of the mountain itself.

Grinding her teeth, she returns to Kristal's side and tugs on the elbow of her cloak to display her annoyance. Kristal pays her no mind. Instead, she observes the partners striking, blade for blade, or the older centaur children who wave wooden swords at the barking order of the weapon's trainer, Fawn's frequent beau.

With a huff, Nefari settles in beside her. There's delight in the woman's eyes, the sheer joy of the practice reflecting within them.

"Do you know how to use one of those?" Nefari eventually asks, nodding toward the nicked and aged swords tossed haphazardly in the wagon off to their left. Fawn will have a fit when she sees the mess the others have made.

Kristal's only answer is a reluctant look of longing.

"I thought handmaidens weren't trained to defend themselves."

She peers at her from the corner of her eyes and then raises her bound wrists to scratch at her filthy cheek. "They are if they're handmaidens to the daughter of a hated Queen."

Nefari cocks her hip forward and crosses her arms. "So, you hate your queen?"

"Don't you?"

"She killed my people. Of course, I do."

Nodding, Kristal returns her attention to what's in front of her. An idea forms in Nefari's mind, and she strides over to retrieve two swords from the pile. The pile falls apart, and swords scatter when she tugs two pommels from within. The snow crunches on her way back to Kristal, and she stuffs one in Kristal's hands.

"What are you doing?" Kristal asks, gripping the pommel with familiar ease.

"Seeing how well Salix trains their people." She twirls her chosen practice sword, and it glints like it's taunting Nefari's own sword strapped to her hip. No way is she going to use the inferaze sword for sparring. No way is she going to get it dirty with Salix blood. Not when she's not allowed to kill the woman. It would be a disgrace to the sword itself.

"If it's anything I've learned by how poorly they train their soldiers," she adds, "then I'll pretend not to be disappointed."

Kristal scowls and raises the sword questioningly. "And you trust me with this?"

A thrill thrums in Nefari's heart. She crouches and prepares herself, circling the girl with her sword poised to strike. "I trust you value your life enough to not cut your binds. If anyone around us saw you attempt it, they'd strike you down before the first strand was severed."

"How am I supposed to duel you like this?" Kristal hisses, eyeing all those around them. The others are trying not to watch – trying not to be noticed that they're watching – but their attention is obvious. Their wariness about her is etched in every single one of their expressions.

200

A snarky tone seeps into Nefari's voice. "As I trust that you value your life, I also trust you're inventive. After all, you managed to escape the Salix court and your charge. How did you manage to sneak past all of the court's guards anyway?" Kristal's jaw ticks, but she doesn't take the taunt. "I imagine you have a few tricks I'd like to know about. I imagine you have a few secrets I'd like to know about, too."

"Is that what this is?" Temper flares in Kristal's eyes. "You plan to whack the truth from me?"

"I'll do what it takes to keep this city – the Rebel Legion – alive." Without further discussion, she rushes the girl. Kristal raises her sword in time to block the strike.

Steel hitting steel rings familiarly in Nefari's ears. She grins brightly and shoves the girl back a few steps.

She's going to enjoy this immensely.

# CHAPTER SEVENTEEN

Nefari Ashcroft spits blood onto the trampled and dirty snow. She continues to circle Kristal while annoyance fills her soul. Both of their swords are raised, and they blink past the blood and sweat dripping into their eyes.

Darkness has fallen across the mountains, and fires are lit around the sparring square, significantly brightening the space.

Normally, practice doesn't run into the night, but the older warriors have extended their training to continue to watch the brawl.

This 'lesson' – this search for answers – isn't turning out how Nefari had hoped. All she's been able to glean so far is that this Salix woman is better at swordsmanship than she had guessed. If she didn't have to concentrate so hard, she might have blushed with embarrassment. Her heavy breaths are mortifying enough, but at least Kristal appears the same.

Twirling her sword in a circle, Nefari lets the fire's light hit the blade just right. A bright reflection bounces off the metal and shines into Kristal's eyes.

Wincing, Kristal looks away. Nefari's heart skips a beat of victory. She dashes to the woman, sword poised, and ready to strike. But she doesn't cross the short distance fast enough.

Hollering, Kristal raises her sword, and the clashing metals boom in Nefari's ears.

"Cheap tricks are nothing I haven't encountered before," Kristal growls, blinking past the fresh tears from the reflection's irritation.

Moments before, Nefari had used her elbow where her sword had failed. Blood dribbles where her elbow had hit, and Kristal wipes it away with a quick swipe on the shoulder of her haggard cloak.

"Who trained you?" Nefari demands, panting. It's been a while since she had been matched so perfectly. *The woman is bound, for Divine's sake.* Even though the sword occasionally wobbles awkwardly, Kristal is still able to hold her own.

If Bastian were here, he'd make a fool out of Nefari for that very reason. He'd throw her into a lesson with himself as teacher, and by the end of it, she'd be sore and nursing bruises for a week. He had trained her, after all, and if he witnessed this . . .

"A handmaiden doesn't receive this sort of attention."

Kristal raises her boot to kick Nefari's abdomen, but Nefari dances away. Her leg flies through the empty air, and she sways as her balance falters. It leaves an opening for Nefari, but she holds back, wanting the answer to her question.

With her sleeve, Kristal wipes the sweat from her brow and turns with Nefari when she circles her again. "They do when they're expected to aid in the protection of a princess."

"Lies," Nefari hisses. "A handmaiden isn't expected to protect the princess."

"Truth! I already told you, the princess is the daughter of a hated queen. Any queen with their wits about them will arm those closest to her greatest assets." Then, with anger coloring her face a shade of crimson, she rushes Nefari on newly steady feet. They meet, sword for sword, dancing across the space left open for them by the others.

Nefari lets her rage fuel her, lets her hatred for the Salix woman sharpen her senses. She can feel her magic stirring inside her, a calm magic that only opens a gentle eye when Nefari gets riled. She pushes it down – her emotions and magic – because here, right now and with the enemy . . . she would be a fool if she were to unleash it.

Kristal swings, and the sword whooshes over Nefari's head. Nefari ducks, swiping Kristal's feet out from under her. The snow crunches as Kristal lands on her back, and her sword tumbles from her hands and slides a few inches away.

Triumphant but panting heavily, Nefari points the tip of the dull blade at Kristal's throat. Her cloak is open, and the lion embroidered on her dress's chest gleams like an insult. "Who – trained–you?"

Snarling, Kristal grasps Nefari's ankle and roughly yanks. She falls to the packed snow, the breath knocked out of her, and wheezing curses fly from her lips.

Kristal scrambles to her knees. She grabs her sword and straddles Nefari's abdomen. She places the edge of the blade at Nefari's throat and hisses, "I was trained by Ostin Markovich!" At the volume of her voice, and possibly by what she had revealed, Kristal's eyes widen.

Those sparring around them have stopped, and Rebel Legion soldiers twirling their weapons inch closer, preparing to deliver the Salix woman's death if she were to make good on her sword's threat. Nefari holds up a hand to stop their advance and pins Kristal with a glare.

"I was trained by the best." The words are like a bad taste on her tongue, and the fight leaves her voice. "I was trained by my father." Slowly, she climbs off Nefari's abdomen and slumps to the snow next to her.

Propping herself up by her elbows, Nefari watches her toss the practice weapon a few feet away. She asks with disbelief, "You were trained by Ostin Markovich? Your father is Ostin Markovich?"

Kristal glances at her from the corner of her eyes. "The Red Reaper himself."

"My Divine," Nefari swears. She wipes a hand across her mouth and runs her fingers through her hair to dislodge the clumped snow stuck there. "So, it's true then? The retired assassin advises the Queen of Salix?"

The Rebel Legion's tale of The Red Reaper had been Nefari's favorite fireside legend even if it was the most gruesome. He's untouchable, a wraith with flesh and voice and thought. Sneaking into a room and remaining unnoticed for hours; then assassinating his target and slipping back into the night before anyone ever noticed . . .

Nefari had gone through a stage of dreaming to be just like The Red Reaper someday. That is until she grew older and realized he was a murderer – an enemy to her own kind, especially when she heard the rumors about him advising the Queen and her wicked ways. But she's never heard the rumor about him fathering a child.

Nefari wonders if The Red Reaper knows the Queen is possessed. He must. He's told to be wicked and insane, the perfect somebody to advise such a dark position. But does Kristal know? Had her father ever told her? No one realized

Despair had possessed Corbin, the Fee who was once the ruler of the Demon Realm for hundreds – thousands – of years. Despair is excellent at trickery. Excellent at fooling those around him into believing one thing when it's really another. Had her father spared her the knowledge? Had he loved her enough to not only train her but to keep her daily life less harrowing?

"It is true," Kristal grumbles. Nefari notes her obvious displeasure. Perhaps it's a reluctance to admit a murderer with no conscience shares the same blood as herself. Perhaps it's embarrassment for knowing him personally. Nefari can only guess.

Kristal rubs at the dried blood on her lips with her fingertips. "He was never my favorite person, but he was always kind to me."

"Oh?" Nefari presses. She gathers herself to her knees and grabs her sword off the ground. While she waits for an answer, Nefari wonders if this is knowledge she should pass to Bastian, but then she quickly swipes the thought away. Who trained Kristal doesn't matter – who fathered her doesn't matter. The fact is that the woman can defend herself. If she were to ever be punished or put to death, she'll take down whoever is closest to her in an effort to preserve her life. The Red Reaper would have taught her exactly that. He would have put the girl into situations where she'd have no choice but to engrain it in her mind as instinct. That sort of person is a dangerous person, but it explains why Kristal is so tight-lipped.

"He was a bastard to everyone else," Kristal says. "Still is, I imagine." Wincing, she stands, and Nefari rises with her, quirking a brow at the girl's pain. A slice across Kristal's arm bleeds sluggishly, and they both peer at it together.

Reaching, Nefari pokes at it. Her finger comes away bloody, but Kristal's yelp has a satisfying effect for not having bested the girl.

"Apparently, the Red Reaper didn't teach you how to hide your pain," Nefari goads, dusting snow from the backside of her cloak.

"What the hell was that for?"

Nefari grins. She starts to walk away, tossing the sword back in the pile along the way. "Come on, Salix. I have a friend who can stitch that up."

The Kadoka tavern's warmth swaths Dao Pyreswift, and it nearly lulls him into a dreamy state. He and Cyllian are seated at the bar while the other citizen's loud and jovial voices wash over them as nothing but mere background noise.

They sip from their ale, content with saying nothing at all to one another.

Dao's day of searching for information about Nefari's sword and the inferaze itself hadn't been fruitful, but he hasn't given up. There are several shelves he hasn't checked yet – several dusty and ancient books and scrolls he has yet to open. He'll find something. He has to. Having a Divine object can't be anything but dangerous, he's sure of it.

An hour ago, Cyllian had arrived at Swen's hut, asking if he would like to get a drink with her. Haggard and wary from his unsuccessful day, he agreed.

Now, sitting next to her, he's aware that the day has not been kind to her either. She's spent it restocking her elixirs for the next Rebel Legion's departure. On the way over, she had told him as much, admitting to accidentally ruining several batches. The head healer had given her a good scolding for it, too, but with the day's events, Dao isn't surprised she had been unusually distracted.

Turning on his stool, he observes the centaur's standing at the tables throughout the room. Some centaurs gamble good coin.

Others drink in silence, and a few harlots lean into prospective suitors.

There are a few shadow people disbursed throughout. They're barely noticed, but there, seated on logs in the dark corner, is Kaymen and his usual three friends.

Feeling Dao's brief stare, Kaymen raises his gaze from the mug of ale settled on his knee and looks him square in the eye. Kaymen abruptly stands, passes his mug to another, and begins striding purposefully toward them.

Dao curses, swivels back in his seat, and mutters to Cyllian, "Incoming."

Cyllian squints over her shoulder and scowls when Kaymen squeezes in beside her. "Kaymen," she greets nastily. Dao hides his smile in his mug.

"Dao. Cyllian." Kaymen frowns at them. "I would have thought Nefari would be joining you tonight with her new pet."

Rolling his eyes, Dao thumps his mug back on the counter, earning a glare from the bar's keeper down the way. "Not now, Kaymen."

"I only speak truth, and you know it." His words are slurred, affected by his ale. He leans into the counter next to Cyllian, and she tilts away from him.

"You know," she begins, pausing until Kaymen's attention returns to her. "Your desire to beat Nefari into submission will only make matters worse."

"Someone has to." He waves his hand in a circle. "You two dance around the topic and pretend all is well with our people and our princess's choice to twiddle her thumbs inside the safety of the mountain."

"Like she said," Dao responds. "You're making matters worse."

Kaymen's barking laugh startles Cyllian. He bends in closer. "Sometimes, I feel like I'm the only one who cares what's happening across Widow's Bay."

Between clenched teeth, Cyllian says, "Don't you think if you approached the matter more diplomatically, Nefari might actually listen?" Kaymen frowns, and she presses on. "Have you tried sharing a piece of yourself with her? She dislikes you so much because she sees you as an equal. Or have you failed to notice? We are her only friends if you can call us that. But if you tried, just for a second, to pretend you knew what she was feeling inside, and then discussed it with her, perhaps you could actually get somewhere on the topic of saving our people. Instead, you chuck your hatred around for everyone to endure. Your attitude is no better than Nefari's. You're the other side of her selfish coin."

Pride and surprise fill Dao; although calling Fari selfish doesn't sit well with him despite knowing it to be true. He studies Cyllian's soft features, splotched with an angry red, the ferocity of which matches her words.

She straightens her spine. "Maybe Fari's new duty will be good for her, and you won't have to spill your guts. If she's forced to endure someone who has never been free…" she lets her voice trail off. Nothing more needs to be said.

He blinks at her but doesn't get a chance to respond because a hairy hand slaps down on his shoulder. The three observe Patrix whose grin fades with the obvious tension. There are bruises on his face, and Dao studies them. "How are we doing tonight?" Patrix asks quietly. Behind him, Emory shifts on his feet nervously.

"We're fine," Dao murmurs. "How was your trip? It looks like you —"

"The trip was most enlightening."

*The bruises tell another story.*

Patrix's astute eyes shift to Cyllian and soften with a warmer expression. Out of all of the two-legged women Patrix runs into, she isn't someone he's tried to climb into bed with. Perhaps it's her innocence. Perhaps it's because she's normally too shy, but either way, Dao is glad of it. His wanton behavior can be most daunting at times.

"Do you want me to tend to those?" she asks Patrix, grinning as she reaches and pokes a particularly nasty looking bruise.

"Oh, no. Not me. But our princess, however, has engaged in a duel with our guest." Dao's shoulders slump, and he exhales loudly. Nefari would. She would challenge the girl. "A healer sent me to retrieve you, Cyllian. Some wounds need to be tended and mended."

"For once, I wish she would leave well enough alone," she grumbles under her breath, bringing her mug to her lips, and drains the rest of her ale.

# CHAPTER EIGHTEEN

The head healer had personally shown both Kristal and Nefari to Cyllian's personal healing room and then left quickly, shutting them inside with the assurance that Cyllian would be along shortly. They hadn't been here long, but from the window Nefari was peering out of, she had watched Dao escort Cyllian to the entrance.

She had expected jealousy to rise in the suit of Dao's chivalrous gesture, but instead, Nefari finds herself . . . glad. Cyllian is finally expressing her interest in Dao, and that, in itself, is a victory in Nefari's eyes. Hopefully, Dao will direct his attention and affections toward the healer, and not herself.

Now, darkness seeps through Cyllian's healing room's small oval windows. Darkness and stars and the sparkle of the big and bright moon hanging in the clear sky. But Nefari is only vaguely aware of it because Cyllian's sharp jabbing glares are directed at her while she threads a needle and string through Kristal's split skin.

Nefari says nothing to her, gives no excuses for her behavior. Instead, she studies Cyllian's workspace as if she's seeing it for the first time.

The fireplace is small and insignificant, and on the other side of the room, the tiny, corked bottles of elixirs glint dully on their many shelves because of it. She has no idea what the elixirs do, but their many colors are fascinating.

Three trunks squat along one wall and a few stools Nefari ignores on the other. In the center is a table with a blanket draped over it. Kristal sits on top of it, trying desperately to hold her arm still while her other hand grips its edge.

By her hip, Cyllian's instruments lie.

Once they pass their training, each healer is given their own room, but they all look the same to Nefari. The same size, the same contents, the same sagey smell. She had heard Cyllian was a quick study in her youth though she shouldn't have been as surprised as she was when her fellow shadow person surpassed the head healer herself. Cyllian's thirst to help others had never gone unnoticed, and her need to keep people alive after what happened in their past . . .

Nefari clears her throat to rid the recollections threatening to surface.

In truth, every time she'd been in here, she was too busy biting back her shouts of pain while a wound was being threaded back together. Nefari rarely gets injured – Bastian had seen to that by making sure she was capable of caring for herself when he couldn't be around to protect her. But every now and then, especially lately, a harvestman or a Salix soldier throws a surprise her way. Each of them died shortly after his attempt at taking her life, but the fact still remains, Nefari is getting sloppy.

Standing by the elixirs'' shelves, she succumbs to her desire and touches one of them. She circles the tip of her finger over the rough and dry cork that confines the blue liquid within, marveling at the dancing hues that splash together on the wall behind them.

Each kind of elixir is in some sort of order, but as Nefari squints at the vials, she can't, for the life of her, figure out how they're ordered. They certainly aren't labeled.

She glances at the healer from over her shoulder. Does Cyllian truly memorize them? Indeed, she's as good as they say.

"Don't touch those," Cyllian orders without even looking.

Nefari whirls around with a cocked eyebrow but relents. She leans her back against the wall, crosses her arms defensively, and bites her tongue. She reminds herself that most people don't like their things touched and she should provide Cyllian with the same courtesy. After all, she wields a sharp needle.

Kristal winces every time Cyllian pokes her skin, but Cyllian, half concentrating, doesn't pay much attention to the girl's pain.

"Have you always wanted to be a healer?" Kristal asks through clenched teeth.

Without pausing, she answers, "Not as a child, no."

"If I remember correctly, you wanted to be a florist," Nefari interrupts. "You always did love the galaxy roses."

"Galaxy roses?" Kristal asks, her expression morphing to delight and pure interest. "Like the stars? A rose made of stars?"

Nefari nods. "Roses as black as night. And they sparkle."

A painfilled grin spreads across her lips. "That sounds fitting. Is that in the Shadow Kingdom?"

Both Nefari and Cyllian stiffen. "Yeah," Nefari says uncomfortably. Kristal blinks at the sudden tension, but thankfully, she doesn't inquire about it.

After a few seconds, Cyllian sighs. "It matters not. It was a foolish dream, and the kingdom already had a florist. There was no need for another."

213

Nefari shifts against the wall, remembering the florist's shop well and the way it had smelled. It smelled like hope. That's what flowers are given for after all. *Hope.*

Bright Diabolus Beetles were also sold there, lanterns full of the big and glowing poisonous bugs found in the Shadled. These lanterns were to replace torches and limit the chances of a blaze.

She won't admit it, but it was one of her favorite shops to visit. A warrior doesn't admit to having a fascination with pretty, pretty flowers.

The shadow woman who tended the flowers always had sugared nuts for any child who came into the shop with their parents. Her father would take her to buy flowers for her mother, usually as an apology because they often didn't see eye to eye. Nefari may have been young, but she remembers their arguments – arguments that circled around Nefari and her future.

She wasn't as close with her father as she was with her mother, but on their way back to the castle, he would let her pluck a petal from the rose he had bought. She'd keep the petal until it crumbled, but by then, she'd have a fresh new petal to press to her nose. She never had a reason to be sorrowful about the petal's death, for there was always another to replace it.

"When I came here," Cyllian says. "I was injured by a crone." She moves the sleeve of her dress aside and reveals teeth marks along her upper arm. Nefari studies it closely from afar, tracing the jagged edges. She had never asked to see Cyllian's injury when they were brought back here, but from the looks of it, it had been severe.

"It is rare to survive a crone bite," Kristal says. "Everyone I've seen bitten by one has succumbed to a fever as wicked as they are."

"Most kingdoms don't have elixirs for that, but we do, among other tonics." Cyllian covers the scar and readjusts her dress.

214

"It's how I came to be involved with the healers of the city. They took me in that day, and I found joy by giving relief to others. I found a place. A purpose." She peeks at Nefari from under her lashes.

"That's kind of beautiful," Kristal bravely confesses.

"It wasn't," Nefari grumbles, rubbing at her arms and the goosebumps that rose. "It was bloody. It was messy. And we – we lost a lot of people that day." She pushes off the wall and throws a few logs onto the fire. They track her every move without saying a word, and when she returns to the wall, she adds, "It wasn't beautiful. Nothing about what we have come to be is beautiful."

Kristal eyes her with sympathy and perhaps understanding. "It was a result of the means of surviving."

Dumbfoundedly, Nefari blinks, then nods curtly. Survival must be something the girl understands, and for a moment, and only a moment, Nefari's hardened heart softens. She quickly squashes this new feeling down deep inside her. It sidles up next to her suppressed memories.

"And you?" Cyllian asks while she ties the last stitch. At Kristal's frown, she clarifies, "Do handmaidens have a choice in being handmaidens?"

"Oh," Kristal breathes. The stitching finished, she redresses her upper half. "No. No, we don't."

"I see." She packs up her things and places them gently on top of a trunk. She lingers there. To the wall, she adds, "Not many people do these days. We all have that in common, it would seem."

Kristal studies her feet, twisting her ankles to examine her boots. "I suppose so."

Straightening her spine, Cyllian turns back to them and places her hands her hips. The mood lifts considerably as she changes the subject. "Now, let's talk about your illness."

Nefari pushes off the wall, interested in this new turn of conversation.

Kristal shrugs indifferently but remains seated on the table. "I've been sick since the day I was born."

"And what are your symptoms?"

"It's nothing you're going to be able to fix."

"Just tell her," Nefari barks impatiently. "She won't leave you alone until she can find some way to fix you."

Wetting her lips, Kristal takes a moment of consideration and then lifts her bound wrists to remove the hair stuck to dried blood on her cheek. "I get tired."

Nefari snorts. "Don't we all."

"It's not like that. It comes and goes against my will, drains me of my capability of doing the very simplest of tasks." In a quieter voice, she adds, "It's not some frivolous matter that can be easily fixed."

"I see," Cyllian says. She passes Kristal a wet cloth to clean the dried blood from her face. She does not offer Nefari the same kindness. The look she gives Nefari could scare the hair off a cat. She supposes she's lucky Cyllian hasn't had her escorted out yet.

"And . . ." Cyllian pauses, returning her interest to Kristal and tempering her tone. "And the Salix healers couldn't find what was wrong?"

She shakes her head. "It wasn't noticed until I was in my adolescence. They claimed I was born this way. The more active

I became, the more noticeable it was. I didn't truly know something was wrong until I was six."

Nefari puckers her lips. The girl was a handmaiden – a replaceable servant. She should consider herself fortunate that she even saw a healer; unless her father had a hand in that and insisted so. No one in their right mind would refuse the Red Reaper's request. Even so, they wouldn't have given her more than five minutes before they considered her a lost cause.

The pity in Nefari's gut is unwelcome, and she flexes her jaw to push it away.

For the next hour, Cyllian and Kristal discuss the ins and outs of Kristal's condition. Nefari hadn't been able to bear the conversation for long and had returned to the window to watch the moon sluggishly move across the sky.

At some point, leaning against the window's pane, she had drifted in and out of sleep where the flickering dreams of screaming shadow people surfaced. Just flickers. Snippets. Painful jabs.

*The sway of her dresses while she hid under them in her closet with Vale. The echoes of the dying gusting down the hall. The sound of Amoon's crying. And the deep tenor of Bastian's voice as he handed Amoon over to the crones . . .*

*"Don't worry," Vale reminds her, his child-like voice so crystal clear inside the spacious, pitch-black closet. The voice turns male, and Vale grows in size beside her until he's an adult instead of the child she remembers. "I'll protect you."*

*Vale. Sweet and kind and courageous Vale.*

Someone grips Nefari's upper arm, and she startles awake, her hand flying to the pommel of her sword. She blinks bleary eyes at Cyllian and sighs relief.

Cyllian frowns. "Are you okay?"

217

Nefari pushes the hair from her face. "I will be."

The frown remains even as Cyllian asks, "Are you ready to take Kristal home? I'll have someone bring you your meals to Bastian's hut and . . ." She sweeps Nefari's face and the sweat developing across her forehead. Her earlier hardened attitude is all but gone, and Nefari wonders if Cyllian knows what she was dreaming about. Had she been talking in her sleep? "There's no need for the city to believe the rumors about both of your bruises, cuts, and bloody faces. If you want, I can clean you up."

She cocks her head as she considers the healer and the discrete glance she throws toward Kristal. She nearly chuffs when Cyllian crosses her arms uncomfortably. She cares for the Salix woman. She cares what the others think of her, and if they stride out of here all bloodied and haggard, the rumors will turn hostile.

The healer always did have a thing for the weak. Someday, it will get her killed.

Nefari straightens her shoulders and rolls her neck. "Home?"

"Yes," Cyllian barks. "The place you will *both* sleep."

She hadn't considered the fact that Kristal would be sleeping under the same roof as her. She squints at the girl in question, watching her fidget as she becomes the object of attention and not for the reasons she might like.

"What the hell am I going to do with her? Let her sleep in the same bed as me?" Nefari would rather die.

Cyllian invades her space, anger radiating off the tiny woman. "Get over it. Bastian gave her to you, and you'd be wise to listen to him at least once in your life."

218

# CHAPTER NINETEEN

Grumbling under her breath, Nefari leaves the healer's hut, Kristal in tow, without much of a goodbye. They travel through the city, noting the few people's blurred faces who are out under the darkness of the night. Huts are lit within, and their torch lights splash across the snow, lighting their way.

The shadows bend toward her in her obvious annoyance, but thankfully, Kristal is too busy perusing the centaur's homes to pay attention to Nefari.

She curls her lips at the shadows. They reach up the side of the huts and curl away from their roof until they almost form a bridge of sorts that blends with the night.

Why won't the shadows leave her alone? What do they want from her? It can't be magic, per se. Not normal magic. Otherwise, the wraiths would have come a long time ago. It's not like she can necessarily control them, not that she's tried. In truth, any shadow that isn't of her own making seems alive, and it unnerves her.

The minute Nefari closes the door to Bastian's hut is the minute Kristal's shoulders slump in exhaustion. The fire is nothing but bright shifting embers, the logs glowing with orange ash. It's enough to light and warm the space, however, and Kristal strides to the embers and warms her hands over them.

Seconds tick by, and with her back to Nefari, she mutters, "Thank you." Nefari says nothing, so she turns. "Even if it is your duty, thank you for giving me a place to sleep."

"Let's get one thing straight. I am not your friend. I am not your protector. Everything I do is for the interest of my people and this city. No amount of built relationships or wrought sympathy from the others will make me see you any differently." Nefari crosses the room to the small pile of logs.

"I wasn't trying to . . ." Kristal moves aside as Nefari squats and places the logs strategically on top of the embers. Immediately, sparks rise in the chimney, and ash billows into Bastian's living space. "Does it offend you that Cyllian has warmed to me?"

Nefari grinds her jaw at the growing flames. It certainly does bother her, but she's not going to voice that aloud. Cyllian isn't grasping how dangerous Kristal can be, and now, not only does she have to look out for herself, but she has to make sure Kristal doesn't hurt Cyllian. Thankfully, everywhere Kristal goes, Nefari will go too. Keeping an eye on her won't be difficult.

Standing, Nefari dusts bark from her fingertips. She turns, avoids eye contact with Kristal, and unfastens her cloak. "Bastian may not be home until late." She moves to the hallway, but Kristal doesn't follow.

"What?" Nefari demands, peeking at the girl still frozen by the fireplace. "What more do you have to say?"

"Are you always this rude? Or is it a defense to something I'm not aware of?"

"You know nothing about me, and I prefer to keep it that way."

"Fine." Huffing, Kristal gazes about. "This is Bastian's hut?" She twines her fingers tightly together. "My – my mother used to tell me about him as a child."

"Don't tell him that. It'll go to his head." Nefari steps into the dark hallway, but then she stops. Over her shoulder, she tentatively asks, "Just out of curiosity. What stories did you hear?"

Kristal is lighting an unlit torch in the flames. Once it's lit, she shuffles across the space between them. "The usual. His adventures in his youth. There was a time, long before the slave trade, when Bastian actively served the Urbana court. When the royals started dipping their fingers into slavery, Bastian left and went to the mountains where he rose in power and became the leader because of his legendary skills." Kristal twists her lips to the side. "Is it true?"

Nefari shrugs. "I've never asked." Indeed, she had heard these stories. The descendants of the Urbana's royalty who had implemented slavery had continued the tradition and trade. There's far too much coin in selling abled men, women, and children than to give it up. There's no way Bastian would have any part of it back then.

Before her birthday ball, she had heard her mother talking with the Urbana King, pleading with him to stop this prosperous business and turn to more morally uncorrupt trades. The citrus fruits grown there make them enough to sustain the entire realm.

Toward the end of the conversation, it had sounded like he might agree to give up the business, but then . . .

He was one of those who had died that day, hacked down by a crone or a wraith or maybe even Nefari's mother's magic. His son, Mixael Uba, the spoiled eldest of the Uba royal family, had risen to sit on the Urbanian throne. When his father left for the Shadow Kingdom, Mixael knew his father and mother would never return. He had made a deal with Queen Sieba Arsonian –

221

sided with her to ensure his profits. And over the last decade, he's been just as determined to sell the innocent as his ancestors who founded the trade. He and his dark ways had not shared the same sympathy as his father.

Nefari often wonders how Queen Sieba Arsonian has convinced Mixael Uba to remain faithful to Salix. He doesn't need her. He has the wealth. Perhaps it is with threats. Perhaps it is adoration. After all, he was a new King. Nefari will never know, nor does she care to truly understand. The spoiled child-like man will someday rot in the Death Realm, and it's the only comfort she has on the matter. Nefari can't comprehend how Patrix can be in Mixael Uba's presence.

"Well, is it also true he taught all of the Shadow Royals? In swordsmanship, I mean."

Nefari snatches the torch from Kristal. "Yes," she softly says. She stares at the torch for a moment. The fire in the living space cracks and pops, and it fills the void of their silence.

"You lost people you loved that day, didn't you."

And though it wasn't said as a question, Nefari doesn't know why she answers – doesn't know why she feels relief as she murmurs to her enemy, "We all did." There's no fight left in her voice. Her mother's face flashes in her memory, and Nefari works to shove the image down, down, down to the place inside her that's as cold as the mountain's snow.

"I'm sorry," Kristal says. The light of the torch shines in her brown eyes.

Nefari hardens her features and snorts. She marches down the short dark hallway, her skin crawling as the shadows seemingly swallow her despite the torch. She pushes open her bedroom door with her shoulder, hangs her cloak on a protruding nail, and immediately crosses the cold room to her barren fireplace. She tips the torch to the logs that nearly resemble bones.

"So, where do I sleep?" Kristal asks in the doorway.

Nefari slides the torch into a holder along the wall. She glances about her room and then strides to her trunk. When she opens the lid, the hinges creak, and the smell of old leather and cold metal tingles her senses.

Inside is an old, wool blanket that chafes the skin. Nefari snaps it free and drapes it on the floor with extra flourish. "Your bed," she says cheerfully, sweeping her arm out in a bow.

"For Divine's sake, Fari." The words are an angry hiss. "You cannot be serious."

"As serious as a march of slaves up a gangplank."

Kristal blinks at her. One of her nostrils twitches. "You and I have a lot in common, you know."

Sliding off her boots, Nefari kicks them into the corner. Her socked toes flex along the floorboards. "You and I have nothing in common."

"I may have been born in a different place than you, but you . . ." she takes a deep breath and tries again. "You and I were trained by great warriors." She awkwardly removes her cloak and hands it next to Nefari's.

"*I* was trained by a warrior," Nefari corrects, pointing her thumb at her chest. "You were trained by a murderer – an assassin who happens to be your father. There is a difference. A large one, in fact."

"Is there?"

"Yes," she hisses. "One has honor and fights for theirs and other's freedoms, and the other covets wealth in exchange for

223

death. You and I are nothing alike. We were not raised the same."

"Is there honor if you're getting paid for ensuring other's freedom? I noticed you don't have any mirrors. Is that because you don't like what you see? Or is it because your own reflection reminds you of someone?"

Nefari sneers, but she says nothing, gives away nothing.

"We are exactly alike. The only difference is, I know who I am. I embrace where I came from so I can do better – can *be* better. You seem to run from it all. And you want to know something else? I'd wager there's more to you than you're sharing, too, and it's the sole reason you find fault in me."

Nefari breathes slow and deep, hands loose at her sides. "You don't know what you're talking about."

"We're all broken inside, Fari," she adds harshly. "You and I are broken. What matters is what we do to mend it. And if that means letting go of the shame we carry so we may stitch our hearts back together and forge something new, then no one can fault us. You cannot fault me for my blood. You cannot fault me for my heritage. I am not defined by them, and frankly, neither are you."

She doesn't get a chance to respond, even if she could think of something nasty to say, because hooves plod down the hall. They're too light-sounding to be Bastian's, but Nefari is grateful for the intrusion just the same.

They turn toward the bedroom doorway.

"Ladies!" a jovial voice says from the dark hallway. Patrix emerges from its shadows, takes in the scene with grim amusement, and rests his elbow against the doorframe. "I could feel the tension three huts down. I had thought it was passion, but now I'm disappointed to find that neither of you is naked."

"What are you doing here?" Nefari snarls.

In his free hand is a tray of food, and he holds it up. "Providing basic needs, of course." He sweeps Kristal from head to toe. "So, it's true. My surly friend is indeed childminding a Salix woman."

"Not funny." Nefari crosses her arms over her chest and cocks a foot out in front of her. The room's smothering emotions evaporate as she exhales.

Squinting, he tips his head to the side, inclining it toward Kristal. "Have we met before?"

"I think I'd remember meeting a furry man with pointy ears and a memorable beard."

Leaning into the room, he whispers sidelong, "I'm a man of many disguises and talents. I don't have to be just a satyr if you don't wish it."

Nefari rolls her eyes. He truly can't help himself, and he doesn't care about shame. He's the most shameless person Nefari has ever met. But deep down, Nefari knows Kristal speaks the truth on the matter. Being shameful is pointless. Perhaps Patrix knows this, and that is why he flourishes about from woman to woman.

Still, he should refrain from trying to bed Kristal.

Striding forward, Nefari snatches the tray from his hand. He chuckles, straightens his posture, and adjusts his tunic. "Testy," he chides.

"What do you want?"

He ruffles Nefari's hair, and she chomps the air between them. "To check on you, of course. The last time we were together, you weren't too happy. But I can see your mood has not improved. It is distressing that you're becoming an old coot with every passing year."

"You were on a mission," she grumbles. "You've missed much. It hasn't exactly been normal circumstances around here. The conditions warrant irritable behaviors." She places the tray on the wooden chest and gestures for Kristal to pick out what she'd like to eat. Kristal does, watching the exchange with interest as she lifts a loaf of bread and bites a chunk off the end.

"Ah, yes. My favorite little shadow doesn't like it when her routine changes," he says conspiratorially to Kristal. Breadcrumbs tumble from her mouth when she grins.

Nefari spies him with suspicion. "Why are you back so early anyway?"

He shrugs, props himself against the door, and crosses a hoof over the other. "It turns out I didn't have to travel far to get the answers I needed. Thank the Divine for that. Court posturing is never my favorite activity. It takes far too long for their tongues to waggle with secrets."

Chuffing, Nefari unties her sword from her waist and sets it, still sheathed, by the fireplace. The aroma of the food makes her stomach growl, but she pushes her hunger away. She bites the inside of her cheek and glances discretely back at Kristal. How much can she ask with the girl in the room? "Did the Urbana general's son meet you halfway?"

He grins. "In a way."

"And I assume he wasn't the one who gave you those bruises." She waves her hand at Patrix's face where the shadows of the room nearly conceal the yellow and purple splotches.

"Have you seen the boy? He'd break a nail if he took a swing."

Suspicious, she watches him from the corner of her eye. "And the horse? It wasn't yours. Where did you get it?"

His nostrils flare, and he narrows his eyes as he considers her uncharacteristic distrust toward him. "Ever the observant one,"

226

he mumbles. "No. My horse was stolen when I slept along the forest's path. I hadn't heard the sneaky, thieving bastard. I had to walk for half a day before another crossed my path. It was like magic." He splays his fingers in jovial emphasis.

"Another horse just crossed your path?" Kristal asks with disbelief. "Out in the middle of the woods?"

Nefari would like to know the same. The trail leading from the mountains to Urbana only has one true wooded area – the Shadled. Gentle creatures such as horses aren't known for wandering into the Shadled. . .

"Indeed, a stroke of luck. Found the mare munching on tree bark at the edge of the Sea of Gold. Did you see the horse? It's the largest one I ever rode, but alas, I'll have to return it to the rightful owner. Or, at least my guess at the rightful owner." He pointedly looks at Kristal.

"What?" she asks after a moment of silence, the bread poised halfway to her lips.

"Why, lady, did your horse have a Salix brand on the rump?"

Around a mouthful of food, she shrugs and says, "All Salix horses do."

"Sorrel and white coat? With a mane as white as snow?"

Her eyes widen, and she nearly chokes. "And a pink muzzle with a four-pointed brown star between the nostrils?"

As if to poke her from a distance, he jabs the air between them. "That's the one."

"You found Joana?"

"Well," he grins and then strokes his beard. "She found me. But if you want her back, I can –"

"Yes! Yes, thank you! Where is she?"

Nefari openly gapes. She cannot believe this. His grin is as genuine as his flirtatious generosity. The bastard is betraying her. *Bonding with the enemy over a horse!* Nefari thinks. *What a ridiculous evening.* First, she appealed to Cyllian, and now . . .

At this rate, the whole city will be bowing at Kristal's feet by breakfast.

"She's in the stables, getting her fill of oats," he reassures her.

"But . . . What about you?"

"I'll just have to acquire another lost little pony frolicking off the beaten paths now, won't I?" Kristal blushes to his sultry words that drip with interest and foul implications.

"If the horse is so precious to you, how did you so easily lose her?" Nefari barks.

Kristal glares. "I told you. Sometimes, I get ill. One of the nights I was traveling alone, I became particularly weak and slept for an entire day." She dismisses Nefari with a lift of one shoulder. "She wandered off and I couldn't find her once it had passed."

"An illness?" Patrix asks, uncrossing his hooves and ears perking with fascination. "Should I be concerned? Do I need to find someone to heal this fair maiden?"

"No," Nefari quips at the same time Kristal tucks her lips between her teeth to hide her amusement. "And don't be kind to her. A Salix woman is no one to adore."

"Fari . . ." He rolls his eyes until they pin her with a chastising stare.

"Don't 'Fari' me. This girl may still be a spy." She jabs him in the chest, and he grunts. "You should know this better than anyone."

"I am not! Why won't you believe me? What do I have to say to convince you that I don't want to murder or get anyone murdered? For Divine's sake! I just want to be safe!"

228

Outside, the noise of the passing centaurs slow at the rise in her volume. The fire crackles and pops while they stare at her, her chest heaving.

"Everyone from Salix is a liar. You have slaves, you obey that *queen*, and you –"

"Endure Despair?" Kristal challenges, and Nefari blinks.

"You know Queen Sieba is possessed?"

She sets the half-eaten loaf back on the plate and rubs her fingers together to rid them of crumbs. "Of course, I do. I lived in the castle, remember? It's hard not to notice the dark magic. Even more so, she doesn't really hide it anymore. Not like she used to."

"What do you mean?" Nefari mutters, not entirely sure she wants the answer.

"Well, those blessed with other abilities like magic or shadow jumping," she waves her bound hands at Nefari's body, "can't use magic. I don't know why, and frankly, never tried to discover why, but it makes it obvious when she uses hers. Or Despair's, I mean."

She ignores Nefari's huff.

"And what about everyone else?" Patrix asks. "Does all of Salix know? What of the slaves?"

Scratching her chin, she seats herself on the trunk next to the tray. "Probably. I didn't interact much with anyone else, but most of the slaves are harvested. I never left the castle, so I don't know about Salix's Crown Capital's citizens, but the princess, some of the servants, and the prince all know." Kristal's eyes cast to the floor, and her brows pinch together. "It truly is a horrid place. Sometimes, I would see the slaves from the castle window. Nefari's kind, I mean. Your people have it worse than the Loess and Sutherland slaves – the humans. I tried not to look. I didn't want to see what was happening outside of the castle, but some days . . ."

"That's my point," Nefari says to Patrix. "We cannot trust someone who was raised in a castle of darkness. Someone who did nothing to help them, nor had the interest in doing so. You've seen the true and wicked desires of Urbana. Urbana suckles on Salix like a newborn to her mother's breast. The two are truly no different, so why do you see this girl as anyone else?" Patrix raises his eyebrows. "It's not just my people in shackles, Patrix. It's yours, too. It's everyone's."

"Am I to condemn the general's son, too? After all, Emory is Urbanian."

"Well, no." She fidgets. "He's helping. He's trying to make a difference."

"And are you?" he mutters. "Are you trying to make a difference?" Nefari splays her arms to encompass Kadoka City and the Rebel Legion. Patrix sighs. "Look, Fari. If I didn't find the good in some people, I'd have no one I could stomach long enough to spy on." He reaches and grasps her shoulder. "Not everyone is bad. And even those who do bad things aren't truly bad. Most of them are just lost."

"That's what I've been telling her," Kristal mutters.

Exhaling loudly, Patrix pastes on a fake grin and slaps his thighs. "You should be happy I'm here, Fari. I made it in time for the Shadow Mourn Eve, as promised."

"Hmm." Nefari crosses her arms, her anger not so easily diverted.

"The what?" Kristal asks. She rises from the trunk, lifts her skirts, and lowers herself to sit cross-legged on the blanket laid out for her.

"Shadow Mourn Eve," Patrix says again. "Why, it's a party in the streets of the city to celebrate the memory of the great Shadow Royals and the people they lost ten years ago. It's tomorrow night."

"I've never heard of it."

"Well, now you have," Nefari blurts. She turns, grabs the fire poker, and stabs at the smoldering logs.

"Do I get to attend?" From the corner of Nefari's eye, she watches Kristal raise her wrists and nod toward the rope.

"No," Nefari says at the same time Patrix cheerfully answers with, "Of course!"

"Absolutely not, Patrix," Nefari growls, whipping around to pin him with a stare. She doesn't want Kristal to taint one of the only things she has left of her past.

Beseechingly, Patrix holds out his arms. "Well, she must!" Nefari's expression does not surrender. As he slides his hands into the folds of his cloak, he says with little patience, "You and I both know you can't leave your prisoner unattended. She's coming."

Patrix Eiling shuts Bastian's hut's door and stares out into the dark streets. He's to return to the tavern and finish his drink with Emory, but at this moment, his feet feel leaden.

Standing in the snow, he touches a bruise on his cheek. He had lied to Nefari. So many lies. He withheld the truth, and not because Kristal was in the room. He withheld it because of who he is: a professional liar and deceiver.

May the Divine have mercy on his soul if any of his secrets were to come to light. Nefari would never forgive him. She'd hold everything against him. The secret the crone shared with him, the visit with the pirate queen, the drugs . . .

He hadn't gotten himself caught by the pirate queen to ensure the rumors were true that she's dipping into the slave trade. It was what Bastian had asked of him, and he could have done that by squatting inside Deeds and eavesdropping on the conversations. Instead, he wanted to look Luxlynn Billihook in the eye and discover if she knew the Queen of Salix is her mother. He wanted to know if Luxlynn had finally discovered the truth about her own blood. He had gotten his answer by the look in her eyes – by her avoidance of discussing it in front of her crew.

It's a card Patrix has been waiting to play because on one very drunken evening, when Savage had joined him in drinking fine ale and lying with beautiful women, Savage let it slip that he'd once shared a bed with Queen Sieba. Patrix hadn't forgotten it, had tucked the information away to discover what he had suspected at a later time.

And now he knows for sure.

Luxlynn isn't the real Salix princess, but she is the daughter the queen had kept from everyone. The year Nefari was born, Sieba birthed twins. The one night she had spent with Savage Deeds hadn't been blossomed from true love. As soon as Luxlynn and her son Philip came screaming into the world, she passed her daughter over to Savage with the condition that he leaves and never returns.

But now, Luxlynn is connected with her mother – with Despair. He has no doubt that they're allies, two dangerous people in a world already so dark. Her deal with Urbana is only a front.

He should consider himself blessed Luxlynn didn't know who Nefari truly was because soon, Nefari will leave his mountain to complete her fate. He knows it. Sibyl has warned him about it.

And if – when –she does . . . well, she'd learn who Patrix truly is. Luxlynn will find her, and Nefari will know exactly what was stolen that day at the gambling tents.

And then, Luxlynn will discover who Nefari is.

His heart patterns unevenly for a second, but he takes a deep breath, squares his shoulders, and convinces himself lying is what's best for him and for her.

# CHAPTER TWENTY

The next morning, Nefari rises before the sun. The fire is still a significant size, its flames a comforting orange. Someone – probably Bastian – had dropped a few logs in during the night.

From her bed, she watches Kristal sleep. The girl is a tangle of limbs, sprawled halfway off the blanket. The words she told Nefari echo repeatedly inside her head. They had haunted her dreams made of the usual memories.

*"We're all broken inside, Fari. You and I are broken. What matters is what we do to mend it."*

Broken. She is broken. There is no honor or worthiness in her life, past and present combined. Her worthiness died the day she accepted shelter among the Rebel Legion and allowed herself to be lulled into a sense of safety and righteousness. And now everyone expects her to be what her mother and Fate had wanted.

When she grows sick of her own thoughts, and the world outside her window brightens, she pushes the blankets off her and roughly washes herself. Kristal does not rise to the splash of water.

She stares at her, dripping rag in hand. Her eyes jerk to the sword by the fire. It stands straight, confident, and gleams the flames along the twisting pommel.

What does a Salix woman know about being broken anyway? What does she know about having everything taken away from her? A little voice in Nefari's head tells her how wrong she is. Kristal was a servant – a slave in all intents and purposes. She knows what it's like more than Nefari to not be free.

In her free hand, she twirls the ring on her wet finger. She brings the ring to her face and presses the diamond to her lips. *Be brave*, the words of her mother whisper into her mind from the memory of an innocent and happy eight-year-old.

Sighing, she rises from the washbasin and toes Kristal in the shoulder. She startles awake and blinks blearily up at Nefari. The beginnings of purple circles squat around her eyes, and she rubs at them with the heel of her bound wrists.

"Get washed. We have things to do."

It doesn't take Kristal long to clean and re-dress herself, but she moves slowly like her joints are pained and working improperly. Perhaps the floor was a bit too much for her and whatever illness she has.

"Do you know you scream a lot in your sleep?" Kristal asks while she travels to her cloak. She awkwardly swings it over her shoulders.

Nefari straps her sword to her waist. She curls her top lip. "Did you know you snore? Perhaps you should fix that before you talk to me about what I do in my sleep."

While she crosses the room and unhooks her cloak, Kristal considers her sidelong and then quietly asks, "What were you dreaming about?"

Nefari doesn't return her gaze. She snaps her cloak and settles it over her shoulders. "None of your business."

"What has you so frightened that it slips into your dreams?"

Hand paused and outstretched to the doorknob, Nefari debates not answering her at all, but something . . . something inside her – perhaps her weakened resolved to her earlier thoughts – compels her to. "The dark," she answers because it's true. She grasps the handle and holds on tight. "You were right. I am broken. I have been for a long time, and the darkness . . ." Nefari cannot say more, not without telling the girl who she really is.

"Okay," Kristal says, her voice small and understanding.

Warmth pumps through Nefari's heart, and instead of embracing it for what it is, she swings the door open and steps into the hallway. She doesn't want to dwell on her enemy's sympathy, nor the silence that follows.

As soon as they stride out of Bastian's hut and into the bustling paths, Nefari wordlessly leads Kristal through the throng of merchants selling their wares and heads directly to the stables. She hadn't shown it to her the previous day because there had been no need. Kristal didn't have a horse, and Dao had tended to Astra's evening meal and stall mucking.

They dip into the stables through the wide-open door, and immediately, Kristal dashes to a stall, lifts the lever, and plunges inside. After a few moments, Nefari follows and peeks over the gate to witness Kristal resting her cheek against the horse's wide jaw.

The horse, Joana, is a beauty, strong and well-built for long travels. She's fit for any royal court. Perhaps those riding with the princess of Salix are provided with some luxuries.

Without commenting, Nefari heads to Astra's stall. She feels a bit numb as she treads through the scattered straw and hooks a rope around Astra's neck. Each step is echoed by the words 'broken' and 'brave.' And while they clean their horses' stalls in silence, this numb feeling never ebbs.

At some point, Kaymen had strode in with his followers. Kristal had been brushing Joana down while cooing sweet nothings to her mare. He sneered as he passed her.

Nefari had watched the exchange from inside her stall – had tensed as soon as Kaymen's foot stepped on the straw littering the path between stalls. For once, Nefari understood his anger, and just for a second, when their eyes locked from over the stall's gates, there was an understanding in Kaymen's eyes. A moment of unity and mutual hatred he believed they both shared. Nefari isn't so sure she truly hates Kristal anymore. Not in the same way she had when the girl arrived.

He ignored them for the rest of his duration, caring for his own steed in silence with his three friends completed their chores beside him. Minutes later, Nefari listened to his horse's hooves clomp while he headed out to check on the herd.

The rest of the day passed by in a blur of snow and wind. When they trekked through the morning market, Nefari said nothing when Kristal stopped to peer at the items in awe. Shortly after, they stomped their feet inside the mess hall to free the snow gathered on their boots.

Breakfast had been awkward, and the stares and the whisperings were persistent, but at the end of their meal, a young centaur delivered them a message. Fawn had requested help with mending arrows for a Legion group. The group would be leaving that afternoon to check on Chickasaw.

On the way to Fawn's, Nefari had watched the group from a distance. They shoved and joked with one another before dipping inside the Council Hut to be briefed on any situation they may find themselves in. She itched to be part of that group.

Itched and grumbled the rest of the way because doing something was better than feeling numb.

There would be no point in asking if she could be counted among their numbers. Bastian would refuse because her task has yet to show any results. Kristal hadn't given much of anything of use, besides her parentage, and since their short exchange this morning, they've said nothing to each other.

Perhaps this evening will be more profitable. At the Shadow Mourn Eve, there will be rich wine, fine ale, and, most likely, Diabolus Beetles tossed into the fire. Nefari doesn't particularly care for the Diabolus Beetle smoke – it makes her fuzzy – but the others seem to enjoy the temporary and harmless euphoria that comes with it. Perhaps if she can get the girl drunk and happy, she will spill her secrets. And then, she can leave the girl in Bastian's hands.

In the armory, her brooding had inevitably irritated Fawn. The situation would have been laughable if Nefari weren't in such a horrid mood. Fawn had snatched the tip-less arrow Nefari had been relentlessly twirling, shooed them out into the cold, and slammed the door while grumbling something Nefari couldn't make out.

The rest of the day, Kristal never commented on Nefari's lack of interest in anything. In fact, the girl was content to watch and absorb her surroundings. The more time they spent outside and around the other centaurs, the more they grew used to her, too, as if she were nothing more than Nefari's shadow. A few of the children, those she normally taught, even waved – *waved* – at Kristal.

Nefari had nearly hissed when she waved back but clenched her jaw to keep her displeasure inside.

The evening meal had come and gone, and now, Kristal and Nefari watch as the last touches of the Shadow Mourn Eve's celebration is assembled under what would be a full moon if the clouds weren't so thick.

Diabolus Beetle lanterns are strung in the area where everyone will gather. Snow lightly falls, a backdrop to the grins that are spread across the faces of those gathered in the streets.

Outside the mess hall doors, two skinned and gutted sheep turn over spikes, and barrels of wine and ale surround the roasting meat while wives shoo away their husbands and children.

Ale splashes and splats on the snow melting by the fires. Centaurs are already filling their hallowed horns and wooden mugs, swapping tales about the years before when their friends had made a fool of themselves on Shadow Mourn Eve.

Nefari moves away from the mass, striding to the other side where no one lingers. She inhales the scent of the roasting sheep as she passes it and slowly exhales through loose lips. The scent had mixed with the crisp, chilly air and worked to relieve her rising and strong emotions that always come with Shadow Mourn Eve. She much prefers the numbness to this.

Here, on the other side of the gathering, it's shadowed. And here, Nefari can watch and tuck away the feelings as she does every year.

Kristal absentmindedly follows, watching a few centaurs check their loots and drums in front of the Council Hut. Soon, the streets will fill with boisterous music and dancing. The fires will grow so hot that the snow on the streets will melt completely and trickle down the dark path beyond.

In front of the Council Hut, Kaymen leans against the shame post with a few others readying their instruments. His grin is wide. Whatever the others are discussing must be particularly funny in order for him to crack a smile. He polishes his flute with the edge of his cloak, and a great belly laugh emits from all of them, including his friends who linger behind him.

Shadow Mourn Eve has never affected him. Not in the way it does Nefari. She envies it, and if Kaymen can find some joy this evening, then perhaps Nefari can dig deep for some as well. Or at least, she can try. She can pretend. She can convince herself.

Everyone wears an array of painted etchings across their face, symbols spread across their cheekbones, foreheads, and eyelids. Nefari prefers her own, the traditional black diamonds around her eyes she frequently wears when she participates in missions.

Tugging her cloak tighter, she shoves these thoughts away and glances at Kristal. She can. She can indeed find some joy, if anything, for her mother's honor.

Only reluctantly will she admit that Kristal's face paint is intriguing. The Salix woman, giddy to see the happenings of the evening, had painted her entire forehead. The black paint stretches past her eyebrows and fades midway through her eyelids. White paint, acquired from Cyllian, is dotted where her eyebrows are. It makes her brown eyes drastically pop.

Cyllian had promised her the white paint was mixed with an elixir that would take the edge off any headaches she'd have this evening. Understandably, Kristal jumped at the chance and snatched the bowl from the healer's hands.

Kristal's amazement is palpable. She bounces on her toes, her excitement contagious. Nefari can't help but feel affected by it, and soon her troubles fall away. Anticipation rises in its place.

Her gaze moves to the shadows, trembling with the reflection of the flames. The urge to make them dance is strong, and it nearly startles her.

A Shadow Dance is a tradition of the Shadow People and hasn't been performed since Nefari's birth. Her mother told her stories, though. When a shadow person dances, sways like smoke, the shadows will curl around them like ribbons. But this is already similar to what happens to Nefari without a dance, and therefore, the urge is concerning. She's never wanted to reach out to the shadows before.

*And I shouldn't do it now,* she tells herself.

"You're squinting at the flame's shadow like they're going to bite you," Kristal says, her voice filled with humor. She tips her head to the side. "Why? Are you one of those shadow people who have shadow magic?"

Nefari crosses her arms, feeling uncomfortable. "No," she lies. "Only shadow royals have magic. And I wasn't *squinting* at them. I was merely observing." How long had she been watching them? The number of centaurs has doubled in size, the streets full, loud, and already melting. Long enough, apparently.

Pushing her hands through the opening of her cloak, Kristal scratches her chin uncomfortably. Through the opening of her cloak, Nefari spies her dress.

The dress she had worn when she arrived is now clean and spotless. To Kristal's delight, and to Patrix's prompting when they ran into him earlier in the day, they had visited the launder hut. Kristal had waited, naked, for her dress to dry by the hot fires while Nefari watched her closely and polished her leather armor. Her own tunic and pants had been drying next to Kristal's dress.

"I thought the shadows draw your kind," Kristal says tentatively as if she's asking Nefari to give away her deepest secrets and unsure if Nefari will be offended. Yesterday, that would have been the case, but tonight . . .

"In the past, and on nights like tonight, the shadows are particularly difficult to ignore for any shadow person if that's what you're asking."

Kristal nods solemnly. "When the slaves started arriving – the shadow slaves, I mean – we had heard stories about shadow traveling in the castle. I was just a child then, but I remember them well. Is it true? In your shadow form, can you fold a shadow around yourself and move to another?"

Dao waves from down the street, and Nefari waves a small greeting. His own paint consists of slash marks that stretch from the top of his cheeks to the edge of his jaw. Nefari tucks her hair behind her ear and answers honestly, "Yes, it is true."

She remembers what it was like to travel through the shadows – to tuck herself inside them and move from one place to another. Her mother had often warned her about it, advised her to never travel to another shadow she could not see or be sure of. She hasn't shadow jumped since her mother was alive. In the shadows, it's dark, and Nefari doesn't know how she'll handle it.

"I'm sorry," Kristal whispers.

Shocked, Nefari whips her head to her. *She's sorry?* It's the last thing Nefari thought she'd say.

Kristal fidgets with her fingers and shifts her posture. "I'm sorry you cannot be who you were meant to be. I'm sorry you're hunted for slavery or for being a threat, or whatever the reason the Sieba Arsonian decided. But," Kristal pauses, seemingly gathers the nerve, and turns to face her. "I know you're keeping something from me. And I really, really wish you wouldn't."

"Oh?"

"Sometimes your face . . ." Kristal squints at her. "It's shadowed. Like now, the shadow of your nose is longer than it should be. The shadows of your brows are darker than your hair. It's – Look, I know the signs of someone trying to hide themselves in plain sight, but I want you to know; you don't have to with me."

"You may have had a solid point last night, but it doesn't make us friends."

Kristal shrugs. "Fine. I've done nothing but obey and be kind, but still, you insist on grinding me under your shoe." Her sarcasm is a palpable thing, and Nefari bristles at it. "You truly are broken," she adds under her breath. "Broken and frightened and incapable of trust."

Nefari opens her mouth to say something – anything to defend herself – but nothing comes out.

A vibrant and jovial song starts to fill the streets. Laughter and hollering quickly follow, and friends and lovers are tugged toward the music. Soon, the wet streets are filled with dancing. All of it washes over Nefari.

*Broken, frightened, lonely, all things of great truth.* She closes her eyes while she twirls the ring on her finger.

# CHAPTER TWENTY-ONE

Bastian watches the celebration unfold in the small path between the mess hall and Nio's hut. With his arms crossed, Patrix observes with him, Emory at his side.

The satyr is far more well-groomed than usual. His beard is neatly combed, and his unruly hair is slicked back and tied neatly at his nape. When he touches his hair to ensure that it's indeed in neat order, it makes Bastian grunt. Who could he possibly be trying to impress here? Centaurs aren't his usual trope.

"Are you going to tell me what happened in the Black Market?" Bastian eventually mumbles. His deep tenor is nearly lost in the noise, but he knows Patrix will be able to hear him.

Patrix's bruises have faded, thanks to Cyllian's elixirs. If it were up to Bastian, he would have forced him to wear the bruises until they healed on their own because he surely deserved them.

Patrix glances at Emory and juts his jaw in silent request for the young man to leave them. "Which particular event do you wish to know about?" he asks when Emory tucks himself into another crowd, mug glued to his lips.

"The part that resulted in the bruises." Bastian glances down at him, an eyebrow quirked. Patrix studies Bastian's thick legs

244

instead of meeting his suspicious gaze. Undeniably, the satyr has been up to no good.

"A run-in with the pirates," he admits. He sighs as if the declaration was difficult to bring to voice.

Bastian huffs. "I assume it's because of the drugs you stole."

"How did you know about that?"

"I know everything, Patrix Eiling. Like any leader, I have many spies. You are not the only one, but you are one I care about. I keep eyes on you."

"You don't trust me?"

"Are you worried you don't deserve the trust?" The question hangs heavy in the air. "I keep eyes on you to make sure you don't get into an abundance of trouble."

A centaur's hip bumps into a barrel of wine, and liquid spills down the side. The women curse at him and dump one of the many buckets of water at the ready, washing the red wine away.

"Are you going to tell her?"

"No," Bastian answers immediately.

"No?"

"You're a buffoon. Nefari sees you as a brother, Patrix. If you care for her, you will tell her the truth. She has had enough betrayals for a lifetime. She doesn't deserve yours."

Patrix tucks his lips into his teeth and turns toward the celebration, peering down the street to where Nefari stands with Kristal and Dao. There's a haunted look formed in Nefari's eyes, one that's been there all day. Bastian doesn't know what to make of it.

"Yeah," Patrix finally mumbles. "Yeah."

From the other side of the gathering, Nefari Ashcroft watches Emory Vinborne give a wide berth to dancing partners. With the snow melting, the path underneath is slushy and slick with mud. Emory's boots slip and slide, but the youth, already influenced by the strong ale, barely notices this hindrance. His mug's contents slosh in his hand and splash across his cloak.

Someone catches Emory before he falls on his rump. He hangs on to his upper arm until he's steady, and then Emory thanks him with a sobering face.

Nefari watches the entire transaction with interest. She feels horrid for him. Daily, he witnesses the Black Market's dealings. He sees the slaves being whipped and starved before they're loaded onto a ship and sent across Widow's Bay, and in order to do some good, he has to pretend he doesn't care. At least, he has the Rebel Legion to find his reprieve.

He heads to the musician's platform, sets his mug down, and begins clapping his hands to the beat. Nefari shakes her head when his movements become more animated, his mood infectious. Kaymen's annoyance is a gleeful sight as he glares daggers at the drunken Urbanian.

Nefari hadn't realized she was starting to bounce with the rhythm until Kristal asks, "Do you dance?"

"Not with my enemy," Nefari answers. The glance she slides at the girl softens the words. She doesn't have it in her to fight anymore.

Kristal snickers when Patrix, dancing his way over with two ales, grins brightly at her. Dao is behind him, shaking his head at Patrix's antics. He had retrieved Patrix upon Nefari's request when it had looked like Bastian was giving him a hard time.

They cross the rest of the distance and join the women. Nefari reaches for the second ale in Patrix's hand, but he pulls it away and passes it to Kristal with a flourishing half-bow.

Dao chuckles and hands Nefari the second ale he had brought. "You know him, Fari. He's always trying to impress a lady."

Nefari grumbles into her mug as Kristal raises her own and tastes the ale. "This is . . .," Kristal's voice trails off, but her curved upper lip completes her thoughts.

"It's practically piss, is it not?" Patrix asks enthusiastically.

"Well . . ." Kristal shrugs. "Yes."

"All ale is." Patrix leans in conspiratorially. "But, I assure you Kadoka's ale is the finest across the realm. Now," he barks the word and stands fully erect. "Tell me about yourself. Do you like adventure? Romance, perhaps?"

"I've had neither," she confesses. "The most adventure I've had is through the castle, chasing the thieving cat."

He gasps. "A great beast roams the castle of Salix? Do tell!"

"It's the princess's." Kristal giggles. "Not a great beast. Heifer is a pet."

"Heifer? I thought you said it was a cat?" Dao questions.

"Yes, I did. Heifer is the name of the cat. A real tosser and an accurate title for the little bastard if I do say so myself. She's always causing trouble, sneaking into places long forgotten and stealing roasted chickens from the castle kitchen's counter."

"Perhaps you should have killed it then," Nefari grumbles. "Pets are disgusting things." Patrix and Kristal turn to frown at her. "Well, they are! They relieve themselves everywhere. Who started this 'pet' thing? Which fool first brought a wild animal into their home and allowed it to drop its feces in a box in the same room they slept?"

Blinking, Kristal's laughter fills the space between them, and despite her resolve, Nefari can't help but grin at it. She hides her smile inside her mug and nearly chokes on it when Dao bumps her shoulder in good nature.

"Well, to be fair," Kristal adds, "The queen would love nothing more than to put the cat's head on a spike. She hisses at her every chance she gets."

*Perhaps this 'Heifer' isn't so bad, then.* She'd bet the cat can sense the darkness within her, too.

"And what of your mother," Patrix presses. "How do you two fare?"

Kristal drags her top teeth across her bottom lip. "My mother and I have never seen eye to eye. It wasn't always that way. As rubbish as it sounds, I remember how loving she was when I was a young child." She scowls while staring at the space between Nefari and Dao's head, tracing her memories back to her youth. "But then, one day, she changed, and I became nothing but another body in the castle halls, forced to endure the cruelty she inflicted on others."

A Salix citizen inflicting cruelty? Nefari isn't surprised. She snorts, and the sound refocuses Kristal's gaze.

Patrix grimaces sympathetically. "How unfortunate." The words were overly exaggerated.

Curious, Nefari studies him. *Is he . . . is he putting on an act for this girl?* Her thoughts are confirmed when Patrix winks at her, and her face softens. So, he doesn't truly desire her? He's . . . he's a spy. . .

*Of course, the sniveling lunatic.* Everything is a game with Patrix, and she feels a sucker for doubting his doting on the girl.

Pursing her lips to distort her relieved expression, Nefari says, "Then, I suppose it's a good thing you're no longer roaming the same halls as her."

"That's a foolish thought." Kristal flits her mug and stares inside it.

"It is?" Dao asks.

"Our mothers are always with us even in death. We hear their voices all the time, do we not? Just because she isn't physically here doesn't mean she isn't mentally." She taps her temple. "The memory of their voices and the rubbish they said, anyway. I'm sure we all have that in common. The things they said shaped us into who we are, and that notion doesn't end with our mothers. It includes people who hold power over us. Take your lost queen, for example. She shaped the darkness – turned something impossible into a little hope for those she could save such as yourselves. You're standing here because of her. Her actions are what influenced who you are today, but that doesn't mean she's not with you. The memory of her will never disappear. Her strength is the podium you stand on."

Nefari is too stunned to answer, but thankfully, Dao replies, "I suppose so. You must have heard the stories then?"

"They're kind of hard to ignore. Ten years later, and Salix still tells the tales." She breathes deeply and then changes the subject. "Am I allowed to dance?"

The satyr grins widely behind his beard, and the toothy exchange evaporates the tension in their circle. He takes the mug from her hand and sets both his and hers on a barrel behind them. Then, he guides her, dancing, into the wet streets.

Once they're gone, Dao places his hand on Nefari's shoulder. The warmth from his body seeps through her cloak, a comfort for the goosebumps crawling up her back. "Breathe, Fari."

Nefari guzzles her ale quickly. She wipes her mouth with the edge of her cloak and grunts, "I know what he's doing."

"Patrix?" Dao lowers his hand. "It took you that long to figure it out?"

"Hush. I honestly thought he was, well . . . being Patrix. You know how he gets."

She turns to Dao and watches him lick his lips. The thoughts churn in his head, and she waits for him to spit out whatever sentence he's trying to form. "He's no doubt doing that, too. Just because he's a spy and has an act to play, it doesn't mean he won't follow through with it."

"You don't know that."

"Don't kid yourself," he adds quietly.

Her earlier sense of betrayal returns. She's been on missions with Patrix – has witnessed his need for women and general chaos. She just thanks her blessed stars he doesn't see her as anything more than a sibling. And as a sister tucked under his wing, the closer he gets to Kristal, the more hurt she becomes. She may not see Kristal as a bloodthirsty Salix native anymore, but she still doesn't trust her. She hasn't earned it, and therefore, Patrix should consider Nefari's hesitation as one he should take for himself.

Dao must have caught on to Nefari's thoughts because he murmurs, "You don't hate her, you know." Nefari frowns up at him. "You don't hate Kristal. She's done nothing to deserve it. You hate what she represents. The blood in her veins is the same blood as those who destroyed our kingdom. She's a totem to pound your fists against."

"She's hiding something, Dao. Even Bastian knows so."

"Aren't we all, though?" He lifts an eyebrow, and she huffs.

"What do you want from me?"

"What your mother would have wanted. She wouldn't like to see you like this."

"Do you think she would have wanted me to befriend our enemy?"

"She would have wanted you to be courageous enough to try." He sips from his ale, scans the celebration, and bumps his shoulder against hers. "You know I'm right. She tried to too, at the end. She knew if she wanted things to change, she had to have faith."

*And look where that got her.*

She grumbles under her breath. She won't admit it out loud, but maybe he has a point. *The enemy of my enemy is my friend,* Nefari thinks, and Amala Ashcroft was smart in thinking so.

Could Kristal be an asset as Dao implies?

At some point during the day – perhaps when Kristal showed nothing but respect, gratitude, and curiosity – Nefari started drawing a parallel between them. And with that parallel and what Kristal said about their mother's shaping who their children are . . .

A small part of her mind believes that if Kristal ever found out about the truth of Nefari's birthright, she'd understand her hesitation far more than anyone else here. Inadvertently, she's helped Nefari see things from a different perspective, and perhaps that's a tribute to consider.

*You are broken.*

Perhaps she doesn't have to be. Perhaps letting go is as simple as taking action.

Will Nefari truly ever trust the girl? No, but they can find common ground to live among each other, as Patrix had pointed out.

She watches Patrix, listens to his great laughter. The mud splashes around him with each hoof stomp, caking clothes and cloaks. "I'm glad he's back, though," she sighs out. And then, a thought strikes her. "But why? Why is he home so soon?"

"You didn't hear?"

"No." She flings her arm toward Kristal and Patrix. "I've had a prisoner. Nobody has been particularly forthcoming with information."

"Patrix hadn't made it to Urbana's Castle in Vivian." Dao clears his throat and leans to whisper, "The general's son had found him first." They both steal a glance to where Emory Vinborne now dances with Cyllian Timida. Her long white hair whips around with each twirl to the beat of Nio's drums.

"Yes, yes." She waves her hand impatiently in the air. "I know about the General's son. But what happened?"

"Emory left the castle as soon as he overheard the news. The court riding to the fades in search for that Divine object? It's the Shadow Kingdom Crown. They believe the shadow kingdom crown will point them in the direction of the Choice-chosen, and the Hope-favored."

Nefari nearly chokes on her own spit. "The Kingdom's crown?" she hisses. "My mother's crown? Haven't they heard? It's dust!"

"They don't think so, and neither does Sibyl." He shrugs. "In fact, she visited with Swen today about it. She was quite angry when I told her it wouldn't have survived the blast of your mother's magic."

A surge of jealousy and possession rises in Nefari. She growls, "Even if it were still whole, they can't have it. It's my mother's."

"I know," Dao agrees. "But Urbana and Salix – even the pirates – are searching for it."

"The crown has been in my family's possession since the beginning of time, Dao. It's not Divine. It has no magical properties. I can attest to that."

"But they believe it does."

"Well, good luck to them when they try to get into the Shadow Kingdom."

Dao hesitates, shifting nervously on his feet. "They'll find a way, Fari. Why do you think they need the crones?" It wasn't a question. It was a statement, words that raise gooseflesh over Nefari's skin. "The crones would have seen it when your mother gave Wrenchel Withervein a tour – they would know what it looks like."

"Is this what Kristal is hiding?" Nefari asks under her breath.

"Maybe. Bastian isn't certain. You know him. As of right now, this is pure fable. And before he sends anyone to search the Shadow Kingdom for it, he wants to be sure."

Nefari nods and chews on the inside of her lip. Traveling through the Shadled would be treacherous. He's wise to be reluctant.

"Fari," Dao adds hesitantly. By his tone, she braces herself for what he's going to say next. "I know you said all is forgotten, but I truly am sorry for yesterday morning. I hadn't meant to . . ."

"I know, Dao," she groans. "You don't need to keep apologizing. What's done is done."

"Can I –" He wets his lips. "Can I ask – is it because of Vale?"

Nefari breathes in the smoke of the fire and exhales it slowly. She doesn't want to answer him, but he's always been loyal to her. He deserves the truth. "Partly, yes."

"He's dead. He's dead, and I'm here. You need to let him go."

"But I can't. And truthfully, Dao, I don't want to talk about it." Truthfully, she doesn't know how many ways she can tell him she's not interested in anything more than friendship without it coming out hurtful and harsh. Talking about it is exhausting. Discussing Vale is exhausting. Remembering that he's dead because of her is exhausting. Blaming Bastian for it is exhausting. Today, she just doesn't have it in her to add another exhausting thing to her list.

Dao allows the silence to linger between them. Then, he sets his mug down. "Okay. Then, we'll dance."

He grabs her empty mug and sets it down beside his. "We'll what?" Nefari shrieks as he tugs her into the celebration.

"Come on," he says, laughing and heaving her by the arm. "You sit on the sideline every year for fear of attack, and every year, you miss out!"

"But –" Her words are cut off when his last tug nearly flings her into a dancing couple.

# CHAPTER TWENTY-TWO

Sibyl Withervein hears the celebration from on high. As near as she is to the entrance of her cave, she's not surprised, but the tune is boisterous and too jolly for her tastes. She harrumphs at it and begins muttering incoherent things.

Under the light of her torch, she examines her drawing along the tunnel wall. The picture doesn't feel complete – this she knows in her soul and in her visions.

Her mutterings become louder as she dips her fingers into the bowl of thick liquid and smears the dull color across the rocks. "Shadows not made of shadows and rock not made of rock. Stars and lions and things scattered in wait. Rings of truth. Crowns of lies. Dark, dark, dark deceit."

A slight breeze curls around her exposed ankles. The cold doesn't bother her. Like all crones, she prefers it. And despite her distaste, the chill and the hushed music seep into Sibyl. Soon, her tense muscles loosen.

The beat of the drums sways her body, easing the lingering anxiety permeating the air, but not for long.

*Two days, and so much has changed.* Two days, and Sibyl is nearly choking on the darkness she tastes in each breeze.

"Bah," she spits aloud. The wretched Salix woman taints everything, even the food Patrix had brought to her cave.

She looks down her tunnel, past the skulls, and into the pure darkness of her home, as if she can see the basket squatting by her mirror. He had come earlier in the day to confess about a crone he found at the edge of the Shadled, and it had taken all of Sibyl's patience to not beat the satyr with the skull of omens. Patrix didn't tell Bastian and probably won't, but he should have told her as soon as he arrived in Kadoka City.

Everything the crone told him is distressing. If they know Nefari is alive, why haven't they killed her yet? They've had plenty of opportunities, albeit none where she was alone.

How does this all fit? The Shadow Kingdom crown is believed to be a Divine item that Despair searches for in hopes of finding his godly siblings. The inferaze with unknown magical capabilities. The handmaiden's sudden arrival. The allies forged across the seas. Nefari, and the crone factions knowing she's alive. It has to form a picture, but what? What picture? What truly motivates each and every piece?

Sibyl had been born deformed and was cast out from the crones because of it. The crones are as much of an enemy to Sibyl as they are to the rest of the realm. Bastian may have made up an elaborate story about her reasoning for living among the centaurs, but only he and Sibyl know the absolute truth. The crones hadn't wanted her – had heard the faster beat of her red heart and cast her aside to be eaten by the bone criers. She cannot begin to understand the impulses of hearts so black, nor what their inaction implies.

Sibyl coats her fingers again, the color as blue as twilight, and brings it to the wall. She mindlessly adds the pommel to the sword she saw on the fate card.

Every time she sleeps, she sees this sword in her dreams. It's surrounded by darkness and shadows and a crown made of just the same. She fears for Nefari's life every time she witnesses it – wakes in a panic and a level of anxiety no crone should ever feel. Because Nefari is the sword, and the crown belongs to her, and she doesn't know what any of it truly means. Theories, yes. But no facts. It scares her that the crone factions may know more than she does, and when she voiced her concern to Patrix, he dismissed it quickly.

*Fools. Fools!* Sibyl thinks to herself even as she rotates her neck to ease the returning tension. *All of them!*

The pieces of this puzzle assembling in her head are starting to form pictures such as the one before her, and they want to dismiss it. But she knows better.

Sibyl pauses painting, stares at the blue smudges on her fingers, and slowly straightens. She backs away from the sword cloaked in a swirling black. She stares at the black swirls for seconds or minutes, she isn't sure, but soon the black warps itself, moving like a wind-blown fog in Sibyl's mind's eye.

Breathing evenly, Sibyl keeps her mind open to the vision forming.

The black swirls push away from the wall and reach out to her like grasping fingers. She holds still, refuses to blink or to turn away from it for worry she may miss something entirely.

Inside this blackness is a stretching scene of Kadoka City. Streets covered in melting snow. Huts with high pointed roofs. Hooves that slosh in mud, and laughter that fills the in-between. In Sibyl's mind, she inhales this darkness to learn more. The vision moves to the dark sky and the snow that drifts down from its inky blackness.

*The blackness* . . . Sibyl mentally cocks her head. *Does the blackness . . . writhe? Is it . . . breathing?*

257

The vision abruptly ends, and the black ink that had appeared to drift toward her snaps, flattening itself against the wall once more. The shadows of Sibyl's torch reflect on the wall, and she looks to the hand that once held it, open and grasping nothing. She had dropped the torch at some point, but she hadn't noticed.

She peers down and finds it on the floor, the flames awkwardly reaching for the cave tunnel's ceiling.

The vision – what was it? What was it showing?

"The city. . ."

Nausea swirls inside her, and she can feel the letters on her forehead rearrange and quiver.

Quickly, Sibyl picks up the torch and uses the cave wall to keep herself upright as she hustles to the entrance. The wind tunnels through and pushes at her face and tangled hair. She breathes it in, tastes the smoke from the fires below.

Once there, she peers down at the city and their celebration. All appears well, but her pounding heart and ravenous instincts say otherwise.

"What is it? What is it?" she begs her visions.

Sibyl squints at the horizon, and her breath is stolen from her lungs.


Patrix and Kristal taunt one another. They move like dancing partners tailor-made for one another, and they bicker as all lovers do at the beginning of a promising relationship. But, thanks to the smoke swirling around them, Nefari finds herself . . . sedated to the insufferable annoyance of it all.

Dao twirls her, and she laughs, their damp cloaks billowing about them like great ballroom dresses.

Harvested Diabolus Beetles were poured into the fire minutes before. As the dead bugs roasted, the smoke rose to mingle through the celebration. The smoke dulls the senses, and the grin on Nefari's face spreads wider by the second. With the smoke, she feels freer. She feels less burdened, and all her troubles just "wash away."

"Did you say something?" Dao asks. The fire's shadows bend across his face as he peers down at her. She hadn't realized she said it out loud.

"No, nothing." She giggles. Are the shadows on his face truly reaching for her? She blinks, and the effect is gone.

There were a few times Nefari and Dao swapped partners with Patrix and Kristal. The two women had laughed uncontrollably as the men spun each other around. They laughed even more when Patrix planted a big sloppy and mocking kiss on Dao's cheek. Dao had turned a bright shade of red.

"Come on, ya saps!" Patrix says to them before bumping his shoulder into Nefari's and nearly knocking her to the ground. "I need another drink if I plan to keep up with Salix over here." He jerks his thumb at Kristal, who's struggling to push her hair out of her sweaty face.

"Can I please take these off? Just for a moment?" Kristal whines while following Patrix, Nefari, and Dao back to the barrels.

Nefari stumbles on a lump of mud, giggles uncontrollably, and then turns to squint at Kristal's binding. *Perhaps the girl will be more fun if she wasn't tied up like a pig ready for slaughter*, Nefari thinks as she snatches Kristal's wrists. She examines the rope.

"Don't even think about it, Fari," Dao grumbles. He slaps her hands away, and she scowls up at him. "Bastian would kill you for defying his orders. Don't squint at me like that. You know it's true! He's tolerated your disobedience and your blatant dislike for him, but he won't tolerate this."

"He'd really kill you?" Kristal murmurs, accepting her mug from Patrix. Someone had filled them, no doubt a centaur wife content on doting on others. "Wait, why don't you like Bastian again?"

Nefari waves a hand in the air and ignores her second question. "Of course, he won't kill me."

"He's killed others for less," Dao grumbles into his ale.

Patrix slaps him on the back. "That he has!"

"My death wouldn't be so fortunate," Nefari interjects. She swirls her ale, the inside of her mug too dark to see the contents.

This far away from the smoke, and with each passing second, Nefari's head begins to clear. Her cheeks ache from smiling, and the ever-lingering anxiety slowly returns. "My death won't be clean. My fate is certain of that."

Silence stretches between the four. "Your fate?" Kristal asks.

Nefari blinks at her foolish slip-up. Licking her lips, she adds, "Well, we all have fates, right? Destinies?"

"What she's saying is that by how reckless she is, she'll probably be gobbled by a bone crier this time next year," Patrix says, the lie rolling off his tongue too easily. *Or maybe it isn't a lie*, Nefari thinks. He could be right.

"Sounds bloody," Kristal murmurs, unconvinced.

"What about you?" she asks Nefari. "What do you think your fate will be? What mess will become of your corpse and by whom should I eventually thank?"

Kristal rolls her eyes, and Patrix jovially says, "By the sounds of it, the person you'll have to thank will be yourself."

"I've never been so lucky." Nefari raises an eyebrow at Kristal's snort.

"As a Salix woman and a runaway at that, my bet is your fate will end at the hand of Despair," Dao interjects, tipping his ale in a toast to Kristal.

"Point taken," she grumbles. "Despair can't be beat, and with his possession of the Queen of Salix, he's stronger than ever. If only Fate had lived on through the Shadow Princess, maybe we could have stood a chance, but . . ."

Nefari fidgets uncomfortably. She continues to be surprised by how much a Salix servant knows about her people's history. "You truly believe the shadow princess could have killed Despair?"

Kristal shrugs. "A girl can dream of a better future, right? But there's no point, I suppose – in dreaming. The shadow princess – whatever her name was – is dead. The only thing we can do is prolong the inevitable and live while we can. It's not like we have enough of that stuff to stop him." Kristal nods at Nefari's sword, and the group looks at it.

"What do you mean?" Patrix, Nefari, and Dao ask at the same time.

"There's a tutor who teaches the old history despite the Queen's forbidding of it." Kristal pushes the hair from her head. "He said all the fee who once walked this realm feared Despair the most. They were all created by the Divine, you know." At their nods, she continues, leaning in to have a better foreboding effect. "One of the fee learned how to keep Despair away, how to keep him subdued and afraid. And though she wasn't the brightest of the five fee, she was smart about this."

"About what?" Dao asks skeptically.

"About the inferaze, of course. She made her entire realm – the Dream Realm - out of the stuff. Despair is weakened by it. When Despair had possessed the Fee of the Demon Realm, he could not fully possess that fee while in the Dream Realm."

All this talk about fee and their magic sets Nefari's nerves on end, and she searches the shadows as if the dead fee are watching from within. "I thought you said you didn't know anything more about inferaze?"

Her blink is slow and long. "I lied."

Nefari narrows her eyes, but deep down, she knows she wouldn't have told her enemy either.

"Some believe the Fee of the Demon Realm had slipped his brother and other sisters some of the inferaze in hopes he could be himself while around them," Kristal continues. "Some believe he was trying to prevent his fee brother and sisters from being possessed themselves. But all along, the Fee of the Dream Realm knew of her brother's possession. She had feared Despair the most and had learned the signs."

"But she teamed up with Despair anyway," Patrix says, challenging her story.

"She did." She nibbles her bottom lip. "Despair promises things. She wanted more power. She wanted to rule over the other fee – over all the realms. Despair let her believe she could." She sips her ale, and Nefari starts to wonder how this girl could know so much about Despair. Perhaps secrets are hard to keep in a castle. "I'm only saying that maybe the inferaze stuff could make a difference here like it did for the Realms War. Maybe it can keep Despair away. It's worth looking into, especially if it's considered contraband."

Nefari turns away from Kristal to peer at the dancers once more. Patrix and Dao strike up their own conversation, great stories each have heard about the fee. She tunes it out.

How can she beat a Divine God who so strategically played all of his fee children, none of which are still alive? And how can she do it while keeping her life in return? Those fee rulers are dead – replaced by Fate before he gave himself and his magic over to Nefari. And her prophecy . . .

Her fate will indeed be messy, especially if Despair learns she's alive, and he surely will if he finds a Divine object capable of displaying such things. It won't matter if Nefari's sword can make a difference because Nefari is only one woman. One person. All the magic she has within her can't be enough.

But maybe Sibyl was right. Maybe if she found Choice-chosen before Despair does. . .

"I think –" Kristal begins. She steps closer to Nefari. "I don't think my fate will end by your hand."

"No?"

"I think my fate will begin by it."

Nefari glances at her. Kristal's hair hangs around her face, but the sweat that had beaded at her forehead is gone. "Are you trying to tell me you're in love with me?"

Kristal chuckles. "No. I'm saying that ever since I arrived here, I've lived more than I have in all my seventeen years. You've given me that. I just thought you should know. You gave me purpose where I had none, and what I said before in your room – "

"Was the truth." Frowning, Nefari whips her head to Kristal. "You're seventeen?"

Kristal nods, and as her head shifts in the fire's wavering light, Nefari notices the exhaustion etched across her face. The purple bruises blossom under her eyes, and the stiffness when she moves her head is quite evident. "I'll be eighteen in two months."

"Not even a full adult, and you've already run away from home."

"You would too if you had to live in that castle. Look," She pushes the hair from her face. "I didn't mean what I said. I mean, I did, but I can see now there's more to the story you're not sharing. And you're not sharing to protect yourself, just like I am. Maybe someday, you'll share it with me, but it wasn't fair of me to label you."

Nefari says nothing. She doesn't want to think about the door Kristal just opened. The door that glitters with the possibility of friendship beyond it.

"Salix doesn't have any parties like this," Kristal says. A lazy grin spreads across her face, and a wondering twinkle sparks in her eyes.

"Nobody does."

"They should. The shadow people in Salix certainly don't dance like this."

"I doubt they do any dancing because they're slaves. It's part of my people's traditions. Queen Sieba wouldn't allow such a celebration – such a tradition. Traditions blossom hope and provide comfort, and the slaves are meant to have neither."

Kristal sighs. "You're right. She wouldn't."

Nefari nibbles on the inside of her lip. After a few moments, she points and says, "See the shadows? For my people, the drug is making them move. It's making the shadows appear to dance, but in the Shadow Kingdom, they would dance on their own. You cannot get that anywhere else. You cannot replicate it, not truly."

"I'd love to see that." A small grin starts to form on Nefari's lips while she studies Kristal's frown. Maybe a friendship wouldn't be so bad.

"Shadow Mourn Eve is to celebrate those we've lost," a deep voice says behind them. They startle together and then turn and peer up at Bastian's face.

"You shouldn't sneak up on people," Nefari barks. She knows what that look is. It's caution. Caution for the blossoming friendship. A warning that Kristal is the enemy. A reminder she has a job to do. How long had he been watching them? Listening to their conversation?

"I didn't sneak." He steps out of the shadows. "You make a habit of pretending I don't exist."

"Yeah, well . . ."

Patrix and Dao pay him no mind, continuing their animated conversation. Kristal, having shrunk in on herself at the hulking presence of the centaur leader, excuses herself. Nefari doesn't watch her head to the barrels of ale and wine. She's intent on holding Bastian's gaze, a clear challenge.

When Kristal is out of earshot, he murmurs, "What have you learned?"

Nefari crosses her arms and briefly watches Kristal giggle with Cyllian while they pour more ale into their mugs.

Clenching her jaw, she refocuses back on Bastian. "Nothing of use. She's tight-lipped and won't give away more information than what she can. All I know is stories of the castle and snippets of her youth, but I think -" Nefari swallows thickly and presses a rock into the mud with the toe of her boot. "I think she's telling the truth. About who she is, I mean. About why she's here."

Telling him she's the daughter of the Red Reaper would cause more trouble than problems solved. And telling him about Kristal's knowledge of Nefari's sword would be just the same. She'll wait. She'll wait until she's sure of everything before divulging any information. Besides, none of this information is what Bastian seeks.

"We're running out of time."

"Story of the decade," Nefari grumbles sarcastically. "Would you like me to wear the shadow crown and frighten the girl enough that the truth tumbles from her mouth?" If the black smoke of the crown doesn't frighten the girl, knowing she has befriended a long-dead princess will.

He ignores her, and Nefari knows it's because he's trying to keep his temper in check while tucking away what he truly really wants to say. He's been watching her all day, and honestly, Nefari had been waiting for him to approach her. "We need to know why they believe the crown is a Divine object. We need to know their plans so we can take action with minimal casualties. We cannot do that until you finish your duty."

Nefari huffs. "It's nothing more than a trophy, Bastian. I've seen the crown. I grew up looking at it. It has no magical properties. Even if they do get it – and I'm not saying I want them to, nor do I believe it still exists – they'd be disappointed."

"You and I both know they wouldn't travel across Widow's Bay without a good reason," he counters angrily. "We need answers. We need to know if . . ." he trails off.

Nefari raises a brow. "What? You need to know if my mother's crown is worth going after?" His lips firm, and Nefari knows she's found the truth. *The bastard.* She glances away and shakes her head. "If you're asking how I feel about it, you don't want my answer."

"Do not dismiss me." He points at her. "I taught you to be nobody to keep you alive while you grew into your prophecy. I broke the blood vow to ensure it, Nefari. I didn't expect you to want to remain nobody, and I certainly didn't expect you to hold saving your life against me."

Leaning closer, Nefari whispers, "Then you thought wrong."

He runs his tongue over his teeth and lowers his hand. "I will wear the reminder of the broken vow forever. Isn't that enough?"

A scream sounds in the distance, and soon, warning horns blare from the watch on the mountain tops. Bastian and Nefari look toward the direction of the scream, but where the fire's light doesn't touch, it's pitch-black.

The music dies away, and the dancing halts. The fire crackling and the collective heavy breathing is the only sound above the horns – the only sound except for the rise in Nefari's racing heartbeat.

"What is it?" she asks shakily. Twirling the ring around her finger, she pinches the black diamond inside her palm until it painfully bites into her skin.

"I don't know," Bastian mutters. He steps forward, squinting into the dark while his hand reaches over his shoulder and wraps around the pommel of his sword.

Behind them, mud squelches. Kristal sloshes her way slowly to them. "They found me," she murmurs, transfixed on the path disappearing into the night.

"Who? Who found you?" Patrix demands.

Raising her bound wrists, she uses one finger to point into the inky blackness of the street beyond. "Them."

Nefari's heart beats loudly in her ears as she turns, a roar that drowns her thoughts and brings forth her memories.

There, coming out of the darkness is one harvested shadow person. She stares at the celebrations with unseeing eyes while treading down the path with eerie grace. Then another appears. Then another, and the march of boots quickly follows.

Patrix curses low and wickedly.

# CHAPTER TWENTY-THREE

They call it a Harvest Storm.

When a village is raided by only harvestmen for no other purpose than the death of the villagers, it is called a Harvest Storm. No prisoners. No one left alive.

Nefari's kingdom was the first to endure a Harvest Storm. And since then, she has only seen the aftermath of one. By the time the Rebel Legion arrives to aid the village, the harvestmen have already swept through like a swarm of locusts. Their orders are to kill and kill only.

Locks of Nefari's hair whip about as the wind tunnels through the path of the huts. She stares at the first line of harvestman and then those immerging behind them. Their cloaks wave like ribbons.

The first who appeared was a woman with the traditional white hair of her people and striking blue eyes to match. To Nefari's dismay, the woman is her age. She even looks like her.

Nefari's heart breaks. She can do nothing but breathe and watch this woman standing among the others. If the woman is her age now, then she was taken from the Shadow Kingdom and possessed as a child. She would have preferred this girl died

268

that day. The Queen of Salix – Despair stole this woman's life. Stole many lives. Death would have been kinder to her. Death would have been a blissful embrace.

*Is there anyone you trust, Nefari,* Dao had asked.

Anger rips through her. Deep hot anger that nearly makes her see red. She flexes her fingers and curls them into tight fists. The nails bite her palms, and the rage builds and surges like high tides. *Yes, I trust death,* she had answered him. And this is exactly why.

And though the queen is indeed the main source of blame, there is some reserved for herself. Nefari has lived ten years freer than this woman has ever been because she has hidden. While she hid, she had sharpened her pain and used it as a weapon to keep everyone and their urgings at arm's length. Their warnings had been frivolous – an annoyance. The rows and rows of harvestmen are their warning given flesh. This is the consequence of inaction. This is the result of allowing it to go on for so long when she should have been actively finding a way to free them.

The harvestwoman has several puckered scars slashed across pale white skin. Her hair is a tangled mess, and her lips, chapped and bleeding, are as relaxed as the vacant look in her eyes. Those behind her appear just the same – beaten and used and ordered to the mountains to . . . *to do what?*

"Bastian," she warns. Why are they here? For years, the Rebel Legion has fought back against Salix. Why are they choosing to Storm now?

She senses something above the city, feels the tendrils of evil curve around her neck and dip down her spine. She reluctantly peers up. A black cloak whisks by, barely detectable with the dark sky's backdrop. Then more appear, soaring with aimless pursuit. "Wraiths," she breathes. They never accompany the

269

Harvest Storms. There's no reason for them to because no one will be left to harvest.

Fear gathers inside her, a true and raw terror that drains all feeling from her limbs. She doesn't like the darkness. The darkness has no shape. It has no end and no beginning, and there is nowhere for her in between. Death is in the middle. Death or possession.

She had heard once, as a Harvest Storm marched toward a village, that some villagers killed themselves and their families to avoid being harvested.

"Bastian," she warns again, her voice quivering.

Her voice snaps the centaur leader from his frozen shock. "Harvest Storm!" His voice booms down the silent celebration, taken on a heavily tainted gale that warns them to *run, run, run*.

A flurry of motion ensues. The call for arms carries to each hut, shadow person, and abled centaur.

"What do we do?" she hears Kristal ask nobody in particular. Nefari is reminded that she's never seen this side of things – had innocently been stuck in a castle while the rest of the realm quivered in their armor.

"Patrix!" Nefari barks, "Get Kristal, the women, and the children to Sibyl's cave!" The princess pulls her blade from its sheath and crouches, waiting for a harvestman to twitch, but they just stand there like trees in a forest.

A cold and nervous sweat beads across her torso. Is this what her mother felt like? Is this how her mother took on the Harvest Storm in the Shadow Kingdom?

In the second she allows herself, she finally admits she understands. She understands why her mother sacrificed herself because behind Nefari is her entire world. They're the only people she has left to call family, and if it takes her dying breath

270

to keep all of them alive and end the torment of the harvest, well . . . she'll pay it. Because she owes them. Because she loves them. Because it's the right thing to do.

Tonight, in this second, she understands. It wasn't just about Nefari. *She died to save what little hope was left: Me.*

And then, without a word or a cry of war, the harvestmen rush. Nefari's heart quickens, and a roaring floods her ears, but she's ready.

She widens her stance.

Arrows whiz over and past her head, a song of death. They whistle as they cut through the wind, and it floods Nefari with adrenaline. She tightens the grip on her sword and then slowly exhales.

The soaring arrows embed themselves into the heads of the first line. Bodies fall.

The harvestwoman, however, continues unharmed. The arrows had narrowly missed her. In her mad dash to Nefari, her arms pump, and heavy breath mists in her wake. Closer and closer and closer . . .

The woman pulls the sword from her sheath. Nefari screams a cry of war. Whirling, Nefari slices her blade through the air. Her feet are soundless, a deadly dance, and soon blood drips from the sword. The woman's head, free of the body, tumbles to the ground.

The volume of the battle rises throughout the city just as the woman's head comes to its final rolling rest at Nefari's boots. The woman's expression had never changed. The jaw never slackened or tightened. Her voice never uttered a word. A spark of rage never glinted in her indigo eyes. And now, those same eyes stare at the stars.

"Fari!" Dao calls from behind her. "Fari, you have to run!"

Nefari whips her attention to Dao. The fires still roar in the background, and her heart pounds against her ribs.

In the path, centaurs make a line. They had dipped their arrows in the fire, and now they poise their bows and release as one. Dao's own newly acquired bow is raised, the string pulled taut, his wrist resting against his cheekbone. He releases it, and the arrow zips past them.

"Run?" she asks. He reaches to the quiver strapped to his back and plucks another arrow. She flicks her dripping sword, and the excess blood splats against her pants. "I'm not running!"

Fury contorts his features, and he pins her with a hard stare. He lowers the bow, the tip of the arrow pointing at the ground. Nefari squares her jaw and wordlessly beseeches him to challenge her on this.

"Hold!" one centaur yells. "Release!" The city lights once more, flaming arrows like comets.

Fawn gallops to them, water from the puddles splashing every which way. Her face is set – hard and blank as the best warriors out there. She takes her place next to Dao and wears no armor aside from her usual leather breastplate. The black markings drawn across her face for the festivities are smeared.

"Get her out of here!" Fawn orders Dao. Arrow after arrow zips from her bow. "Go!"

"I'm not going anywhere!"

Crossing the short distance between them, Dao grips her upper arm and draws her closer. "You have to!"

She tries to rip her arm from him. "I won't."

Other centaurs rush past them, swords raised. Nearby, there's a cry of pain.

"You must," he adds more gently.

272

"You're my friend, Dao. If you're not running, neither am I. I won't – " She peers past his shoulder to the trail where Patrix is herding women and children to the safety of Sibyl's cave. To her surprise, Kristal is aiding Patrix, shouting for them to hurry and rush and be quick. She leans against the tree, looking as though at any moment, she may collapse. She appears . . . sickly. Pale.

She raises her gaze to Nefari. They hold each other's stare, and a fierce sort of determination is there, lingering with the fear of what may become of this Storm.

Nefari traces the path down to the city. Kaymen and his friends are there, blocking the trail up to the mountain where a cluster of harvestmen tried to race after those fleeing. Their swords match strike for strike, battling against the possessed skilled in combat and unafraid of their own death. So far, they're holding the line, but how long will their efforts last?

Nio is down the way, passing out arrows by a fire while Bastian points and barks orders to all those who are near.

Breathing heavily, Nefari looks back to Dao. "If people die while I hide, I won't be able to come back from it. My mother didn't hide. She stood between them and her people. I can't be a coward. Don't ask me to be."

Her words sink in, and he slowly releases her elbow to gently grip her chin. His eyes swim with words she knows he won't say. "You are the only shadow royal left," he begs. "We need you alive. I need you alive. Our people need you alive, if for anything but a figure of hope – a starlight for those unpossessed to gaze upon. Please, Fari. Please hide."

An idea forms. She never did see her mother's display of starlight magic when she died. She had only felt it and pictured it in her mind's eye.

"A light," she whispers his words back to him. He releases her chin as her eyes cloud with stars, and the wraiths above scream at the sensation of magic. The darkness may not have an end and a beginning, but maybe something could cleave it. Shape it. *Someone.* Sibyl had told her as much.

"A light," she says again. There's so much determination behind the two words that goosebumps crawl up her arms.

"Nefari, don't release it," he warns.

"If I release it, I can end this!"

"If you release your magic," Fawn growls, "You will doom us all. You will not be saving us. She will know you're here, and her darkness will follow tenfold!" Nefari swallows thickly and looks at the female centaur. "Do not do this."

Frustration threatens in the form of tears, but for once, she listens. She sucks the magic back inside herself and deeply inhales the smoke around her.

Dao's face pales when he glimpses something behind Nefari. "Behind you!" he shouts.

But his warning is too late.

Mid-whirl, and out of the corner of her eye, Nefari catches sight of the approaching harvestman. She raises her arm to cover her head and prepares for the strike of the harvestman's raised sword.

The world tilts when she's knocked to the side.

She slams into the mud, and the breath leaves her lungs.

# CHAPTER TWENTY-FOUR

Sibyl watches from her cave entrance, clutching the thigh bones of her skeletal centaur guards. Prayers are whispered from her tongue, pleas she knows will go unanswered.

Women and children and a few of the elderly rush past her, their hooves echoing in the cave's tunnel as they seek the only shelter the Kadoka Mountain has. She's been ignoring her intruders, gaze frozen to the chaos below.

The fire from the lit arrows brightens the streets considerably, and the army of harvestmen still march into the Rebel Legion's masses. It's not a big army – she's seen larger Harvest Storms in her visions, but it's a sizable one. Enough to cause damage. Enough to cause death.

But this Harvest Storm wasn't made simply to destroy the city. *That* she is sure of. No, it had to be made to create blind panic. It had to be made to send a warning. There is no other explanation. Sending them here was near suicide.

Could this be retaliation because of the Rebel Legion's persistence in pushing the raiding armies out of their territory? Or could it be because the enemy knows they harbor a runaway Salix servant? Or is this the crone's doing? Had they followed

275

Patrix back to the city? Sibyl can't be sure. She can't be sure at all, but none of it sits well with her.

*Oh, there are too many moving pieces.* Too many ifs and mights and maybes.

Vision after vision tries to take hold of Sibyl's mind, but she shoves them aside. Now isn't the time to indulge in such luxuries as the scent of death rises to her nose. What could a vision possibly show her that isn't happening before her very eyes?

Children's cries filter out of the cave's tunnel from where they squat with their shushing mothers. The war cries from below carry up in the breeze pushing up the mountain. A few wraiths shriek from above as they swoop and dip and dive. None have attempted to possess yet. For that, Sibyl thanks her blessed stars because it means the harvestmen have yet to add a centaur among their numbers. If they did, if the wraiths possessed a centaur, well . . . The battle would be lost, and many battles that follow. None would cut down their friend, and a single centaur is as formidable as three human warriors.

The young crone's attention moves to someone dashing down the path of the mountains and back to the city, cloak billowing in their haste. Patrix yells at this person, his voice carrying to the heavens while he demands they stay with the group. The person doesn't listen. Doesn't stumble, either. Instead, they dash into the city, weave between the swords, duck under arrows, and continued on until –

Sibyl's eyes widen when this person shoves Nefari to the ground. The Divine sword flies from her hand and splashes in a puddle next to Dao's feet.

Sibyl can't look away. She can't! Because in the place where Nefari once stood is . . .

Her fingers touch her chin, shock stiffening her muscles and joints. "The Salix woman." Her voice slithers into the night.

Filth cakes Nefari Ashcroft's eyes. She had been about to be cut down, but Kristal had come out of nowhere and . . .

Nefari prepares herself. Had the girl gone mad? Is she going to attack Nefari? With a swipe of Nefari's hand over her face, she clears the mud from her vision. Kristal isn't standing above her, a sword raised. She isn't poised to end her life.

The harvestman's sword slices through empty air right where Nefari had just stood. Kristal ducks. The blade swipes where her head once was, and when she rights herself, Dao tosses her Nefari's sword. She catches it with ease, but the wet pommel wobbles awkwardly in her bound grip.

Nefari scoots back, sliding through the muck when Kristal screams and thrusts the blade forward, right into the heart of the harvestman.

When she yanks it out, she doesn't watch the man fall.


Sibyl inches closer to the edge of her cliff and watches with her keen vision as the girl's eyes fall to the blade soaked with harvested blood. Kristal's bewilderment is clear while she examines it, lifting and twisting as if it's the only object in the world. It's as though she's seeing something others cannot – feeling something others do not.

It's not shock, exactly.

Sibyl cocks her head to the side, considering. *It's* . . . *amazement. Awe. Wonder.* What is she seeing?

She tips her head in the other direction. Behind her, she can hear the hooves of someone dashing through the tunnel. Patrix approaches, his breath heavy.

277

"I got them all," he says hurriedly. Items jostle in his grip. "Right? Did I get them all?"

Sibyl quickly turns and peers at the items he's gathered for her. The girl and the sword can wait.

She says nothing and gestures for him to splay these items at her feet. He frowns at first, and when she snarls at him, he hurriedly bends to do as she asks. The items scatter in every direction, inches from each other.

Kneeling to the cold stone, she hastily spreads them out further and arranges them in order. They're an array of shells, tiny rodent bones, and small pebbles.

"Sibyl . . . What are these? What – What are you doing?"

"The shells were gathered from the shores of Divine Islands, the rodent bones from the Shadled Forest, and the pebbles from various kingdoms across the realm." She places each item just so with trembling fingers. She's never used this sort of magic before. She's only studied it in the books Patrix had stolen from the Black Market. She had a feeling that someday, this specific magic would be needed.

The wraiths gather by the numbers above the village, the few's presences and Fari's brief bout of magic drawing more of them to the city. The song of death is calling them, and if Sibyl doesn't do something fast . . .

A clash of swords ring behind her. She whirls in her crouched position, her nose inches from Patrix's blade crossed with a harvestman's. The possessed man's eyes are fixed only on Sibyl, and a pent-up breath escapes her mouth in a hazy cloud that's immediately whisked away.

How had this man snuck past Kaymen and the others?

A second later . . . If Patrix hadn't heard the man and was a second later in raising his sword, Sibyl would be dead.

Patrix thrusts his weight into the harvestman with a grunt, and the harvestman stumbles back. Raising his sword, Patrix strikes. His center of balance wavers when the swords slam together once more, the force of the harvestman's blow outmatching the satyr's. Patrix grits his teeth, the match picks up pace, and Sibyl grips her knees as she watches it unfold.

Cloaks whirl, grunts, and groans with each blocked strike. Patrix hollers when the blade slices into his shoulder, a narrowly missed strike to his neck.

Sibyl's nails dig into her knees.

A young man leaps from the trees' shadows on the path. Emory Vinborne's short sword glints, and he screams a childish rage. The young man thrusts his sword into the lower back of the possessed man. The harvestman doesn't even clutch his stomach, doesn't look to the tip of the blade protruding from his ribs. He just slowly turns.

The harvestman steps toward Emory and, frightened, Emory retreats. His back bumps into the leg of the centaur skeleton.

She must do something. She must help!

She focuses on the items around her feet, plucks up a shell, and slices a deep gash across her palm. Then, she squeezes her fist, and blood drips to the stone. With a little magic, the blood moves quickly, traveling across the stone to the centaur's hoof, up his bones, and to the skull.

Emory cowers when the injured harvestman raises his sword, and upon descent, it's met with the skeleton centaur's. Emory screams and ducks, covering his head.

Before the skeleton can kill the harvestman, as Sibyl intended, Patrix tackles him to the ground. Snow puffs about, and they slide a few feet away.

Quickly, heart pounding, Sibyl slams her fists against the stone, and the centaur retreats back to the lifeless statue it was seconds ago.

With Patrix straddling the man, Emory's blade shoves all the way through and to the hilt. He grabs the harvestman by the collar of his tunic and demands, "Why are you here?"

Wide-eyed, the general's son quivers at the happenings around him, but slowly, he inches his way closer to Patrix. Sibyl wipes her bleeding palm onto her pants, waiting for the answer she knows won't come.

Harvestmen don't speak.

"Tell me!"

"He cannot speak to you, Patrix," she reminds him. "We've tried this before, remember?"

He thumps the pommel of his sword against the man's cheek, cutting a gash. A trail of red stains his white hair. "Why? Why have you invaded the Kadoka Mountains? Tell me!"

Sibyl shakes her head, and while she does, something catches her eye. A piece of parchment is poking from the man's cloak pocket.

Crawling across the stone, she reaches and seizes the paper. The breeze tries to snatch it from her fingers and she quickly unfolds it. There, drawn across the parchment, is a crown.

Sibyl nearly drops it in her surprise.

"What is it?" Emory asks, voice squeaking.

It's a crown Sibyl recognizes. "The shadow kingdom crown?" She holds it up and waves it. "We do not have the shadow kingdom crown, you fool! No one has been to the kingdom since the day your queen destroyed it!"

Patrix slowly releases the man, and the man slumps back to the snow. Blood seeps into the fabric of his tunic. "No," he whispers, shaking his head. He looks at Sibyl. "No one has because no one can get inside besides . . ."

Blinking rapidly, the breath seizes in Sibyl's chest. "The Shadow People." She glances over her shoulders and down to the battle below. This is why they are here: To claim them.

"But they have Shadow People in their harvestmen's ranks. Why don't they use them?" Emory asks meekly.

"Unless they can't." Sibyl spins back to Patrix. "Unless the possession makes them nothing else but ordinary. After all, there is no light inside pure darkness, and . . ."

"You cannot cast shadows without light. A shadow person cannot shadow jump while in the grips of such darkness." Patrix swallows thickly. "We must tell Bastian – we must –"

"No!" Sibyl barks. She stuffs the parchment into her cloak pocket. "We must first move forward with our plan. Kill the man."

There's no hesitation when he quickly thrusts his sword into the neck and leaves it there. He walks back to Sibyl while poking at his own wound. The wound isn't deep, but it's enough to seep into his cloak.

Sibyl is breathing as hard as Patrix, and they exchange looks, knowing now this invasion – this storm – is not typical. There are worse things than death, this Sibyl knows. This, she sees.

"It is too much," Emory murmurs to himself. He clutches his head. "It's too much. I need to leave. I need to leave."

"Are you sure this will work?" Patrix asks Sibyl, ignoring Emory's mutterings. He kneels next to her, and she whirls back around to her shells, bones, and pebbles. "Whatever you have planned, are you sure Fari will understand?"

"She is no fool," she grumbles. She doesn't know how he came to the conclusion that whatever she's going to do next is for Nefari's benefit, but the satyr's mind has always been sharper than his blade. "If I do not give her the chance, many will die."

"Okay," he breathes. "Okay. But do it quickly." He peeks over his shoulder at Emory. The boy is still falling apart at the skeleton centaur's legs. "Pull yourself together! Go inside and guard the women and children!" The buffoon trips and stumbles his way into the cave.

She scoops up a handful of rodent bones, cups them to her lips, and whispers. Her voice echoes in her palms while Patrix watches on with fascination.

Magic stirs in the air, thickening the freezing breeze, and once the goosebumps rise across her flesh, she drops the items. The bones scatter in every direction, and as they do, a path between every item glows. She hears Patrix gasp, but she ignores it. Anxiously, she waits for the magic to be ready – to grow and develop as the books had stated.

Seconds tick by as it builds. Precious seconds where below, the sound of many dying reach their ears.

"Come on," she murmurs. Her childlike voice seems insignificant in the chaos, but the grave tone cannot be denied. Patrix shifts his balance, and Sibyl slams her palm on her knee. "Come on!"

*There!* Sibyl's heart leaps in her chest, and relief floods her. The seashells glow brightly, and then the pebbles, and then lastly, the bones. All of the items tremble along the stone, quivering and shivering. Their light stretches up, up, and up in hues of shimmering yellows.

"My Divine," Patrix curses. He steps away when the magic builds before their very eyes.

"Shield your eyes," she warns.

"Why?"

Standing, she turns and snarls in his face. "If you'd like to keep your sight, shield them!" She can see her reflection in his wide eyes. The words shift and rearrange on her forehead until they recede into her dark hairline like fearful rabbits in the presence of a predator. The pasty whiteness of her skin is all that remains until her earlier words flow from temple to temple, carved into her forehead's thin flesh.

She reads them aloud while blood trickles from her nose. There's always a cost for such powerful magic. Sibyl had anticipated it because nothing is free in a realm so dark. "Shadows not made of shadows and rock not made of rock. Stars and lions and things scattered in wait. Rings of truth. Crowns of lies. Dark, dark, dark deceit."

The light explodes in a silent burst, and Patrix barely covers his eyes in time. Sibyl's hair is thrust upward, and when she turns, she raises her arms and embraces the magic before her just as the book had said.

A pulsing throb of blinding light blankets the village. She grits her teeth, trembles at its immensity and addictive qualities, and swallows her scream as she guides the magic.

# CHAPTER TWENTY-FIVE

Nefari peels herself from the ground when the sky becomes brighter than day. A wave of the light washes over everything, a burst dam of illumination.

The wraiths in the sky can no longer hide within the darkness between the stars. The light outlines their figures, pulses through their wispy midst. She shields her eyes because it's like gazing at the sun.

*What is happening?*

This wave of light rushes at the city, surrounds Nefari's every limb, and she gasps at the majesty of it – at the pleasure of raw and potent magic. Every warrior ducks and covers their face. Everyone, except for those born in the shadows. Kaymen, Dao, Cyllian, and the others . . . they feel it. Nefari knows they do.

Kaymen spares her a glance from where he still guards the beginning of the path up to the mountains. His chest heaves as the harvestman he was fighting shies away from the light. The harvestman's sword drops, and he bumps into his brethren behind him, clawing at his eyes.

In a daze, she looks at Dao, but his gaze is cast to the mountains where the light originates.

Kristal screams through gritted teeth. Her face is shoved into her palms. "It burns!" she yells.

"What is happening?" Nefari demands, her voice loud to be heard above the rising agony.

"I do not know," Dao murmurs. He points to the mountain. "But look!" She does, and there, at the edge of the cliff and before the stunning magic, is a figure.

"Sibyl," she whispers. Her hands are raised and her hair with it. What is she doing? Why is she putting herself in danger? Why . . . Oh.

"It burns!" Kristal yells again. The harvestmen stumble blindly about, swords splashing in the mud left forgotten.

Flicking the brown goop from her hands, Nefari quickly snatches her blade from Kristal's grip. She watches the magic leave Sibyl's small body – watches as her mouth widens in a scream. The wraiths above the light veer away from the magic, shrieking in pain like the others. The combined noise makes Nefari's ears ring.

Something gleams at the top of Nefari's vision. She looks up. There are more wraiths than there were before, but now, having made it past the shield of light, two brave wraiths rush toward the city itself.

One is closer than the other, a gruesome hand outstretched for Dao.

"No!" Nefari screams. Her heart shoves its way into her throat, and her body moves on instinct. As Dao turns to Nefari, she jumps and slashes her blade above his head. It cuts through the wispy cloak of the wraith Dao hadn't seen coming, and then . . . then something spectacular happens. The sword glows with the ring on her finger, and the wraith bursts into pure smoke. The

285

echoes of its squeals die out, and its smoke disappears into Sibyl's light magic.

Nefari blinks and blinks hard. She peers down at her sword and ring and swears she feels it hum and vibrate inside her palms. *Never has . . .*

She lifts her gaze to Dao, wide-eyed and shocked. His arms are raised to protect his face. He lowers them and mouths the word, "How?"

"Make it stop!" Kristal drops to her knees.

Heads bent, eyes shielded, harvestmen begin retreating as the sky continues to brighten.

Nefari ignores the girl and the frightened harvestmen because there, traveling quickly, is the second wraith. And it's headed straight for Nefari.

The world slows around her, or maybe her thoughts move quickly. Nefari isn't sure which. But she thinks, she envisions, she plans her split-second decision, and barely hears Dao when he reminds her, "This Fate-blessed princess of rage and wrath. Rage and wrath, Fari!"

*Rage and wrath . . .* Nefari blinks, and behind her eyelids, she pictures Vale, Amoon, her parents, her kingdom. Gone. All of it, gone. She lets the magic shimmer across her skin, gathers it at her fingertips, and then . . .

"Fari!" Dao ducks, covering his head once more as the second wraith's cloak nearly touches him while it swoops by him for her.

"Now, Nefari!" Kaymen yells from across the way. Nefari grits her teeth and shoves her magic forward. Her skin turns as black as night, and the sparkles along her flesh reflect the light of Sibyl's crone magic. The world comes into sharper focus with brilliant hues and vibrant details. Her chest bows with the swirling starlight within her.

286

Chest heaving, nostrils flared, Nefari raises a hand. The magic within her swirls and coils with a tidal wave of rage and memories, a bottomless pit ready and willing for her to use. She grasps it, mentally takes hold, and thrusts it down her arm.

The starlight pumps from her palm. The wraith veers backward, narrowly missed by it. It soars for her once more.

She drops her sword and raises her other hand. The sword splashes in a puddle by her feet.

She screams her agony. She screams her internal pain. She unleashes it all.

Another pump of bright starlight magic leaves both of Nefari's palms, joining together for a larger blast. The light strikes true, but Nefari doesn't see what happens because the wraith's cloak had touched her cheek.

Her world warps, stutters until everything is slow and unusual.

*Cold, like a lick of mist.*

A sense of frightening calm pushes away her rage as the wraith's touch begins to take effect. The *wrongness* of it winds through her veins, and a blanket of black descends over her vision. She can feel it – the evil. The darkness. The wickedness mixed with despair and the sorrow which weaved together with that one touch.

*It makes sense*, she supposes, a conscious thought whispered in her mind. It makes sense that a creature made from the magic of Despair would feel such a way. And soon, as her eyes adjust to the dark, she can see it.

Solely sucked into her mind, Nefari looks around and sees nothing but many individual swirling shadows circling her. She's inside a murky cyclone of them. They move too fast, blurs of inky black, but carried in them are flashes and snippets of her memories. Slowly, she turns full circle. What is this?

One such swirl pulls away from the others, hovers before her, and takes a distorted shape.

"Mom?" Nefari murmurs, both in her mind and out loud. A lump forms in her throat, thick with grief and relief. Her knees sting as she physically drops to the mud of Kadoka City, mud she cannot see but only feel.

Queen Amala Ashcroft is a jumbled smear, but her hair curls in a non-existent breeze. Nefari can tell that she's smiling, though, a sweet motherly smile that blends with her obscured features.

Nefari had forgotten. She hadn't realized it, but she had forgotten what her mother's smile was like and how it felt to have it directed at her. In this cyclone, she cannot pick out these details. Not clearly. And it's painful.

But why is she smiling? The wraith had touched Nefari, and now she's being harvested! She's failed! Why would this warrant a smile?

A memory pulls away from the cyclone and plays like a scene behind her mother. It's also jumbled and distorted, but it's a cherished memory just the same.

*"When you're afraid, I want you to press your lips to this ring and, remember that you are as sturdy as the silver of your ring, as sharp as it's stone, and as wise as all those who have worn it before you." Young Nefari says nothing, too transfixed with the ring resting against her chest. "Nefari? You need to promise me."*

Her mother's mouth had moved to the words in time.

"I will, Momma. I'll remember," Nefari promises both now, and as a child, where present and past collide.

Nefari mentally reaches for her. Amala shakes her head, smiles once more, and then her whispered voice carries to Nefari. "Be brave, Nefari Astra Galazee Ashcroft. Be brave, my daughter."

"I'm trying." She covers her mouth and sobs. She's here. Some part of her mother is here. "I'm trying, but –"

"You must be brave," she says more fiercely. "Be the sword who cleaves the darkness."

And then she's gone, tugged back into the cyclone and carried away. Nefari doesn't have a moment to adjust or call out for her because Bastian's tall and wide frame fills her mother's place. Not the real Bastian. This one looks as regal as the day he stood before the flock of sheep, waiting for her and their lesson to begin.

Bastian says nothing to her – no greeting, no wisdom, no sympathies. Hovering shadows of sheep bounce behind him.

"Is the sheep truly troublesome?" she asks him, peering past his wide frame to scan the wispy flock.

"Only if the sheep continues to believe it's only a sheep," he murmurs, his voice deeper than usual. Nefari blinks, and then his distorted face is directly in front of hers. "Cleave the darkness, Nefari. Cleave it!"

"How?" she asks him. *"How?"*

Faintly, and from outside her dark, harvesting mind, she can hear Dao call her name. It sounds foreign like he's underwater or trying to shout through the cyclone. There's so much fear in his tone. A fear Nefari understands.

"They need you. Make a choice before it's too late." He is pulled away as her mother had been. She can feel herself losing control – feel the dark cyclone inch closer, further invade and wrap around her memories. The black shadows smother them, shrinking them until they're tiny, little pieces.

*The darkness is going to devour them.*

She panics and screams into her mind. Those are her memories! Those are the pieces of her life! She has to get out of here. She has to break free before it's too late! She reaches for the cyclone and her fingers are zapped.

Dao yells her name again, but it's not strong enough. His voice, his plea isn't strong enough to pull her from the harvesting. She can feel the wraith's possession work its way through her physical body, to her shoulder, her elbows, and finally, her hands. It's cold, as cold as she imagines the Frozen Fades to be.

Through tears and gritted teeth, she tries to touch the cyclone again, but the zap is stronger than the last. It travels through her, steals her breath away, and the wraith's magic works faster, closes in quicker.

"Embrace your fear, little one," Sibyl's voice echoes in the cyclone, breaking away from the shrinking memories. Her face does not appear like Bastian and Amala's had, but her words come through crystal clear as if Sibyl is standing right behind her. "For if you do not fear, you have nothing left to lose and no one left to love. If you don't embrace your fate, it will embrace you. You are Fate-blessed, and if you so wish it, the Queen of the Shadow People. There is nothing more powerful!"

"I can't!" she says both outwardly and inwardly. She spins full-circle and beseeches her friend's voice. "I can't do it!"

Outside her mind, she hears the squish of mud as someone settles in behind her. She feels arms wrap around her torso in a tight grip, and Kaymen shouts into her ear, "You can, Nefari. I'm right here. I'm right here with you. Push it away! Stand for yourself, you insufferably stubborn fool! Beat it back!" His grip tightens until it's painful. "Come on, Nefari! You have to believe in yourself!"

*I can do this. I can do this! I am starlight. I am the Queen of Shadows.*

One breath. Another breath. How is she going to do this? Nobody escapes a harvest. And then she remembers. "When you're afraid, I want you to press your lips to this ring."

Nefari glances at her ring. It shines despite the dark. Could it be so simple? She brings it to her lips, and while she does, the cyclone screams like an army of wraiths. She presses it harder to her lips. The shrinking memories extract themselves from the cyclone and then dive into her chest.

*It's working!*

When she moves the ring away from her lips, a bright and blinding sword is in her hand.

"My magic?" She had forgotten about it. She had forgotten, but there it is, ready and waiting.

Hope blossoms in the cold places where the wraith's magic had spread throughout her body, an undeniable fiery warmth. Kaymen releases her when she rises to her feet in the real world.

Nefari musters up all the energy she has left, raises her magical sword to the closing in walls of the screaming cyclone, and slashes at it. She doesn't know if her actions are happening outside her body. All she knows is the starlight sword cleaves holes in the dark walls, cuts it like a knife to butter, and with each slash, the volume of the screams decreases.

As she swings, tears stream down her cheeks. The cold retreats from her arms, her legs, and finally, her mind. Her vision returns. The first thing she sees is Dao, a blurred expression of terror stretched across his face and the blinding light of the sky behind him. She looks at her hands, and there, grasped between them, is the starlight sword.

Startled, Nefari releases it, and the sword winks from existence. The ring on her finger glows a great and brilliant blue, but then its hue winks, and the stone is a flat black once more.

*It stopped the possession.* An unsettling feeling curdles the ale in her stomach. Without the ring's magic – without it . . .

Before she can think on it further, her shoulders are roughly grasped. "Fari!" Dao yells in her face. His fingers dig into her muscles, and he crouches to be eye-level with her. She blinks until his face comes into focus, dropping her hand back to her side.

"I'm okay."

Relieved, he pushes the hair from her face, murmuring curses. "Are you sure? The wraith, the harvest –"

"Y-yes," she stutters.

The light from the top of the mountain sputters, and then it's gone, Sibyl's magic evaporating in a blink. The black sky looms once more, and the loud noises of screaming, agonized warriors diminish entirely.

The world . . . *it is so quiet.* So quiet, Nefari swallows, both in awe and distrust at the same time.

"Your skin, Nefari," Kaymen warns into her ear. "Change it back." Nefari does so, and her skin returns to pale white.

"She did that for you, didn't she?" Dao mutters. "She made the light so you could use your magic."

The warriors shakily rise, and murmurs spread.

"Yes," she breathes. Bending slowly, she wraps her fingers around the pommel of her inferaze sword. Her knees wobble as she does so, and she grunts when the tremble reaches her other limbs. Kaymen helps her to her feet.

Indeed, Sibyl had gifted her a situation where she would be able to unleash the starlight within her and none would be the wiser. Not even the wraiths, except for the one a moment ago.

Nefari scans the cliff where she finds Sibyl slumped to her knees. The lingering pound of her heart still thuds through her veins. Gratefulness swells in her chest. Gratefulness to the child crone for many reasons.

"I've never seen the crone's display of magic – nothing of that magnitude," she murmurs so quietly that she isn't sure if Dao or Kaymen heard her. And as she stands there, listening to the warriors help their friends rise, she thanks her blessed stars Sibyl exists.

# CHAPTER TWENTY-SIX

"What was that?" Kristal demands. Nefari had nearly forgotten about her, and Dao, herself, and Kaymen turn to look at her.

A hot tear makes a trail down the bridge of Kristal's nose, and she peels herself from the mud. Her cloak and the skirt of her dress are completely ruined and stick to her legs. The black paint on her face is smeared, and her eyes are wide and wild as they survey the ruins of the celebration.

Nefari and Dao shift uncomfortably. Nefari wets her lips, preparing for a lie, any lie, but Dao touches her elbow and answers for her, "That was Sibyl."

"The child who doesn't like me? The crone?"

Even from this far down, Nefari can see Patrix helping Sibyl stand. The display of magic had to come with a price, and now, Sibyl is paying it. She'll never be able to repay that debt.

"The one and only," Dao says.

"She's lucky she's still alive," Nefari murmurs, glancing at him. The wraiths know Sibyl is here now – know a crone protects the city.

"She's aware of the consequences that might arise," Dao mutters back.

"Why was there a Harvest Storm?" Kaymen asks.

Nefari peers once over her shoulder and meets his murderous stare. "I don't know." In truth, there could be many reasons, but if one – just one – of those reasons was because they know Nefari is alive, at least now, they have no proof.

*It could have gone terribly wrong,* Nefari thinks to herself. If her magic had been faulty, Sibyl could have been captured once her magic depleted.

"She shouldn't have done it. She shouldn't have been willing to . . ." *Sacrifice herself.* Kaymen seems to understand because he grasps her upper arm and squeezes once.

She has so many questions with few answers. In this city, she will get no answers. Answers lie in ash and ruin. Answers lie in what's left of a dead queen's last stand, but there is one thing Nefari now knows. Her mother knew she'd need the ring and had told her how to access its magic.

Nefari nibbles on her lip and peeks at the cave one last time. Standing with Patrix's support, Sibyl stares back. She was right. Sibyl is always right, and fate indeed found her. She just hadn't thought it would be so soon, or raw and brutal, forcing her to confront everything she was clinging to.

Logs that were once stacked for the fires are scattered in every direction. Centaurs weave between them, leading the injured to the healer's hut. Above, embers from the flames soar in every direction, and below, arrows poke from the mud. The buildings remained unharmed, though, a miracle in itself.

Down the path leading toward the city's tunnel, Bastian returns with a group. Anger stretches across each of their faces, their weapons clutched in their grips. They must have followed the Harvestmen out, cutting down those too slow to outrun them.

They pass them without a word.

Nefari traces her shaky fingers across her brow. All around her lay dead harvestmen, and Kristal studies them with tears in her eyes.

"I heard the wraiths," Kristal says. "I smelled them, too." Her voice trembles as much as Nefari's legs, and she turns her back on the dead to face Nefari once more. "I know the Queen of Salix made them, but they don't come to Salix often. And when they do . . . How did you . . . Where did they go?"

"The sword," Nefari says, half lying. "There were two who managed to get past Sibyl's light. The sword destroyed them, and the rest fled with the harvestmen."

Dao subtly stiffens beside her. "It's true," he adds tightly. "I saw it."

Kaymen plucks an arrow from the mud. Blood seeps from his mouth, and a bruise blossoms on his cheek.

"You okay?" Dao asks him. Kaymen nods and wipes at his mouth with the back of his forearm. The bow and arrow strapped to his shoulder jostles, and he stares at his sword lying ten feet away. He had helped Nefari, abandoned his weapon to pull her from a place so dark and hopeless.

"We got lucky," he grumbles. Nefari can see the memories swimming in his eyes – memories from the past better left buried. He turns his attention to her. "Really lucky."

"The others?" she peers around him and searches for his companions, but no other shadow person is in sight. Kaymen shakes his head. His jaw ticks, a telling sign of his grief, and Nefari's heart sinks.

296

There, under the shadow of the trees sprawling up the path, are all three of his friends. "They're dead," she mumbles. Her voice sounds hollow.

"They were protecting me. The Storm – we were distracted. They came from around the hut, and we didn't see them until . . ."

Tears spring in Nefari's eyes. She roughly wipes her eyes with the heel of her free hand.

"I don't know how many of our people survived," he adds. "But we'll find out."

"How did this happen?" Kristal demands. "I thought this place was a fortress, as foreboding as the Fades."

"Clearly, it's not," Kaymen snips.

Nefari studies Kristal, wondering which of the two of them the harvestmen were truly after. If she trained with The Red Reaper, surely fear over battle and possible death hadn't affected the girl in such a way. Surely, she wouldn't be unraveling at the seams.

Looking closer, Nefari breathes a sympathetic sigh. *It's the illness*, she thinks to herself. The weakness she had seen earlier during the festival. "Are you okay? You look . . . do you need a healer?"

"I'm fine." Kristal rubs at her eyes. The skirts of her dress are torn, but she doesn't seem to notice. "I'm fine."

Bastian calls Kaymen's name. The centaur leader is still surrounded by his angry warriors, their heads bent as they discuss the audacity of the Salix Queen and her attempt to take the mountains. Some of them watch Nefari. It makes her question if any saw what she did or if they know she was nearly harvested and somehow escaped the darkness's grips.

Whatever the case, Nefari hopes they keep their mutterings to themselves. If Kristal were to overhear . . .

Before Kaymen leaves their side and sloshes sullenly through the mud now mixed with blood, he turns to Kristal and says, "Thank you."

Taken aback, Nefari asks, "For what?" She doesn't think she's ever heard him utter those words.

Kaymen's attention remains on Kristal. "For saving Fari."

Upon passing, he locks gazes with Nefari. Something passes between them – something that has never been there. *Respect,* perhaps? Nefari understands though, and she's grateful to him for what he had done for her tonight. Differences aside, he was there when she needed him.

"That was strange," Dao comments when Kaymen reaches Bastian's side.

Nefari doesn't answer him. She grasps Kristal's hand with one of her own and peers at the burns and cuts along her wrists. "Don't dismiss my question. It is the illness, isn't it?" she asks so low it's barely a whisper.

From under her lashes, Kristal peeks at her. "Yes."

Dao leans closer. "Are you sure you don't need a healer? Should I fetch Cyllian?"

Kristal shakes her head. "There's nothing she can do for me. It'll pass with rest. And the wrists, well, they'll heal."

"But –"

"Let it go, Dao. If she wants to suffer, let her suffer."

Kristal clears her throat and makes a sad attempt to straighten her hunched posture. "So, it's true? The inferaze contains magical properties?"

"It would appear it is truly Divine." Nefari releases Kristal's hands and lifts the sword so they all can examine it. Blood is still slick across the blade, but it's drying in some places. "Why hasn't anyone discovered this?"

Dao shrugs and adjusts his quiver strap. "Because everyone thought the wraiths could only be destroyed by magic – the purest form like the shadow royal's."

"Kaymen is right. I owe you my gratitude, Kristal."

"For what?"

"For saving my life."

"Perhaps you can show your thanks by removing these." She gestures to the ropes.

"We will do no such thing," Fawn barks. None of them had heard her approach, and all three jump at the abruptness of her tone.

"Why?" Dao asks suspiciously, his brow raised. "She's proven herself to be on our side."

Squeezing her way between Dao and Nefari, Fawn glowers at Nefari. She squares her jaw in challenge while wordlessly beseeching her to see reason.

"She's right," Nefari intervenes and returns her attention to Kristal. "The rope stays until we're told otherwise."

Shocked, Dao places his hand over his heart. "The great Fari is obeying rules?" he asks, flabbergasted. Then, he sobers. "Seriously, the girl has done nothing –"

"Leave it, Dao," Nefari growls for the second time because, down the path, Bastian heads toward them. There's a look in his eyes Nefari doesn't like, one that makes her heed caution. Other centaurs surround them, each in an array of bruised and beaten and bloody. They all stare at Kristal.

Kristal backs up a step and bumps into Nefari. "What's going on?" she asks as she steadies the girl.

Bastian leans to sneer in Kristal's face. "Did you bring the Harvest Storm?"

"What?" Kristal whispers.

Nefari steps away from Kristal to peer at her expression. True fear lingers there with the purple splotches squatting above her cheekbones. "What is this, Bastian?"

Through his teeth, he says, "I'm asking the question, Nefari. I demand an answer."

"N-No!" Kristal's gaze flicks wildly to Nefari, Dao, and Bastian.

"Then, how did they get here?" He crosses his arms. "How did they find the entrance? How did they know when to strike? Where to strike?"

From within the crowd, Nio's voice rumbles after Bastian's, "One raven would have been all it took."

Searching the muck and the boots caked with it, Nefari quickly thinks back to the time she's spent with Kristal. "She never sent a raven, Bastian. Not once."

"That you saw."

"I don't –" Nefari begins, but Bastian cuts her off with a swipe of his hand through the air. Angry murmurs agreeing with him sound at the leader's back.

"I never sent a raven," she pleads. Kristal clasps her hands as if in prayer. "You have to believe me! I didn't do this!"

Do they truly think she did this? Nefari searches the crowd for Kaymen. When she finds him, they share another look, but Nefari cannot read his expression this time. It's blank. No anger, no guilt. Nothing.

She can't believe this. If Kristal had brought the Harvest Storm, why would she save Nefari?

"Forgive me if I don't believe you," Bastian growls. "Take her," he orders the warriors. Knocking Dao and Nefari aside, they reach for Kristal and roughly grab her upper arms.

"No!" Kristal shouts to the crowd. They tug her away despite her heels firm in the mud. "I didn't do it! I swear on the Divine!" She peers over her shoulder to Nefari. "Please! You have to believe me!"

When they're far enough away that the beseeching shouts and Kristal's pleas fade, Dao asks, "What do we do?"

"What can we do?"

His nostrils flare, and he spits on the ground. "They'll tie her to the shame post, and then the council will decide her manner of death."

"I know."

"Kristal will be made an example of," he presses. "Her death will be –"

"I know."

He turns to her. "And you're going to do nothing?"

Nefari glares at him. "What am I supposed to do, Dao? Rescue her from a dozen angry centaurs?" She shakes her head slowly. "I am not the leader here. I am not in charge."

Exasperated, he flings his arm in the direction of the crowd. "She saved your life, Fari. They're wrong. They're wrong, and you know it."

"I know," she agrees, guilt-ridden.

"Stop!" a male tenor shouts. The word booms into the village. "Stop!"

Nefari and Dao whip around. Traveling quickly down the path, aiding Sibyl and her hobbling steps is Patrix. He holds up his

301

hand, waving a piece of parchment in his grip. "Don't kill her! Bastian, stop!"

At the base of the path, Sibyl weakly pats Patrix's arm. "Let me go." Patrix does, his hands hovering around her space until he's sure she won't fall. "Go! Show them what we found."

Nefari rushes to Sibyl's side and replaces Patrix. She ignores Sibyl when she slaps away her hands for keeping her upright, gripping Sibyl around the waist instead.

As Patrix crosses the village, Sibyl whispers, "I saw her."

"Who?"

"Kristal. With the sword. Inferaze is Hope's rock, remember? She's drawn to it, Nefari. You must keep it close."

"You think . . . what? She wants it for herself?"

Sibyl peers up at her. "I think if she was ever to return home, she'd attempt to bargain with her life. What better way to bargain for one's life than with a sword made from Hope's island?"

Nefari closes her eyes and sighs deeply. "Because the Queen of Salix has Hope, and the sword would make a better trophy than Kristal's head."

Sibyl nods. "Remember the fate card, Nefari. Remember Hope's prophecy. We mustn't let it come to light in a way that could make it impossible for you to find her."

"Wait, wait." Nefari adjusts her grip on Sibyl's waist. "You think my sword *belongs* to Hope?"

"I think it was meant to find Hope. I think your fate is intertwined, and things do not happen by coincidence. Not with you. Not with the Fate-Blessed princess. Things are stirring, Nefari. Pieces are moving across the board, and if we do not play the game right . . ."

Blood dribbles down Sibyl's nose, and by the evidence of the smeared and dried trail across her cheek, it looks like it has been bleeding for a while. Nefari doesn't comment on it. Instead, she says nothing and takes on the girl's full weight. "Come on," Nefari murmurs.

They follow Patrix's hoofprints and approach the crowd. Up the way, the sounds of children and women filter down into the village. They're still hiding up there, a fact Nefari is grateful for. It'll take a while to clear away the dead bodies, and though those children will someday grow to be great warriors, they don't need to see this. Not yet. Seeing the dead and how they died, well, Nefari knows firsthand it's something no one can forget.

"Look!" Patrix demands, thrusting the folded parchment at Bastian's chest. When Bastian takes it, Patrix puts his hands on his hips and breathes heavily.

Silence falls over the crowd as they wait anxiously.

Unfolding the parchment, Bastian frowns at it. "What is this?"

"Just look!"

Huffing, Bastian holds the parchment up higher and squints at it. "The Shadow Kingdom crown?

# CHAPTER TWENTY-SEVEN

*My kingdom's crown?*

Nefari's heart fractures at the mention of it. She doesn't need to study the picture to remember what it looks like. But how did Patrix get it? Better yet, why is there a drawing of it?

Quiet chatter spreads through the crowd while Patrix explains everything. "They weren't here for Kristal, or . . . any other obvious reason." He spares Nefari a moment's glance. "They were here to steal a shadow person. They needed a shadow person to lead them right into the ashes of the Shadow Kingdom."

*And all for a crown of a long-dead queen.* Despicable. Disgusting. Nefari's anger returns tenfold.

Dao, Kaymen, and Cyllian come to stand by Nefari and Sibyl's side. Sibyl grips Nefari's waist tightly. The squeeze she gives is a welcome pressure that banks her emotions. It's a reminder, a consolation, to keep her wits about it.

"Is it true?" Cyllian asks Sibyl quietly.

"Of course, it is." Sibyl peers at her through the fallen hair draped over most of her face. "Those men and women were harvested.

304

They were all your own people. They were sent to find you, which means Despair knows you're here. Their presence was meant to break you – to make you hesitate and tremble long enough to be captured. I'd bet my last coin if we examined every pocket of every harvestman, we'd find the same parchment."

Nefari doesn't doubt Sibyl, and she trusts Patrix.

Patrix goes on to explain how a harvested shadow person wouldn't be able to travel through the shadows; otherwise, they'd never come to Kadoka. Not if they had the means to find the crown themselves. Because Despair wouldn't bother with a few protected shadow people when he has the majority.

It explains why, when touched by the wraith, Nefari hadn't remembered her magic. Her mind had been disconnected from her body and her memories – the things that make her who she is. And without the ring, she'd still be stuck there.

*My Divine!* Her mother knew. She had to have known what it could do!

On some level, Kristal knew, too. She had told the story about the fee and how one particular fee had built her entire realm out of inferaze to ward off Despair. Despair had been hunting the Black Market for the odd merchant who was selling the substance. The harvesting *is* Despair's magic, an extension of the God himself, and therefore, the inferaze is truly, and undeniably, his weakness.

What does this mean for her? Despair knows they're here. When she was in that cyclone, was he able to tell who Nefari was? Or had it not reached that point?

Around them, healers are picking up the dead and carrying them to two separate areas. One is a pile of harvestmen to soon be burned, and the other is the healer's hut where the priestess will bless their bodies and prepare them for a ritualistic pyre. Some of the younger warriors are helping, not caring about the drama unfolding in the crowd.

"So, what do we do?" Dao crosses his arms and sighs heavily through his nose.

"We wait for instruction," Kaymen murmurs.

When Patrix is finished answering any and all questions to his and Sibyl's theory, Bastian glimpses Nefari from over Patrix's shoulder. Patrix turns to look with him, his face solemn and grave, while Bastian's is still etched with rage and distrust. She understands the rage, feels it waiting inside her, too, but the distrust is misplaced. Kristal had nothing to do with this.

"The crown isn't theirs to take, Bastian," Nefari growls. "No matter how they found out about us, the crown takes priority."

Satisfied with her answer, Bastian folds the paper and hands it to Fawn. "Take Kristal to the healer's hut with Cyllian. Get the girl patched up."

Pinching it between her fingers, Fawn takes it carefully and peers wearily at Nefari. "And the ropes?" she asks him.

"Leave them. For now."

Relieved, Cyllian rushes to Kristal's side, and the warriors gripping her upper arms release her. She murmurs to Kristal as they head toward the healer hut, Fawn following close behind.

"The rest of you, make yourselves useful." Without challenge, the crowd disburses to aid in gathering the dead. There are mothers and children tucked away in Sibyl's home who will need to be told about their husband's or brother's or friend's death, and Nefari's grateful the task won't fall to her. Feasts will need to be prepared in their honor. Someone will have to find Swen, too, to record the names.

And as for Kaymen's friends, Nefari's own people . . . Well, she doesn't want to think about that. Not right now. Not tonight.

As one, Patrix and Bastian approach her.

"Go with Cyllian," Nefari says to Dao and Kaymen. "Take Sibyl with you. See if they have something to ease her pain." She passes Sibyl off to the men and then crosses her arms under her cloak to soak in some of her own warmth.

As soon as they're out of earshot, Nefari squares her jaw. "The other shadow people in the city?"

"Alive," Bastian murmurs. "They're in the mess hall, awaiting instruction.

"What do you want me to do?"

His nose twitches as he considers his answer. "I will be sending both you and Kristal to retrieve your crown." He put emphasis on the word 'your,' and it coils tight in Nefari – a fierce possessiveness over the crown.

She expected it to hurt. She knew he'd send her to retrieve it the moment it was mentioned, and she expected the idea to be a painful reminder of the past. But something changed inside her tonight. A switch had been flipped, and now . . . now, everything she didn't want to be doesn't hold the same significance as it once had.

In that cyclone where the darkness was obliterating her memories, she was reassembled. Those painful memories were reformed, and all the things that had once been too heartbreaking to recall don't hurt so much anymore. The things she once feared are insignificant thoughts in the back of her mind, and she feels *different*. Whole. Purposeful. Brave.

She wants to do this. She wants to go *home* and see what remains. She needs to even if it'll be dangerous. Who better to bring along than someone who might know Despair – the Queen of Salix – inside and out? Kristal can be an asset.

She nods to Bastian.

"Why can't Nefari and myself go retrieve it?" Patrix asks. "We've always worked well together in the past."

"You will be escorting Nefari and Kristal to the edge of the Shadled. Afterward, you will leave them to their task. You have a role to play, Patrix, and I expect you to do it."

Patrix grumbles under his breath. "And Emory?"

His front hooves stomp in the mud as he angles his body to the satyr. "Get the general's son out of the mountains and away from the Rebel Legion. The last thing the boy needs is to be suspected as a traitor. Take him wherever he is meant to be, and do it quickly. Stay with him for a few days so you may also build your own alibi. What happened here tonight will reach the edges of the realm before next week's end, and you mustn't be part of that rumor."

He heeds without further argument. "Is there anything you want me to listen for during our travels?"

"Yes," Bastian murmurs. "Listen to everything. Pass me everything." Patrix nods, glances at Nefari, and grips her shoulder as he strides to greet Emory treading down the mountain path.

"And what about Kristal and the information she might have?" Nefari asks, narrowing her eyes.

"After today, I do not believe Kristal will be willing to tell us much of anything, but she might tell you if there is anything left to tell that we don't already know."

"You're angry with her."

"Indeed," he spits. "If she had told us it was the crown they were after, we could have taken measures to protect –"

"That wouldn't have stopped the Storm, and you know it."

There's a pause between them, and they listen to the soft voice of the priestess praying to the Divine over the nearest dead body. Her billowy velvet cloak drapes over her equine shape and drags along the wet ground.

*A lot of good that'll do them,* Nefari thinks to herself. Nefari is fate, and she's never once felt the prayers. Praying for the dead is pointless.

"You really think I can do this? Steal the crown before they get to it?"

"*Your* crown," he corrects. He rests a heavy hand on her shoulder. "This is an important step in the right direction. For you, for your people, for the realm . . . I think you know that. It's the best plan we have. *You* are everyone's best chance."

"And if I get caught?" Nefari peeks up at him. "Their armies are practically everywhere now, and the crones have taken over most of the Shadled. What happens if I get caught?"

Bastian's jaw ticks at the mere thought of Nefari being in danger. But he can't guard her forever. Even he knows this. "Then, you will burn bright, Nefari. You'll have nothing left to lose and no secret to keep if they catch you." He pauses again, and she watches his thick throat bob in a swallow. "If they catch you, and you live, they'll take you to Salix. I do not believe you'll be ready to stand against the queen. Not with shackles. Not without allies. Not without the other Divine."

"Bastian …" she begins.

He grips her chin. "I'm asking you to stay alive, Nefari. Not just for me but what you could do for our future. After tonight, I know you don't have it in you to stand by and watch anymore. I see the spark in your eyes. It's the same spark your mother had when she first heard your prophecy. You're determined and stubborn, and once your mind is made up, there are no other choices." Tears spring in Nefari's eyes, and Bastian smiles sympathetically. "Do you remember the lesson with the sheep?" Nefari nods. "You chose to save the one. Your mother chose the same fate with her own people because she knew that 'one' would inevitably save them all. You are brave enough to do this, Nefari. You are so much like her that some days, it doesn't feel as though she's gone but living through you."

"You think so?"

His grin broadens. "I see her here." His hand hovers over her eyes. "I see her here." His hand moves to her jaw. "And I see her here." He places his hand over her heart. He grips her chin again. "You aren't nobody, Nefari. You are special, just like her, but greater. You are someone who has the power to make a difference, and no matter where your future takes you, she will always be proud of you. As will I."

Having left Sibyl with one of the centaur healers, Dao strides into Cyllian's healing room. Kaymen hadn't stayed with the crone for more than a second before he left back into the city. He hadn't said where he was going either, but by the look in his eyes, he definitely had a destination and purpose in mind.

Dao wasn't interested in following him. He's bone-numb and weary from the night's events. *Harvested.* She was almost harvested! *And Kaymen . . .* Shame fills Dao. He should have been the one who clung to Nefari and demanded she fight for herself. But he hadn't. He'd been too shocked to move, too stunned to do anything but scream her name.

Cyllian looks up from bandaging Kristal's wrists, her fingers fumbling around the ropes still tied there. Kristal's legs dangle

310

over the side of the table, her spine hunched. She appears exhausted.

Wads of bloody bandages are at Kristal's hip, and she stares at them. He gets the feeling she isn't actually studying them but allowing her mind to drift and come to terms with everything that happened to her tonight. It makes him wonder if she's grateful she's here or if she's regretting ever leaving the Salix court.

"Is Nefari –" Tears threaten to spill from Cyllian's eyes.

"She's okay," he says right away. He leans against the door frame and crosses his arms. The fire crackling in her hearth licks at his cold skin and dries what mud remains on his clothes.

Her shoulders sag with relief, and she turns her attention back to her task. "You need to respect your limitations, Kristal."

"I'm trying."

In a motherly quality, Cyllian snorts. "Not hard enough. You should have gone with the women and children to Sibyl's cave. Nefari could have taken care of herself."

"She saved Nefari's life." Both women peer at him, but his attention drifts to the flame writhing against the logs. "Nefari wouldn't – She would be dead right now if it wasn't for Kristal."

Grabbing wool from a bucket by her feet, Cyllian says nothing. She slides the wool over fresh bandages and secures them. When she moves to rebind Kristal's ropes, Dao startles her by saying, "Don't."

"But, Bastian –"

"She can't go on the journey bound like a slave." Cyllian considers him and then gently drops the rope to the floor. He continues, "They'll send you with her, you know."

"With whom?" Kristal asks. "To where?"

"Nefari." He pushes off the door frame and heads to the fire. He hovers his hands over the warmth and then rubs them together. "They'll send you with her to retrieve the crown."

"She can't travel in this condition, Dao."

He turns away from the fire. "She'll have to if she wants to live." He doesn't have to explain that though Kristal is innocent of what they blamed her for, they won't want her here. If she stays any longer, she'll wind up dead, her body shipped in pieces across Widow's Bay and straight to Queen Sieba Arsonian's castle. She's lucky there haven't been any attempts thus far.

The centaurs respect the healers, however. None would barge into their hut and charge down the hall. Cyllian's room is the safest place for her at the moment.

Kristal closes her eyes, submitting to her fate, and twists her hands to ease her stiff wrists. "Is it possible . . ." She swallows and then opens her eyes to study the logs stretched across the ceiling. "Is it possible there might be something out there to cure me? Something magical?"

Cyllian pauses, and Dao stiffens. They glance at each other, and Cyllian softly answers, "I don't know. Do you have reason to believe there is?"

"No, no." Kristal shakes her head. Her voice is toneless, distant, when she adds, "It was just a thought."

Licking her lips uncomfortably, Cyllian adds, "I don't want you to worry about the journey, Kristal. I'll send some elixirs along. Those will help take the edge off. It's not magic, but it'll have to do."

Disinterested in their journey, Dao makes to leave, but in the doorway, he stops. Over his shoulder, he asks Kristal, "What happened? When you touched the sword, what happened?" That sword had done the impossible. He could ask Nefari, but he's not sure he'd get the truth.

"Magic," Kristal breathes. She studies her palms, and Dao, knowing he'll get nothing more, leaves.

# CHAPTER TWENTY-EIGHT

Having departed with Bastian, Nefari strides through the village.

Exhaustion has settled into every bone and every muscle, and her boots slop through what's left of the mud. Her legs feel weighted and her hands heavy, and as she trudges between huts and by a cluster of sobbing centaurs, she doesn't even glance at the pyres lit in a small clearing where the sheep usually come for their evening oats. They're burning the harvestmen, and the scent of their crispy flesh lingers everywhere she goes.

Large enough spaces to safely burn them are limited. Some centaurs thought taking them out of the city would be best, but others argued against it. "Tales would begin spreading too fast about what happened here tonight if we burned them out in the open," Nio had barked. Nefari agreed with the butcher, but at the same time, Sibyl's light had probably been seen all the way to the Black Market.

It wouldn't look good for the Rebel Legion if the villages they protect learn Kadoka had been invaded. She's honestly surprised the ravens haven't already arrived. Perhaps none were awake when Sibyl's blast blanketed the mountains. Nefari can only hope.

That particular argument had shifted into silence, and the true work had begun. Women and children were told of the dead, and their names were recorded by Swen as they were carried away.

Upon passing, Nefari had heard they were storing the bodies of the dead centaurs and Kaymen's friends in the temple until the healers could prepare their bodies. She passed the temple a few minutes ago, refusing to look inside.

With the brisk wind still howling and the sky still dark, the pile burns quickly. She does her best to keep her mind on her destination. It won't do her any good to remember the harvested shadow people's faces, but some part of her knows they'll always be there in a pocket of her mind. They deserve to be remembered even if they did try to kill everyone.

*But it wasn't them,* she reminds herself. It was the Queen of Salix's dark magic – Despair's magic – and now Nefari knows first-hand what a sliver of possession feels like. Death had been a kindness to them, but maybe death isn't their only option anymore. Maybe death isn't the only answer to set them free.

Nefari kisses her ring when she arrives at the armory. The windows glow with the fire within, and the sound of metal hitting metal vibrates the pane. It's a welcoming sound – a normal noise when matched to the sobs of women and children who pass by.

Stretching her neck, she pushes open the armory door. She's swathed in warmth as soon as she steps inside.

Stone-faced, Fawn doesn't turn from the sword she's molding, bright with the trapped heat. Her hammering replaces Nefari's thoughts with its jarring repetition, and normally it would help release the tension inside her if Fawn hadn't been hammering so furiously.

Sighing, Nefari leans against the wall next to the door and wipes a dirty hand down her face. Her fingertips come away black from the paint, and she stares at them, remembering the swirling

315

darkness and the shadowed faces who whispered the words she needed to hear.

Eventually, Fawn pauses. She twists the hammer in her grip, fixated on the flames. Her jaw flexes, and Nefari finally speaks, "Are you okay?"

Her tail swishes, and she lifts her gaze to Nefari. "No. And neither are you."

Nefari settles in deeper against the logs, but she can't squash the truth from her words when she replies, "I'm tired. So, so tired, Fawn."

"Devastated. Life altered. Lost," Fawn adds to the list. She carefully sets down the hammer and wipes the sweat from her face with a nearby rag.

"All those things, too, I suppose." Nefari pushes off the wall and heads to the table directly in front of her. Sprawled across the surface is all the material she needs to clean her sword, so instead of meeting Fawn's rare, sympathetic expression, Nefari pulls her sword from its sheath and begins the task of cleaning it.

Dried blood is caked along the surface, obscuring the glittering inferaze within. The sound of the cloth against the metal sends goosebumps up her arms.

When the sun finally rises, they'll have a meeting in Bastian's hut. She's supposed to be sleeping right now, preparing her mind and settling her soul for the journey to come. But sleep won't help her. It won't calm her mind.

"Things could have gone very, very wrong, Nefari." Fawn's voice drips with anger. "Your magic is great, I will not deny it, but it could have gone wrong. You could have called more wraiths. You hardly ever use your magic – you never practice – and a mistake could have easily been made. You could have injured any one of us."

"You don't have to remind me of any of that."

"Dao told me what happened. He told me about the wraith. Look, Nefari, I'm not trying to tell you to not defend yourself and the others, but I'm frightened."

She grins without humor and grabs the wetting stone. "You? Frightened? I never thought I'd see the day."

"And . . ." At her hesitation, Nefari looks up at her. Fawn studies her blade. "And I feel like we've made you small while you've lived here. I feel like we've fit you into this tiny little box, and now we're pulling you out and expecting you to grow in size. We're expecting a warrior to be Divine, a princess to be a queen. So, yes, I'm scared. I'm scared of what it all means. I'm scared of everything. And I'm scared for you."

"Me too," Nefari whispers.

Fawn's tail swishes softly when she sluggishly approaches the table. She rests her hands on top of Nefari's, halting her in her task. "You're my friend, Nefari. You're not just the realm's only hope. You're my friend, and I need you to be okay."

A small, sad smile tugs at Nefari's lips. Dropping the wetting stone and her sword, Nefari turns her hands over and grabs Fawn's. Her small palms are dwarfed by Fawn's. "You know, tonight, when I was touched by the wraith, I saw my mother." Fawn blinks at this, but Nefari pushes on, her voice thick with emotion. "She told me – She told me to be brave. Over and over again, she said it. Sibyl is right. Bastian is right. I can't keep hiding, and I can't keep pretending I'm not meant to do this. And just because all of this wasn't what I wanted, it doesn't mean I won't be okay."

"And if it gets you killed?"

Nefari shrugs, the gesture small and insignificant. "Then, I'll make sure it won't be in vain."

In a rare show of weakness, Fawn's eyes line with tears. She sniffles, gently pulling her hands from Nefari's, and slides them into her apron pocket smudged with soot and singed from sparks long since passed. "When do you leave?"

"I'm not sure. We meet with Bastian tomorrow."

"And Patrix will go with you?"

Nefari shakes her head. "Only in the beginning. Eventually, he will head further South to put Emory back where he belongs. I think Emory is broken." She chuckles half-heartedly. "He's still trembling. At least, Nio has taken sympathy on him. He shoved a bowl of soup under the boy's nose laced with sedatives and demanded he drink."

Fawn nods solemnly, unaffected by Nefari's attempt to lighten the mood. "And the Salix girl?"

"She'll be with me." Nefari holds up a hand to Fawn's incoming protest. "She saved my life, Fawn. She's capable of protecting herself and anyone else."

There's a taut silence only the crackling flames fill. "Fine," Fawn finally grumbles. She runs a hand over her braided hair. The weaves are a frizzy mess. "I'll get the packs ready then. What weapons do you need? What supplies should I grab?"

Nefari rattles off the weapons she desires and the food that will last until they make it to the first village. It isn't much. Nefari prefers to travel light.

While she names them, Fawn treks to the wall of weapons and plucks a few from their hangers. She gathers them in her arms. "Leave your sword with me. I'll finish cleaning it. You need to get some sleep or you'll fall off Astra before you make it to the base of the mountain." Nefari doesn't move from her post next to the table. Fawn glances over her shoulder. "Go! I mean it, Fari. Get some sleep."

She gently traces the pommel. "Thanks, Fawn," she murmurs, and then she heads to the door.

When her hand is wrapped around the handle, Fawn calls her name. The centaur strides to Nefari, dropping the weapons onto the table as she does so. She wraps her in a tight hug. Nefari squeaks as the air is squeezed from her lungs, her cheek squished against Fawn's leather.

"Fawn, I can't breathe."

She squeezes harder. "You may think you have no friends, Fari – you may think you're alone – but you're not." Fawn rests her chin on top of Nefari's head. "Remember this while you're gone."

"Okay." She pats Fawn's back. "What is this?"

Fawn snorts. "Can't I say goodbye?"

"Sure. But –"

"Death may be your end, but I can't stand the thought that you might march toward it. I need to know you won't be reckless. I need to know you won't be another body I'll have to watch burn from my window."

Tears prick the corners of Nefari's eyes and she stops resisting Fawn's affections. "I'll try."

Nefari leaves soon after, unable to endure these rare emotions of Fawn's.

Instead of going to her hut, however, she finds herself at the top of the mountains overlooking the Shadled and under the stars twinkling above the purple-leafed trees.

She absentmindedly twirls the ring around her cold finger, remembering the glow, its warmth. There are forces unseen. There are trails left by gods long since gone. Steps had been taken to ensure the realm lives another day, and Nefari is one of those assurances. The inferaze is another. If armies had more of

319

it, the difference it would make when the Harvest Storms invades would be astronomical. And what if . . . what if she slides this ring on a harvested's finger? What would happen?

She huffs at the sky.

"I haven't seen you look over your home since the first week I brought you here."

Nefari glances over her shoulder to the voice she knows so well. Bastian stands not ten feet away. His hair is tied back tightly, but tendrils escape around his forehead and flap with the breeze.

She had heard his approach a few minutes ago, knew he was standing there watching her – waiting for her to turn and greet him.

"Is it settled then?" She pulls her cloak tighter and turns back to the scene. The sun will be up soon, and the true work will begin. "Is everything ready for our departure?"

"Yes." She listens to the sound of his hooves packing down snow, and when he's beside her, he sighs and studies the territory he helps protect. "Nefari, about the blood vow . . ."

"I know why you broke it."

"Oh?" He looks sidelong at her, brows raised.

"It's the same reason Sibyl risked herself tonight. She was trying to protect me."

"Indeed." She can feel his eyes searching her expression. He will find nothing there but understanding and acceptance.

"You both care for me. You both love me, and love should never be punished. I was wrong to do so."

Her shoulders sag, and the cloak slips. Nefari doesn't want to punish anymore. She doesn't want to hold anyone else at arms-length who has done nothing but show concern for her. Not

320

everyone is untrustworthy, and those closest to her have proved that time and time again. Patrix, Dao, Cyllian, Fawn, Bastian, and now, Kristal and Kaymen.

"And through all the hatred I have had toward you," Nefari continues. "I'm grateful because I've lived an ordinary life. You gave me that, and more. You allowed me to blame you for what I had lost so I could cope."

"So, you're accepting your fate, then?"

She shivers once and hunkers back into her warmth. The cloak is soft as it rubs against her chin, but it smells of blood and smoke. "I don't know. Maybe. Probably. I may not have a choice. Today –" she blinks at the fading stars, "Today, I was reminded of what I have ignored because fear is just anger turned inside out. I was reminded of what all this felt like, to have my home invaded and my people killed, and then realized it doesn't have to be this way. That's what my mother was trying to tell me when she gave me this." She holds up her hand, and Bastian flicks his attention to the ring. She tucks it back into her cloak. "She was telling me to be brave enough to move on. She knew, even then, I'd grow up without her. She was telling me to let her go, to let my anger go. She gave it to me to protect me."

Bastian hums. "But our home wasn't taken. People were killed, yes, but we still stand proud and strong."

"It could have been." Nefari focuses on him now. "Just like all the other villages they've managed to wipe out over the years. It could easily have been taken. A Salix woman saved my life, Bastian. A Salix woman!"

"I know, but tell me what this means for you now."

"That things are no longer what I thought they were. And I think," she swallows thickly. "I think if we don't do something, the darkness will continue to spread until nothing is left."

321

"We know, but what are you getting at?"

She internally grimaces. "I . . . have something to tell you. I haven't been completely honest."

After a deep exhale, she confesses about the inferaze and its magical properties. She tells him how the Divine magic can change everything. She admits to him about the wraith who had touched her and how the wraith died. It wasn't until she went into detail about how she killed the second wraith and remained unharvested that true anger bubbled inside him, turning the skin on his cheeks three shades darker.

Bastian grips her shoulders. "You kept this from me? Have you no sense?"

Ashamed, she glances at her boots, the toes buried in snow. "I thought it was all nonsense. I'm sorry. I hadn't been sure until the ring . . ."

Bastian hisses and releases her. He paces a few steps away and then whips back to face her. "This could be valuable. This could change everything." He strokes his beard as he considers her. "I understand why you kept it a secret, Nefari. Hope can be dangerous."

"I know."

He quiets his voice. "Do you realize what this means?"

"I do."

"Until now, I believed only your magic could rid the realm of them, your mother's and Fate's magic; though I'm a bit reluctant to believe Fate gave you any significant gifts you weren't born with. But –"

"About that. . ." Bastian quirks a brow at her interruption. "I don't know exactly what Fate's magic has done to my own, but there is something else I've kept from you. The shadows? The ones you've seen move? That's happened for as long as I can remember – well before I turned eight."

His brows fall into a frown. "I thought –"

"I know. I hadn't told my mother or father, either. I knew it wasn't normal, and I didn't want to frighten them, but as Sibyl had told me, Fate's magic had mixed with my own." She peers at the nearby trees to ensure they're alone. "They move like living things, Bastian. They bend toward me."

"Interesting," he murmurs, sweeping his gaze across the planes of her face. "All the time?"

"No, not all the time. Mostly when I get angry or agitated. They're attracted to it – to the magic within me that rises when I feel those emotions."

Sighing, he pulls her into a hug. "Do not fear them, Nefari. Sometime soon, you should explore them, but for now . . ." Nefari sniffles against his stomach as tears spring to her eyes. "Don't dwell too long on it."

Nodding against him, Nefari pulls away and swipes at a tear rolling down her cheek. "We'll have to get more. The inferaze, I mean. As far as I know, it's only sold in the Black Market by one guy. Hope's island is filled with it, though. At least, no one knows about the magical properties, but if you magically find the man who sells it, buy mass amounts, others will catch on. They will inquire."

He adjusts her cloak. "Then, perhaps, we will have to mine the inferaze ourselves. Make allies with those who have ships."

"Easier said than done."

# CHAPTER TWENTY-NINE

When the sun rose, its rays spilled over the village's many paths. With the fires diminished and the freshly falling snow, the mud had begun to harden. The flakes fall slowly, leisurely, but its gathering masses erased the evidence of the Storm.

A cold and brittle breeze seeps into Bastian's hut and claws fingers down Nefari's spine. She sits on a large stool she had dragged over from the table to the barren hearth, a blanket wrapped tightly around her. The stool was made for her long ago and rocks precariously from uneven legs at any twitch Nefari makes.

Kristal wanders about in Bastian's living space, blowing at the dust on the empty shelves and combing her fingers through the blankets of fur squatting by the massive cushions Bastian never rests on. Nefari wonders what she sees here. Does she see a home? Does she know that the fur she touches is the pelt of Nefari's first hunted bear? Does she know the cushion by her feet is where Nefari would lie some nights, staring at the stars outside the window?

"Are you sure we can't light this?" Kristal points at the charred logs with a single hand. A particularly strong breeze had tunneled down the chimney and curled around their legs, but

Nefari hadn't truly noticed. The girl looks odd without her ropes, but she's glad Dao intercepted on Kristal's behalf. She didn't want to endure the long conversation with Bastian about it, not when her forgiveness was still so fresh.

"There's no point." Nefari turns on her stool. "We'll be leaving soon."

Twisting her lips to the side, Kristal nods and tugs her cloak tighter around her. The door to Bastian's hut opens, the wind pushing Patrix and Emory inside. Emory hastily shuts it behind them, and they both dust the fresh snow from their shoulders.

"It's going to be an unpleasant journey down the mountains," Patrix says under his breath.

Nefari rolls her neck and then leans on her seat to better peer out the window. All she sees is white snow and red roofs. "Astra's not going to be fond of it, but it's nothing we can't handle. Where is Bastian? He was supposed to meet us here by now."

"Why isn't the fire lit?" Patrix gasps dramatically and crosses the living space. Kristal moves aside as he points to the pile of charred logs. "Emory! Get over here and light this."

Rolling his eyes, Emory does what Patrix asks. "I'm not your servant, you know." His tread is much lighter than Patrix's hooves. He squats to the hearth, packs it with kindling, and sparks a flame.

Nefari sighs at their insufferable bickering. "Patrix, where is Bastian?"

He waves his hand in the air in a dismissive gesture. "Council. He assured me he'd be here any –"

The door opens again, and the centaur in question strides inside. Dao, Fawn, Cyllian, and Kaymen follow. Bastian's living space

325

becomes crowded. Nefari rises from her stool and slides it to the wall.

Dao moves to her side and taps her nose as if that'll erase her newly acquired frown.

"What's going on? Why are you guys here?"

Cyllian and Kaymen settle on the cushions while Fawn stands between Kristal and Patrix. Emory rises from the hearth and tucks himself in the corner of the living space.

"I don't know," Dao murmurs. "Bastian and Fawn dragged us out of the tavern."

Tucked under Bastian's arm is a large roll of parchment. He spreads it across the table and pins it down with mugs. He waves everyone over, and once there, Nefari cocks her head to study the parchment properly.

It's a large map of the Divine Realm that proudly displays all the countries' names.

Salix squats to the east across Widow's Bay and just under the eastern edge of the Frozen Fades. Loess's words are faded as if water had splashed across it ages ago, a southern country whose sole trade is fish. Okaton wobbles underneath Salix, and Sutherland curves underneath the Divine Islands, which are tucked in the bay between Sutherland and the Shadled.

Bastian smooths his hand over the surface.

"What are we all doing here?" Fawn asks him.

He peers up and meets everyone's gaze. "In light of the situation, each of you will now be playing a vital role." He looks directly at Nefari. "Patrix and Emory will travel with Nefari and Kristal to the edge of the Shadled, in which they will then head to the Shadow Kingdom to retrieve the crown.

"We know this," Nefari murmurs, wondering what else Bastian had concocted in the council meeting.

"Patrix and Emory will then travel further south." Emory inches forward at the mention of his name. "He had told his father he was traveling to Loess to meet with the princess. Rumor has it, the boy is courting her."

Emory blushes and nods. Patrix slaps him on the back. "We'll get you to your lady, and I'll make sure you woo her properly. You're a seasoned warrior now, Emmy! She'll be smitten."

Nefari, Kaymen, and Fawn snort at the same time. The group quietly chuckles, but Bastian's expression holds utter disinterest. "Patrix will be staying with you, Emory, to build his own alibi. Nobody must know what happened here last night."

"They'll figure it out soon enough," Kaymen grumbles.

"That they will, but we need to control the situation as best as possible. If others believe we are weak enough for invasion, Salix's harvestmen won't be our only problem."

The group nods, and Dao and Nefari glance at one another. "And when we are successful in retrieving the crown?" Nefari asks.

"Then you come back here where we can protect it. You must stick to the shadows, Fari. Do not be seen."

"And what do you wish for me to do while we are in Loess," Patrix grumbles. Nefari puckers her lips, remembering how it's Patrix's least favorite place to squat. It's where he was born and raised, and unless Bastian asks him to go, he keeps well away.

"What we've already discussed." He scans Fawn, Cyllian, Kaymen, and Dao, "You four will travel with Patrix where he will leave you at the Black Market to find a seller named Savage Deeds."

"I don't think –" Emory begins. He shares a look with Patrix, and Nefari catches the subtle shake of the satyr's head. She frowns.

"The pirate?" Dao is incredulous.

"You want them to negotiate with the old pirate king?" Nefari can't believe what she's hearing. When they went to the Black Market, Patrix had refused to go near the man's tavern. "The one whose daughter overthrew him, kicked him into Widow's Bay without legs, and he miraculously survived? That pirate king?"

"I've met the pirate queen before," Kristal whispers. "If he's anything like his daughter . . ."

Bastian ignores it all. "With sufficient payment, he will provide a small ship and someone to navigate you to Hope's island where you'll acquire more inferaze. He will be well paid to behave, and he owes me a favor. He will do what I ask."

"And once we have it?" Fawn asks. Her spine is straight and confident in the task she's been given.

"You will bring it home and forge blades. There are many without the means of magic. If we can tip the scales by wielding blades and wearing rings of inferaze –"

"We'll stand a chance," Kaymen finishes. He nods and steps closer to the map, approving of Bastian's plan. "When do we leave?"

"Today, after the ceremony." He stares at them, long and hard. "We do not have time to wait."

Nefari agrees.


Patrix Eiling's chest tightens while he gazes unseeingly at the map. The group disperses, chattering among themselves about the things they'll need to pack as they head out into the city. Bastian follows them out, shutting the door quietly behind him without another glance. The only ones who remain are Patrix and Emory, and as soon as the silence stretching between them becomes taut, Emory steps closer to Patrix.

"Dealing with Savage Deeds is a bad idea. We should tell them."

Patrix sighs and tugs at his beard. "No. We won't tell them. By the time they find Savage, you and I will be long gone. He won't know we're associated with them. They'll be fine."

"And the crone who knows about Nefari? What if they find her in the Shadled?"

Admitting that the crones are after Nefari would mean admitting that he told them she's alive in the first place – the ultimate betrayal, held high above all his others. Shame colors his cheeks, but in addition, he knows that if Nefari caught wind that the crones are aware she still lives, she'd further resist her crown, and her fate, just to remain alive. He turns to Emory. "She can take care of herself. She'll never allow herself to be caught. She's scrappy and resourceful. I have no other reason to believe otherwise."

Emory's eyes narrow, but he relents. "I can go to Loess myself if you don't want to see your father."

Patrix raises a brow. "Who said I would see my father?"

"You're the son of the Loess Queen's brother. You're cousin to the princess I'm courting. How would you not run into him? Do you think you can avoid him? Skirt around conflict?"

Swiveling, Patrix watches the embers devour the logs. "We will take it as it comes."

Throwing up his arms, Emory scoffs. He leaves Bastian's hut and slams the door behind him. Patrix doesn't flinch.

Indeed, he will take it as it comes because he has no other choice. He knew someday his secrets may come to light. *He knew*. Now, he just wonders how much it'll cost him.

Nefari and Kristal had barely left Bastian's and there were already messengers hunting her down. "What is it?" Nefari asks a young boy impatiently. He had hollered her name as he galloped down the path, stopping them near the stables. The horses whinny from within, and the snow stings their cheeks.

There is something in the boy's left hand, but his palm is too big to see what is inside. She squints at it when he finally comes to a stop before them, huffing with exertion.

"Here." He drops a purse in Nefari's hand. "Bastian told me to give this to you."

She curls her fingers around the leather purse. It's heavy, and the coins clink against each other within. Nefari nods her thanks, and the boy takes off toward the temple where others are already heading.

Kristal waits until he's out of earshot and softly asks, "Who is Bastian to you, Fari?"

She watches him go until he disappears into the gathering crowd. "My guardian," she answers truthfully. Because he is, always has been, and forever will be.

Smiling to herself, she turns on her heel, and Kristal wordlessly follows her the rest of the way to the stables. Her smile fades at the barn's entrance, however, because Kaymen waits there, his shoulder leaning against the stable doors. They slow as they reach him. What could he want?

"Go inside and start mucking the stalls," she tells Kristal. Despite the horse's noise, she can hear the soft chatter of Dao and

330

Cyllian inside. Kristal does as she asks without protest and dips inside.

Kaymen straightens when she asks, "Why don't you blame me? For all this, I mean."

His lips twitch. "Because ten years ago, my grandmother stood by and watched as the Shadow Kingdom was destroyed."

She huffs. She remembers his grandmother well. The elderly had served on the Shadow Council and certainly wasn't in any shape to take on the wraiths and harvestmen who marched into the castle that night. She died just like the others. "That's hardly her fault, and it was a long time ago. What does this have to do with me?"

He sighs deeply. "My grandfather shielded her. Instead of fighting, my grandfather shielded her. His wife was more important than everybody else, and there's shame in that. Until last night, I had drawn a parallel between you and Bastian and them. I thought it a disgrace, but you saved Dao at the expense of yourself. You drew the wraiths to you. You stood."

"That's hardly heroic." She blushes. "What you did for me, however . . ." she lets her wordless gratitude hang between them.

A sympathetic grin lifts his cheeks. "You would have done the same thing for me if I had been touched by a wraith."

She wrinkles her nose mockingly. "Would I have?"

"I saw your face when the first harvestwoman attacked," he says, sobering. "Guilt had almost rendered you immobile. The fact that you felt guilty, you felt responsible for her situation, is all I needed. It's all I've ever wanted. Responsibility."

"Well," Nefari blows out a breath. "If I didn't feel guilty before, I sure do now."

331

"That's not what I meant. I meant you felt something on someone else's behalf, and you and I both know that that means something."

"This - I - this isn't me claiming my birthright, Kaymen. The crown, I mean. My fate I've accepted, but I don't know if I have what it takes to lead anybody."

He smirks. "Sure, Nefari. Sure." He leaves her and heads into the stables.

With the breeze pushing her every which way, she stares at the spot he once stood until Fawn comes along and slings a saddlebag over Nefari's shoulders.

"You ready?"

"Actually, will you take this inside and get Astra ready? I'd like to see Sibyl before we leave."

Fawn frowns. "Sure."

Nefari passes the saddlebag back into Fawn's hand and turns on her heel, dashes through the streets, and begins the climb to the mountain.

# CHAPTER THIRTY

Sibyl can feel Nefari grow nearer – knows she travels up the hill instead of attending the ceremony for the fallen Rebel warriors. She waits at her table, eyeing the fate card with suspicion and fear. She's been staring at it for a while now, not wanting to pick it up and decipher what it might show her.

The skull of omens rattles when Nefari enters the tunnel of her cave and then settles once more when Nefari's soft footfalls echo into Sibyl's living space.

Sibyl glances up upon her entrance and blinks in surprise. The shadow crown flares on top of her head. *Without hesitation? No tantrums? No fits?* Sibyl cocks her head to the side, and the letters across her forehead quiver and rearrange to Nefari's prophecy.

"This Fate-blessed princess of rage and wrath, indeed."

"Hush."

She remains seated, doesn't rise to properly greet the princess. "To what do I owe this unscheduled pleasure?"

"I wanted to say goodbye." Nefari holds a basket. She raises it for Sibyl to see, and Sibyl sniffs at it. Apples and bread from the smell of it. Nefari sets it down gently and shoves her hands into her cloak pockets.

"And here I thought you'd forgotten about me."

Nefari shifts her weight. "I could never forget about you. I, um, I actually wanted to thank you. For what you did, that is. I wanted to –"

"Stop." She waves a hand dismissively in the air. "I was doing my duty. I was protecting you. It is nothing that needs gratitude."

"I think it was more than that. I think you care for me more than you'd like to outwardly admit."

"Bah!" Sibyl spits. She grinds her jaw. "And the ring? Did it survive?" Nefari inclines her head and Sibyl's lips curve. To anyone else, the grin would look wicked. "I told you. The ring was a gift."

"And?"

"And . . ." Sibyl rises from her chair and touches the tips of her fingers to the table. "It may not protect you from everything. You mustn't believe it will. I won't be there to protect you. Bastian won't be there to shield you. When you leave, you are on your own, Nefari. Do not gamble your life because you have the ring."

Nefari crosses her arms and glances at the bending shadows. "And what makes you think I'll need help?"

Sibyl's chuckle echoes around the cave's space. "Oh, my Fate-blessed child. You're wearing your shadow crown and without my demand for it. You've changed. You're different. And now you're about to embark on a journey, not only for your crown but to find a new you."

"I didn't come here to hear what I already know."

"And you didn't come here for goodbyes, either."

Nefari returns her gaze, and for a moment, a thousand tiny stars dance within them. Sibyl observes them, moving away from the table to cross the distance between them. She grabs Nefari's chin and peers into the stars. "Do you know why it is okay to perform magic in my cave?"

"Because of your magic."

Sibyl smiles and releases her chin. "Yes. *My* magic. But my magic is nothing compared to the three crone factions combined. Someday, you may find yourself facing that magic."

Nefari cocks her head to the side. "What do you mean?"

"It is not my story to tell. But I will also warn you of Salix. Magic is broken there – broken by more magic conjured by the crone factions."

"Why are you telling me this? Better yet, what aren't you telling me?"

"There are things that have been kept from you and for good reason. The magic being broken in Salix is one of them. Bastian had feared, in your youth, you'd seek revenge on the Queen before it was time. He kept this from you – the broken magic – to keep you as –"

"Nobody," Nefari hisses. "To keep me as nobody."

"Yes," Sibyl answers gravely. "Because, no matter his past, he loves you as his own."

"So, even if I do pick up my crown and march against Salix with all the starlight I can muster, I would be useless?"

Sibyl abruptly grips her upper arms. "No! We will do what we can here with the inferaze, but you must find the others. You must find the Choice-chosen and free the Hope-blessed. And when you do, the three of you can find a way to break this magic."

"And how am I supposed to find them, Sibyl?" Nefari rips her arms away from the child crone.

"You are Fate, child. *Fate!* They are as destined to find you as you are to find them!"

Behind them, the skull of omens speaks. "She will shape the darkness – this Fate-blessed princess of rage and wrath – for she is the crown of endless night and the memory of woeful shadows. Echoes of clinking chain and metal. The sharp sting of leather. The bitter taste of tears will feed despair, but the hopeful shards of a broken kingdom will find the fated queen, and then death will yawn and swallow the realm."

Sibyl turns back to her, her grin wider. She watches Nefari's throat bob at the skull that was not touched and prompted to speak. "The hopeful shards of a broken kingdom will find the fated queen," she repeats. "I told you."

An hour later, Sibyl watches from the wind-whipped entrance of her cave. Nefari Ashcroft mounts her mare and nudges the horse to the others who wait for her down the path. Dao, Kristal, Cyllian, Kaymen, Patrix, and Emory wait, twisted in their saddles to peer at her oncoming approach. Fawn meets her halfway and then escorts her to the front of the group.

Every horse's rump is covered by plump saddlebags, supplies they'll need for their journey, and every rider wears layers of fur to stave the gale outside the mountain.

She told the princess that her journey will be more than gathering a crown. This Sibyl knows as fact. But, as she knows this, she also knows Nefari will accept it, once the crown is in her hands.

Before the princess had left, Sibyl made her promise to send word through the shadows if she ever found herself in trouble. Without the protection of the Rebel Legion, Nefari isn't safe. She needed the reassurance because, just as she had told Nefari that the pieces of the puzzle were forming, she withheld the information that some of these pieces flitting around in Sibyl's foresight felt evil and dark. Nefari doesn't need the weight of it on her shoulders, not when so much is already settled there.

A movement beside Sibyl catches her eye.

There, on the skeletal centaur's shoulder is a bone crier. The massive bird's black feathers ruffle as it, too, watches Nefari leave with her group. Fear patterns in Sibyl's heart, and as if sensing it, the bird takes flight into the snow that's falling heavily from plump clouds. It swoops over the city and then heads north into the Fades.

She knows what this means and hobbles hurriedly down her tunnel, to her domed space. She nearly trips over a chair by the table when she scrambles for the fate card she's been avoiding. As her fingers wrap around the card, the misty swirls within begin to churn.

Sibyl drops it back to the table when an image appears.

*A heart as black as coal.*

We hope you have enjoyed The Shape of Darkness (Heavy Lies the Crown). Please leave a review to help other readers who may enjoy this series as well. The next book's publishing date is projected for Spring 2021.

*For series order, visit dfischerauthor.com.*

*Take a moment and follow D. Fischer on Instagram, Facebook, or Email. If you'd like to connect more exclusively, join her Facebook group, D. Fischer Reader's Group.*

# ALSO BY D. FISCHER

| THE CLOVEN PACK SERIES |

| RISE OF THE REALMS SERIES |

| HOWL FOR THE DAMNED |

| HEAVY LIES THE CROWN |

| NIGHT OF TERROR SERIES |

| GRIM FAIRYTALES COLLECTION |

# ABOUT THE AUTHOR

Bestselling and award-winning author D. Fischer is a mother of two very busy boys, a wife to a wonderful husband, an owner of two sock-loving German shorthairs, and slave to a rescued cat. Together, they live in Orange City, Iowa.

When D. Fischer isn't chasing after her children, she spends her time typing like a mad woman while consuming vast amounts of caffeine. Known for the darker side of imagination, she enjoys freeing her creativity through worlds that don't exist, no matter how much we wish they did.

Follow D. Fischer on Facebook, Amazon, Bookbub, Goodreads, and Instagram.

DFISCHERAUTHOR.COM

CPSIA information can be obtained
at www.ICGtesting.com
Printed in the USA
BVHW040211290722
643319BV00001BA/3